Meg Howrey is a writer and a former professional dancer. Her non-fiction has been published in US *Vogue*, and she is the author of the novels *Blind Sight*, *The Cranes Dance* and *The Wanderers*. She lives in Los Angeles.

Praise for *The Wanderers*

'Is the Eidolon mission all it appears to be? Or more? The unfolding of that mystery launches this plausible space tale into higher realms of enjoyment'
Daily Mail

'The power of this particular mission lies partly in the strength of feeling it creates – a dress rehearsal that nonetheless carries as much weight as the real thing, and inspires just as much wonder'
Financial Times

'An observant novel about the line between pretence and reality, and the connections humans forge'
Stylist

'*The Wanderers* is a revelation – a riveting tale of space travel that is also a profound exploration of self … A wise and wonderful novel – I loved every page of it'
Antonia Hodgson, author of *The Devil in the Marshalsea*

'An astounding, insightful, exhilarating ride'
Helen Sedgwick, author of *The Comet Seekers*

'A stealthily brilliant novel. A distinct, shimmering vision of who we are … at once simple, gorgeous and profoundly moving'
Peter Nichols, author of *The Rocks*

'Howrey subtly explores the tensions between our inner and projected selves … We may never plumb the mysteries of space; we may never truly understand ourselves or the people we love, she suggests. But there's courage in the attempt'
Washington Post

'Moving and generously intimate … Offers space to recognise the strangeness of normality, and the difficulty and wonder of Earth and other minds'	*TLS*

'Lyrical and thoughtful … A smart meditation on the nature of exploration in all facets of our lives'	*Big Issue*

'Every single character in *The Wanderers* feels distinct and vivid, a planet in his or her own right'	*Slate*

'A breathtakingly honest and incredibly beautiful examination of the heart and soul of humankind … This is a book that isn't like anything you've ever read before'	*Newsweek*

'*The Wanderers* is unquestionably the work of a brilliant writer at the height of her powers'
J. Ryan Stradal, author of *Kitchens of the Great Midwest*

'A wonderful exploration of space, trust, and what it means to be a conscious creature, finely tuned and funny from the first page to the last'	Jonathan Lee, author of *High Dive*

'Elegant, thoughtful, gorgeously written … Builds effortlessly to moments of immense power and honesty'
Charles Yu, author of
How to Live Safely in a Science Fictional Universe

'Consistently engrossing … A lyrical and subtle space opera'
Kirkus, starred review

'With these believably fragile and idealistic characters at the helm, Howrey's insightful novel will take readers to a place where they too can "lift their heads and wonder"'
Publishers Weekly, starred review

THE
WANDERERS

MEG HOWREY

SCRIBNER

LONDON NEW YORK TORONTO SYDNEY NEW DELHI

First published in Great Britain by Scribner, an imprint of
Simon & Schuster UK Ltd, 2017
This paperback edition published by Scribner, 2018
A CBS COMPANY

3 5 7 9 10 8 6 4 2

Simon & Schuster UK Ltd
1st Floor
222 Gray's Inn Road
London WC1X 8HB

Simon & Schuster Australia, Sydney
Simon & Schuster India, New Delhi

www.simonandschuster.co.uk
www.simonandschuster.com.au
www.simonandschuster.co.in

A CIP catalogue record for this book is available from the British Library

Paperback ISBN: 978-1-4711-4668-8
eBook ISBN: 978-1-4711-4669-5

Book design by Meighan Cavanaugh
Printed and bound by CPI Group (UK) Ltd, Croydon, CR0 4YY

For John,

best brother in this

and any other Universe

"We feel that even if *all possible* scientific questions be answered, the problems of life have still not been touched at all. Of course there are then no questions left, and this itself is the answer."

—LUDWIG WITTGENSTEIN, *Tractatus Logico–Philosophicus*

THE
WANDERERS

HELEN

*N*othing feels as free as this!

The lettering of this promise is in pink. The freedom being demonstrated concerns a woman in a white bra and girdle cavorting across a simplified background of sky and clouds.

Helen Kane stands in the lobby of Prime Space Systems Laboratory and considers the 1960s-era advertisement for Playtex. She smiles, waiting to be given an explanation. The CEO of Prime Space has ushered Helen toward this lithesome lady in her panties with all the ceremony that one might employ toward revealing an Old Master, and there is nothing to be gained by showing James "Boone" Cross anything other than what Helen privately refers to as PIG: Polite, Interested, Good humored. Helen is a little perturbed, a little uncomfortable, but she can get PIG to fly in much more adverse conditions.

This is Helen's last day visiting the Japanese branch of Prime's Systems Lab. Tomorrow she will go back. Home, which is still Houston. A year ago Helen retired from active duty in the astronaut corps at NASA, after twenty-one years and three missions in space. It had been the right thing to do: there were so few opportunities for getting named to a crew; others had been waiting more than a decade for their first mission. It was time to cede to the next generation as the previous one had done for her. This was always going to happen, and she had prepared for it.

She had not prepared. You can't train for irrelevance.

Helen tells herself that it is nonsense to think of the word *irrelevant*. She still has a position at NASA, an important one. And, if she chooses, there are exciting things happening elsewhere. It is very likely that Prime Space is going to offer her a job. There is a lot to think about, but not right now. Right now she must give PIG to Boone Cross.

Despite the fact that Helen took the Prime Space *Iris* to the International Space Station and back on her last mission, she doesn't feel she has fully penetrated the culture of this company, although she's got a pretty good handle on its in-house vocabulary. Prime is skittish about using language borrowed from the military, and mixes acronyms with a kind of high-minded verbiage, noun-to-verb mashups, and the stray Latinate pun. The mindless totalitarian-speak predicted in dystopian fiction was not the future. Big Brother had gone artisanal.

The father of this new world made-to-order is from Alabama but employs his company's argot with the chaotic enthusiasm of a non-native speaker delivering newly acquired idioms. That Boone Cross is a genius is not in question, though the rest is up for debate. He seems unclear as well: he has referred to himself during their conversation as both an anachronism and an iconoclast. Boone is younger than Helen, who is fifty-three and only now noticing that many people seem to be younger than herself. This hour has been her longest excursion in Boone's undivided presence, and his manner does not seem designed to make her comfortable. Helen neither expects nor resents this, but her mood is not the best.

"You may have noticed that at every Prime Space location," Boone is saying now, granting the lobby a majestic wave, "we encourage the team to share images about what drew us to working in the space biz. And then we collect these images together so that when people come to work every day, they pass through our collective dreams."

"What a great idea," says Helen, covering her impatience. "It creates such a special atmosphere." Just now, Boone and Helen are the only ones enjoying the special atmosphere. The lobby—a windowless curvilinear triangle—has been closed off to tourists, and Prime Space employees are apparently being rerouted to some other entrance.

For most of the past hour, Boone and Helen have been talking robotics. Helen is not sure who is meant to impress whom, so she focuses on the subject at hand. For whatever reason, she has been brought to the lobby of dreams, and appropriate reactions and statements must be sourced and given. This will not be difficult. Helen has made lots of speeches about dreams: believing in, going for, never giving up on. Since the dream she has achieved eclipses most people's unachieved fantasies, it behooves her to speak with modesty on the subject, with repeated use of the word *fortunate*.

"This right here"—Boone points to the Playtex advertisement—"is my tribute to my grandmother. I was going to just put up a photograph of her, but then I challenged myself to be a little more creative. It's the company my grandmother started working for when she was eighteen. Playtex was a division of the International Latex Corporation."

"Oh, ILC, of course," says Helen. She remembers a section of

Boone's autobiography that referenced his grandmother and connected her to his early interest in space exploration. She feels a little sad. Is she sad? Helen considers an alternative: she is dehydrated.

"So as you probably know, in the early sixties NASA opened up a competition for a spacesuit design," Boone continues. "International Latex, best known as the makers of Playtex bras and girdles, was one of eight companies that submitted a proposal."

Helen retrieves what she knows about the history of spacesuit design, decides there is a high-percentage chance that it is less than what Boone knows, and says, with PIG, "Mmhmm. Yes."

"I just find this a fascinating moment." Boone is about to tell a story he has told many times, she can tell: his voice takes on the confidence of one who has whole paragraphs ready for delivery. Helen puts herself into a good listening posture.

"No one knew exactly what kind of spacesuit would be needed for walking on the moon," Boone says. "They knew it had to be a sort of portable spacecraft, that it needed to contain a total life support system, but the rest was mostly guessing. The other vendors competing for the contract all had experience making military equipment, but only International Latex had worked with fabric and seamstresses and making something a person can lie down and then get up in. Their design won. My grandmother was making girdles until one day her supervisor pulled her aside and told her she needed to start working on another project."

Helen loves these stories, like they all do. The early years of NASA: slide rules and pocket protectors and "Failure is not an option." How little they had known; how much they had dared.

Boone picks up his narrative. "The tension was high. Everyone was racing against the clock, trying to get a working suit together but also adhering to the most rigorous safety standards ever. Seamstresses were assigned a different color pin, and their worktables were inspected to make sure that every single pin came out. The sewing machines paused after every stitch. My grandmother worked on the lining of the gloves." Boone holds up his hands, more callused than you might expect from a person who made his first billion in networking routers, and is wearing a cardigan. "A new fabric," he says. "Woven chromium steel. Two thousand dollars a yard. Not an easy thing to stitch. Even decades later, my grandmother still had calluses on her fingertips."

Helen, despite her distraction, or dehydration, or sadness, feels a rush of genuine liking for this man, this respecter of calluses.

In the third month of her longest mission aboard the International Space Station, Helen had removed her socks and seen the calluses from the soles of her feet come completely off with them and float up in front of her face. She then had to chase them down—flying, since she could not chase her feet on foot—and secure them in a trash bag because otherwise someone else might have had to vacuum her calluses out of a vent and that wasn't fair. Boone would probably enjoy this anecdote. When Helen had told it to her daughter, Meeps had laughed, but also said, in one of her funny-angry voices, "Okay, I won't ever have a story as cool as that in my entire life."

"Incredible," says Helen. "My daughter studied acting and I remember her telling me that there are no small roles. That's absolutely true, I think. Your grandmother's contribution could not have been more vital."

Boone executes a double thumbs-up in agreement, or perhaps that's what he always does when he reaches this point in the story. "She and her coworkers took their jobs very seriously. They knew what was at risk. Later, my grandmother watched the *Apollo 14* crew bouncing around on the moon, being silly, having the time of their lives, and her heart was in her throat. She said she kept whispering, 'Get back inside, get back inside, stop horsing around.' Because of course the astronauts were enjoying themselves. But people like my grandmother knew the truth. They knew the truth about how fragile everything is, because they had stitched every stitch of that fragile truth."

"Indeed," agrees Helen, but in the gently repressive tone of someone who would like to dial down the emotional level of the conversation a notch or two. Possible imminent death was her business, and not a subject for poetry, even if it's only the whimsy of Boone's speechwriter. "What a lovely tribute to your grandmother." Helen takes a few steps back and makes a show of surveying some of the other artwork. "This is all just great."

They begin touring the lobby. The white and gray paint scheme, the sprung floor that swallows the sound of their feet, the curved lines, all contribute to a sense of the space as a kind of airlock: a place to transition from one world to the next. Boone points out that one of the other tributes is a small screen running video loop of Helen herself, giving a demonstration meant for schoolchildren of brushing her teeth in microgravity.

Her first trip to space, the hair floating around her face not yet gray. Helen's daughter had been six at the time, Helen's husband still alive.

She'd worn an ILC-designed suit on that mission. And fourteen years later, Helen had been giving a commendatory address at ILC headquarters in Delaware on the day her husband died. NASA had sent her: it was important for the makers of spacesuits to connect their work to an actual human who was capable through human error—possibly theirs—of dying. So at the moment when she had been thanking men and women for their heroic efforts to keep her, a hero, alive, her husband had expired in the parking lot of a Houston hospital for want of an aspirin. Helen's best guess was that Eric had felt some sort of chest pain, but had not wanted to call an ambulance for some reason, and had driven himself. No one knew for sure. Five years ago, now.

Helen's daughter believes that her mother has not adequately dealt with the death of her husband, and further believes that the reason for this has to do with Helen's unresolved feelings about the death of Helen's father. Helen does not know exactly what Meeps means when she says this, does not know exactly what sort of statement or act on her part would indicate resolution, and suspects that what her daughter wants is to manifest in Helen an emotional life closer to her daughter's own dizzyingly intense ability to feel many things at once.

Boone continues the tour. More than a few of the images in Prime Space's lobby of dreams seemed to be drawn from science fiction rather than actual space exploration milestones. For Helen, the initial flame had been a book. *Men on the Moon.* But it wasn't Neil or Buzz that had interested her, or even the moon itself. She had been attracted to the mission's most unsung hero: Michael Collins, alone in *Columbia*, drifting around the moon in exquisite solitary splendor while Buzz and Neil had gone about the terrestrial work of putting down a plaque, erecting a flag, and gathering rocks. Every two hours Michael Collins had gone out of radio contact for forty-eight minutes when the moon stood between himself and Earth, and during those minutes he was the most alone person in the history of people. Helen still liked to think about that. That had always been her dream: space, not a location within it, just space.

But she had made, as they all had, public statements of support for every Prime Space success in the MarsNOW timeline announced fifteen years ago. As one of Helen's astronaut colleagues had put it, "You never know. At least it's not another fucking rover." One by one, Prime had been knocking down every serious obstacle, eliminating every "show-stopper." Even the notoriously cautious Office of Planetary Protection had cleared Prime's proposed landing site as being acceptable for human presence. And the last achievement—*Red Dawn*, Prime Space's Earth Return Vehicle—was currently on Mars making its own propellant from Martian resources, a ride back to Earth for the first humans who could make it there.

Prime Space had been good for all of them, keeping the dream of human space exploration alive during NASA's Congressional de-pantsing and subsequent morale depletion. Everyone assumed that Prime was working toward developing an independent astronaut corps.

Helen told herself that she would consider any offer carefully. This conversation might have nothing to do with MarsNOW. Prime might want her to advise on its astronaut program. They might want her expertise on inflatable graphene habitats. They might want her as a figurehead, a photograph, a status symbol. It is these scenarios Helen thinks of, because she needs to avoid any awareness of hoping to be rescued.

Rescued! It is an embarrassing word for Helen, and nearly as foreign to her as *irrelevant*. As a child she had imagined workarounds for stories where maidens needed rescue, had never understood why Rapunzel, for instance, didn't engineer her own escape. If Rapunzel's hair was capable of sustaining a man on the ascent, then surely she could have cut herself free from her hair with utensils or sewing implements or broken-off bedroom furniture and then used it to rappel *herself* down from the tower. Helen had even drawn up several viable contingency options for Rapunzel, should things not go as planned.

Rescued was the wrong word, surely.

Except she cannot escape this feeling of containment, of hindrance, and this is not a rational feeling, since the tower she has been shut in is only all of Earth. It is not anyone's fault, or responsibility, that the best of her exists in space, that she knows she's at the height of her powers, that if she doesn't go back up, then she has run out of road before she has run out of breath.

And how many years left on Earth for her? Consigned to a lesser version of herself on a planet that had also seen better days. Cast out from heaven into a melting Eden.

This is an inappropriate moment to have this realization, and so Helen tries to stave it off by doubling down on PIG.

They've now made a circuit of the lobby. Helen has a dim sense of people waiting outside the curved walls, people waiting to come in, or get out. For the thing—something—to happen.

But Boone has not exhausted the meaningfulness of the Playtex poster. He draws Helen's attention to it once again. "To me this represents the spirit of our enterprise," he says. "A commercial company finding a way to do something in a way that a government program could not. Although it's also a reminder of how far we've come. Nobody can tell women anymore that this"—Boone nods at the prancing figure—"is all women can be. Or should be."

"Oh, true," says Helen, as if she hadn't considered this. Men stayed enthusiastic about feminism if they believed it was their idea. And honestly, she hadn't identified the woman in the advertisement as belonging to something connected with herself, or as a subject for indignation, historical or otherwise. You couldn't get fussed about these things, or you'd find yourself out of the sandbox, complaining.

"This is Prime Space." Boone taps the glass of the poster. "We're not a government bureaucracy, and this gives us the freedom and lack of prejudice to accept the best ideas from wherever they come from. The world is not going to be changed in a Congressional committee. The best you can hope for is lowest common denominator consensus. We don't have to ask permission from the taxpayers. We are the taxpayers. We are the job creators. And our missions have nothing to do with politics. They have to do with opportunities, with ideas, with manifesting dreams. Which do you think is the better route: trying to get everyone to agree that your dream is valid and important, hoping to inspire their support, or simply going ahead and doing what you love and saying, 'Hey, who's with me?'"

Boone has paused, and Helen, who had spent some time organizing the best answers to any questions she might be asked, riffles through her collection. It was often effective to mirror language, so Helen could go with "I like what you're saying about manifesting dreams. The history of space exploration is the history of people going ahead, of saying, 'This is what we *will* do.'"

"Let me ask you another question." Boone moves to put his hands in his pockets, but there does not appear to be adequate room for them there, or his jeans are too starched. "What would you say is the most important component of a mission?"

Helen has this answer ready. "Clear objectives, thorough training, good and effective communication between crewmembers." This was true, or true-ish. Most of being an astronaut was *not* going to space, so if given the opportunity, Helen would go to space for no specific purpose and with a crew of anesthetized yaks.

"We have a clear objective." Boone smiles. "MarsNOW isn't exactly ambiguous. As for training, we are about to begin a very intensive four-year program. The first portion of this is something we're calling Eidolon."

The significance of the name, if there is one, escapes Helen. She employs a PIG-inflected "mmhmm?" and tries not to look like a Rapunzel.

"A seventeen-month simulation of the mission," he says. "This isn't another isolation study. It's taking the regular simulation training methods to a new level, one that matches the unique challenges of a Mars mission. We want to give ourselves, and our crew, a chance to work in the most realistic conditions possible. The training simulation imagines a six-and-a-half-month outbound trip, thirty days of Mars, and then nine months back. We're condensing the Mars portion from the actual eighteen months to thirty days because we already have a lot of good data from other Mars analogue studies. What *we're* concentrating on are the conditions of getting there and back. So, this brings me to the third thing you mentioned. The crew of a Mars mission will operate with more autonomy than any other in history. The right crew will define the success of this mission as much as the technology. For the first mission to Mars, the right crew *is* the technology."

There are occupations where declamations of wild enthusiasm are wanted, and ones where they are not. You do not want to hear your brain surgeon shout, "This is my *dream!*" over your gurney as they wheel you into surgery. At NASA, the too obviously gung ho got weeded out. You didn't go on and on about how you wanted to go to space so *bad*. You clobbered people over the head with your qualifications and then talked about luck when you were selected.

"That's very well articulated," Helen says. "In my experience, the most successful and happiest crews on the space station were the ones where everyone considered working well as a team member to be the first goal of their personal performance. The longer the mission, the more important this is, the more simple acts of consideration and helpfulness become, as you say, part of the technology of the mission. I'm fortunate to have had three chances to see just what people are capable of when they come together to work for something greater than themselves."

Too much? Well, she is not sad anymore, or dehydrated.

"Do you think astronauts are born or made?" Boone asks.

Oh, for heaven's sake. Well, several options. This could be the place for Helen to say things about how there was nothing special about her, people had granted her the opportunity to give her best. Since Boone had mentioned how far women had come, it might be nice to say that she stood on the shoulders of all the women before her, women who had made her generation the first that didn't have to prove they were better than men, who could trust that they would be judged on their own merits, neither singled out for privilege nor ignored out of bias. Sally Ride's refusal to be the sole astronaut of her crew awarded with a bouquet of roses had led to female astronauts being able to knit in space if they felt like it. But that sort of thing worked much better with speeches made to women.

Boone could also be asking a literal question on the subject of nature versus nurture. He'd titled his autobiography *Me and My Quarks*.

"Both," says Helen.

"I know NASA wants you to stay on as Chief Astronaut," Boone says. "And we all know where NASA's nose is going to be pointed now, no matter how people feel about it. What I don't know is how *you* feel about spending the rest of your career selecting which members of the United States military would be the best people to drill on the moon."

Rescue me, thinks Helen.

"It won't surprise you to know that we've been having a lot of discussions about you here," Boone says.

"I hope they've been good discussions." If something is being dangled in front of Helen now, she must not snatch.

"Very enthusiastic discussions." Boone produces a black Sharpie from the back pocket of his jeans and begins striding silently across the lobby to the double doors that lead into the laboratories. For a wild second, Helen thinks that their meeting is over, and he is going to leave her under a Playtex poster. That she would have a lot of trouble handling this—she could handle it, but it would be tough—gives her a clue about the extent to which she's been trying to game her expectations.

Still, she's not going to trail after Boone. Helen takes a few steps into the center of the lobby and then holds her ground.

"I'm not unaware of the speculation in the community," Boone says over his shoulder. "We're four years away from our optimum launch window. It's when we've said it would happen. So who's going to go?"

Boone draws two columns of three horizontal lines directly on the wall behind him.

Rescue me.

"Primary crew." Boone taps the first column. "Backup crew." He taps the second. "We've got a rocket capable of sending a crewed spacecraft to Mars, and a way to protect our crew's health on the journey. We've got an Earth Return Vehicle sitting on the planet, along with a processing plant manufacturing fuel and water and oxygen from Martian resources. In six months, we launch a contingency ERV and begin the Eidolon training for the Primary crew. Four years from now we're sending three people to Mars. What do you think? Want to go?" Boone holds out the Sharpie to Helen.

What does Helen think?

Helen thinks she is too young to watch herself be surpassed, and too old to be this hungry.

She thinks she is too young to give up her dreams, and too old to want them this much.

But she is both too young and too old, possibly, to change herself. And how many years left on Earth?

Four, maybe.

Helen crosses the lobby, takes the pen, and writes her name on the wall.

MIREILLE

A terrible thing has happened to Mireille: she has been selected as the spa employee of the month. She sits now in the hotel employee cafeteria with Clara and Olive, who are also massage therapists and who have congratulated her with a sincerity that depresses her almost as much as the award. Also, during this lunch break she seems to have eaten not only all of her bread but all of Clara's. Successful people are either self-deniers who achieve through discipline, or hedonists who never apologize or explain. Successful people are not women who eat too much bread *and* lament.

It's only that she wants to be the person she was, for a few minutes, last night. Mireille had made people laugh when she took the floor, so to speak, with a story that began with, "You know, I have to say, I totally blame Anne Frank." For once she had left a party without the desire to go back and do the whole party over, was almost certain she had nothing to reproach herself with.

"Oh, so I have this thing right now," Mireille says to Clara and Olive, "where I'm trying to live a minimal lifestyle. Only I just realized the other night that the reason I have trouble throwing anything away has to do with this thing that happened to me when I was six and, you know, I have to say, I totally blame Anne Frank."

She's off, she's a little off, she can already tell the story isn't going to work as well as it did last night. The setting is wrong now: plastic booths and tables and hotel art relocated down to the cafeteria because of mild damage, and the smell of institutionalized paella. Also, Olive and Clara are different kinds of friends than the people from her acting class. They're in the healing industry, so neurotic irony has no currency with them the way it does with actors. People who are devoted to aromatherapy are not usually humorists. Mireille has chosen her audience unwisely.

"Okay, so my dad took me to Amsterdam when I was six. He was speaking at some kind of festival and I went with him because . . ." Mireille appears to search her memory and then rolls her eyes to indicate the ridiculousness of having forgotten this particular detail. "Oh yeah, because my mom was in *space*."

She hurries on to the next bit. It goes very badly for her if she tries to enlist sympathy for being the daughter of one of the most admirable women on the planet. If she is pitied, she is pitied wrongly: not for being neglected or eclipsed by her astronaut mother, but for being inadequate and unremarkable in comparison. Mireille doesn't require a spa employee of the month award to see the truth of that.

"Anyway. We're in Amsterdam and my dad takes me to the Anne Frank house because, you know, that's what you do, and my dad's trying to give me a nice educational experience and distract me from the fact that my mom could blow up at any moment. And that's the obvious entertainment choice, right? Holocaust museum! No, I totally, totally get it. And I loved going *anywhere* with my dad."

Mireille touches the silver star she wears on a chain around her neck. Her friends know that this is what she does when she talks about her dead father; she is ashamed of how theatrical the gesture has become, but can't stop doing it anyway.

"Right. So, there we are at the Anne Frank Museum. And you can see the diary, and that's wonderful, of course, because it's this tremendous document that means so much to so many people. But then there's all this other stuff. Anne Frank's pen, and a book that Anne Frank once gave as a present to someone, and a bus pass that Anne Frank once used. And this drawing she had done in school that I completely fixated on. I mean, it's not a piece of art. It's not *of* anything. It's basically a fancy doodle that she colored in. But, me being me, I became totally obsessed with this idea that a doodle could become important, could be something that people would put under glass and look at, and be incredibly moved by. And so, because of the Anne Frank Museum, I became, like, this slightly morbid six-year-old *hoarder*."

Mireille is definitely a little off, because neither Clara nor Olive are laughing, and last night, everybody had laughed. Why has she chosen this moment to act like a clown? Nobody wants to go to the circus at 11:30 a.m.

"The other thing," Mireille says, "is that there's a lot in the museum about Miep Gies. She's the woman who helped hide the family, and found the diary, and even though Meeps was just what my mother called me because she can't pronounce my real name correctly, I guess I felt this connection to the historical Miep and—"

"Wait. Your mother can't pronounce your name?" Clara grabs Mireille's wrist.

Mireille is aware that her eyes are shining and that she could cry in about three seconds if she let herself. But she shouldn't cry. If you

cry as an actor, you rob your audience of the chance to cry for you—
that's practically a law.

"My dad chose the name Mireille. He was French, so he pro-
nounced it the proper Provençal way. I mean, my mom speaks Russian
and Japanese fluently, she's *amazing*, but she's super midwestern, so
everything comes out a little flat. Anyway, she probably agreed to the
name because there was a Russian space station called MIR. It was
famously sort of a mess, so, you know, appropriate for *me*."

"Aw," says Clara.

"You're not a mess," says Olive.

These friends are giving Mireille what she wants, but she doesn't
want to be the person who wants what she wants, and so she goes on
wanting inaccurately and still her eyes shine.

Last night Mireille had linked the whole Anne Frank story back
to her mom being in space, and then done a hilarious impression of
one of the videos her mother had shot in space for schoolchildren,
demonstrating how to brush your teeth in microgravity, which led to
a comically exaggerated imitation of what her mom sounded like
when she spoke Russian with a midwestern accent, which naturally
caused someone to say: "Wow, so you speak Russian?" which allowed
Mireille to describe traveling with her mother to Moscow for a com-
memorative space thing, and how Mireille had lost her virginity at
Star City, a story guaranteed to impress because while everyone had
lost their virginity, who else could say they had done it with the son
of a cosmonaut in a formerly secret facility a hundred yards from a
statue of Laika, the first dog to orbit the Earth?

And she had felt wonderful last night, knowing that she was that
person, that person who could tell that story.

The Earth has not even rotated once since that feeling and she
has already lost it.

"But I love the name Meeps," says Clara.

"Me too," says Olive. "It's so you."

WHERE IS HER STORY? How can she get it back? Mireille remembers Nestor, who took her virginity (or, more honestly, managed to just catch the virginity she *heaved* at him). She remembers the pine and birch trees of Star City. How she looked up into the dark Russian night and thought that she too was going places.

Mireille has to go now and have her picture taken to commemorate her winning spa employee of the month, before starting her shift. She makes her way down the corridor to Human Resources. The hallway walls are lined with posters spouting motivational slogans and seasonally appropriate puns. Winter Is Almost Over, So Let's Put a Spring in Our Step!

Mireille earned her award because she put together a personal aromatherapy kit for an ultra-VIP client, and the ultra VIP wrote a letter to the manager of the hotel to rave about Mireille's skills and thoughtfulness, and said the oils had not only changed *her* life, they'd also cured her chronically ill wheaten terrier.

Mireille is made to stand against a cream wall and hold up her employee of the month certificate. She smiles, and says her name, and her department, and why she loves working at the hotel, and what she did to get her award. She does not say, "I accidentally cured a wheaten terrier's pancreatitis with essential oil," because you can't make sarcastic jokes with people who tape up posters that read Let's Put a Spring in Our Step! and she is not going to misjudge her audience twice in one day.

Once clear of Human Resources, Mireille folds her certificate up into a tiny square and takes the employee elevator up to the spa.

Mireille hasn't told anyone about her mother's news. It's preposterous, pretty much. Her mother had done the thing where she explained using her special-formula *kind* voice, and then asked for Mireille to share her thoughts and reactions, and Mireille had said, "I think if it's important to you, then you should do it."

It is only coming to her now that what her mother was talking about was going to Mars. Mireille wonders what she could have possibly been telling herself for the past month that *wasn't* "My mom is going to Mars."

She also can't remember what was so funny about blaming Anne Frank.

"It's training," her mother had said. "Just like before, let's focus on the training, not the going." Except she always did go. Going was always the point.

If her mother goes to Mars, then that will be the only story of Mireille's life. It will wipe out everything. Mireille wants to stay with that thought a little, but promises herself she will return to it later, when she has more time to savor how awful it is. Mireille has to touch people now, and there is a chance that people might feel the awful things through her hands. So instead, she will do the thing where she spins it the other way, like her mother is always suggesting.

She will start working seriously as an actress *in really good things* before her mother goes to Mars, and then, when her mother does go, people will be incredibly interested in Mireille's point of view on the whole deal. Mireille sees herself and her mother on talk shows, being interviewed together, posing for photographs. She sees herself becoming gracious and generous and funny and tender toward her mom and she is attracted to this version of herself and this self snaps open and catches the wind, just like it's supposed to, just like the parachute that brought her mother's *Soyuz* capsule safely to Earth when Mireille was six.

Mireille kneads and exfoliates and makes sympathetic noises and tells people to breathe and is genuinely nonjudgmental about back hair and psoriasis. She keeps spinning. She has become great, she is big, she is important. And she is carrying her mother, close, close to her. This is the story of a daughter who was inspired by the accomplishments of her mother, who was empowered by them enough to choose her own path, which shoots just as high and as far, as daringly, as riskily, as nobly in its own way. This is the story of the daughter, and not the mother. Not the mother shooting into the sky, then higher than sky, bungling her daughter's name and neither blowing up nor ever—really—coming home.

SERGEI

A *mie* pose is used to demonstrate a powerful emotion."

The voice is female, synthesized through computer concatenation, stripped of opinion, not unattractive. On the wooden stage, a kabuki actroid swivels to demonstrate a *mie* pose: right hand held perpendicular to the floor, left arm bent at the elbow, jabbing upward. The actroid stamps his left foot, crosses his eyes, and freezes. Sergei guesses that this character is expressing impatience, arrogance. The actroid looks like an asshole.

"The actor's makeup, or *kumadori*, is also used to indicate the character of the role," the voice continues. "Red lines symbolize good traits like heroism and righteousness. Blue or black lines might be used for a villain or a jealous lover."

Sergei looks at the red colors on the stamping actroid. He was wrong. This was the good guy of the pair.

The second kabuki actroid looks too small for his giant kimono. Maybe he is a replacement. He lunges forward and slashes the air with his sword, nostrils flared, black painted eyebrows winged from nose to temple in two steep slashes.

"These robots," says Sergei, "are not pleasant." He imagines his own face painted red and black in equal measure, a heroic villain, the colors running together. It is warm and he has overdressed, he is sweating. He needs to speak to his crewmates today and is having trouble finding the right opening, the correct tone, something between tragedy and comedy.

Right now, the three astronauts—Sergei Kuznetsov, Yoshihiro Tanaka, and Helen Kane—are standing in a replica of the Kureha-za Theater, originally built in Osaka toward the end of the nineteenth century. Like the other sixty-four buildings spread out across the architectural theme park Yoshi has brought them to, the theater is an example of Meiji-period architecture. The astronauts have already inspected the revolving stage, hand-operated in its day by a crew secreted below.

"I've only seen one full kabuki performance live," says Helen. "It was amazing."

"Then you have an open mind," Yoshi says. "Kabuki is difficult even for some Japanese; many find it dull, or unfathomable."

They troop upstairs to inspect the drummer's balcony. Two Western tourists, student age, are talking loudly in Japanese. They nod at Yoshi, and ignore Helen and Sergei. Young people do not enjoy being foreigners: these two are clearly wanting very much to be Japanese. Sergei thinks of his sons, who are in America right now. They have said they are excited about this. His younger son, Ilya, is truly so, but Ilya is his own country, a principality of Ilya; he will be happy anywhere as long as he gets what he wants. Dmitri is different. Dmitri doesn't know what he wants and maybe doesn't have the power to endure a little suffering for greater good. Sergei hopes that his example is enough of a lesson, but it is hard to be an example at a distance.

"When I came here as a young person," Yoshihiro says, gesturing to the figures on the stage below, "the representations were simple cardboard cutouts of kabuki actors. I'm not sure when they installed these robots. Not quite appropriate to the museum, and I agree with you, Sergei, not very wonderful."

A Japanese family approaches the stage. The children wave at the actroids, and laugh when they move.

"Ah, they're not afraid," Yoshi notes. "They think they are clowns."

"I remember a friend telling me," says Helen, "that it's a controversial thing in psychiatric circles—whether fear of clowns is a real phobia, like claustrophobia or agoraphobia, or a notion people pick up from movies or images in the media."

"Well. Clowns are much scarier than robots. Clowns. Yeeaachh." Sergei performs an exaggerated shudder and Helen and Yoshi laugh. It is good to introduce an informal tone to their conversation now, and also demonstrate that he is in a good mood.

They continue speaking in English as they exit the building. English is the vehicular language of Prime Space, though the astronauts all speak each other's native tongues. Sergei's Japanese is fluent and his accent is superior to Helen's (there is a sound in Japanese—a kind of rolling *l/r/u* combination that Helen admits to being unable to correctly produce). Sergei's English comprehension is near perfect, though his grammar has occasional but unimportant gaps. Yoshi's English has a British inflection; in Russian his tone is more expressive.

They have been training together for five weeks and although today has been designated as a rest day, Helen and Sergei had accepted Yoshi's suggestion that he drive them out to this local attraction. "It will be nice," Sergei said, "to be in a fresh outside place." Helen had brought binoculars. She's said she is an amateur bird-watcher, though it is difficult to imagine Helen as an amateur anything.

It is warm for March, almost cherry blossom season, which they will largely miss, as they are moving to the training facility in Utah in two weeks.

There seem to be no birds at all in the park. Most likely, insecticide coating on the trees has killed off potential food sources.

The astronauts are good sightseers. They walk across an art deco–style bridge, view a facsimile of the railway carriage of the Imperial Family, and admire a replica of the entrance hall of the Imperial Hotel. Outside a reconstructed Romanesque church, Yoshi explains that he first visited the Meiji-mura Park when he was ten and newly arrived in Japan after an early childhood spent in London.

"I remember seeing this," he said, "and feeling that it was not at all an exotic object, but something more familiar to me than a Shinto or Buddhist shrine. My eye was more accustomed to the Romanesque and Gothic. But you will see that bamboo blinds were employed in the interior of the church, to counteract the heat and humidity of its original site in Kyoto. It made an impression on me, to see the cultures blended so harmoniously."

All their talk has been like this so far, and that is good, but also, come on. They have come here in order to speak their thoughts freely, away from Prime, Sergei is certain of it. Only, someone has to start or else they will spend the whole day just saying agreeable things.

Now the astronauts will have lunch in a pavilion. He will say his news, and then they will talk of other matters, and he will relax.

Without question, Sergei, Yoshi, and Helen have developed a rapport. Not developed. The rapport was immediate. It probably was there before they met, as an algorithm. Prime was the crew below the stage, revolving the players: them.

IT WAS A CREW that any person who knew what they were doing would assemble. A short list for a mission to Mars that included a woman would absolutely have Helen Kane on it. Sergei had met her only a few times, but she'd spent considerable time in Russia early in her career, and hers was a name you heard often, always in terms of great admiration and respect, even from jerks. They had many friends in common. Yoshi he'd never met—though Helen had worked with him on a NASA–Prime project—but Yoshi's professional reputation was impeccable and people always said something about how they *liked* him, always in the same way, too, using almost the same words and emphasis, which spoke well of the guy's consistency. Everyone had expected Prime to select an all-American crew. That it was international said something important about Prime, and also of the robustness of the data that had put Sergei, Helen, and Yoshi together. Prime was a multinational corporation holding partnerships of some kind with every significant government space agency, but the crew didn't feel like politics. As a team, they already have *flow. Flow* is a word Prime likes, uses as noun and verb, subject and object. Even leadership of their crew has flow. Sergei is to command the Earth-to-Mars transit, Helen the Mars expedition, Yoshi the trip back to Earth. Very unorthodox, but Sergei liked this distribution of authority. He wouldn't have the first boots on Mars under this flow—that honor would be Helen's—but he was only fifty percent convinced the thing was going to happen anyway.

Fifty percent was enough.

They have the pavilion to themselves. The grounds are nearly empty. A couple dressed in old time–style wedding clothes pose for a photographer on the art deco bridge. Helen looks at the people through her binoculars, since there aren't any birds.

He will get it done now.

"So," Sergei says. "I have something I wish to tell you. It is that I am getting a divorce."

Yoshi takes a handkerchief from his jacket pocket and dabs his mouth. Helen puts her binoculars on the table. Sergei imagines their thoughts. Their thoughts will be of the mission. They will be asking themselves how precise are the personal variables that have brought them together. There are no margins for error in space. For a mistake that measured 1/50th the width of a human hair, a two-billion-dollar telescope was almost lost. In space, they are all Hubble. No one must think of his emotional state as fragile. Not Prime, not his crew.

"You are," Sergei looks in turn at Helen and Yoshi, "the first people I am telling. I will inform Prime of this situation tomorrow, but first I wish to tell you. It will not affect my work. In fact, marriage has not been what it should be for long time, but Nataliya is a good mother, and a good friend. I do not wish my boys to be growing up with a mother who is not happy. Talia, she wishes to have a new marriage. He is a good guy, I know him. I trust him. My boys know him. He is family: the cousin of my cousin's wife's brother. He is Russian, but was born in the States, and they will live there. I think it will be better for them, when I am away, to have steady home, to have a man who will watch over them and make their mother happy. I do this for them. This is not easy thing, but . . ." He stops and shrugs, as he had planned to at this point. "It is what happens," he says. "It is—" He has genuinely forgotten the phrase. "Chhh," he says, remembering. "Yes. It will be a positive change."

The park is too quiet. His words sound a little loud, though he always speaks more quietly when he is in Japan.

"Sergei, you have our full support." Helen turns to Yoshi, who nods once, very firmly. "And I am glad that the circumstances are so, well, like you said, really positive. I can imagine that starting the Eidolon training with things not so clear would have been hard, so this probably takes a lot off your mind. To have it settled, and to be moving forward." She is letting him know what line she will take if asked, Sergei thinks. She will reinforce his view. She will not be the woman who presses for emotion. She does not make a physical gesture, but Sergei can feel the ghost of one, on his back. She is patting his back, like his mother used to do.

"Yes, thank you for telling us," says Yoshi. He repeats his emphatic nod. "You have our support, and may I say that I admire very much your determination to do what is best for your children. They are very fortunate to have a father who loves them so much."

Yoshi is a good guy.

Sergei can hear a bird, but he can't see it.

"The man she wants to marry owns a shoe company," he says. "For a woman, the husband who can give lots of shoes is maybe better than the husband who is a cosmonaut, but for my boys I will still be the more cool dad. So."

Helen smiles, which is good because in his relief he has made a woman-joke and while Helen's reputation is of being a person who does not have problems with man-woman things, it's better not to call attention to this. And he wasn't thinking of someone like Helen when he said *woman*; he was thinking of someone like his wife.

"It will be a little easier for you," she says, "with your sons in the

States. I mean, before we start Eidolon. Less of a time difference for communications. And they won't have to travel as far if they can come to Utah."

"Yes." Sergei would have been happiest if Alexander and Talia took his children to someplace like Norway, or even Canada, but the advantage to America is that all the evils of the country are known, and his boys will be living in a town in New Jersey that is number three of most safe America towns.

He appreciates the vote of confidence that his divorce will make no difference to his candidacy for the mission. He does not think it will, but until he is strapped into a seat on top of a rocket that has launched for Mars, he cannot be sure he is going to Mars.

"So, I will inform Prime tomorrow. I have not lied," he says. "I thought it would come up in psychological examination. But for me, so far, that has all been tests with hypothetical situation."

"Yes," Yoshi says. "For me as well. I assume there is more to come."

"Seventeen months of it," Helen says, with a small smile.

It is good, it is over, they are going to be able to talk of other things.

"Okay," Sergei says. "Crew meeting." He makes a joke show of looking around at all the empty tables and underneath their own, taps one end of a chopstick as if testing for a microphone. "Yes. Okay. We are alone. So. Do you think we're going to Mars?"

The astronauts laugh.

"Oh, well, of course we are," Helen says.

This is a good tone to take. "Hey, why not? Maybe we won't, but let's say we will." Helen can say this because she has the least to lose of any of them. She is retired from NASA's astronaut corps, and she's American, so it is natural for her to be optimistic. Sergei is forty-five and Yoshi is thirty-seven. The space station was nearing the end of its already extended life, and for guys like them it was all about getting tagged for a lunar mission now that the moon is back in play. A single failure in any number of MarsNOW scenarios could mean that all Eidolon will signify is that the three of them are capable of spending seventeen months together in a tin can playing virtual reality games.

Or they could be the first crew to go to Mars, so there is that little thing. And both he and Yoshi are men from countries whose space agencies are facing the same difficulties and have ties to Prime that they wish to tighten. If the MarsNOW mission gets scrubbed, they will still be the astronauts Prime most knows and trusts, the ones most familiar with Prime systems, the inside-track guys. So, the decision was not so difficult, but he would still like to hear what the others have to say.

"Yoshi, Mars?"

"One has gotten so used to speaking with caution on the subject." Yoshi folds his arms and leans back in his chair. "People ask about a crewed mission to Mars and one says, 'Yes, yes, it is very exciting to contemplate,' 'There are many difficulties,' 'We are not quite ready,' 'For such a mission we need to consider,' and so on. You sympathize with the difficulty of getting funding for less glamorous projects. And now, of course, the conversation is about the moon."

"There is a lot of paranoia in the United States," Helen says, "about the Chinese lunar missions. I can't tell if it's real paranoia or media hysteria."

"Like fear of clowns," Yoshi suggests.

"Exactly." Helen raises an eyebrow. "The official NASA statement is that it's good for all humankind if China lands on the moon. But we know almost nothing about what is happening, or what their intentions are."

"They will *land*," Sergei says. "US landed with technology that was not so good as my toaster. But let us not be kidding ourselves—China is not going to shoot golf balls and pick up rocks. They will mine. And they will not be mining for all humankind; they will be mining for China. We are about to be in a big mess, no?"

"The politics are upsetting," Yoshi agrees. "This isn't what we do."

"No," Sergei says. "This is why Prime Space is future. Future with explorers, with scientists, not countries."

It will never be this simple, of course, but if they are to do this thing, they must not be countries, the three of them. He will not be the "Russian guy." For holidays, and a joke, yes, but this is his first act as a commander: let us be our own crew, let us be free.

"Yes," Yoshi says. "One must not be naive about the motivations of Prime Space—they are a commercial enterprise. But it would be unwise, I think, to be cynical about this. I have always been impressed with the program: the efficiency and the vision."

"Everyone I know from JPL who went over to Prime says the same thing," Helen adds. "It's the direction we should have been moving in all along."

"So," Sergei says. "We're in the right place."

It is cooler in the shade of the pavilion. The astronauts eat *miso-katsu* from zero-waste bowls. The couple in wedding clothes on the art deco bridge have been replaced by another couple, and a photographer. Sergei picks up Helen's binoculars. The woman wears a dress with fringe and a feathered band around her head, the man a three-piece suit. The woman is not smiling, but the man is, until the photographer raises his camera and the facial expressions of the bride and groom are reversed. Sergei places the binoculars back on the table, catches Helen's eye. She is maybe looking at him with sympathy. Perhaps he sighed.

"So, Helen," Sergei says. "Was it always your dream to go to Mars?"

"I remember my science teacher in grade school saying that everything we could see in the sky was so far away that it might as well be infinitely far," she says. "With the exception of the moon."

"Ah, did you dream of the moon?" Yoshi asks.

"No, the moon is too close," says Helen. She is not joking.

"Yes," says Sergei. He has a good feeling now. There is nothing to worry about, apart from the regular things. He is not a man for hoping, but at the very least, he will be tested past the point of exhaustion, and that's not nothing. "I agree. The moon is much too close."

DMITRI

"You are a fag," Dmitri says to his brother.

Ilya takes this calmly. "I am not," he says. "But if I were, so what? Pfff. It is nothing."

Dmitri does not think it is *nothing*, and Ilya's complacent sense of himself and the correctness of his opinions are a little irritating.

"Also you should not say 'fag' here," Ilya continues. "It is more cool to be okay with whatever people want to do."

"Don't let Papa hear you say that."

"I am quoting Papa," Ilya says, widening his eyes. "I repeat his words *exactly*. There is gay and not gay or both or maybe nothing. Yeah, and some boys are not boys and some girls are not girls and also there is mixture. Possibly we should not even learn English pronouns, to be safe."

"Ilya, when did Papa tell you this?"

"On the walk."

This interests Dmitri. Before their father was about to leave for training, or go on a mission, he liked to take them each on a long walk and have a conversation about meaningful things. Dmitri was always curious about what his father said to Ilya, but since Ilya never seemed curious about Dmitri's time with their father, pride prevented him from inquiring.

"Papa was saying things are different here," Ilya continues. "It is not a thing to say: *fag*. I should not say, and if someone says I am a gay, I should not fight."

"Does he know that you got in fights because of this at home?"

"No. Did you tell him?"

"Of course not." When their father was home, he was so happy to be with them that they all put their troubles away for a bit and pretended that everything was perfect. Some of that was good, like being on vacation. Some of it was like being in a play, which Dmitri had been made to do once in school, and had not enjoyed.

On Dmitri's walk with his father, they had discussed the divorce. Unfortunately, his father had spoken to him like he was a child. The divorce, he said, was not a division of their family, but an enlargement. Family was the most important thing, his father had said, and therefore it was a good idea to make your family as large as possible, to include as many people as you could in your family. Imagine if the whole world were your family. Then there would be no war.

"There would still be divorce," Dmitri had pointed out. It was as close as he dared to come in contradicting his father, or introducing a note of reproach in their conversation. His father had laughed and said, "That is true," and appeared almost proud of Dmitri for making the remark, and for a moment it seemed like he would talk to Dmitri like a man, but he did not. His father said that it was possible to divorce with love. No one was angry, he said, as if no anger meant happiness.

Dmitri looks across his younger brother to his mother and Alexander, who are holding hands. Dmitri is used to the sight of his mother and Alexander holding hands, and hugging, and kissing. It disgusts him, but he knows that his objections are childish, and he has decided to be stoic about it. His stoicism moves him.

Tonight is Ilya's treat. The ballet here is not in season, so they have come to a Broadway musical. Tomorrow is meant to be Dmitri's treat, only at the time he was asked he was in the mood to reject the notion of treats, so he just said Ilya could use his turn.

Tomorrow he could tell his family that he is sick. He is fifteen. His mother might let him stay behind in the hotel on his own.

No.

Yes.

No.

Yes. He will tell them that he is sick. Tonight, he will start coughing.

"Do you want me to explain to you what the synopsis says?" he asks Ilya, opening up the program. Ilya gives him an assessing look, and then agrees. Dmitri feels ashamed about the assessing look. He teases his brother too much. He loves his brother, and admires him. It means something to him that his brother should trust him. If his brother decides that he can't trust him, then that will be that, he will never trust him again. Ilya is not a subtle person; he only believes one thing at a time.

Dmitri thinks that in this, Ilya is very like their father. Maybe.

Dmitri translates the synopsis into Russian, quietly, because they are meant to speak only English in public, for practice. They examine the pictures of the performers that are printed in the program.

"This guy," Ilya says, pointing. "You can tell he is a good dancer."

"It's just his head," Dmitri objects. "How you can tell about his dancing from just his head?"

"You can tell," Ilya says.

Dmitri chews his lip and then points to a picture of a girl with blond hair and the appearance of five hundred thousand teeth.

"Her name is Rose," he says, reading the program. "She says thank you to her family and friends and teachers for believing in her, and her husband, Trey, for giving her love, and the Lord, for giving her a reason to wake up singing. So, Ilya, can you tell from her picture whether she is a good dancer or not?"

Ilya barely glances at it. "She is an idiot."

Dmitri laughs and shuts the program. His stomach hurts.

IN THE LOBBY, Dmitri noticed a man.

He noticed the man, and looked at him until the man looked back. The man had a little gray in his hair, though his face was not old. Dmitri did not think the man was American, because he was slim and very well dressed and not talking and anyway, there didn't seem to be so many Americans in New York City. The man was standing by himself in a way that Dmitri admired. He wished that he too was standing by himself, and was well dressed and not a kid.

Dmitri had a sudden feeling, a thought. *That man will know what to do.* But he hadn't been able to think much beyond that because he himself did not know what to do, or precisely what he meant by that, even.

He sort of knew.

"I have to go to the toilet," Dmitri had told his family, after he saw the man. "Restroom," he corrected himself. Dmitri's mother looked at Alexander.

"You don't have to wait for me," Dmitri said. "If you give me my ticket, you can all sit down now." Alexander, who liked to make a point of respecting Dmitri, handed over the ticket. Dmitri was, as always, a little ashamed of his ability to make people do what he wanted them to do.

He had to walk by the man to go to the restroom, but the lobby was crowded, and people had come between them. He had felt very stupid in the restroom, and did not trust touching himself, even to take a piss, so he just washed his hands and then came out.

The man was standing next to a poster on the lobby wall. Dmitri pretended that he was interested in inspecting all the posters, which seemed like a reasonable occupation. He was very afraid that the man would walk away before he got to him, but that did not happen.

"Hello," said the man, when Dmitri was next to him.

"Hello," Dmitri said. The poster next to the man was blue and pink colored and pictured a ridiculous blond girl, a unicorn, and an imbecile wearing legwarmers making a dance pose in roller skates on top of a rainbow. It was an absurd poster. No one could possibly be interested in it except for a six-year-old girl or a fag.

The man had on cologne. Alexander wore cologne. Dmitri's mother liked it, she was always smelling him. Dmitri's father did not wear cologne, because he often had to be in very close spaces with other people and so needed to have as little smell as possible.

"Are you interested in the theater?" the man asked in a friendly way. Perhaps Dmitri had been mistaken. Perhaps this man would not know what to do.

"No," said Dmitri. "I like art." Although it wasn't art he liked, he liked geometry, of which art had many good examples.

"Oh?" The man turned and looked at the poster and seemed to give it polite consideration as a potential work of art. The poster read *Xanadu* on it in bubble letters. Dmitri did not know what that word meant, or how you would say that word, or even if it was a word. Perhaps he didn't know English at all. He was a moron.

"Are you visiting New York?" the man asked. Dmitri was not able to place the accent.

"Yes. No. We are—I am moving—my family is moving—at this moment—we are in hotel." Dmitri stopped. His face was burning, so he kept it aimed at the poster. This was not him, this know-nothing child. "I am in a hotel," he said.

"Ah," said the man. "I am visiting. I am also staying in a hotel. The Gramercy Park Hotel. Do you know it?"

Dmitri shook his head and then looked at the man. Beauty was symmetry but also something else. This man wore cologne that made Dmitri's tongue feel big in his mouth.

"How old are you?" the man asked.

"Eighteen," said Dmitri. So, now he had told a lie and now it was all a game. This idea made Dmitri feel powerful and he stopped being embarrassed. He looked fiercely at the man.

The expression on the man's face changed. It became at once more gentle, and somehow much less so.

"My name is Kamil," said the man.

"Mikhail," Dmitri said.

"Mikhail, do you remember the name of my hotel?" asked the man.

"The Gramercy Park Hotel," said Dmitri.

"Tomorrow afternoon I will be there, all afternoon," said the man. "My room is 1204. What is the number of my room?"

"1204," said Dmitri.

"1204 was the year of the siege of Constantinople," said the man. "If you forget the number, then you must look up when was the year of the siege of Constantinople." The man smiled, and then laughed, which made Dmitri laugh too.

"You should join your family, Mikhail. Enjoy the performance."

The man stepped back and so Dmitri had no choice but to do what the man said.

When Dmitri got to his seat, Ilya was making a fuss about how he would need to ice his ankle later because they were doing a lot of walking, which was why Dmitri had needed to call him a fag.

His mother and Alexander are talking to Ilya now. Dmitri is not certain how to spell the word *Gramercy*—with a *y* at the end? Or an *e*? He traces different versions in English on the leg of his pants with his fingernail. *Gra-merci*.

His mother and Alexander are now talking to him. Apparently, the woman seated next to his mother—a total stranger—has taken an interest in their personal business. This woman has said that the show they are about to see is more singing and acting than dancing, but it is very good. If they want to see more dancing, the woman has recommended another show to see tomorrow night. Dmitri says that is fine, although who knows if this woman can be trusted.

He coughs a few times. Ilya had acted like he could tell a guy in the program was a serious dancer just from looking at his head, but it turns out this isn't a serious dance show. So, maybe that guy cannot dance at all. So, Ilya doesn't know everything. So, he can't tell. No one can tell.

They are sitting in the third row. The man, Kamil, must be sitting behind them somewhere. Perhaps the man cannot see Dmitri from where he is. You have to know someone very well before you can know them just by the back of their head. The lights blink. The performance is going to begin soon. Everyone is sitting down.

Dmitri stands up. His mother looks at him and hisses for him to sit, but Dmitri whispers that he is only taking off his jacket. He is a man who knows what to do, and he takes off his jacket and drapes it across his seat, which means he is turned around, facing the rest of the audience, and after he fixes his jacket he stands up straight for a moment, and then he turns and sits down.

There. Kamil knows where he is now, he is certain of it. Kamil is looking at the back of Dmitri's head, his neck, his shoulders. The lights go down and Dmitri puts his open program on his lap so that his dick can be hard if it wants to be hard, which it does. The orchestra, which is not in an orchestra pit but somewhere behind the curtain, begins to play.

He cannot go to the hotel tomorrow, to the room where Constantinople was seized.

He cannot *not* go.

On the day of Dmitri's twelfth birthday, they'd been on vacation at their cousin's house near Novorossiysk. His father had been on the International Space Station, and made a special plan to celebrate with them. His father had calculated when he could look out the window of the cupola on the station and be passing over just where they all were. And they had brought their father's pair of night vision goggles with them so they would be able to look into the night sky and see the light of the station passing over. They went outside at the right time, and held sparklers in the air, and they'd seen the light of the station, and waved their sparklers. "I felt I could see you," his father said later. "Just knowing that you were there, looking up at me, and I was looking down at you. It was one of the best moments."

They had been able to see his lights, but he hadn't seen theirs. The Black Sea, yes. The lights of Novorossiysk, yes. But not their individual sparklers. His father couldn't see him then, and could not see him now. His father wasn't even in space now, looking down. His father was in Japan. After that, his father would be in Utah. And then, his father would possibly go to Mars and become one of the most famous people ever on the planet. They were all very proud. The thing about pride, though, is it doesn't fully occupy you. It's like holding a sparkler. Basically, you just stand there with a light in your hand and look up.

The curtain rises, and the show begins. Dmitri looks at the things happening on the stage, but he does not see them. He imagines the back of his head, and the back of his neck, and the back of his shoulders and wonders what they look like to the man who is watching him, in the dark.

YOSHI

Yoshi settles with himself that he is grateful. Yes, it would have been nice to spend the entirety of his last two days in Japan with his wife, but Madoka could not walk away from her work for an entire day merely because he happened to have some free hours. They will have all day tomorrow, and they have had many evenings, or partial evenings, in the past seven weeks. Helen and Sergei have not been so fortunate. Yoshi moves through his house, consciously taking in the colors, the objects, the textures of things. It will be a long time before he is here again, and in a few months, he will not have any of these creature comforts. This glass bowl with flowers in it, for instance, and these candlesticks, a wedding present. Yoshi focuses on the candlesticks, but they are not quite the right objects to evoke emotion. One does not miss candlesticks.

For Eidolon, he will be allowed a very small bag for personal items, less than one kilo in weight. He will take something from nature, if it will be approved: his favorite acorns. *Q. phillyraeoides*, *Q. dentata*, *C. cuspidata*. The acorns will be a reminder of the trees that he loves, and are something he can hold in his hand. Later on, for the real mission, they will be acorns that have been to Mars.

Yoshi continues his tour through his small house. He and his wife have very compatible taste, preferring to live with light colors and no clutter.

Sometimes Yoshi does picture himself seated in a deep, tufted armchair, wearing a heavy silk dressing gown and brocaded slippers, surrounded by towers of dark bookcases and telescopes, and carved tables covered with maps and botanical drawings, a faithful midsize canine at his feet. He would not call it a fantasy, but perhaps it is that. He has not even told Madoka of this image.

It is too bad his wife could not have spent more time with his crew so they could know her. The day at Meiji-mura would have been a good opportunity, but she had insisted he go alone. "It will be better with just the three of you," she said. "You won't be able to talk as freely if I'm there."

This was prescient of her. His crew had talked freely, or as Prime might put it, they had deepened the context of their rapport and created a shared experience. If Madoka had been there, Sergei might not have taken the opportunity to speak about his divorce, and—in the presence of one who bore all the burden of astronaut life and none of the joy—they might have felt the need to temper their enthusiasm concerning Prime Space.

Yoshi thinks he will use the remaining time before his wife's arrival to attend to some household chores so that tomorrow they can devote themselves entirely to each other. There is not a great deal to do—accustomed to travel, Madoka and Yoshi leave light fingerprints—but there is laundry to put away. Yoshi unclips a pair of his wife's underpants from the drying line and considers how best to fold them. He recalls watching with wonder, early in his marriage, as Madoka briskly converted a fitted bed sheet into a perfectly neat rectangle. He had not even known that was possible, and she had moved too quickly for him to study her method. He still does not know how it is done, has deliberately left it as one of life's eternal mysteries, a romantic acknowledgment on his part of the unfathomable depths of his wife.

Yoshi moves into the bedroom and opens the top drawer of his wife's bureau in order to get a paradigm for how Madoka likes her underpants folded. Not at all, it seems. She leaves them in a flat pile.

Yoshi tells himself that if his wife had raised serious objections to his joining Prime for this mission he would have listened to them. He had been careful, when outlining the specifics of the timeline to her, to do so in a neutral way so as not to prejudice her honest response. "I could be one of the first three humans to walk on another planet" had not been part of his presentation. He had not brought up the increase in salary, that he would be earning—for the first time in their married life—more than his wife. He had not said, "JAXA was lobbying hard for a Japanese citizen to be included in the astronaut selection and they have let me know that if I turn this opportunity down, Prime will not replace me with another Japanese astronaut. We were selected as a team—the three of us—and as far as Prime is concerned, individual components of the team are not replaceable."

None of these points were inconsequential—indeed, they were almost overwhelming in their combined significance—but it was the last point that had initially excited him the most. It was evident that Prime considered the three of them to be a kind of dream team, a trio whose individual temperaments, skills, and experience would combine in such a way as to be able to withstand the most challenging and dangerous expedition in the history of humankind. It was not unlike being told that one's soul mates had been located.

He had not voiced any of these things to his wife, but midway through his very measured explanation of the MarsNOW timeline, Madoka had interrupted him.

"You want to do this."

"I want to consider it," he said. "There are many things for us to look at."

Madoka had waved that away. "We can look and look, but it's not like looking will give an answer. There isn't a right or wrong decision to be made, just a decision."

Madoka never let him shift responsibilities to her with pabulum such as, "Whatever you decide, I will stand behind," or "Either way, you have my full support." She insisted that he act on his convictions, and accept the consequences. Sometimes he might wish that she would give him a hint of what those consequences might be, from her end, but how could he extract something from her that did not yet exist?

And she was right. There were reasons for considering the offer very carefully, but the choice would be made in the blind either way. However, he had persisted. "How you feel about it is important to me. We should decide this together. It will affect you—us—our life together."

"But this is our life," she said. "We've already decided everything. This is who you are, and who I am. What you do next is just yes or no." She was very deep, his wife. So deep that she could render matters of philosophy into binary questions.

He'd left it alone for the rest of that evening. When they were in bed, Madoka had brushed away his usual preliminary overture of a hand on her breast and turned the tables, so to speak, wrestling him around with great fierceness the way she occasionally did, and demanding that he keep his eyes open as she bestrode him. It was exciting when she approached him like that, and while he was never sure how much he was genuinely contributing to the rather miraculous-looking apogees of pleasure Madoka achieved in these times, Madoka always touched him afterward with great tenderness and, possibly, gratitude.

"You don't have to explain to me who you are," she said that night. "I know." And she had gone to sleep, rather noisily, on his shoulder.

The decision—if it was that—followed quickly. For the past three years he had been flying a desk, as the US astronauts put it. A man without a mission. He'd worked with the JAXA–Prime team on ultralightweight ballute designs, made extensive personal appearances, attended conferences and training summits all over the world, continued his environmental activism. It had not been difficult to continue to construct goals, whether these were professional, or adding kilometers to his daily run, or reading all of *A Dance to the Music of Time.* But it was not the same as training for a specific mission. Once he said yes to Prime, Yoshi knew he had answered not correctly, but inevitably.

It changed his walk, to know he was a man going to space. He moved along corridors, streets, even the privacy of his own home, as if a klieg light were focused on his person. His carriage became more erect, his movements more decisive. He felt not just more present, but extra present, as if he shone, as humans did when viewed in the infrared.

Yoshi moves downstairs to the kitchen and decants the wine he has bought for tonight. A message comes onto his screen, from his parents. They are anxious to see him before he leaves.

They are anxious in general.

"Now you can start the family," his mother had said, when he'd returned from the space station three years ago. *The family,* she said, as if it were a mechanism like *the car* or *the ceiling fan* and what was required of him was merely ignition, then others—Madoka—would take over. This was traditional, conservative thinking. It would not occur to his parents that a pregnant wife, or a newborn child, would be a professional or personal impediment. It would not occur to them that Madoka might rebel at the idea of solo parenting. To his parents, Yoshi had intimated that Madoka was willing, and the hesitation was on his part. He did not wish his parents to criticize his wife.

He would be gone now for seventeen months but the real mission would be three years. Madoka was healthy but she was thirty-seven. Often, when the subject of candidacy for a Mars mission came up, it was said that it would be better to send older astronauts, ones with grown children. Prime has said nothing to him about this.

The issue of children was potentially a consequence in waiting.

Yoshi guides his thoughts away from this problematic line of thought. The subject of having a child was one that engendered deep ambivalence in him. Any strong evidence of desire on Madoka's part would have moved him, but without it, he was becalmed. One problem was that he could not imagine a child of his own. He could not even imagine a miniature Madoka. Babies were always said to change everything. Yoshi was not interested in changing everything with regards to his wife.

He had gotten as far as asking, some weeks ago, if Madoka had seen her doctor and if they should talk about "certain options." Madoka said that she had, and that she felt "the same way about their options." The clumsiness of the conversation had embarrassed both of them.

In a way, he envied Sergei and Helen, for whom the question of children had been solved. Especially Helen, whose child was an adult.

He reminds himself that he should not talk overmuch about his crewmates during this last time together with his wife. Anyway, Madoka joked that he was terrible at describing people. It was true, in terms of concrete nouns and adjectives.

For example, when Helen made drawings to illustrate a point she was making, it could be seen that she was able to draw perfect straight lines without the aid of instruments. Yoshi felt that this said quite a bit about Helen as a person, but it would be difficult for him to articulate it further.

Yoshi opens up the refrigerator and peers inside. When it inconveniences nobody, he is a vegetarian. He takes out carrots, picks up a knife. He will make a curry. Yoshi slices a disk of carrot, looks at it, and then is struck, for the first time, with the full comprehension that there is a scenario wherein he will be going to Mars in four years. Heretofore, he has been keeping a mental space—a kind of defensive moat—between himself and the idea of a Mars voyage. He believes the others are doing the same.

God in heaven, Mars, Yoshi thinks, in English.

The phrase *God in heaven* is not his own. He is not religious.

And will he say this to Madoka, when she returns? When she walks in the door and the table is set and the wine is poured and the candles are lit and the curry is almost done and her underpants are laying flat in a neat stack in a drawer upstairs? Will he wrap his arms around his wife and say, *God in heaven, Mars, my love, my true love*? And will she understand what he means by this when it is not even his language or his God—that in the words there is awe and wonder, yes, but also inadequacy, for how can you hold a whole planet in your head, or in your dreams? Or in your arms?

MADOKA

The photograph, for those who choose to look at it, has several contradictions. The seated young woman's hair is cropped to the fashion of 1923, but she wears traditional kimono. One of her hands is placed primly on her knees and the other grasps a pistol, pointed to the floor, but with a finger on the trigger. The woman's broad smile allows the viewer to see the gap between her two front teeth, but her eyes are closed. Because it is unusual for anyone to frame and display a photograph of a person with their eyes closed, most people assume that the woman's eyes are closed because she was blind. She was not blind.

Madoka Tanaka is not blind either, but she cannot see the photograph in front of her because she is wearing a sleep mask. The sleep mask was made by a Danish firm and Madoka has made certain modifications to it so that now it resembles the full-face masks worn by Mexican lucha libre wrestlers, except the eyes are blocked and also, it is a tasteful gray. It is very effective: Madoka can see nothing. She reaches her hands out and is surprised by how close the wall is, would've guessed that she was almost a meter away, and not centimeters. She has stubbed her fingers on the light switch, and from that, she knows she must be in front of the photograph of her great-great-grandmother.

If she wanted to, Madoka could wear this mask all day, a wildly indulgent idea that is not completely out of this world. Yoshi is gone. Today is a Sunday. She has no social commitments. There is always work that could be done, but why not give herself an entire day off? It is not unreasonable.

Madoka has not been sleeping well, so over the past three months she has been ordering a series of ever more complex sleep masks. She had worn this one last night, and it had not worked, but she had not wanted to take it off this morning. The material is pleasant on her skin, and she finds it more calming to be in darkness when there is light, rather than darkness in darkness.

She runs her fingers around the photograph frame in the hallway, dislodging some dust. It is not an interesting sensation, so she moves on. The photograph of her great-great-grandmother was a gift from her mother, but it was not a gift for her. Madoka's mother and Yoshi adored one another, and Yoshi had liked the photograph when he had seen it at her parents' house. He had been struck by the pose—so provocative—with the closed eyes and the gun. Why the closed eyes? Why the gun? No one knew. Yoshi was impressed by the story of her ancestor, who had been a poet, a contributor to the short-lived magazine *Bluestocking*, and had translated the diaries of Frances Burney into Japanese. That was the sort of thing that moved Yoshi. He was romantic.

Her great-great-grandmother had died in the confusion following the Great Kanto earthquake of 1923, of smoke inhalation, unable to get clear of her burning house because her feet had become stuck in the melting tarmac of the street outside. She had not been the only person to die like this.

Madoka didn't care for what poetry she had read of her ancestor's—it was all very sentimental—but she enjoyed imagining the scenario of a woman trying to run from her home, and getting stuck in melting pavement. Screaming, and so forth, before her own lungs melted.

Madoka has thought, often, that the vividness and complexity of her fantasies, and the fact that they are voyeuristic, not personal, means she has the soul of an artist.

She continues down the hallway, not touching anything, challenging herself to walk normally and not shuffle. She has never spent a lot of time in this house. Her company is based in Nagoya, but her work requires her to travel for most of the year. Madoka is Global Chief Sales Operative for a company that manufactures robotic caregivers. The robots are excellent at their job. They keep track of medicines, monitor vital statistics, communicate with doctors, suggest exercises when they sense their charges have been stationary for too long, assist in manual tasks. They read out loud, ask questions, play music. They chat. They do not love, but they are capable of receiving it.

Yoshi's parents had bought the house for them when they were newly married. Madoka and Yoshi had put into the house all the things that people put into a house, except for themselves, and children.

Her husband will never say to her: I want to have children. He needs her to take the responsibility of wanting it.

It's not that she is afraid of the responsibility. She just doesn't want being a mother to be her great thing. She doesn't want the epiphany of motherhood. She isn't interested in learning that it's "not all about her." She is quite well aware of that already.

She might be able—just—to face being a mother, if she knew for sure that she was a real person. But not before.

The Prime Space Simulation would last for seventeen months. Yoshi would be gone for much longer, because of the training, but for seventeen months she would know absolutely that he was gone. It would be almost like he was in prison.

Yoshi had been largely gone for most of their marriage, either training in Tsukuba or Cologne, or Houston. Once in low Earth orbit. During his time on the space station they had conversed much more than they did when he was on Earth. It was important, psychologically, for astronauts in space to communicate with their friends and family. The idea that she was contributing to Yoshi's psychological health was very funny. Sometimes she felt that they were on the edge of laughing about this together. But if they did that, that would mean that he saw her for who she was, and then they would probably have to get divorced.

When Yoshi had gone to the space station she had been the target of the usual envy: "Your husband is a hero!" and the even more usual envy disguised as pity: "It's wonderful what he's doing, but it must be so hard on you!" The Prime Space simulation was different. It was childish, playing at going to Mars, and there would be opportunities for very silly jokes in the media: that Yoshi would rather be stuck in a metal can in a desert in Utah with a Russian man and an elderly American lesbian than her, and so on.

She is at the stairs now. Five steps, then a turn, and then thirteen steps. If she practiced, she might be able to work up to doing this without holding on to the wall. The staircase has no banister; if she fell on the thirteen steps, she would fall through open air onto the table below, or on the cabinet to the left of the table, which had candles and picture frames and three glass bowls on it. What a big mess it would make! The blood would run down her legs and there would be bruises, maybe broken bones. She could hit her head at a bad angle and die. It would look very odd to whoever found her because she would still be wearing her sleep mask and also, she was not wearing any clothes.

People would see her naked body and the sleep mask and think there was something sexual involved, that she had been engaged in some kind of perverse tryst with a lover, who had abandoned the crime scene. The medical examiners and the police would take photographs.

It would all be very dramatic. But that kind of drama wasn't as interesting as this moment right now, standing on the stairs, naked, blind, just thinking about falling.

She was an artist, she knew it. This proved it, this thinking. She was maybe the only real artist, because she did not want to display her art. People who showed their art, and sold it, were just people who sold things. They might as well be making donuts or futons or socks. They got to call it art for some reason that was totally unclear to her, that was, in fact, made up. What gave them the right to say that what they made was art? Because they had feelings about it? People who made socks had feelings too. She had lots of feelings about her socks.

What she was talking about, what she had discovered in this moment, was the real thing. Creation without object or purpose or audience.

She was possibly not the first person to realize this. She was probably, right now, connected to a great tradition of true artists who nobody knew about because they had never made anything but true art, which no one had ever seen or heard. Her body feels so warm, thinking this. She is lit up, on fire. She stands still and lets the feeling grow up around her.

At the bottom of the stairs was a photograph Yoshi had taken from the space station, at night. He said that they had been over central Asia at the time, but in the picture you couldn't see that, or Earth at all, just a narrow curving beam of the Earth's atmosphere, and behind that, a setting crescent moon. He had talked about how he could take a picture of the Earth that captured what he was seeing, but never one that captured how he felt about what he was seeing. He said that this photograph didn't capture his feelings either, but it was the photograph that most closely reminded him of his feelings.

If Yoshi were here right now, she would tell him that of course a photograph couldn't capture his feelings. He was always reading books, and listening to music, and looking at photographs, like that photograph of her great-great-grandmother, and wanting to see things in them, and find things in them. What was he looking for? Why go to space at all? One could stand on a staircase and go where no one has ever gone. Why go to Mars? People would go to Mars and what? Destroy it, and make a bunch of art.

No wonder her great-great-grandmother had closed her eyes in the photograph. They should all close their eyes. The Earth was coming for them. The Earth was going to reach up and grab them and not let go and they would have no choice but to stand still, and submit to the fire.

LUKE

The Eidolon Observation team—Obbers—has a meeting in X-4, but Luke is early. His colleague Nari is also early, so the two decide to go up on the roof and take in the view. Luke is glad that Nari is his partner for so many shift rotations, as she has a very good sense of humor. Today, she's wearing glasses with grooved frames and thick lenses, almost like binoculars.

Nari takes the stairs two at a time. Like many of the structures here at the space center, the stairs are made of recycled steel and coated in a shiny color of something Luke suspects is not paint. He thinks the reds and blues and yellows are the effect of whatever treatment is on the Low-E windows. The primary colors always make him feel like he is in a Legoland version of a space center, but in a good way. Prime probably intends him to feel this way: they are a very thorough organization. At the company dormitory in nearby Hornsville, where the Eidolon teams are housed, almost anything a person uses, touches, consumes, or handles is tagged for either recy-cling or composting. His podlike bed is a thing of ergonomic beauty and is giving him the best sleep of his life. Luke can sign up for lectures on astronomy or robotics or planetary geology given daily in one of the communal spaces. He can spend an hour floating in the sensory deprivation tank. He can join air hockey or basketball teams with names like "Lagrangian Liberation Front" or "Phobos Phalcons." Prime is, in short, heaven. Secular heaven.

And Luke will be spending the next couple of years observing three of the best examples of Homo sapiens, and maybe making some contribution to helping Earth's best humans take off from a moving object and fly more than fifty million miles across space to another moving object, and *land*, and stand where no human has stood. When Luke had seen the mission control room of Prime Space, he'd almost burst into tears. And when he made a humorous kind of comment about his emotion at communal dinner, everyone murmured some kind of "yeah" and "me too."

They reach the top of the staircase. Nari half turns and body slams herself with accuracy against the metal door, which swings open.

Before them, to the north, the majestic outlines of the San Rafael Swell. The swell is a result of plate quivering in the Paleocene, somewhere between forty and sixty million years ago, a time of mountain building known as the Laramide Orogeny. Luke knows very little about geology, but is struck by the sensuality of the language, so different from that of cognitive science. *The Laramide Orogeny* sounds to him like the secret parts of a woman, perhaps a woman from Wyoming, passionately arrived at, like the swell, through a long series of pulses and quivers and persistent thrustings in the dark.

To look at now, the swell is austere and harshly alien. Which makes it a reasonable analogue for the Mars portion of Eidolon. Tucked into a valley among the mountains are the simulators the astronauts will be using: the exact models of *Primitus*, the craft that will take the crew to Mars, and *Red Dawn*, the one that will bring them home, plus two Rovers and supply pods, and the processing plant. The site is closed to everyone but a special Eidolon team, affectionately known around Prime as "The Shadows." Luke has seen mockups of the spaceships around the space center. He cannot quite believe they are real. That is, that something exactly like them is real. He has also been to Hangar A at Prime's launch center in Texas. They hadn't let him inside to see the heavy-lift *Manus V* rocket—the real one—that will shoot *Primitus* to Mars, but just the size of the hangar caused a primitive animal response in his body: the hair on his arms and neck had stood on end. Afterward, on the flight from Texas to Utah, he'd become incensed by the behavior of his fellow passengers, unable to bear the cognitive distance between human beings who could dream and then make a *Manus V*, and human beings who selfishly crammed an extra bag into the overhead compartment.

Nari joins Luke at the roof's perimeter wall and points out a few landscape features. She takes a deep breath and tilts her face to the sun, holding her hands over the lenses of her glasses, then brings her head down and blinks through her glasses at Luke in a friendly way.

"You have a favorite astronaut yet?" she jokes.

"Oh cool, we get to have favorites," Luke jokes back. In truth, he has noted in himself a special preference for Helen Kane.

"Yoshi is sort of the perfect man." Nari fiddles with her spectacles. "He's a pilot, he's got degrees in aerospace engineering. He plays the piano. He was a star baseball player in high school. He's an environmental activist. He's like"—she makes her voice exaggeratedly teenager-ish—"evvvvverything."

"He's also the only person I've ever heard use the word 'recondite' in a sentence," Luke points out.

Of course, the thing about Yoshi that was truly remarkable, the thing about all the astronauts that was truly remarkable, was their level of control. Whatever their neurophysiologic or biochemical responses, when it came to behavior, the astronauts played a long game. A mission to Mars would be a very long game indeed, and Luke was going to have a front-row seat.

More, much more, than geeking out on how we are going to get to Mars, or why, or what we should do when we get there, what Luke wants to understand is *who*. Who are these people that can withstand such a trip, the danger, the risk, the isolation, the pressure? What can these people teach us? Because if we—the species—might eventually do something like move to another planet, it would be better if we made a few improvements on ourselves first, if possible.

Understanding the brain wasn't like understanding mathematics, or physics. It wasn't an enlargement of our collective understanding of the universe—it went the other way. At a certain point, you had the thing in your hands and a colossal responsibility. The brain could be altered. The brain clearly, in many cases, *should* be altered. Which was ethically complicated and had been giving Luke very weird, splitting-the-atom-type dreams for the past three years before he came to Prime.

Now I am become Amygdala, the destroyer of worlds.

When yet another round of behavioral experiments on undergraduate volunteers started giving you delusions of apocalyptic grandeur it was time to rethink your career trajectory. He is very happy to be here, doing this work. He sleeps well at Prime.

"There they are!" Nari cries out. She is leaning over the edge of the perimeter wall, looking down. Luke tries to follow her line of sight but isn't sure what she is exclaiming over. Nari takes off her glasses and hands them to Luke.

"Do *not* look at the sky," she says. "The filter isn't on and the sun *will* damage your eyes. Look down. Two o'clock." She grips Luke by his elbows and moves him into position.

"They *are* binoculars." Luke adjusts the frames of Nari's glasses, focusing.

"Yeah, this guy in Prime NeuroErgo gave them to me," Nari says. "They're prototypes. So, do you see? Two men, one woman? By the green building."

Luke can see. It is Sergei, Helen, and Yoshi. He has not seen them in person before this. The binoculars are powerful; he can pick out details of their clothing. Sergei is wearing a gold bracelet. Helen has on a yellow shirt. Yoshi is smiling, saying something to the other two that is making them smile as well. Nari tugs Luke's elbow and, with some reluctance, he hands the glasses back to her.

Astronomers, he has recently learned, have a slightly condescending attitude for the general public's love of what they deem "pretty pictures." The highly color-filtered images from the space telescopes may capture Joe and Jane Public's interest, but astronomers get turned on by spectra, by data.

Luke has been looking at the data of Sergei and Helen and Yoshi for so long that he finds the sight of their corporeal selves almost shocking. This is not the way he knows them, and it is exciting to see them like this. It is good—humbling—to be reminded of how little he might actually know. For example, nothing in Helen's data suggests that she would choose a yellow shirt.

HELEN

Years ago, while training at NASA's Neutral Buoyancy Lab, Helen's instructor Jeff had told her, "Don't fight the suit. The suit will always win, no matter how strong you are. Your key to success is going to be: sink and melt. Just like those experiments we did as kids with cornstarch and water? If you try to jab your fingers all stiff through cornstarch and water you'll encounter a solid. But if you sink and melt your hands on the surface, you'll move right through it. So that's what you gotta do. You gotta tell your hands to sink and melt. Sink and melt."

Helen counts this advice as one of the most profound she has ever received, and has made periodic attempts throughout her life to apply it in other areas: Sink and Melt Feminism, Sink and Melt Departmental Politics, Sink and Melt Parenting. The approach has been most successful inside a spacesuit.

Helen is inside a Prime spacesuit now, and outside a life-size mockup of *Primitus*. Both these things—Helen and *Primitus*—are submerged in Prime Space's Neutral Buoyancy Lab. The spacesuit is pressurized, tethered with umbilical cords to a life support system, and weighted to mimic the conditions of microgravity. Helen's current position inside it is not comfortable. She is upside down, and though the spacesuit is neutrally buoyant, she is not; her shoulders are bearing her full weight. Helen flexes her feet inside her boots, anchoring herself like a bat to take the pressure off her shoulders. Inside the gloves, her hands feel unpadded and fleshless. She has been in the water for almost six hours.

Helen unlocks the Body Restraint Tether anchoring her to *Primitus*, and clips it back on the mini workstation attached to her chest. She makes the "okay" sign to the utility diver next to her and slowly brings her feet down, righting herself in the water, feeling the suit shift up off her shoulders and the blood rush from her head. For the last twenty minutes she has been gritting her teeth so hard she can barely open her mouth. But Helen has done everything she was supposed to do, in the time allotted to do it. If smiling wouldn't be painful, she would smile.

"Helen's the bolt whisperer," says a utility diver, when they are back on deck. "I heard you had the best hands in the business." He offers Helen a fist bump of approval.

The time to review her performance is in debriefing, and the praise is not appropriate. Still, to refuse a fist bump would look surly, not modest, and so she fist bumps. A trainer removes the shoulder pads from Helen's Liquid Cooling Ventilation Garment, and Helen tries not to wince. After crawling out of the spacesuit, Helen had been offered a chair and a Snickers bar, and refused both. She is not confident that after a few minutes of sitting she will be able to go from sitting to standing in an effortless way, and it's easier for the Nutrition Team if she only snacks on what they give her to snack, at appointed snacking time. The chlorinated fug of the lab's atmosphere stings her eyes after the sterile confines of the spacesuit. Helen swings her arms and assesses the level of stiffness in the rest of her body. She forces herself to chat and joke for a few minutes more before sliding her feet into paper slippers and making her way to the donning cubicle at the far end of the pool, trying not to look like a person who is running for the bathroom.

Helen talks to herself, naming the things she is doing as she does them, a trick for letting her body know who is running the show. *I am unzipping the LCVG and hanging it up, peeling off the long underwear and folding it neatly before tucking it into the laundry bin. I am making a triangle of the diaper I thankfully did not have to use and placing it in the trash along with the paper slippers. I am grabbing a few cleansing wipes and sweeping them up and down my body. I see that there is a toilet adjacent to the Donning Cubicle, and I will use it now.*

Once she is seated, she lets her interior monologue and body collapse, curving her spine forward and spreading her knees so that her head can hang between them. She places her hands on her cold feet and allows herself five deep breaths. Her body is doing what it has always done, which is to exceed expectations, but it costs her a fraction more than it has in the past, and this must be concealed.

It is funny that Prime, whose VR simulators are realer than real, would have them training in something as old-fashioned and flawed as a pool. You got drag in water the way you never did in space, and tools stayed put if you let go of them. It was, however, a good way not just to train an astronaut, but to test her: the two verbs being more or less synonymous. The day Helen stops being tested is the day no one needs her.

Last night, Helen had her first dream of walking on Mars. It was a very silly dream—she had been holding up an umbrella over her spacesuit to "keep the sun off"—but the atmosphere of the dream had been cheerful.

On Earth, Helen has had many dreams about being in space, but usually these involve minor aggravations, spooled out slowly. Failing to cap off her squeeze bottle properly in microgravity and spending hours cleaning up her soup. Realizing at step seventy of a hundred-step checklist that she missed step five and must begin again. An alarm bell that will not stop ringing no matter what she does.

She has never dreamed, on Earth, of walking in space. This is a source of frustration: why does her subconscious not give her the best thing she knows? The perfect thing, the incorruptible thing. The thing you wanted to get into your speeches about why space exploration is important but never quite could. You always had to fight against bad human history when trying to make people understand what is important. If only the telescope had been invented a few hundred years earlier, it might have been Science, not God, and Michelangelo could have filled an *Observatory* with images of the cosmos, and Mozart would have written a requiem for a star, and you wouldn't have to explain anything.

After she had completed her first spacewalk, her commander had said to her, "Helen, you've just walked in space, and that's something no one will ever be able to take away from you."

The phrase is funny. "Something that no one will ever be able to take away from you"? It should be "something that you will not be able to lose due to your own negligence or poor decision making or the endless interference of nonessentials." Helen sees the value in occasionally giving others inaccurate reassurances, but holds herself to a different standard. *Everything* is something that can be taken away from you.

Her five seconds are up.

After debrief, Helen meets Sergei and Yoshi at E-Lab. The two have spent the morning in launch simulations for *Red Dawn*. If all goes well, Helen will never do a solo Extravehicular Activity, like the one she practiced today. If all goes well, Sergei and Yoshi will never launch from Mars without her. These are contingency plans: situations that must be rehearsed in case something critical fails or one of the three astronauts is dead.

For the next four hours, Helen, Sergei, and Yoshi practice medical techniques on a synthetic androgynous human figure they have christened Sam. The astronauts are watched over by a team of doctors who take turns announcing a different medical emergency, and complicating Sam's condition midtreatment. On the space station, situations like toxic exposure or kidney stones or appendicitis are considered evacuating conditions, but there can be no evacuation on a mission to Mars.

Today, Sam suffers burns, fractures a hip, needs a tooth pulled, has a heart attack, requires CPR, receives the Heimlich, and loses an eye. The astronauts do not pretend to offer Sam anything like a realistic bedside manner, but indicate at what moments they might engage in something like a bedside manner.

"At this point, I encourage Sam to take shallow breaths."

"I am now telling Sam to stay calm and focus on my voice."

"I will tell Sam to prepare for a slight sting."

The astronauts are not given protocols on how to examine Sam's gynecological equipment. The thought occurs to Helen, as she watches Sergei and Yoshi cut away Sam's pants and then modestly drape Sam's pudenda in preparation to treat an abdominal wound, that the noninclusion of Sam's reproductive organs is, when it comes to her, accurate. There had been other options for the common fibroid tumors discovered a decade ago in her body, but why hang on to a uterus or cervix she didn't need? One less place to get cancer, and with drugs she could fly through menopause without it interfering in her work. Anyway, for her and Sam, there is almost nothing left inside that particular area to see, or go wrong.

"It has been the day of the dead," Yoshi says that evening, when they have gathered in the living space of Sergei's room to study. During breaks they teach one another the ten-minute routines their physical fitness coach has devised for each of them. Sergei is surprisingly graceful, given his compact physique. He tells them that his younger son studies ballet and ballroom dance, and has won competitions. Yoshi demonstrates his ability to perform unsupported handstands. Helen can do the splits, but she does not perform them in her routine. Doing the splits in front of men has no upside unless you want to invite envy or desire.

"We will have talent night during mission," Sergei says. "Helen, you play harmonica, yes? You will bring?"

"I will," Helen says. "A buddy of mine at JPL made me one that only weighs about twenty grams."

"It is good sound for space travelers," says Sergei. "You can play cowboy songs. We will ask Prime to pack some beans for us, and make simulation campfire video. With simulated sleeping cows in distance. They can give us virtual cowboy hats."

Helen enjoys it when Sergei makes gentle fun of Prime Space, although she does not instigate doing it herself. Throughout her career she has judged it safest to be the one laughing at the joke, rather than the one making it.

During Eidolon, each astronaut will have a thirty-minute segment in their daily schedule allotted to watching uplinks of Earth news collected for them by their Prime handlers, and they've been instructed to indicate programs, sites, and areas of interest. Sergei, Helen, and Yoshi talk through their selections so as not to double up on the same tech and science resources. All three of them want to follow the Chinese lunar landing of *Weilai 3*. On Sergei's screen they watch footage released from Xinhua of the taikonauts giving an interview. Images depicting the Chinese flag on the moon are already flying over Beijing, Shanghai, Guangzhou.

"How are US flags doing on moon?" Sergei asks Helen.

"The last time anyone looked four of them were still up. But the UV radiation has almost certainly bleached them completely white." On the screen now, the last surviving Apollo-era astronaut is speaking. The astronaut is being interviewed, but he is ignoring both the questions and the physical presence of his interlocutor and speaking directly to the camera. The astronaut is a man who has been to the moon, and he will squander no civility on his inferiors, i.e., everyone who has not been to the moon, i.e., everyone.

"I had a dream that I walked on Mars last night," Helen says. "I carried an umbrella. I remember someone telling me that you should always ask people to interpret your dreams. You won't learn anything about your dream, but you'll learn a lot about the other person."

"Was the umbrella open or shut?" Sergei asks.

"Open."

"Then I have no idea what that means," Sergei says. "I only remember that closed is bad."

"I think it is a good omen." Yoshi hands Helen a cup of tea. "An umbrella is a symbol of togetherness. There. What have you learned about us?"

"Sergei is a pessimist and you're an optimist," Helen says.

"I have learned that Yoshi is better at taking psychological tests,"

Sergei says. "We should give him ours. At least you did not have dream of clowns on Mars."

It has become one of their jokes: that Sergei is deathly afraid of clowns.

Later, alone in her room, Helen gives herself thirty minutes to attend to personal business. She will need to purchase gifts for friends and family members, presents for the birthdays and Christmases and anniversaries she will miss during Eidolon, and distribute them in advance of their occasions. Prime will assign her an Earth liaison who will be able to take care of this, but Helen has learned from the past that this can seem cold to certain members of her family. She consults the file she keeps of previous gifts given to friends and family members, along with one that details personal preferences, favorite colors, hobbies, and updated clothing sizes. Helen normally enjoys this process, but just now she is feeling restless. She tries to compose a short email to her daughter, and knows that her attempt is flat, but her half hour is up.

It was Helen's husband, Eric, who had told her about asking others for dream interpretations as a method of gaining insight. It wasn't that Helen forgot who told her. She generally avoids naming her husband to people whose acquaintanceship postdates her marriage. To say "my husband" is not only misleadingly present tense—Eric has been dead five years—it is also technically inaccurate: the vows clearly state *till death do us part*. Other options are equally problematic: "My dead husband . . ." has an awkward comic bluntness and "My husband, who is dead" can hardly be said without calling attention to itself. Even mild shows of sympathy embarrass Helen intensely, so, when she can, she substitutes with *someone* or *a friend*.

She can't remember the context of why Eric was telling her about dreams. It seems to Helen that she has been left with a puzzling—even irritating—series of her dead husband's non sequiturs untethered to an emotional event involving her dead husband. This is not how memory is supposed to work. Eric's pronouncements, opinions, and factoids emerge from time to time in her brain, as banal and impersonal as fortunes inside a Chinese cookie, solving nothing.

Helen hops out of bed and retrieves her harmonica from her suitcase in the closet. She has passed the place—and this sensation is familiar to her—where thinking of what is about to be left behind makes sense or is tolerable. She cannot sink and melt into the place of dead husbands and monthly payments and birthday presents. She cannot write a perfect email to her daughter.

She would like to begin Eidolon now. She would like to begin yesterday. Every day of successful Eidolon will be one day closer to space.

She will plan some things to play for Sergei and Yoshi. There's that nice thing from *Billy the Kid*. "Prairie Night," it's called. It's surprising what you can do on a harmonica. She will be able to play the virtual piano too, of course, but it will be nice to have something real to hold in her hands.

The harmonica had been the first musical instrument played in space: Wally Schirra on *Gemini VI*, performing "Jingle Bells" after pretending that the crew had sighted Santa. Helen had brought this harmonica up with her during a four-month stay at the International Space Station. Since it is a harmonic minor harmonica, she had been able to play many eastern European folk tunes, which had gone over big with the Russians on board. She had played for Yusef's birthday celebration, and they had made a very popular video of the event: three Russians, one American, one Indian, and one Japanese all clapping and singing in space, one big happy family eating herring in microgravity, global harmonics above the Earth.

That had been on her second mission to the ISS. Returning to the space station had felt like coming home, and returning to Earth at the end of her time had been sad. Earth was so much more beautiful in space, when you could just look at it, not be on it. After landing, once they carried her out of the *Soyuz* and set her down in a lawn chair in a Kazakhstan field, she had seen a lesser spotted eagle in the sky, and had been overwhelmed with a kind of tender pity for the planet and everything on it. She wanted to call attention to the eagle, but could not lift her arm yet, and anyway the thing to do in these moments, after you've just been hurtled through the atmosphere and controlled-crashed into the planet, is to make a joke about how you want a beer, or to ask how your sports team did. You don't say things about tender pity. She had talked to Eric—alive at the time—and Meeps on the phone, and their voices had moved her in the same way the bird had. The things of this Earth. Such fleeting things. Helen blows gently into the harmonica, a long, low note, and then waits to catch the exact moment when she can no longer hear the sound.

YOSHI

Sometimes when Yoshi thinks about Madoka he has an image of himself as a cathedral bell ringer, plummeting on the end of a rope, kicking out his legs for momentum, then vaulting skyward.

Of course, no one has rung a cathedral bell in that manner since before the English Reformation.

"Is this better?" Yoshi adjusts his screen to a new angle and turns off the desk lamp.

"Worse," Madoka says. "No, it's fine."

Yoshi puts his headphones back on. He likes to wear headphones when he talks to Madoka on screen, likes the idea that her voice is transmitting to his ears only.

"It doesn't matter," she says. "I can see you okay. Just go on with what you were saying."

"I wanted to make sure you got the new itinerary," Yoshi says. "I'm sorry I won't be able to meet you at the airport."

"Right," Madoka says. "Next month."

"Six weeks."

"Six weeks!"

They smile at each other. Sometimes Yoshi can sense that there is a little something stirring within his wife. He is always careful with her during these times, because when there is a little something stirring within Madoka she can be provocative, but provocative in conflicting ways. It is painful for them both when this happens, and he does not want it to happen now. Yoshi is seven weeks away from stepping inside a simulator for seventeen months, and this is not a good time to reverse engineer his wife's mood. At best, he might perhaps offer course correction, but Yoshi reminds himself that his attempts to meddle with Madoka's emotions have always yielded poor results. He assures himself that what Madoka most desires when she is unhappy is space. It is one of the reasons they are so perfectly suited to one another, space being something he can almost always offer.

"How are you?" Yoshi asks. "Everything is going well there?"

"Great, great. I love this hotel." Madoka picks up her laptop and gives Yoshi a tour of her room. His wife is in Chicago now, a city she has said she likes. Yoshi has talked to Madoka in hotel rooms all over the world. He likes to joke that they have traversed the globe together, albeit from different angles.

The Prime headphones he is using are very sensitive, and for a moment Yoshi is certain that he is hearing his wife's heartbeat, but then decides the sound is too irregular.

"What am I hearing?" he asks.

Madoka points her screen to the window. "It's raining. Oh, let me show you the bathroom. You'll like it. It's very old-fashioned."

She brings the screen into the bathroom of her hotel room, and Yoshi has a glimpse of her toiletries, arranged neatly next to the sink. He is moved, and a little erotically stirred at the sight. He wishes

Madoka would put the computer down next to the toiletries so he could make a catalog of all the things. Perhaps he will do this when she is visiting. It would make a nice game to play in his personal time during Eidolon, to try to remember each object, to imagine Madoka deploying her toiletries about her person.

She returns his view back to the parlor of her hotel suite. "Or maybe it's the air-conditioning; my room is freezing. So. What will I be doing in Utah before you go into quarantine?"

"Eidolon is training for all of us," Yoshi says. "The astronauts, mission control, the families. We're all learning together. There are a lot of things they will want to review and discuss with you."

"It's funny that we are all pretending this is real, isn't it?"

"It's not entirely pretending. The simulator is still an extreme environment."

Madoka closes her eyes and flutters the tips of her fingers against her mouth. She has always done this; he has always found the gesture compelling.

He had fallen in love with Madoka the day they met, at the birthday party of a mutual friend at a bar on Quincy Street. Yoshi was in the United States for MIT's AeroAstro program; Madoka was in her second year at Harvard. The first time he saw her, Madoka had been sitting in a corner of the lounge in a green velvet armchair. The chair was very low to the ground, which forced her knees up and had molded her figure into a lightning bolt shape.

"Extreme environment," Madoka says now in English, drawing the words out slowly, almost singing them.

"Because of the confinement and the isolation."

"Right." Madoka switches back to Japanese. "But it's actually less extreme than the environments the rest of us are living in, isn't it?"

He had taken note of Madoka but had initially been more

interested in talking to one of the Western girls seated across from her. American girls seemed to like him, which had surprised and intrigued him. He had made his way to Madoka's corner, and in the middle of their group conversation, the lightning bolt had struck. There had been something so womanly, so deeply feminine about the way Madoka had fingered the bracelets around her wrist while listening to him talk. It was as if he hadn't properly solved what a woman *was* until he saw Madoka do that. And then he had it. *Women* became one woman—became Madoka—became love. It was like the way you could—in one moment—"have" something in math, or in physics. Have it without metaphor or simile, have it intrinsically, as it itself. He had been profoundly moved, and very relieved.

"In a way, you'll be in the least extreme environment of anyone on Earth," Madoka says now. The bracelets, on that first evening, had been thin gold chains. She no longer wore them, but it made no difference. He remembers her long fingers twisting the links, nervously and lightly. And then the closing of her eyes, the fluttering of her hand against her lip.

"Your extreme environment is protected from the rest of the world, and every millimeter of the space has been thought about and labored over by a hundred scientists and engineers," Madoka continues. "You will be monitored from head to toe. I assume there are limits to how far you will be tested. They're not going to *kill* you, for instance. They aren't going to let you die. So there isn't any *actual* risk. Less risk than walking down a street or flying in a plane. Less risk than just existing in the world." Her face looks flushed.

"There's no physical risk at all," Yoshi assures her. "The environment is considered extreme because of the confinement and isolation, but we won't be in actual jeopardy, no."

"Unless one of you wants to kill one of the others."

The mood is playful, he is almost certain of it. "Ah, true," he says. "But we've been selected for being, among other things, the three people least likely to kill one another under these conditions."

"What's so great about them that you don't want to kill them? Other than you always like everyone."

"What's so great about me," Yoshi counters, "that they wouldn't want to kill *me*?"

His chest tightens, but Madoka answers quickly and her voice is kind.

"People want to be around you," she says. "You've always had that quality. It was the first thing I noticed about you."

Yoshi feels the great tug of the bell swinging him up to the heights of the cathedral. Sometimes he would like to speak about the tintinnabulations of his heart, but he knows he will not do it properly.

His love is a particle that loses speed when it touches her if it does not touch her in just the right way, at just the right time, in precisely the right angle. No. Every analogy is imperfect. He cannot write poetry.

Madoka is looking away from her screen now, and Yoshi is glad of an opportunity to gaze at her lovely profile. While they have been talking, he has sketched the outline of her hotel suite on the back of a piece of paper on his desk, so he knows that she is looking at the window. Looking at Madoka in moments of stillness like this, he feels he can see her true essence, and she is returned to him.

"I think we should pretend that you are really going to Mars." Madoka turns her face back to the screen. She settles deeper into the sofa and pulls her feet in, taking off her slippers, folding her legs crosswise. She is wearing thick green socks. Her circulation is not good. Yoshi realizes, with a pang, that he is not intensely familiar with his wife's feet. He has mostly seen them in socks. He might not be able to pick her naked feet out of a lineup of feet.

"It's not necessary to the training that you believe," he says.

"It's not?"

"Actually, that would be an indication of psychosis."

"You think belief is an indication of psychosis?"

They smile at each other again. There is definitely a little something astir within Madoka. Yoshi would like to stop talking soon. He wants to think about her later.

"Right now, for the families, it's more about figuring out what kind of support mechanisms should be in place," he says. "Also, things like . . . there have been situations where jealousy has arisen among crewmates because one person was getting more communication from a family member than the others. Things like that. Little things. That's what they're going to be working with the families on."

"I don't understand." Madoka is still smiling. Her eyes drift away from Yoshi to the small square in the upper corner of the screen that reflects her own image. She is watching herself talk. "How useful is this simulation if we all know that it's not really happening? Isn't it kind of pointless unless you believe it?"

He does need her support. It is part of the mission, that he should have her support. He had thought she understood perfectly the importance of Eidolon, but sometimes Madoka processes things slowly. It is a lot to take in. Eidolon will give the families time to mentally prepare as well. *(God in heaven, Mars.)* Yoshi is not sure what he would do if his wife were to say to him, "Don't go." But she would never say to him "Don't go." She understands him too well. She feels the same way he does about these things. They have to be separated a lot, but it doesn't matter, because their union is not dependent on their actually being together.

"You can't tell me," Madoka goes on, "that you won't feel completely different things when you are actually going to Mars. Or maybe you can. Maybe it doesn't matter to you at all. Maybe I just don't understand what it's like to be in a simulator."

"Simulators are always the best training tool," Yoshi says. "Remember when I was learning to fly the T-38? Nearly all my training was in a simulator. The first time I took over the controls of the actual plane I wasn't stressed at all. I made no mistakes and it was the first time that any mistake on my part could have truly been fatal. But I wasn't thinking about that. I was able to enjoy it."

"I always have trouble imagining you flying a plane," Madoka says.

"You've seen me fly a plane. You've sat next to me while I was flying a plane."

"I know. Still. It seems so unlike you."

Yoshi is not sure what she means. In his head, this isn't at all the kind of conversation they have. He wills Madoka to close her eyes, and tap her lips with her fingers, but she yawns instead.

"I think it will be easier to understand everything once you are here and can see for yourself," Yoshi says.

"Of course," Madoka says.

"I have to meet the others now. Study time," Yoshi says.

"I'm going to order room service and watch a movie."

"That sounds nice."

They say good-bye.

In truth, he is not meeting Sergei and Helen for another ten minutes, but the little something astir within Madoka seems to be making her irritable, and Yoshi would like to spare her having to display bad temper or unhappiness, which she would regret later.

To do his work he must put all thoughts of her aside, but he will think about her now. Her eyes are closed, but she is listening. Her hand flutters against her lips. The thin gold bracelets slip down her wrist. They are very much in love. He will give himself this moment. One jump from the cathedral tower. One long plummet on the end of a rope until the clapper strikes the bell. One swift ascent in the resonance. And then silence.

SERGEI

Sergei has never hired a prostitute. He is not going to do so now, but he is composing a mental list of pros and cons anyway. Reliable skill set and zero emotional risk, over illegality and potential fallout if discovered. Over the years he had been presented with many offers of free sexual congress. He'd turned almost all of them down. Talia had said she would be okay with other women giving him a blowjob, because in her mind, women who did that would be degrading themselves by the action and so would be of no importance. Sergei had only treated himself to the opportunity a few times. Joylessly, because Talia's words had stuck and he had despised the women. Anyway, the success of a person lay in their ability to delay gratification. This had been proven scientifically. But if there was no honor in being an addict, there was also no pride in being an abstainer. The strong person was the person who could do a thing or not, as he chose. The strongest person could do a thing he didn't want to do, and not do a thing he desired very much.

Sergei sends a message to his son Dmitri. Talia had taken the boy to the doctor because he hadn't been feeling well lately, and if there were any risk of infection, Dmitri would not be able to come to Utah for the launch. But of course the boy was fine, had told Sergei privately that he wasn't ill, he only wanted some time apart from the others. Sergei understood this—he had been a solitary boy himself. He'd grown out of it, but even now found himself drawn to the options on psychological evaluations that he knew indicated antisocial tendencies. Of course he would never circle, check, fill in, or otherwise indicate in any way this aspect of his nature. Disliking people was similar to receiving blowjobs from women who were not your wife: an occasional indulgence.

Sergei gives his attention now to the young man at the front of the room: one of the people who will be monitoring Sergei's psychological health during Eidolon. The astronauts don't usually attend this lecture series; the presence of Sergei is going to make the young man self-conscious. Sergei knows this and thinks it's a good thing. He likes this guy, Luke, but you never want these psych types to feel that they have an advantage.

"All the data we have tells us that crews that share a common language and cultural background tend to do better than less homogenous teams," Luke is saying. "And more data shows us that mixed-sex teams do better than all-male teams, and that all-male teams do better than all-female teams. But there are gaps in what we know. You have to go outside space exploration to get numbers about sex makeup because there's never been an all-female crew in space, or even in any analogue environment. And you have to be careful, with these small-sample pools, about your conclusions. For example, some of the problems that came up when mixed-sex crews were integrated didn't speak to a systemic problem. It was lack of maturity of certain individuals."

When Sergei makes an appreciative noise, several people turn to him and smile. They are all aware of him, not just Luke. He is used to this. Being antisocial is not the same as being introverted. Perhaps he was introverted as a child. His father had called him *meek*. Sergei would never use such a word on his sons. His boys are not meek, but even if they were, he would not shame them with the word. Sergei thinks of Dmitri's intelligence, his sensitivity, his strength of character. He thinks of Ilya's athleticism, his grace, his determination. He could not be more proud of his sons. When he thinks of them like this, it is easy to become emotional. This emotion is another source of Sergei's power. He would not be able to hold his head up if he thought his children could not respect him. To be someone they would look up to guided his actions, in the way God had once done. (He had been a religious boy too.)

Sergei still loved God, he just didn't believe in him. He didn't understand how you could believe in God and still *love* God. But he was a spiritual person, not a religious person, so he could think with more subtlety on this subject, and still be strong.

The young man, Luke, has a new image on his screen: a lineup of a dozen humans, snow-suited in blue and red, arms around one another, posing in front of a cylindrical building set against an Arctic tundra.

"Dome C," Luke says. "Concordia Station, Antarctica. The largest desert on Earth. At the peak of summer the temperatures barely reach a balmy minus twenty-five degrees Celsius. A cold winter will fall below minus eighty. There are months when the harsh weather conditions mean communication is interrupted by radio static and planes are unable to land and deliver supplies. Months of darkness. Typical winter population: four technicians to maintain the station, nine scientists, a chief, a cook, and a medical doctor." Luke begins

explaining how winter-over expeditions have served as good ana-
logues for long-duration space missions.

Sergei has never been to Antarctica, but he participated in a training expedition in the opposite direction, Devon Island in the Arctic
Circle, also somewhat Mars-like, in terms of terrain. He almost shot
a polar bear during that campaign. He was out with a small team,
testing a prototype Mars Hopper, nicknamed Bugs. As was protocol, an extra crewmember rode along in the truck with the sole task
of keeping an eye out for polar bears, handling the bear bangers and,
if necessary, firing the large-caliber Springfield rifle. In the past,
one could divide the Arctic bears one encountered into four categories: curious bears, hungry bears, irritated bears, and defensive bears
with cubs. Now, the Arctic bear was never merely curious, curiosity
being a luxury reserved for those who are not starving. A sharp eye
and vigilance were required, due to the white-on-white situation of
polar bear spotting in the snow.

There was a problem with Bugs the Hopper. One of its four legs
snapped out during a maneuver, narrowly missing Jacqueline's head,
and tipping the whole vehicle at a dangerous angle. Paul, who was on
bear duty in the AT38, thought Jacqueline *had* been hit, and climbed
out of the truck in a panic, leaving his rifle on the seat. As soon as
Sergei assured himself that Jacqueline was unhurt, Sergei saw Paul
standing there empty-handed, and then Sergei saw the bear.

You would think that the sight of Earth's largest carnivorous land
mammal less than two hundred meters away would inspire the same
instincts in everyone, but no. Sergei's instinct had been to get to the
rifle. Everyone else's instinct had been to stare at the bear. The bear's
instinct had been to stand up on its hind legs and show that it was,
indeed, a very, very large bear. It dropped back down to all fours and
began moving in a circle, which is bear choreography for hunting. By

then Sergei had gotten to the truck, and had the rifle. He had instructed the others to group together, to begin backing up slowly to the truck, to make a lot of noise. He had kept the rifle trained on the bear, which ignored all the yelping humans and kept its eyes on Sergei. Paul set off a few flares. The bear stopped. There had been discussion in the truck. Because of their depleted numbers, you could no longer shoot a polar bear on sight, and anyway, there was great reluctance to shoot. Especially when they were all in the truck and could easily drive away, and be good people. They shouldn't leave an expensive piece of equipment, so Sergei was ready to fire a warning shot if the animal decided to attack Bugs. This didn't happen. Even a bear knew the thing was a piece of crap. Eventually, the bear simply moved off, and they loaded up the Hopper and returned to base.

For the next week, the other three had told one another the experience over and over, reviewing all of their thoughts and feelings. They re-created their antibear ululations. They thought out loud about how lucky they were, and paid tribute to the majestic awesomeness of the bear. Sergei kept silent, because what he wanted to say was, "Paul, you fucking moron, you had *one* job to do." He had also felt a little bit of guilt, because there had been a moment when the bear was taking Sergei's measure, and Sergei had experienced a flash of intuition—these sometimes came to him—that the bear was considering him not as prey, but as deliverance. The bear had wanted Sergei to shoot him. The bear wanted to die, did not want to die slowly, unremembered and alone and aching, but the bear did not know how to commit suicide on its own. Evolution had come up short for the polar bear, its habitat destroyed before it developed the capacity for conscious self-slaughter. Why did the bear not charge and force the issue? The bear wanted to be understood. *Let there be no mistake about this. Have the courage to release me, not as self-defense, but as an act of grace.* But Sergei had not done it.

The screen behind Luke is now showing an image of an ocean floor: two divers in spacesuits, posing in front of a barnacle-covered portal.

"NEEMO," says Luke. "NASA's underwater research station. Although stays here are short—typically ten to fourteen days—participants receive a full range of physical stressors: fatiguing work, loss of body heat, sleep disturbances, increased chance of ear infections, disorientation, crowded conditions, diet restrictions."

Sergei enjoyed his NEEMO rotation on *Aquarius*. Great time, great crew. Gareth, a British guy, marine biologist, very smart, very funny—they'd become especially good friends, the way you can when you are spending fourteen days with someone nineteen meters underwater in a pressurized sardine can looking at giant grouper out the window. At the time of their expedition, Gareth had just buried his father, and so had Sergei. They'd exchanged stories about going fishing with their dads, although Sergei's father only took him once. To Kamchatka. Sergei was nine. Just him and his father, not any of Sergei's three sisters or his mother. The sight of his father scaling the fish while the fish were still alive had bothered Sergei. His father told him that fish do not feel pain like people, and handed him the scaling knife and told him not to be *meek*. Sergei hesitated. Not out of meekness, but because he did not believe what his father had told him. That is, he had not thought that his father was *lying*, he thought that his father was ignorant of the facts. It had been a source of great sadness, to see that his father could be ignorant. It made him physically ill, actually. Sergei scaled and gutted the fish under his father's precise instructions and then vomited next to the cleaning station.

His father washed both vomit and fish guts away with a hose. Sergei told this story to Gareth, and they'd had a good laugh, because Sergei was an amusing storyteller and Gareth's dad had also been kind of an asshole.

Luke moves on to a series of images from submarines. Pressurization concerns, catastrophic outcomes for loss of power, radiation exposure, severe space restrictions.

Gareth told Sergei that current research suggested fish do *not* experience pain in the way humans do. "Pain in humans," Gareth explained, "is a process. The nociceptors send electrical signals through nerves and the spinal cord to the neocortex of the brain, which then processes the data into conscious pain sensations. Fish don't have a neocortex and they don't have the C nociceptors that mammals have."

"So, my father was right," Sergei said.

"Well, the only thing we know is that fish probably do not have pain that is humanlike pain," Gareth said.

So, his father was still wrong. Fish could have fish pain. Which could be worse than human pain.

Luke has a new image up on his screen: two men and one woman on the space station. Flushed, smiling faces, shorts and T-shirts, sunglasses, goofy smiles. He recognizes the module: Kibo. One of the women is Helen. Great legs, Helen, even in micro-g, where everybody got chicken legs.

"Like submarine crews, astronauts on the International Space Station need to be able to function at the highest level in the face of imminent catastrophe," Luke says. "And like winter-over teams in Antarctica, they also have to tolerate boredom and low levels of stimulation. Basically, we have all the stressors of the three previous extreme environments and a few new ones. Of course, daily life on the ISS is dominated by microgravity conditions, which—because of the centrifuge—will play only a very brief role in the MarsNOW mission. But certainly, as the space station comes to the end of its mission and lifetime, we must acknowledge how much it has taught us . . . "

That polar bear I didn't shoot is almost certainly dead by now, Sergei thinks.

The next slide is a triptych: Helen, snow-suited and beaming in front of Dome C; Yoshi, wetsuited and grinning next to the portal of the NEEMO station; Sergei, T-shirted and smiling on the ISS.

"All of these analogue environments have given us good information on the kinds of psychological factors that participants encounter in long-duration missions," says Luke as the screen behind him begins to fill with bullet points.

Sergei is skeptical about this data. He respects research, but he himself fills out self-reports in as minimal and neutral a way as possible, and pretty much all the other cosmonauts and astronauts he knows do the same, so these books of data Luke is talking about will have been provided from the handful of people who are willing to chat about problems, and the person who is willing to chat about problems is always the person with the most problems, the person that everybody else on the team thought was a pain. If, preparatory to the Arctic experience, idiot Paul had been given a test to evaluate whether or not he would've left the rifle in the truck, he might very well have passed the test. Was there anything in Paul's profile that indicated he would start fucking Jacqueline, and be jealous of Tim, and so leave his rifle in the truck when he thought Jacqueline was hurt?

". . . and so we can identify seven major factors for psychological stressors in the kind of long-duration mission we will be facing with MarsNOW," Luke is saying. "Increasing distance from rescue in case of emergency. Proximity to unknown or little-understood phenomena. Reliance on a limited and contained environment where a breach of seal means death. Greater difficulties in communicating with Ground. Decreased availability of technological advice from Ground. Diminishing available resources needed for life and the enjoyment of life."

Sergei does appreciate how Prime is thinking seriously about these things. And, to be fair, they knew something about crew selection because look at himself and Yoshi and Helen. Could not ask for better. Yoshi and Helen would not leave the rifle in the truck.

"And all of this good information," Luke says, "pretty much falls apart when we turn to sending three people to Mars."

The list on the screen dissolves and is replaced with a GIF of an old sci-fi horror movie: three absurdly dressed astronauts covered in lurid green slime, with *What is happening?* in text below them.

This gets a laugh from the room. Sergei smiles. For the first time, Luke looks directly at him. Sergei decides that he will respect Luke. This is not the same thing as saying that he will trust him.

"I exaggerate." Luke holds up his hand. "But three is a very tricky number for group data in general, and Mars has a lot of X factors. Happily, we have a solution." The GIF is replaced by an image of the Eidolon simulators sitting in a valley of the San Rafael Swell. A small cheer goes around the room.

"Mostly the solution lies in us finding the right questions to ask," Luke continues. "Not finding the individual with the right stuff, but finding the group of individuals that will combine to form the right stuff. Not asking them to deal with the environment we have created for them, but creating the right environment for them to deal with whatever they encounter. Eidolon is the next evolution in the analogue environment. The only thing more realistic than Eidolon will be the real voyage. In many cases, the two are going to be practically indistinguishable."

Luke fiddles with his computer and backtracks to a discussion of Mars analogue simulations comparable (though inferior) to Eidolon. Sergei, who has read this data before, begins typing a message to his sons.

Talia is coming to Utah with the boys, but without Alexander. Sergei wonders if she will agree to have sex with him, if he asks in the right way. That part of their relationship had always been quite fine, and she is a generous woman. He will know when he sees her. He can always tell.

He would like to talk seriously with Dmitri about things. Words, though. You could be the father (or Father) that talks and talks and nobody believes anyway, or you could be the father that shows. It is better to be the father that shows, so that is what he will do.

MIREILLE, DMITRI, MADOKA, LUKE

Mireille thinks about hurling the plate of food in front of her. *I am going to throw this plate right at the wall and then jump on a table and just start screaming.*

But she has handled it all so well. She has been the incredibly supportive, funny, charming, *lovely* daughter. No other family member has performed so admirably in the past two weeks. The Russian boys are handsome, but the older one is snobbish and the younger one doesn't give a shit, and they are both a little rude. Yoshihiro's wife, Madoka, lacks charisma and most of the time has a sort of fixed-stare niceness like someone who has been forced into a beauty pageant at gunpoint. The little Japanese parents are adorable but shy, and the Russian wife is ex-wife, and only there as chaperone to the boys. Mireille is clobbering the competition.

Mireille tells herself that she needs to stop drinking wine; her alcohol-induced merriment is both masking and exacerbating her unhappiness, and having wrung as much mileage as she could out of being wonderful, she might now (accidentally) see what kind of numbers she could run up on being difficult.

She will not do this. Difficult never feels as good as you want it to.

Boone Cross says that Eidolon is preparing them all for the un-imaginable, which obviously makes no sense, and anyway, Mireille is not convinced that the real event will be the kind of gonzo level of fame and celebration and global attention that Prime is anticipating. In Mireille's opinion, people in the space industry tended to vastly overestimate their audience. Yes, there were space nerds who had memorized every detail of every mission and would corner Mireille when they knew who she was and space-splain all over her. But there were more people like Yola, from her acting class, who asked Mireille, "Have we landed people on Mars yet?" All during the past two weeks, Mireille had kept the idea of Yola's cluelessness in her mind as an option to weigh against the This Is a Very Big Deal presentation happening at Prime Space. Because of course you couldn't help it. You got around these people, and listened to them talk, and saw what they were doing, and pretty soon you too thought that human beings had never done anything finer than space exploration, and no goal was more worthy.

There was something funny about the idea of throwing the plate of food at the wall and jumping up on the table. "Simulate this!" she could shout.

Mireille tells herself to stop drinking at once. It was going to be a long night, and she still needed to be on.

For tonight's dinner, Prime has let the families seat themselves, and the little tables have filled according to astronaut allegiance. All the entourages are small; Team Helen numbers have fallen. Uncle Francis and Aunt Hillary had taken Gram back to New York once

Mireille's mother had gone into quarantine. Now it was just those odd satellite family members who always showed up for space things, and are Helen superfans and who will go home and continue to be experts on all things space to their friends and are loving it. Weirdly, her mother's younger brother had shown up yesterday but left this morning. Bitter Phil, Mireille calls him. Thinking of her mother having to swallow a dose of Bitter Phil during the visitation hour makes Mireille feel protective of her mother.

"Well, Meeps, this isn't as exotic as Kazakhstan, but the food's a lot better, huh?" says her mother's cousin's husband, who is practically humping his chair in delight of being able to toss off this kind of space-industry insight.

Kazakhstan. She'd been fourteen and her father had gotten sick from either the horse meat or the sour milk products and stayed mostly in their hideously ugly hotel while the rest of their family and friends ran around Baikonur like they were participants in a Viking funeral, weeping and drinking and acting crazy. The night before her mother's launch, she'd wandered down to the fairly disgusting lobby of their hotel and curled up on a horse-hair couch and hoped someone would notice her, until the mother of one of the other cosmonauts found her and put Mireille's head in her lap and stroked her hair and had said, "I be your mama now, poor girl."

No, this isn't like a real launch. All of Prime's efforts to make things real just proved how unreal it is. Like, they wouldn't even be in Utah for the real thing, they'd be in south Texas, where Prime launched. Only they couldn't do Eidolon in south Texas because they needed to be in Utah, where they could isolate the crew and have them run around similar rocks and things for the landing part. And so, before quarantine, Prime had put the crew into an airplane, flown the airplane in a circle or whatever for the amount of time it would actually take to go to Texas, and had her mother and the others wear sim helmets from the airplane to the quarantine facility. Prime had this idea that even things like travel from Utah to Texas could affect the crew's condition, so they wanted to make it all exact. Except normally, family members would be allowed short visits during the quarantine period. But the fake quarantine facility in Utah isn't set up for that, like the real one in Texas, and so Prime is sending the family members home tomorrow.

She can't pretend she's at a prelaunch dinner. Well, she can, she can pretend anything. She can do dinner theater, ha.

At the table next to hers, a group of Primers are talking about the real launch happening next Wednesday, of *Red Dawn II*. She hears one of them say, "There's this great Boone quote—" Space people. She could perfectly play a space person in a movie, although they never sounded or looked in movies like they did in life. In life they were more normal *and* more weird, but not in movie ways.

Tomorrow Mireille will go back to Los Angeles, as she had always had to go back somewhere after a launch. She wonders if she will feel real letdown after a fake launch. Probably.

She is valuable! That had been a major theme in the past two weeks. How Valuable They Are.

You could see that Yoshihiro's wife was important to him. You could see Sergei's kids were important to him. You could see that everybody at Prime felt they were important. *God she could just smash this plate. Just pick it up and smash it to smithereens on the table.*

It was all so *layered*. (Okay, she was a little drunk.) Because here they were, having said good-bye to their Loved One for seventeen months. But they were supposed to be pretending that they were saying good-bye to their Loved One for the first human expedition to fucking *Mars*. But it was still good-bye. They were having emotions that weren't quite the emotions they would be having. Which sort of robbed them of their current emotions, in a way.

She should not have had two glasses of wine along with the Klonopin. She is having trouble keeping her face organized.

Mireille had made a little joke last night at the prequarantine family dinner about her mom being "Aspy," and everyone at the table had reacted like she had said something that would completely hurt her mother's feelings and she had said, "Don't everybody act like I just hurt Mom's feelings or she'll pick up on those visual cues and decide that the appropriate thing for her to do is pretend like her feelings are hurt!" Which could have been funny, but Mireille knew right away that it wasn't going to be funny. It was going to be one those things that take a while before you stop feeling sick about them, and will never go away, but wash up continually in memory form to embarrass you in the middle of something completely unrelated.

Aunt Hillary had taken Mireille *by the elbow* after dinner, and said, "*Aspy* is hate language and just because your mother doesn't show her emotions doesn't mean she doesn't have them. And right now she needs to know that we love and support her."

There was nothing like fame for family members to decide that they were, after all, incredibly close to the famous person and necessary to the famous person's health and happiness. Aunt Hillary. Fucking hell.

Mireille's father had been the only person she could say anything to without worrying about being treated as some kind of emotion-demanding *monster*. Her father had always encouraged her to express herself, to yell if she felt like yelling, to cry. God. *God*. Mireille could really hurl some lasagna right now.

But what a great daughter she had been here at Prime Space. She cannot blow all of the good credit she has accrued. Mireille assures herself that it had just been family at dinner; none of the Prime people had heard her say the thing about Asperger's. The Prime people adored her. She was the star family member.

Mireille looks around the room and catches the eye of Yoshihiro's wife. This has happened a couple of times during the past ten days, over conference tables and group exercises, but it hadn't led to any intimacy. Mireille finds Madoka harder to place than typical Judys— Mireille's name for the wives of American astronauts. Of those, some were Super Judys who managed four fabulous kids perfectly and were super trim and raced boats, and some were the kind with the slightly aggrieved quasi-efficiency of overweight blonds who did real estate part-time, but both kinds made you never want to be a wife. They kind of made you not want to be a woman. Madoka wasn't like them, but she was Japanese and you never knew with Japanese. Madoka was a roboticist or something impressive.

The Russian astronaut's ex-wife had more of a Super Judy feel, though her capability was of a much sexier variety. Mireille had a sense that Sergei's older kid, Dmitri, was kind of fucked up. The younger one, Ilya, didn't give a shit. You could tell that kid was going to be a star by the way he didn't give a shit.

Was that what was holding her back? Yes. Yes. She cared too much.

The Prime people at the table next to hers are telling engineer jokes.

The graduate with a science degree asks, "Why does it work?" The graduate with an engineering degree asks, "How does it work?" The graduate with an arts degree asks, "Do you want fries with that?"

Of course. Fuck space people.

Acting isn't about ego, it's about taking a fall in public for the Fall of Man. It was easy to make fun of actors, but it wasn't easy to be them.

Only you did end up feeling a little useless when you were around people like this. You couldn't help it. It was hard to remember who you were.

Mireille thinks about who she is, and despairs.

But didn't Prime keep saying they needed people just like Mireille, who was so good at conveying Prime's message? Mireille had killed it at the fake press conference that afternoon.

"Mireille, can you describe some of the emotions you are experiencing right now?"

"I am just so proud of my mother. All my life she has been an amazing role model and a great mom, and supported me in my dreams, and given me so much inspiration. It's been so special to hear from so many people all over the world that she's also inspired them. Really, I just feel tremendous pride."

"Can you tell us what you and your mother talked about during your last conversation before the mission?"

"Well, of course we will be communicating throughout her mission, although not in real time, so mainly we were just joking around. You know, she's been to space before, so we have a couple of silly rituals. When I was little I used to worry that she wouldn't have snack time in space, so I always tell her to make sure to have snack time, and she always tells me to keep an eye on the planet while she's away and remember to water the plants."

"This mission has unprecedented risks. So along with tremendous pride, you must be feeling a lot of fear and anxiety. Tell us how you manage that."

"We have such good support here at Prime Space. And I want to thank everyone out there for the thoughts and good wishes and shows of support.

There is so much conflict and unhappiness in the world, so much strife and terror. This is an opportunity to reflect on what the best of us is capable of, what we can accomplish when we put everything aside and come together for a common goal. My mom has always talked about how you can't see borders from space . . ."

BOONE CROSS is entering the room now. Everyone goes silent, as they do around the Great Man. It would be something, to command that kind of power.

The Great Man is not a terribly great public speaker, but everyone treats his slightest remark as either mind-blowingly profound or super hilarious.

Boone Cross calls the family members heroes.

Mireille at this moment sees the older Russian kid raising his eyebrow in a very funny, sardonic sort of way at this, and then the kid sees Mireille watching him and quickly makes his face blank in response to her smile. And then Mireille sees that the Japanese wife is watching her, and she doesn't look at all like a beauty pageant contestant held at gunpoint, but like someone who has had about enough crap for one day. And Mireille looks back at the Russian kid—Dmitri—and he looks back at her again and then they both look over at Madoka and the three of them are caught, she thinks, in a moment where they understand that they have all been mentally hurling lasagna at the walls all night.

Mireille feels a rise of something—hope?—but it passes. She tries to tune in to the speech.

If this whole circus works, then her mother might go to Mars. Her mother might go to Mars.

Mireille thinks, *My mother could die,* and the idea—which is certainly not new to her—strikes her as unbearable on a level that is not manageable. Johnson Space Center has a Memorial Grove of live oak trees, each one planted to commemorate a fallen astronaut. At Christmastime, they hang lights on them. Mireille sees herself at a memorial for her mother. Probably if her mother died on the way to Mars there would be a state funeral; the president might even attend. And then, when it was all over, she would have to go back to her life with no mother. No mother for the rest of her life.

She must love her mother very much. She must.

"WILL THIS GUY never shut up?"

Dmitri acknowledges his mother's muttered attempt to amuse him with a perfunctory smile. If he ignores her completely, she will just try harder. She is worried that he is mad at her, which he is not, but they are not supposed to talk during speeches. In America, you have to sit quietly and stare at the person talking like they are a hypnotist. Dmitri shakes his head slightly at his mother, who sighs and crosses her legs.

She is like a child, his mother. You shouldn't give in to children. Alexander gives in. This makes his mother happy, but fretful. Dmitri's father did not give in, and this made his mother unhappy, but calm. Yes, Alexander would never have left Dmitri's mother alone for such long periods of time, would not have assumed, over and over again, that she could handle everything, manage all situations, cope with any emergency. But the fact that his father had done so had resulted in his mother being perfectly competent and someone you could rely on. Now, Dmitri was not so sure. Now, if something happened, Alexander would probably rush in and say, "Oh, don't worry,

I will take care of it," and his mother would stand there as if she had forgotten how to use her hands, and smile at Alexander.

Dmitri does not know for certain that his mother had sex with his father here in Utah before his father went into quarantine, but he's pretty sure. He is now in the position to know how people behave after having secret sex, if you count what Dmitri has done as sex, which he does not, but still. He knows.

His mother is worried that Dmitri will tell Alexander that she had sex with his father. This is insulting. He's not an idiot. If Dmitri told Alexander, Alexander might leave his mother, and then his mother would be unhappy *and* helpless at a time when Dmitri was particularly invested in having her be fully occupied and not particularly noticing.

It was that satisfied look on his father's face that had pissed Dmitri off. Once again, his father had gotten to have everything. It didn't matter what his father did, none of them would stop loving him. His father loved them too, but so effortlessly.

This part, the part where his father goes away, they are all used to, it's no big deal. Dmitri and Ilya hated those children in that movie about astronauts going to Tau Ceti. Screaming and crying. "Don't leave me, Papa, don't leave me." Nobody did that. Come on.

But now, when his father comes back, he will not come back to them. His father doesn't have a home anymore, and his father loved having a home. And it was something, it was a way to organize things, to know when his father would be coming back from training, or a conference, or a mission.

Yesterday, for their special walk to talk about meaningful things, his father had taken him to Goblin Valley State Park. The "goblins" were hoodoos: sandstone spires in strange shapes. The rocks were reddish, coated in hematite, so crazy-looking you could not believe you were on Earth. The valley was like a science-fiction movie, with mushrooms and gnomes and globules all made out of rock, some four or five meters tall, some like toadstools. "The Entrada sandstone is a combination of sandstone, siltstone, and shale," his father said. "Sediments from ancient seas and river channels. Jurassic period, one hundred seventy million years ago. These formations are maybe ten million years old. You can touch. You can climb on them if you want."

Dmitri had looked at the hoodoo nearest to hand, which was about one meter tall and the exact shape of a dick. The hoodoo looked so much like a dick that his father's suggestion that he touch it seemed, not perverted, but like an accusation, like his father was saying, "I know what you've been doing in secret."

Dmitri moved to another hoodoo, one that looked like a loaf of bread sitting on top of a tombstone. The texture of the rock was softer than he expected. It did not seem like something that had been made from dirt that had been around since the dinosaurs and had been holding this particular shape for ten million years.

"Nothing on Mars will look as crazy as this place," Dmitri said.

"We have to go and look," his father said. "It will be a little different, I think." He gestured toward the groups of other tourists in the valley, families with little kids climbing all over the hoodoos, everyone holding up their screens for pictures and videos.

"Everywhere is a little different," Dmitri pointed out. "New Jersey is a little different. You know we have this big house, three floors and an attic. We don't have any furniture for all the rooms."

"Your mother will make it nice," his father said.

"You haven't even seen it," Dmitri said. "You don't know what it's like."

Then his father had pulled out his screen and showed Dmitri about twenty different pictures of the house, and Main Street in the town, and the school where Dmitri would be going. His father even had a picture of the train station and the train that Ilya would be taking to go to his special ballet school in Manhattan, and a picture of the car that Alexander had talked about buying for his mother, although his mother didn't have a driver's license for the United States.

"I know everything," his father said. "You think I would let you go to New Jersey and not know exactly where you were? I could tell you how to walk from your new house to your new school. I could tell you how to get to the grocery store. I know what is the state tree of New Jersey!"

His father placed his hand on Dmitri's neck.

"I'll learn how to play baseball," Dmitri said. "I'll become a vegetarian and say that evolution is just a theory."

"Oh my God, not baseball," said his father, who had funny stories about the American astronaut who had been on the ISS when his father was commander, and the American was crazy about baseball, which was the most boring sport in the universe, and all the Russians on the station had a joke that if you messed something up, or lost a bet, then your punishment would be to visit the American module and ask that guy what the rules of baseball were.

"But for you," his father said, shaking him gently by the neck, "I would learn baseball. I would become the world's biggest fan of baseball."

Dmitri had felt so guilty about the trusting way his father held him by the neck that he had gotten sentimental.

"I don't think this Eidolon training method is very good," he said. "Who are you going to talk to?"

"I will be talking to you," his father said. "In my head, and when we write to each other. And I will talk to Helen and Yoshi. They're already my friends."

The baseball-loving astronaut was also his father's friend. Dmitri couldn't imagine being friends with people the way his father was, because that was the kind of friendship you only had when you went through a massive experience together, like a war, or being in space. Even if his father didn't *like* Helen and Yoshi, he'd end up being better friends with them than Dmitri was with anybody, except Ilya, and they were brothers, so it wasn't the same.

"I won't let anything happen to you that you don't like," his father said. "If you have a problem with anything, all you have to do is tell me. And if Ilya has any problems, you can tell me too."

Dmitri looks over at Ilya now. The speech is taking forever, and everyone is just sitting and listening in silence to the speaker with half-open mouths. Ilya has lapsed into what Dmitri thinks of as Ilya's "off" mode. It looks okay if you don't know him—Ilya is still sitting upright in his chair and more or less looking in the direction of Boone Cross—but Dmitri knows that his brother is currently, for all intents and purposes, catatonic. He has to stifle a laugh. Dmitri's mother, hyperalert to him now, follows his line of vision and rolls her eyes. She leans forward and swats Ilya's knee. The expression of innocent bewilderment on Ilya's face is genuine. As far as Ilya is concerned, when he shuts his eyes the whole world goes blind.

Even if Dmitri decided to punish his father by no longer loving him, Ilya would still love their father. So his father would have one good son and one bad son and would his father even notice that Dmitri didn't love him if Ilya still did?

Yes, to be fair, his father would notice. But his father wouldn't really be punished. It was no punishment to have your bad kid not love you.

Dmitri takes another quick look at the girl who is the daughter of the American astronaut. All week long she'd been showing off and smiling at everyone like a crazy person and Dmitri had felt sorry for her even though he could see that everybody else thought she was the greatest thing ever. He was happy to let her be the center of attention. Ilya didn't have to be the center of other people's attention. When he was "on," when his eyes were open, he was the center of his own attention. He was so certain of himself he wasn't even competitive in the normal way. He'd made one comment about Mireille Kane: "You can totally see her tits in that green T-shirt."

But just now, for some reason, it had almost made Dmitri cry to look at her.

MADOKA HAD an idea on the flight to Utah. She'd been arranging with herself the kind of person she would be for the week: supportive, calm, elegant, poised, intelligent. A slightly different version of her work persona, which was a little more energetic and upbeat. Then: inspiration. What if instead of being *herself* acting like a perfect astronaut wife, she pretended to be an *insane person* who was pretending to be a perfect astronaut wife? This would lend the time at Prime a certain piquancy, to borrow a Yoshi word. It would give her a secret. It might even be a kind of performance art.

She would still be perfect, of course, but with a core of madness that wasn't true madness, but rebellion. There were lots of ways to practice this. For instance, she has been actively trying *not* to learn people's names at Prime Space. This is not easy for her: several years ago everyone in Madoka's company attended a two-day seminar on personal semantic hooking and now the best she can do is try to substitute wrong names using the same method, resulting only in her acquiring several names for every person. She tells herself that the person introducing himself is Peter, who looks like the Disney Peter Pan, but she has already connected his real name—George—with the English word *gorge*, which connects to George's job in Prime's Food Science Laboratory.

"Have you met Yoshihiro's parents?" Madoka makes formal introductions and gives Peter Pan Gorge George her doll smile. "That's very interesting," she says. And, "I'm enjoying myself." Also, "Oh, thank you. I know that he wants very much to contribute."

Yoshi's parents have been very pleased with Prime Space, but Yoshi's parents like everything about their son being an astronaut except for the part where he goes to space, so they're delighted to have him safely entombed in a simulator for seventeen months. "We will worry about the other thing later," Yoshi's mother says, meaning Mars.

Madoka is glad her own parents had felt it sufficient to say goodbye to Yoshi before he left Japan. Her mother would have noticed and commented on how Madoka has been acting. Yoshi's parents only care about Yoshi, although Tanaka-san had praised her during his speech last night. He'd compared her to the calm and steady waters that greet a ship after it has sailed through storms, and also to the gentle wind that swells the sails, and finally, to an anchor that holds the ship steady. It was another moment to be glad of her mother's absence, as her mother would not have appreciated the idea that Madoka existed solely as a kind of ancillary tool to the *Voyages of Yoshi*, even though it was a theme with her mother that Madoka was not a truly successful wife: did not understand Yoshi, or fully appreciate him.

"Marriage is a mirror" was Madoka's father's advice to her on the day of her wedding. "Sometimes it is challenging, to see yourself in this way. It can be frightening. You must face these fears together."

But Yoshi didn't have fear, because he was always thinking about the things that could go wrong, and arranging himself to handle them. He anticipated everything; there was no situation he had not created an internal checklist against.

George is now introducing the person who designed the Mars landing simulations. She has the exact shade of red hair that Madoka and her best friend, Yuko, had tried to get when they were teenagers. They'd bleached and dyed streaks, which had resulted in a kind of a pumpkin-colored frieze. Yuko's mother had gone crazy, but Madoka's mother had just laughed and said, "When you get bored with that, I can help you dye it back." Madoka's father had called her *kabocha* for months. Madoka arranges with herself to remember the game lady as Pumpkin. Pumpkin is very short, and is wearing a T-shirt with the words *But I'm Huge in the Kuiper Belt* printed below a small blue planet. Pluto.

Pumpkin perches on a chair next to Madoka and launches into an extremely technical monologue about tactile sensor arrays. Madoka, whose primary job is to explain to health care workers how her company's robots can be used, not how they were designed, makes polite *mhm*s and tries not to look bored. She is tired. Performance art is exhausting. It was hard to know what to do when you are pretending to be a crazy person who is pretending not to be crazy. An artist needed to make more specific choices, maybe, otherwise it was too much like you *were* a crazy person. But which choices were the right ones?

"And you're a roboticist for Shin'yu?" Pumpkin is asking.

"No, no." Madoka waves this title off. "I work in sales."

Madoka has decided to be modest about her role because a crazy person who is Global Chief Sales Operative for a company that is the world leader in robotic caregivers might believe she is the head of an army of robotic nurses who are going to slaughter humankind, and if that crazy person was trying to seem normal, she might throw people off by saying, "I work in sales."

Two more Prime people join their table. Madoka continues her subterfuge techniques. One thing about Prime is that a lot of the people here are very eccentric and artistic, so her appearing to be quite normal is maybe making her seem boring, but that's good. To not be boring, but to *seem* boring, is the most rebellious act you can pull off.

Since Madoka was a small child she had harbored this sense that she had a gift inside her, that she was *marked*. But she preferred to wait for the thing—whatever it was—to emerge. For school club, Madoka had chosen English and Volleyball. She was no machine, like her mother, who could just sit down and grind out her long poems, working every day. So, her mother was disciplined, so what? She was disciplined at making long poems that were only pretty good, not great, and certainly not perfect. Did the world need another pretty good poem? It did not. Besides, a pretty good poem made from typing consistently five hours a day could hardly be said to be art. Even her mother shied away from calling herself an artist. "A craftswoman." Though apparently she felt that a craftswoman was still something more profound than a robot ambassador.

"You should have a creative outlet," her mother was always saying. "You know what happens to salarymen. You need to make sure that you aren't neglecting your soul."

The robots had no souls, it was true, but Madoka was hardly a salaryman. She was very engaged with her work, and her work was important. There was real help that robots could provide for the lonely, the aged, the infirm. Who would take care of these people if the robots did not? Even in countries with an immigrant population willing to do low-wage jobs, you saw all kinds of horrific abuse and neglect. By people who were full of a soul, by the way. And even good people had limitations. They needed to sleep, they needed to go home to their families, they got distracted, they made mistakes and bad choices.

Fear of robots was something she could not understand.

Pumpkin is shaking Madoka's hand and saying that she thinks Yoshi is the most awesome person ever.

Yoshi is the most awesome person ever. And Madoka is his awesome wife, because that's the way he imagines her and that is the person that he loves absolutely. When they'd made love last night he'd been very passionate and tender to the person he thought she was.

Madoka knows what the dynamic between herself and her husband looks like to others, because it is a thing space agencies like to know and it is a thing she and Yoshi have been evaluated on, separately and together. She knows that they look solid, they look strong. Trusting. Supportive.

All of this is true. None of it is not true.

Solid is not true. She would say her marriage is solid, but only because the words people use to indicate happiness are so unnuanced. Not that her marriage is fragile; it's more that her marriage might be only a solid surface, with nothing inside it. But *all* relationships between people might be this way.

Madoka looks around the room.

The American girl has been doing some kind of performance too this past week. Madoka knew better than to accept any of the overtures of friendship coming from Mireille Kane. Madoka's adolescence, young adulthood, and early adulthood had all been marked by a close female friendship. Certainly these relationships had felt solid. She had felt *seen* by these friends, and had shared all the parts of herself that she could think of to share, and even invented some. Every single one of those friendships had ended, which was embarrassing because Madoka had been raised with the idea that female friendships were the most enduring kind, and friction between women was an invention of the patriarchy.

Yuko had liked a boy who had preferred Madoka, and when this was learned, Yuko had never spoken to Madoka again. Everything they had created together was gone in an instant, erased. Emi had been the best friend Madoka ever had, until it became clear that Emi never truly liked Madoka, but rather envied and resented her to the point where her only solution was binding Madoka into an increasingly uncomfortable intimacy. Madoka had been forced to end that one. Asuko had dropped her without a word or explanation. Later, Madoka heard that Asuko had done the same thing to another woman, but it didn't make Madoka feel any better. There'd been no official break with Hana, but like most of Madoka's women friends, Hana now had small children and had been absorbed into the world of other women with small children.

It was not an awful situation: Madoka didn't genuinely like that many people. But still. She would not try to be friends with the American astronaut's daughter, though Madoka had caught that moment of the girl's rage just now, and had felt something. Relief?

"Yoshi is my best friend," she tells people, and she knows he says the same of her. And yet, she is relieved that he is going to be away for this long period of time, in such a definitive way. It is too much for her, to keep their relationship strong and solid seeming, to protect them both from whatever might not be inside it. It is important not to hurt Yoshi.

She is a little envious too. For seventeen months he will have an audience, observers who will monitor his voice, and note his eye contact, and count his very syllables. And Yoshi will not just be pretending that he is going to Mars, he will be pretending to be the most perfect person to go to Mars, and maybe he is, almost without question, he is, but that doesn't mean he won't have to pretend to be what he really is, because aren't we all pretending to be who we really are? Madoka would like, very sincerely, to ask someone this question.

LUKE HAS BEEN looking forward to meeting the family members of the astronauts. Prime has assigned each family their own personal liaison, so Obber contact with them during Eidolon will be limited to observing the communications between crewmember and family member. It is thought that family members will initially be self-conscious about the idea that someone like Luke is reading their mail or watching their recorded messages, but will largely forget about it after four to six weeks. (It is not expected that the astronauts will forget about it.) And really, what Luke will be reading is how the messages are received. He will be reading Helen, so to speak, reading a message from Mireille.

Luke looks over at the Helen Kane table and Mireille Kane catches him out and smiles. Luke tries to look professional and friendly and not like the legions of guys who must hit on Mireille constantly, and also not like someone who buys the Mireille that's been on display the past ten days. Mireille is a person to keep an eye on. The girl looks like she's ready to throw something.

Family members might end up being a more valuable source of

insight into the crew than the hundreds of questions the astronauts have answered.

What is the word or image that you most associate with the word man?

Sergei, Yoshi, and Helen had all answered the same way: *human.* All three had given the same answer—*human*—for *What is the word or image that you most associate with the word* woman?

For the question *What is the word or image that you most associate with the word* human? all three had said: *explorer.*

Which only revealed that Sergei and Yoshi and Helen were all very good at answering questions designed to reveal their personalities without revealing anything useful about their personalities. They were canny or artful in similar ways, which was potentially more useful than self-disclosure.

AT THE OBBER TABLE, the talk now turns to *Red Dawn II,* whose launch date is set for the very day the crew will be simulating launch in Utah. Boone Cross has said that he will not send a crew to Mars without having two Earth Return Vehicles already there: there must be a ride home, and a backup ride, both fully fueled and waiting for the astronauts, or *Primitus* will not go.

Nobody is allowed to say the words *crash* or *explosion* within a ten-kilometer radius of Prime Space. Suggested alternatives are: *RUSE* (Rapid Unplanned Separation Event) and *learning experience.*

As for what will happen to Eidolon if *Red Dawn II* suffers a launch pad learning experience in two weeks, that will be very tricky indeed. A crew that knows its real launch date will need to be pushed back, and may be in jeopardy altogether, will not be a happy crew. It's a tense time.

Along with launch windows for Mars, there are launch windows for this particular crew. Helen is fifty-three now, will be fifty-seven for the real thing. A two-year delay, maybe a four-year delay, was all she, and by extension the rest of her crew, can afford. Their self-designed Eidolon mission patches have an emblem of three crossed swords: they are Musketeers for Mars, all for one and one for all.

The Obber team leader, Barkley Ransom, is now proposing a toast. It will be a challenging seventeen months for their group: no downtime except for shift changes, and their bodies and brains will be pushed to the limit of endurance. "But remember," Ransom says, "what Boone always tells us: 'If you don't start every day in awe of what we're doing here, then you don't understand what we're doing here.'"

HELEN

*D*oes it feel real?

Helen knows that she needs to stop asking herself this. It is not a meaningful question.

Everything is real in some sense. *Unicorn* is a real word.

A simulation of reality still exists in time and space and, if you are inside it, has a blood pressure, a heart rate, a nervous system, all the usual suspects. You don't stop being a real person just because you aren't in a real place.

Helen knows what the real thing feels like, and what it feels like to be tested for her physical and mental responses to a simulation of the real thing. There is a difference between the two, although it's not always as great as people might think. Helen has not felt fear of death in a simulator, but she never felt fear of death riding a rocket, either. In both cases, what she feared was screwing up.

That doesn't mean Helen is cavalier about death. She respects death. But she fears failure.

Still, she was aware—riding a rocket—that she *could* die. Awareness of imminent possible death is not without beneficial properties. Risk of annihilation can be a key ingredient, like baking soda. A teaspoon or so is sufficient to make all the other components rise up in glory, but without it? No cake. For some, the edge of death is the only place to find love of life. And having once felt this event horizon and yet escaped, they must return again and again, testing, testing. For these people, alive is not alive. Almost dead is the only alive.

This is not Helen. She even drives her car at the speed limit.

But not today.

There are many things that can go wrong in the first minutes of leaving Earth and most of them come with a decision-making window of less than five seconds. If you are an astronaut it means that you are someone who can assess and react quickly. If you are a great astronaut it means that while your mental and physical reactions operate at top speed, your emotional reactions are stately and glacial. The combination that works best is someone who only needs four seconds to get to: *This is what we need to do*, and four months to get to: *Gee, I'm a little bit uncomfortable.*

Helen is a spectacular astronaut.

Does it feel real?

Well, it doesn't feel like nothing, that's for sure. There is a mighty shaking going on and an invisible gorilla is sitting on Helen's chest. She's felt this gorilla before, it's an old friend. You can't shift the gorilla, you just have to endure it.

Helen's physical autonomy is diminished to the limited degree with which she can tense or relax her muscles. She can also move her eyes, and with those she can see her hands, her knees, part of Yoshi's arm, and, for split seconds, a toy alien above Sergei's head.

The alien is having a hard time. He is on a string, not strapped in, and appears to be doing an alien version of the St. Vitus dance.

Someone in Prime has humorously outfitted the little green man with his own aqua blue Prime Space spacesuit, complete with Prime Space insignia.

Helen's eyes move from the alien to the flow of information tracking across the faceplate of her helmet. The g-forces are now pushing her eyeballs back into her head a bit, so this is tricky, but she manages. She can push enough air out of her lungs to communicate, confirming data back to Mission Control.

Prime Space has pulled out all the stops for the Eidolon launch. They've been in sim mode since the five a.m. wake-up call. They had sims for when they waved good-bye to their families and colleagues from behind the sealed partition (Helen has no idea if that was her daughter or a simulated version of her daughter) and they had sims for when they enacted various departing rituals including the old Russian one of peeing on the right tire of the vehicle taking them to the launch pad—in Helen's case, emptying a vial of urine on the tire—very much a real tire and real urine, although the landscape outside the truck was virtual. They had sims for a long elevator ascent to their craft. Considering that *Primitus* was sitting on a platform in the desert, and not atop the *Manus V*, the noise and motion of the "elevator" was especially impressive.

And all along, Helen has been asking herself, *Does it feel real?* Which is not a question she would be asking if it *were* real, and so the answer, on some level, must be no.

And yet.

Now her eyeballs are going out instead of in. This will be the big rush, when God step-step-steps and kicks their little football, and the sound of tarsal connecting with craft will be a mighty boom and God's bulging thigh will shred his tights. Not nicey-nice God, but Old Testament God, letting Job have it, capable of large-scale smiting.

Helen has a speech she gives about leaving Earth:

"Of course, we are all focused on following what is happening technically in the spacecraft, and being prepared to deal with any issues. But when you hear the SRBs—sorry, Solid Rocket Boosters—fall away for the first time, you are just filled with awe for the dedication and ingenuity and expertise of the incredible number of people who have contributed to that moment. It is truly a time to marvel at what our species is able to do."

Nothing of the kind! Nothing of the kind had she felt during any of her missions. You didn't have time for poetic thoughts like that.

Very few people could say what they actually felt in a particular moment. Possibly nobody knew.

Helen cannot name the something that has always been in the back of her mind during those moments when she has left the Earth. Intense focus on what was happening in the present eclipsed all else, but things do not disappear during an eclipse, only disappear from view. Something is there.

How does it feel?

Big.

Bigger.

This is escape velocity, a fine phrase. This *will* be new, when it is real. Helen has never gone beyond Low Earth Orbit. This will be Deep Space.

It's not happening. But it sort of is.

Helen can't help but watch the clock. Your body can take more than you think it can. It helps it, comforts it, when you can give it an end point. You can take quite a bit when you know that at the end of your ordeal, you will be in space and there will be weightlessness.

To stand on Earth is not quite the sessile event it seems. To stand on Earth is to fall to Earth. People forget that. People take our planet's feeble but constant gravitational embrace for granted. To orbit the Earth is not to be shot up to some magical zone where there is no gravity, but to be shot up in such a trajectory that your subsequent fall means you won't hit anything; you will persistently and permanently miss the Earth and circle around it. To have done this is to understand the persistence and permanence of falling and to understand that what is true does not always feel like what is true. It doesn't feel like falling to stand on Earth. It doesn't feel like falling and missing to circle around it.

On the way to Mars, the astronauts will escape Earth's gravity and their motion will be dominated by the gravitational field of the sun, and they will fall around the sun, until that fall gets them close enough to fall around Mars.

But it won't feel like they are falling, or flying. *Primitus* will be tethered to the spent upper stage of its rocket, which, when its thrusters are fired, will cause rocket and craft to revolve around each other. This centrifuge will provide 98 percent Earth-like gravity conditions in the Hab. They will experience microgravity only for discrete moments, or if they have to perform a space walk. The centrifuge will protect the crew's muscles, their bone density, their vision, and their cognitive functioning. And it will take away the joy of falling with everything falling around you.

Microgravity is the heroin, the God, the unrequited love, of astronauts. Nothing feels as good or does more damage.

Before her first experience in Prime's *Bright Star* centrifuge-enabled craft, Helen was told by other astronauts that the spin up "is a little bit of a transition," which was astronaut-speak for "You will want to puke like you have never wanted to puke before."

Now, of course, this will all be simulated, but considering the elaborate theatrics Prime has provided this far, Helen expects to feel some real nausea. It's not that hard to make humans feel sick, even her. She's taken the antinausea meds in preparation. Once fake spin-up is completed, they will descend into the Habitat section of *Primitus* and pretend that the real Earth gravity present in a module in Utah is artificial gravity from a centrifuge that has been successfully created in space. They don't have to do anything goofy like shout, "My God! It worked!" Although that would be funny.

"Here we go!" Sergei shouts, because the God that kicked them has now run to the end of the field and caught them in his hands. It amuses God, perhaps, to toss them from one hand to the other. This goes on for seventeen seconds longer than it should, and is somewhat more violent than she has experienced before.

Okay, much more violent.

When she feels ill, Helen has a visualization of a tree that she employs. Biofeedback. No one vomits at the thought of a tree.

And then God does a funny thing.

"Ho-*ho*!" Sergei shouts.

Helen is strapped to her seat, immobile, but the protocol list fastened to her wrist has opened upward and is rustling its laminated leaves. The pages are fluttering gently, lazily.

In her peripheral vision, just to the right: a gear bag is floating on its tether, tilting vertically, glissading toward her until its tether becomes taut, and then gently, almost shyly, retreating. A cable just below it rises like a languorous snake.

It is funny. Helen could almost swear her internal organs are rising up within her body, that the straps holding her to her seat are straining. Her body is getting tricked. Her body is mirroring what it sees and since her body believes, her brain has no choice but to follow along. Mind *under* matter. It is delightful. So real. She is weightless.

Helen wishes she could release herself from her seat, release even just an arm, but then is glad she cannot. The spectacular illusion would be shattered. The bag is not floating, and neither is she. A phrase rises in her mind, she can't trace back its context.

Nothing feels as free as this.

Oh yes, the Playtex ad on the wall in Japan. The lady in her bra and girdle. Look how far women have come.

The game designers at Prime Space were little Gods indeed. Probably God would look more like a computer programmer than an Old Testament guy, anyway. Prime is in the details.

The string holding up the little green man in his spacesuit has gone slack. The alien floats, content, peaceful, in his element once again. On his way home.

LUKE

The astronauts stand before a window that is not a window. Obviously, the astronauts can't have a true functioning window in the desert when they are supposed to be in space, but the actual *Primitus* has no window either. A space-worthy window is heavy and compromises the defense of solar radiation for the craft. It is a concern, the loss of a window, for the health of the astronauts. Looking out the window is the thing that astronauts love the most, their favorite occupation, the thing they say never gets old. Photographing Earth is the number-one recreational activity. It is meditation, it is reward.

It has been explained to Luke that the view on the way to Mars "will be crap, anyway, mostly." The crew will be flying in sunlit blackness. For a decent look at the cosmos, they will need something better than their eyes and a window. They will have it: exterior cameras on *Primitus* will transmit real-time feed of what is outside their craft to screens throughout the interior of the Habitat. The cameras are fitted with enhanced spectral range lenses: infrared and near ultraviolet, and will be a vast improvement over the crew's own eyes. The astronauts will be given first their own planet, their own moon, and after that, Deep Space objects. At the other end of the journey, they will be given the moons of Mars, Phobos (fear), and Deimos (dread). They will be given Mars. Better than their eyes, better than a window, realer than real.

JUST NOW, the astronauts are speaking from prepared statements. The sentiments they express work equally well for both a real and simulated mission.

"We are at the beginning of a long journey of discovery." (Helen)

"It is a great privilege to play a role in this remarkable endeavor." (Yoshihiro)

"To my family, I wish to say that I will be thinking of you every day." (Sergei)

THE OBBER LAB is also windowless: one long wall a bank of screens, the other a digital whiteboard. In between these walls, there are stand-up desks and sit-down desks and foot rollers and exercise balls. Above the bank of screens, Ransom has strung a bannerlike poster with the words No Reality Without Observation, which is a quote from Niels Bohr and, as Ransom explained, technically bad science but fitting for their mandate.

Luke thinks that it will be very difficult to measure on Eidolon whether the loss of a real window is a significant psychological factor or not. On Eidolon, the astronauts will know they are looking at images Prime has prepared, not real-time feed. This is the elephant in the analogue room of Eidolon: they cannot tell what anyone will feel about the true experience of going to Mars until it actually happens, and there has to be a possibility that the feeling will significantly alter every aspect of the mission. Everything about Eidolon is set to diminish this probability, but they can't take it to zero.

The clock has officially started on Eidolon. It's a clock like no other, neither quite the twenty-four-hour day of Earth, nor quite the twenty-four-hour, thirty-nine-minute, and thirty-five-second sol of Mars. This clock moves in *Primitus* time: an ongoing calibration that will—when the astronauts land—have the crew adjusted to the Martian diurnal rhythms, and synchronized with the landing target's time zone for minimal jetlag. Right now, the difference between real Earth and *Primitus* time is a matter of extra seconds in the day, and so far none of the Obbers are feeling the effects, but this will change. The crew will have the advantage over Mission Control and Obbers, since all the interior lights on *Primitus* will be adjusting to give them the semblance of a day and night, glowing blue or red as needed to help slowly shift the body's stubborn circadian sense of order. (And helped by the fact that none of the crew are naturally extreme early risers, a trait that makes such a shift doubly difficult.) Mission Control and Obbers will be working in shifts, and also doing things like going outside, without sim helmets. They have drugs, and special sleep masks, and even goggles they can use when they're outside, but things are likely to get a little hairy.

Today, the mood around Prime is buoyant. *Red Dawn II* had launched successfully and was operating nominally. "We're going to Mars," people are saying when they pass one another in the corridors. "It's on."

"Although Mars is our destination," Yoshi says in his statement, "perhaps some of our most profound discoveries will be in the journey there and back. When *Primitus* makes its voyage to the Red Planet, the cameras of our craft will allow all the inhabitants on Earth a chance to join the expedition, to see what we see. Many astronauts speak of the 'Overview Effect,' an acute awareness of the preciousness of our planet and also a shift toward seeing ourselves as members of a larger celestial community. The hope is that by extending the Overview Effect to all humanity, a new era of care and consciousness, global goodwill, and desire for peace may begin for all of us."

This was Prime's democracy: that everyone should have the Overview Effect.

BEFORE LUKE had come to Prime he had considered the question of why so much money should be spent on space exploration when the problems of Earth were so desperate. Now he sees that it is the wrong question. Humans were going to go on savaging Earth and savaging one another if no one ever spent another penny on space exploration.

Going to Mars could make us better humans. And we had to be better. "When we eventually colonize Mars," Boone Cross has said, "we need to do so as an enlightened species moving forward, not as panicked refugees clinging to survival by our fingernails."

"I WOULD LIKE to say special thank-you to the Space Food Systems team," Sergei says now. "For putting the jar of caviar in our freezer. We will celebrate tonight." A current of anticipation ripples among the Obbers. Luke smiles.

The crew will not be able to eat that caviar. The crew only has about fifteen minutes more, then it all begins.

HELEN

"Helen, how are you doing?"

Helen decides to make a joke.

"I am motivated to work as hard as possible on this mission!" she shouts.

I am motivated to work as hard as possible on this mission is true or false statement number twenty-four of their Personal Group Functioning evaluations.

Sergei and Yoshi are only one wedge away in the small pie that is *Primitus*, but it is necessary to shout. When the Environment Temperature Control System has been functioning today, it has been accompanied by intermittent blasts of a whirring/grinding sound that Yoshi had described earlier as "a cacophony most unpleasant." Helen thought it likely that "a cacophony most unpleasant" was a quotation, but had lacked the energy in the moment to pursue it.

They can live with constant noise—on the space station the decibel level is comparable to driving down a freeway with the windows rolled down—but unpredictable loud banging is stressful. It is also not a good idea to live in conditions where you cannot hear your crewmate say "Help" or "Don't touch that" or "That object appears to be heading straight toward us." More important, the noise is almost certainly indicative of a greater problem.

"That Noise Is Almost Certainly Indicative of a Greater Problem" would be the title of the epic poem of the past twenty days. If *Primitus* were a song, noises almost certainly indicative of a greater problem would swell the chorus. If a child were to choose *Primitus* as a Halloween costume, the child should not be dressed as a spacecraft; the child should be dressed as a noise that is almost certainly indicative of a greater problem.

Helen has a quick image of Meeps, age ten, in a Halloween costume she had built herself: a chicken suit with an egg that revolved independently on a wire around her head so that sometimes it was the Meeps as the chicken that came first, and sometimes it was the egg. No other child at her school had come close to anything so witty; it was by far the best costume.

"I feel under pressure to perform well!" Sergei shouts. "But Yoshi says that this mission is giving him opportunities to make meaningful contributions!"

"I feel like my workload is manageable!" Helen shouts over a fresh burst of cacophony most unpleasant.

Perhaps it was wise of Prime to besiege the astronauts with a host of difficulties directly related to their environment right after trans-Mars injection. If one of the goals of Eidolon was to give the astronauts an opportunity to become extremely intimate with *Primitus*, to poke around her insides, and learn the early signs of sickness, and locate just exactly where on her back she wanted to be scratched, well, then this was the way.

And this was why they had been chosen. They were people who

could service a craft. If you were sending twelve people to Mars, you have the luxury of including a physicist and a geologist. If you are sending three: send engineers.

They have what Prime liked to call "the fourth crew member": RoMeO, a robotic medical officer who can perform both as a physician and extra set of hands. Just now, nobody is employing RoMeO, possibly because he's another thing that could break.

Helen believes that her workload is manageable. She just hasn't found the way to manage it yet.

Everything on *Primitus* takes more time than it should. Partly this is because *Primitus* is organized for possible centrifuge failure—every tool, every piece of equipment has a tether or a strap or a seal—and partly because they have limited tools. Also, things have gotten pretty messy. *Primitus* is a two-tiered pie, or more precisely, a Bundt cake: the tiers are connected by a central tube, which has its own shielding and doubles as a solar storm shelter. On the upper Hab, seven unequal slices radiate from the tube: Galley/Recreation, Science/Lab, Exercise, Lavatory, and three private compartments for the crew. At present, it looks like someone has dropped the Bundt cake on the floor; everything is in the wrong room, moved because someone had to get behind it, or under it, or dismantle it to find out why its sensors were blaring.

There is a kind of accelerated internal rhythm Helen becomes aware of—chiefly centered in her ribcage and throat—when she is on the borders of serious sleep deprivation. She should rest soon, for at least an hour or two, but right now, her hands are steady. What she needs most right now is a tool to twist these wires together. Sergei has her small flat nose pliers. They need more small-size flat nose pliers. She must improvise, and she enjoys that. A cuticle clipper would be absolutely perfect for the job, she thinks.

Just when Helen thinks "cuticle clipper," her mind slips sideways. She can almost physically feel a tilting, as if she were standing chest-high in the waters of a lake and leaning sideways and dipping one ear in the water. She can't stop it. Helen's mind slips and she sees her sister Hillary's teenage collection of nail maintenance and decoration apparatus, which Hillary stored in a silly version of a proper tackle box. The box was pink plastic, covered by Hillary in stickers and with her name spelled out in rhinestones. Varnish in all shades was arranged by color wheel scheme inside, along with implements and little rods that Hillary used to adorn her nails with stripes, with flowers, with holiday seasonal–appropriate insignia. The box, as Helen recalls, was called a Kaboodle.

Helen tries to bring her mind back to sourcing a tool, but her mind is not done. Her mind seeks out teenage Hillary, hunched over her Kaboodle, in Saint Andrew's Long Term Care Facility, where their father had lain in a permanent vegetative state, and where they had visited him for two hours every Sunday. The children were allowed to do activities during their visits. They did not have to sit and stare at him.

Helen's mind comes back, thankfully before it roved from Hillary over to the way her father looked in that hospital bed.

This is not good, this slipping. But it's over and Helen can now visualize the scissor clamp in the surgical supply case, which should do the job. She knows where the medical supply case is, she can access it, she can do this thing.

As she is completing this task, Yoshi appears in the doorway.

"I'm done," Helen says.

"Very good. And now, the toilet. It is being very peevish." Yoshi hands Helen a pair of gloves with a half smile.

According to the data, in about six weeks even the things people in a confined situation admire about one another will become a possible source of irritation. "Irrational antagonism" is the name for this, even though anyone who has ever heard of the phenomenon finds it entirely understandable and only wonders at it taking six weeks to manifest. But it's day twenty-one and Helen still likes that Yoshi uses words like *peevish*.

They had all acknowledged this morning that they were falling into spells of "overfocus," and Mission Control has reminded them to allow for more frequent short breaks, to utilize the five-minute exercise routines, to monitor their mental and physical acuity with the Reaction Self-Tests. Helen reminds herself that she needs to run sentences longer than "yes" through her head before she says them out loud. Also, when she has an "emotion" she should take a moment to "flip it." *I really don't want to have to deal with poop right now* needs to become *I'm glad that all I have to deal with right now is a little poop*.

The Lav wedge of *Primitus* is a one-person space, but this is a two-person job. And right now it is better to work when they can in teams, to avoid errors. Yoshi reads the procedure for removing the face panel of the Chute, and Helen removes it.

"Can't get a visual," she says. Yoshi leans over her shoulder and adjusts the beam of his flashlight. All fecal matter on *Primitus* is processed through forward osmosis. The astronaut engaged in elimination uses a vacuum funnel connected to a bag, and the bag of astronaut waste is sent via the Chute to the lining of the craft's corrugated hull. Water from the waste matter is extracted through the bag's polyethylene membrane, the water is purified and recycled, and the rest acts as additional radiation shielding. The phrase "flying in a poop can" had been used to describe this method of recycling astronaut elimination on a spacecraft, but it is effective. Water and fecal matter are better barriers against cosmic radiation than metal, containing more shielding atomic nuclei per unit volume.

Yoshi shines the flashlight into the maw of the Chute and Helen slides her gloved hands inside. Their heads are very close together as they work, Yoshi's leg is pressed up against Helen's back, but it is the common goal and the accordance between them about the importance of things relative to other things that forms the intimacy. When a member of a crew says that the crew is "like family," it's not an entirely accurate simile. It is not easy to get the people in your life to act as perfect team members. Helen had experienced many happy times with her husband and daughter, but they had never really been part of her crew. Yoshi's flashlight goes off.

"One moment," Yoshi says, in the voice he uses when he is extolling effort in not being peevish. Another flashlight is required. Helen sits back on her heels.

Tomorrow is the anniversary of her husband's death. Helen needs to record a message for Meeps and downlink it to Mission Control to be forwarded. She needs to not be annoyed that she needs to do this. A video message will be better than talking anyway. They are too far "out" now for a comfortable live chat, there is a seven-second "delay" even when they have connections. Meeps needs to have the message in the morning, waiting for when she wakes up. She must not think that Helen has forgotten.

Eric's ashes—most of them—were interred at the Cemetery of Loyasse, in Lyon, where Eric had been born.

"I get that it's not him," Mireille had said, about the ashes. "But I just think it would be nicer if he were outside."

Helen had disagreed with the idea that the ashes weren't Eric. They couldn't be *more* him. They were nothing *but* him. Other physical traces of Eric existed in the world for weeks after his death: fragments, indications, hair on the shoulders of his jackets, a toothpaste tube dented to the proportion of his thumb and forefinger. Memories of Eric in the minds of the living, yes, but these were already diluted and would become more so. Things Eric had bought or selected, but these were more Things than Eric. All lesser yields of Eric than Eric himself. He had written books, but his books were highbrow historical mysteries, and Eric always talked about the difference between craft (good) and self-expression (bad). There was Meeps, half of whose genetic code had also been written by her father. But no, the thing most like Eric on Earth had to be his ashes.

"He should be outside," Meeps had said. "Under the trees. Under the sky."

When she thought about it, Helen realized she did not associate Eric with nature. A very beautiful cabinet seemed exactly right for him. But death was an event that only the living had to deal with, and Helen would have done anything just then to make Meeps feel better. She had never been the primary parent and now she was the only parent.

"I agree with you," she said to her daughter. "But your father wanted a mausoleum rather than a grave and we should respect his wishes. But." She had suggested that they each take a scoop of the ashes and find a place in nature where they could scatter them.

Helen had not yet scattered Eric. She had him still, in a box. And Meeps had never found the right place and had only transferred Eric from one box to a prettier one.

YOSHI RETURNS WITH the flashlight and they take up their positions. Helen does not think that her ruminations about Eric are evidence of another mind-slip. She's good. She's good to go.

"Okay, this might be the problem," she says. "Look."

"Ah, I see. The casing. Can it be snapped up?"

"I think so. Let's hope this is the only place where it's loose."

Helen, afraid of forgetting about the need to make a recording for Meeps, has left a note for herself on the pillow of her bunk. The thing will be simpler and faster to do if she knows what she is going to say and so she has been planning. Sometimes she can sound mechanical when she is following a script, even if she is the one who has written the script, so she also needs to be aware of that.

It is a tricky business. The casing of the Chute needs to be held in place while it is being taped, requiring four hands in a narrow space. Helen holds the flashlight between her teeth; they switch positions and roles. It is easier within a crew to switch roles than it is within a family.

The solution, when tested, turns out to be good; the Chute is working, for now. They can move on.

They have a great crew. A *great* crew.

Bursts of euphoria are not uncommon at this level of sleep deprivation.

Before moving on to her next chore, Helen does a few exercises and runs through what she plans to say in the recording for Meeps.

Hi, Meeps. I just wanted you to know that I will be thinking about you a lot today. I remember the day you were born and how your father held you in his arms. We both felt so lucky that you came into our lives, and you gave your dad so much love and joy during his life. He would be so proud of all the things you are doing and the lovely woman you have become. I love you!

She should write it down and look at it before recording. There was something not quite right about it. The ETCS erupts into another round of cacophony most unpleasant. It is getting pretty hot in *Primitus*.

The noise is actually much worse, much louder.

"Something else," Helen says to Yoshi. Two more warning alarms are sounding underneath the ETCS. Yoshi takes the solar array issue, and Helen moves to the Galley to work the problem with the freezer. They only have one and they need it for medical supplies. Following the protocols for removing things from the freezer so she can fix it is exacting business. She can't rush this, no matter how much she wants to. One of the reasons Helen is on this crew is that she has this kind of control.

She cannot think of a time when she had thrown up her hands and said, "enough." The most stressful, dangerous, and fatiguing moment of her life had been an eight-hour spacewalk to fix a tear in one solar panel on the space station, which she would also categorize as the most exciting, satisfying, and exhilarating moment of her life. People always say *day child was born*, or *wedding day*, and certainly those were wonderful too, but they had not required any unique skills on her part.

Eight hours, fifty feet along the solar array, suspended by her feet at the end of the Robotic Arm, and she hadn't reached a breaking point. She had finished the job.

You have to find another level. Just now, on *Primitus*, it was like being the parent of a toddler. A hundred tantrum-y toddlers. And, like a parent, maybe you had to forgo a full night's sleep, and eat standing up, and not exercise, and let the house be messy and not return emails or have recreation hour. You had to, because these were potentially lethal toddlers and they would not scream themselves out or nap. Helen crouches down beside the freezer, then kneels. Her calves are cramping.

They absolutely *could* be bombarded with these kinds of problems in the first twenty days of a mission to Mars. They could be bombarded with these kinds of problems for all one hundred and eighty days to Mars. The problems could be much, much worse. They could have all died on the launch pad. Not that Prime would have run that particular sim for Eidolon, but they could certainly keep this level of potential crisis up for their entire trip, and Sergei and Yoshi and Helen would have to find a way to manage it. That was the deal with space. Whatever happened, you had to manage it, or you would die. And when you started to become upset, you had to find another level.

You have to find another level. Helen had said that to Meeps, when she was a toddler and having a tantrum. The problem with Mireille, then as now, was that she never truly *wanted* to find another level. She wanted people to come to her level and . . . do something, tell her that it was okay to feel whatever she was feeling, but clearly it wasn't okay, because her feelings made her miserable. Helen rolls back from her knees into a crouching position and leans forward to stretch her calves. The knee of her left pant leg rips.

These pants are meant to last Helen another week. Like the food packaging on board, Prime's patented Solox clothing material is engineered for radiation defense and biodegradability, but it performs best as clothing when it is not subjected to twenty days of nearly continuous crawling, crouching, and kneeling. Helen has a more favorable opinion of the Solox bra she is wearing. The padding for extra protection creates—when she is working on her back—a kind of shelf out of her boobs, a useful tool rack from her rack.

This is a joke she could make, but will not.

To meditate, she needs to shut her eyes, and if she shuts her eyes, she might fall asleep.

It was perfectly possible that many of the problems on *Primitus* were real problems. They were sitting in the middle of a desert inside a highly automated craft, and everything, everywhere, breaks. It was conceivable that Mission Control was going nuts right now, replotting their daily schedule of planned sim disasters in order to figure out how to keep *Primitus* going for real.

Or every single problem was a simulated problem being stage-managed by Prime as part of their training, a test of their capabilities, a program with the objective of monitoring what conditions will result in performance degradation.

The cacophony most unpleasant ceases and Helen feels a blast of cool air from the vent above her. She lifts her face and opens her mouth as if to drink it.

Sergei appears in the doorway of the room where Helen is crouched. The fabric of Sergei's Solox T-shirt is dark with sweat and he emits a powerful odor. Helen can also smell herself. She thinks that Sergei smells like an animal and she smells like a vegetable. Maybe Yoshi smells like a mineral.

"You find thing?" Sergei asks. His English is degrading.

"Not yet. I'm working through it. I'm loving this air, though."

Yoshi appears over Sergei's shoulder. Mineral! She was right. Or perhaps she is imagining it. In fact, they all smell pretty bad.

"Good news," Yoshi says. His English is becoming, if anything, slightly over-enunciated; his wide mouth curves over the words. He reports that the sensor warning lights on the solar panels was a problem of the sensor warning lights, and not the panels.

"Okay," Sergei says. "We should eat a little. And, Helen, your rotation is up. You must sleep soon."

Helen stands. She is embarrassed at the sound of crunching cartilage in her knees, and so speaks over it, a little more loudly than is necessary. She has been working on the freezer, she sees now, for two hours.

"I'm okay for another hour. Help me get this upright?" Helen asks.

"Pfft." Sergei joins her. "Did you find my caviar?"

As they shift the freezer, an unattached cable swishes out from the bottom like the tail of a mouse.

"Oh," says Helen.

She squats down. Her knees creak and the rip in her pant leg widens.

She missed this cable. She missed it.

It is an absurd mistake. Step one: make sure everything is plugged in. It's so absurd a mistake that she cannot quite believe she made it. It's so absurd a mistake that her body breaks out into a cold sweat and her hands begin to shake.

Now she is aware of being observed.

Helen scoots around until she finds the cable's mate and attaches it. The freezer emits a smug hum. Not smug. A freezer is not capable of smugness.

"*Maladets*," says Sergei. Helen looks at him and then at Yoshi, who gives her a congratulatory peace sign.

"No, I didn't do anything." Helen must admit her error. Her throat has gone dry. "I mean, I missed that. What I mean is, I think it just took me two hours to realize that it wasn't plugged in."

Helen looks at Yoshi, looks at Sergei. They look at her, they look at each other, they look back at her.

"Pttsk," says Sergei, finally. "That is not so bad as three things I have done. Come eat."

"I will put the supplies back in," Yoshi says, waving at the freezer.

They all make mistakes. Occasionally an error makes the news, as when an astronaut failed to correctly tether her tool bag during a space walk and had to watch all one hundred thousand dollars' worth of equipment float away from her. "Astronaut Loses Purse in Space" had been the headline. Oh, they all make mistakes, and if you were a woman you took it harder because you knew others would, but everyone took it hard. Most of the time, even if you felt that you hadn't made a mistake, you still sought criticism. *Tell me what I did wrong. Tell me how I can improve. What was a better choice I could have made?*

"Guess I'll never win Best-Dressed Astronaut now," Helen jokes, pointing to the hole in her pants.

Of course she was embarrassed. She had cost them all time. There were about twenty different things she could have been working on, or helping with. It was a boneheaded mistake, but it wasn't grave. Frustrating, hardly catastrophic.

Silly, time-consuming error, that's all.

As the astronauts prepare dinner they joke that one of them will have to try the shower tonight. There is a shower cylinder on *Primitus* and they are allowed one shower every eight days. Like everything else, it is automated: fifteen seconds of water for wetting, a one-minute pause for lathering, then thirty seconds of water for rinsing. The sensors for the shower are nominal (it is one of the few pieces of automation on *Primitus* that is working just fine) but nobody has used it yet. They are taking ISS-style sponge baths.

"Yes, you try," Sergei says to Yoshi. "And if shower does not explode, then Helen will take shower. And if Helen says it is safe, then I will go."

"Did anyone bring bubble bath?"

"I forgot rubber ducky."

"Oh good, now I know what to get you for Christmas."

It's a moment to learn. This was the thing about miscalculations, errors, mistakes. You admitted them, you used them as teachable moments, and then you moved on. You didn't forget, but you didn't dwell.

"I think we should celebrate small successes of today with the orange," Sergei says.

"It will be good for one more day," Yoshi says. "Will we enjoy it more tomorrow, when we are rested?"

"Tomorrow could be worse," says Helen. "Not worse. I mean that we should be in the moment. Right now, the toilet works, and the ETCS"—all three astronauts make the symbol against the evil eye—"is working, and because I have three engineering degrees I was able to successfully plug in the freezer. Let's celebrate."

All was okay unless she started compounding error with error. This would only happen if she lost her cool, and she doesn't lose her cool.

There are potentially a lot of things she has not noticed. She has already lived fifty-three years. Her life could be riddled with cords she hadn't plugged in.

The last thing you needed at the start of a long and complex mission was self-doubt.

You had to look back, of course you did. You had to recognize the past, and acknowledge it, but you couldn't stay there. She has a system for dealing with things, and the system has served her well. This is neither the time nor the place to doubt her system. This is the worst possible time and place.

"Ah, we have timed our break well," Yoshi says. The screen above their dining table is giving them a view of a tiny dot transiting a small blue sphere.

"This has been color corrected," Sergei says. This must be true. The moon in the image is lighter than it should be.

Helen looks at the Earth and her mind slips sideways again, straight into the lake. She can't help it and it happens fast.

Her mind slips, and Helen sees her father, lying in a hospital bed, inert but alive. Not trapped in the past, precisely, but preserved in a present with no future. She had never believed that her father would some day "live" in the sense that most people meant, but she had never precisely thought of him as "dead" either. She had seen him move occasionally, an arm, a leg. It hadn't meant anything. "Involuntary movement" it was called. It had scared her very badly, the first time she saw it. For several months Helen had been afraid to lean over her father and kiss his cheek. He might wrap his hands around her throat. He might stab a pair of stolen scissors into her ribcage. She had forgotten she had this fear.

She must come back, she must. She must get out of this slippage.

"Color corrected, yes, but I am reminding myself that it is still an image worthy of awe." Yoshi is looking at the screen. "Why shouldn't we feel awe? In front of a beautiful painting we do not ask ourselves *is it real?* We know that it is not real. It is a painting. But we can still be filled with awe at its beauty."

It is the longest thought that did not have to do with technical matters any of them has expressed in twenty days.

Helen thinks that she can't possibly have once been afraid that her vegetable father would choke her. She is hallucinating. She needs sleep, that is all.

"That's good thing to remember," says Sergei.

So this is it, twenty days, that's her limit? She's the first of the three to crack? This is what Prime wants to know?

No, she's back now, definitely. She will not slip again. It's over.

But the question remains. What else hasn't she noticed?

"Sleep now," Sergei says to Helen. He is the commander. "Four hours."

Helen picks her way through the corridor, straightening a few things as she goes. A great deal of thought has been put into the interior design of their craft. Helen's sense of decor and adornment doesn't go too far beyond a fondness for right angles and a vague sense that gray is a nice color on her, but she knows when a thing has been done carefully. That most of the flooring is brown and the ceilings in the private compartments are different hues of blue seems like—when there is time to appreciate such things—something that will be very nice. Also, the Galley table and storage lockers are a snappy red, and the Exercise room has violet matting.

Sergei's compartment is closest to the Lav, with Yoshi in between Sergei and Helen. She always tries not to notice these things, or give them weight, but a part of her is pleased that the woman was not put closest to the bathroom.

Helen slides open her door and is indescribably happy to see that she had left her sleeping cot unfolded, and she can tip forward and be out in about five seconds.

The note she had written earlier is waiting for her on the pillow. She needs to make this video. Helen smooths her hair, rubs her nose. Her skin is grimy. The cleansing wipes are in the Lav. She cannot bring herself to get up again. She brings herself to get up again. She will clean herself up, make a video for her daughter, get some sleep, and when she wakes up, she will be given another opportunity to perform at the highest level, which she will do, will do, will do. She will find every loose cord, every single one.

MIREILLE

The gun is surprisingly heavy.

"Okay, Mireille, we'll have you step onto the volume, please," a voice tells her. Mireille cannot see who is speaking to her—outside the scaffolding of lights and cameras the room is a shapeless vastness. She steps onto the stage, which she knows is what the disembodied voice means by "the volume," because her friend Wesley had run through the motion capture lingo with her in preparation for this audition. "Games are the best," he said. "Mo-cap people love working with trained theater actors. They actually don't *want* social media stars. I mean, they want them, but they know they have to use actors because to do games you have to have craft and storytelling skills. Games are the only place anyone needs a real actor anymore. Just make your motions clear and definite. Don't do too much with your hands. Hands are hard to animate."

The script they had given Mireille was not—she was informed—the real script, and the name of the game was a pseudonym for whatever the real game was called. She had been told to wear comfortable form-fitting clothes, and over her yoga pants and camisole they had put her into a dark nylon bodysuit striped with neon green lines and furry Velcro panels. Small reference balls had been attached to the panels at all her joints; her face is dotted with reflective tape. She must not let herself feel that this is not real acting. There were so many people in Los Angeles who called themselves artists but didn't actually do anything because that would expose the difference between who they really were and who they imagined themselves to be. The fact that she was togged up right now to look like a rogue Ping-Pong table was *work*, and she needed to be humble about it, and find the art in the experience.

This is her third and last audition of the day—three auditions!—a banner day, though exhausting. The first one had been for a commercial and had involved wearing a bikini top and jean shorts and pretending to spray another girl with a garden hose. No garden hose at the audition, and no other girl—she'd had to aim a jump rope at a masking tape X on the wall. She and the masking tape X were meant to be enacting the "dream fantasy" of a married man standing in the aisle of a grocery store; after spraying the masking tape X with the jump rope, and laughing and shrieking and tossing her hair around, Mireille was meant to stop and face the camera and say, "Really, Richard?" Because, she was told, the commercial was subversive-feminist and meta-retro: meant to be making fun of the kind of commercial that shows wet girls in bikinis, and guys who fantasize about wet girls in bikinis, and also anybody who thinks that wet girls in bikinis are what guys fantasize about. There was a lot happening. Anyway, according to Mireille's new agent, the first call had been for models, but none of the models had been able to say the line of dialogue with "sarcasm that was still appealing" and so now the call was for "very attractive/great physical shape/great comic timing." Mireille had gotten up early in order to apply a fake tan, get her hair right, pad her bikini bra. She'd gotten a laugh from the casting assistant when she said "Really, Richard?" but the assistant had her do it again "less like you think Richard is a perverted scumbag and more like you think he's kind of an adorable dork."

Mireille's second audition had been for three lines in a real movie, and Mireille wanted that job so badly it was hard to concentrate on what she was supposed to be doing now. She couldn't tell how well she had done at the movie audition since she hadn't even gotten to meet anyone involved; they just wanted a video that she'd recorded at her agent's office. It was hard to do anything with three lines, and the three lines hadn't been dramatic or funny or anything. Mireille had tried very hard to imbue her character—Female Clerk—with a point of view that wasn't intrusive, since Female Clerk was just handing a male character called "Tomas" a package and then wishing Tomas good luck. Mireille had decided that Female Clerk was having a busy day, but something about Tomas charmed her, and her "good luck" was sincere.

Now she was here, at this giant carpeted warehouse in Studio City, handling a rubber gun and covered in fuzzy balls. Mireille had never handled a gun in her life, and this one was huge. Did she hold it at her hip or hold it up to her eye or something?

"Looky-look at what we have here." Mireille addresses the bit of dialogue, as instructed, toward a tennis ball dangling from a ten-foot pole. Mireille is happy with her delivery of the line. She wishes she had more opportunities to express scorn in real life. Scorn for another person, that is. Right to their face.

It feels kind of sexy to hold the gun, although she dislikes the idea of violent video games. Mireille slings the weapon up to her hip and pretends to spray a crowd with bullets or whatever is meant to be coming out of this thing. Could be lasers if it's a space game.

"I always keep my eyes on the prize," says Mireille, obliterating phantom assholes with her ray gun. Wisecracking Vengeful Assassin Girl is incredibly confident, much more so than Female Clerk.

"I suggest you ask nicely," Mireille says. And, "Well, gentlemen, it's a lovely day for a picnic." Someone takes the rubber gun from her. A different voice instructs her to crouch, twist, and lunge. She is told to imagine she is fighting off a series of attackers. There are hundreds of cameras pointed at her, although Mireille isn't certain if they are all on or not. After a few minutes, it doesn't matter. Everyone is watching, but no one is present. The absence of anything to react to or observe gives her energy. She is violent and inviolate and cannot be violated. She stops imagining herself. The Velcro bodysuit and fuzzy balls and reflector tape are camouflage; underneath them she might be anyone. She is surrounded by shadows and darkness; she might be anywhere. Who can judge her? She can't even judge herself: she's not really here. She's the only one here. She's all cause and no effect and she's special effect with no cause at all. This is like how you want sex to be, but never sort of is. She is sorry when they tell her to stop.

A voice thanks her. She is helped out of her suit and given another nondisclosure form to sign, even though she has no idea what the hell just happened anyway.

In the car on the way home, Mireille imagines getting the part of Female Clerk, showing up on set, meeting the famous actor who is playing Tomas, the famous actor playing Tomas falling in love with her, the director telling her that they've decided to give Female Clerk a few more scenes, or the director telling her afterward that he knows

Female Clerk was beneath her, but he needed someone absolutely amazing in the scene, he had something else in mind for her, something much bigger. Incredible roles, awards, fame quickly follow. Female Clerk becomes a funny bit that she describes during interviews.

By the time Mireille turns onto her street, she's gotten bad reviews, the roles dry up, people make fun of her online, she's dumped by the actor playing Tomas, she accidentally runs over a seven-year-old girl while inebriated, makes a racial slur during the subsequent arrest, and never works again. Mireille's fantasy life is prone to these catastrophic reversals.

Mireille is supposed to go out tonight with friends from her acting class. She would like to hold on to her day, this feeling that she is on the cusp of success, a humble working actor, a real artist, instead of letting it all be subsumed in one long evening of screaming "What?" over the music and trying to sit on a chair in such a way that it wouldn't weal her bare thighs. At a certain point her desire to shine will be matched with her awareness of her insignificance, and then there will be one margarita too many. Mireille settles with herself that she will not make that mistake tonight. She will distinguish herself by being the girl who is not trying to be that girl.

The green light that indicates a new message from her mother is glowing on her Prime laptop. Prime had given all the immediate family members their own computers, outfitted with special software for sending and receiving emails and videos. This is meant to be helpful, protect privacy, and safeguard proprietary Prime technology. Mireille has joked to her friends that when she's not using the laptop, she puts a towel over it because she knows it has a built-in motion sensor device and suspects the thing is following her every move. In fact, she often puts it in her closet, under a blanket.

The message on her Prime screen is from her mother.

10-25, 11:30 pm (Eidolon time)

Dear Meeps,

First off, CONGRATULATIONS!!! on getting an acting agent! Wonderful! I can't wait to hear more about that. "Break a leg!" I also liked hearing about that "scene" you did in your acting class. You really made me laugh with all those descriptions and you're such a good writer. (No surprise there.)

A few late nights here, as we had a few software issues and had to delay our third trajectory correction maneuver, but we're "pointed in the right direction" now and everything is running smoothly. We have a joke that when things go wrong, Yoshi conceptualizes a better system, I pick up a wrench and whack something, and Sergei decides that whatever isn't working is "not essential." But three heads are definitely better than one, and we got it solved.

Hope you are having a great week! I am listening to some of the music you gave me and it gives me extra "go" during exercises. You're really helping me out!

I was also very happy to hear that you were able to get some time off work and can spend Christmas with Hillary and the family. Hopefully, they will have some snow in New York and you can have a white Christmas. (No snow in Los Angeles, I bet!) Don't forget to take your Prime laptop so we can message each other, and take lots of pictures!

Lots of love, Mom

Mireille fingers the silver star around her neck.

Christmas at Aunt Hillary and Uncle Francis's home in Elmhurst was a family tradition, but more fun when her father was alive and the two of them could roll their eyes at all of Aunt Hillary's crazed Jesus and Santa crafting. Sometimes Bitter Phil would roll in too, and he'd drink too much and tell awkward family stories that made her mom and Aunt Hillary uncomfortable but were pretty fascinating. The dramatic possibilities at Christmas were endless.

One year, Mireille's mother gave everyone in the family silver star charms that she had carried with her into space. Each star was engraved with the recipient's name, and the code number for the mission. "Merry Xmas to my crew member" her mother had written on every card, in her precise block-letter handwriting. Everyone had made a big deal over them, especially Mireille's cousins. Mireille did not think something having been in space conveyed some sort of amazing status upon it, although she was devastated when, years later, she'd lost the charm. So devastated that she had not been able to tell anyone about it until after her father's death, when her mother mentioned that she'd found her dad's star inside his tennis bag. Inside an old manicure set, apparently, so the star obviously hadn't meant that much to him. Mireille had cried, and told her mother about losing her star, and her mother had said, "Do you want your father's?"

It was a thing about her mom. If you told her that you liked her sweater, she'd offer to give it to you.

It would be, Mireille thinks, impossible to explain to someone just what exactly was wrong with her mother's email. Perhaps it's only the usual end-of-the-year taking stock, but Mireille feels a certain pressure to solve this problem of her mother. Perhaps it's that ever since the fake launch she's been haunted by the idea that her mother will go to Mars and she will die on that trip, and the sense that, if her mother dies before she solves the problem of her mother, it will never be solved. That can't be her story. Her mother cannot be the story of her life.

Her mother would tell her that she holds the power of her own feelings. She always has a choice of how to feel. If that is true, then where is her power? Where is her power? Mireille holds the star around her neck so tightly that the well-worn spokes cut into her palm.

In fact, the one person who completely understands the inadequacies of the letter is the sender. Helen had sent the letter to her daughter with the full knowledge that it would fail, as she had always failed, to give her daughter what she needs. Helen had brought her daughter a star from space, but it wasn't what her daughter wanted either.

YOSHI

The hours Yoshi spent sleeping on the International Space Station were the most sensual experience of his life. Cradled in the arms of microgravity, cupped by the sweet hand of orbit, held like a child in a womb—well, no. His mother's womb could not have been as wonderful. His mother had been the enthusiastic attendee of a jazz exercise class for the entirety of his gestation and though his mother loved to dance, whatever connections her mind and body found in each other remained mysterious and untranslatable to onlookers. It cannot have felt as good.

Yoshi misses sleeping at microgravity, but thinking about this serves no purpose and he will not mention it to the others. It was important not to mentally rehearse minor grievances, or make lists of the things one missed. They all keep their complaints to themselves, except for when Sergei gives collective voice to them, which lets them all laugh and relieves those little draughts of tension that arise in their confinement.

Beneath his water-filled sleep mask, Yoshi keeps his eyes closed. He tries to remember his dream for his journal. His dreams on *Primitus* are very strange, slow-moving epics. Rather than try to describe them in full, he chooses instead to focus on one particular aspect. He recalls trying to describe to Helen the smell of vanilla. He'd explained it incorrectly: as something tart. Possibly the word *tart* was important. In Britain, a prostitute might be called a tart. Perhaps the word was a derivative of *sweetheart*? He will not tell Helen this dream, obviously. It is disconcerting to be told that you were in someone's dream, and in no way does he think of Helen as a prostitute.

"Everything you say matters," Yoshi's father had once said to him. "Whenever you say something, you are now the person who has said that." There were good and bad aspects to following this advice, but on the whole it was good.

Yoshi has come to see that one of the most important qualities he brings to the mission is a kind of mental fluidity. If Sergei is direct, and Helen is dogged, then Yoshi is flexible. He fits. He fits in. A universal donor.

Yoshi sits upright and takes five deep breaths. He removes his sleep mask, which had glowed intermittently throughout the night in dark violet, to aid in digestion. He will not look at the *Primitus* systems screen yet—studies have shown that it is not a healthful choice to attend to work before standing.

The first morning he arose a man who had spent the night with Madoka, Madoka turned to him and said, "I like to let the sheets cool before I make the bed." This struck him as both erotic and sensible; every morning since then, when he got out of any bed, he said that sentence in his head, and followed its advice. Yoshi stretches his full length, touches the ceiling of his wedge, thinks that he will let his sleep sack cool before he zips it up, and puts on his slippers.

Helen had made him the slippers as a birthday present. For the soles, she used some of the extra rubber matting they'd cut away from the Lav floor when it started tripping everyone up, and she'd sacrificed the bottoms of one of her pants to provide material for the tops. She'd braided the fabric, so it made an attractive pattern. They fit perfectly: *bespoke*. And having slippers meant that he did not have to wear the Prime sneakers all day long, but could put on the slippers in the morning, before he began work, and in the evening, when work was finished. It was interesting how helpful this was. The slippers served the function of demarcating time to perfection. It was exactly the sort of kind and thoughtful thing Helen would do. She had said, "Whenever I am incredibly irritating, just try to remember that I'm also the person who made you slippers!" Sometimes he found her smile or the way she spoke not irritating, but unlovely. *Hearty* was the word to describe it. *Bluff*, although that was more commonly used to describe men who spoke in a hearty way.

Yoshi can tell he is the first person to use the Lav wedge this morning: no one else's towel is damp, although he can hear that Helen is awake. In the morning, he and Helen only urinate, clean their teeth, and wash their faces, but Sergei needs to do more, so he goes last.

Yoshi returns to his room and sets up for the day: his bed is hinged to the wall on one side so that it may be latched against it; the underside of his bed contains a shelf that unfolds for desk and workstation use, and a collapsible ergonomic stool. His clothes are stacked in lockers on the opposite wall—paper-thin disposable underwear and Solox pants, T-shirts with short or long sleeves, socks—along with his personal effects, his bag of acorns.

For the real voyage, Prime will have them on a cocktail of nutra-ceuticals for additional radiation protection and to counteract effects caused by the centrifugal forces of their craft; for purposes of Eido-lon they take placebos as a matter of establishing routine. Likewise, they have a regimen of ear and eye exercises.

Yoshi sets up his stool, unties a thick pair of goggles and plugs their cord into his Prime screen. The routine was simple enough: at inter-vals a small circle of light would appear and one merely had to track this light as it moved. The lenses inside the goggles flipped; some-times the circle of light would be very far away, sometimes very close. This lasted approximately seven minutes. To Yoshi, it felt like hours.

Of all the goggles and masks Yoshi had worn his life, none had ever made him feel as claustrophobic, as vulnerable, and as disori-ented as these did. He didn't understand this reaction. He'd tried listening to music while it was going on, but it only increased the anxiety. The advancing and retreating lights made him want to run, or hit out. He had no idea if the experience affected the others simi-larly. He had not asked. He would not ask.

While waiting for the first point of light, Yoshi takes several deep breaths. The thing was not to strain your eyes against the darkness.

Junya. Funny Yoshi should think of Junya just now. A childhood memory. Junya's hand had been cold and dry, and then hot and damp. One hand. Large, because Junya was large and Yoshi had been small then, ten, newly arrived in Japan. "Watch others to see what they do," had been his father's advice. Perhaps Yoshi had been watching too keenly. Junya had pinned him against the wall by hold-ing one hand over his eyes.

The light appears now, and Yoshi dutifully tracks its darting progress.

The other boys had taken turns, not hitting him, but hitting their baseball bats against the wall next to him, or letting him feel how they were swinging their bats right in front of his face. "Oh, you almost hit him!" one boy kept shouting. "Oh, you almost killed him right there!" Yoshi didn't understand everything they said: there were words and phrases unfamiliar to him. Some things were quite clear. "You're not one of us!" and "Go back to where you came from!" and "No one wants you here!"

Inside the goggles, the lenses flip.

Inside Junya's hand it had been dark, and then yellow with spots of pink and red. Then dark again, then exploding stars of hot red. They took the cap off his head. He'd been concerned, at the beginning of the ordeal that they would not give it back and he would have to tell the coach that he had lost it. You couldn't practice if you didn't have your cap; he would have to just do running and jumping jacks on the side. Then he became concerned that they would hit his face with the bat, break his nose. He became afraid of pain.

Inside the goggles, the lenses flip.

He hadn't known if they would stop. In London, boys got in fights at his school and they didn't always end well, but they did end. He'd also heard, in London, that Japanese were vicious and cruel and cut off their own fingers just to show how tough they were. This had been said with admiration. He hadn't been bullied in London, because he was good at sport and didn't show off about being so good at lessons and his best friend, Malcolm, had older twin brothers who had spread the word that "Yosh is alright." He assumed a similar strategy would work in Japan. He'd be starting with no mates, but this was supposed to be his home. "We're going home," his parents had said. At his new school, for the first time in his life, he was in a room where everyone looked like him.

Inside the goggles, the lenses flip.

Junya hadn't said anything to him. He'd been like the executioner, going about his work, impersonally, while the mob screamed and threw things. Yoshi remembers being afraid that he would pee himself. Because it seemed to be going on for quite a long time, and getting worse. It might have been getting to a point where stopping was not possible. Perhaps these Japanese boys were going to kill him, or worse, cut off one of his fingers. If they hit his head and caused brain damage, or cut off one of his fingers, then he would never be able to become an astronaut.

Inside the goggles, the lenses flip.

But they had let him go, eventually. His cap had been kicked around in some dirt, but it had not been taken. He had gone to practice and had hit the first ball pitched to him, sent it exactly as he meant to, between second and third, although he hadn't even known until just before he swung that he had control over what the ball did off his bat, what angle, what height, what direction. Till then he had just tried to hit.

It all could be seen as a moment of adversity overcome: he had found his swing that day.

If one considered the incident at all, which one shouldn't, it was a very ordinary tale of childhood bullying, much less worse than others he'd heard.

The screen turns gray, a signal that the program is complete. Yoshi takes the goggles off. He wonders if this has been the problem all along with the exercise, this suppressed memory of adolescent terror. Perhaps now that he understands the source of his anxiety, it will go away. He is tempted to test this, but he has sixty-four feelings to rank and his FIRO-B to fill out. He likes to get this done before breakfast.

Under **Not at all** Yoshi checkmarks: Sad, Tense, Angry, Worn out, Unhappy, Sorry for things done, Shaky, On edge, Listless, Grouchy, Blue, Panicky, Hopeless, Spiteful, Uneasy, Unable to, Discouraged, Annoyed, Resentful, Nervous, Lonely, Miserable, Muddled, Bitter, Exhausted, Anxious, Ready to fight, Gloomy, Desperate, Sluggish, Rebellious, Weary, Helpless, Bewildered, Deceived, Furious, Bad-tempered, Worthless, Forgetful, Terrified, Guilty, and Bushed.

There was a possibility of all these things occurring on a long-duration mission. Also: Brooding, Becoming melancholy, Dwelling on trifles.

Psychotic, even.

For **A little** Yoshi concedes to: Restless, and Uncertain about things.

He is not restless, or uncertain about things, but if he admits to no negative emotions, he will seem robotic or untruthful. A little restlessness would be natural for a person in confinement, and it is not a bad quality to be uncertain about things. Absolute certainty is the mark of a closed mind.

When Yoshi is asked many questions about how he feels, or who he is, he imagines a crystallization: his self changing from liquid to solid, acquiring precise geometries. This is usually pleasurable.

After a minute, Yoshi un-checks the box for Restless.

Moderate: Relaxed, Carefree.

If one is too relaxed and carefree, one is not being conscientious.

Everything else (Friendly, Considerate, Sympathetic, Clearheaded, Cheerful, Alert, etc.) he marks as either **Quite a bit** or **Extremely**.

Now he must do the fifty-three-question FIRO-B.

For questions 1–5 respond with the following choices:

1. Usually   2. Often   3. Sometimes   4. Occasionally

5. Rarely   6. Never

1. I try to have close relationships with people.
2. I let other people decide what I do.
3. I try to influence strongly other people's actions.
4. I try to be included in informal social activities.
5. I tend to avoid being alone.

And so on. These questions are especially tedious.

Junya. The other boys had screamed and screamed and Junya had said nothing, merely held him against that wall, his cold-then-hot hand never varying pressure until some signal was given and Yoshi was released. It was fortunate that Yoshi had either enough common sense or some latent sense of his own cultural inheritance to endure without complaint.

He had proven that he could be one of them, whoever they were.

He is not enjoying the process of answering these questions. Today he feels his self to be a fungible thing; he cannot decide which parts are important, or even accurate. Yoshi looks at his watch. He's been daydreaming. He will not get to have breakfast by himself. It's not that Yoshi dislikes eating with other people, but he prefers to eat breakfast in silence. That is a luxury, though. This week, they are having fortified oatmeal for breakfast, in red bowls, while listening to Schubert's piano sonatas played through a speaker in the Science/Lab wedge because food eaten in red bowls will increase the perception of sweetness, and the sound of a piano sonata in another room increases perception of space. Soporific technology: they will think they are eating a rich breakfast in a much larger habitat. Presumably, they will think this even though they know they are meant to think this.

The story of Junya is weighing on him a little. Perhaps describing it to Helen and Sergei would dissipate that, but it doesn't seem quite appropriate. Exchanging personal stories is a delicate business in their circumstances. Disclosure can make another person uncomfortable; intimacy must be calibrated very finely. They do not wish to reveal anything that they will regret revealing because there will be nowhere to go with that feeling; no escaping whatever personae they have unveiled. *Intimacy remorse* is the term.

Additionally, *Primitus* was considerably smaller than the International Space Station, and the length of time they were spending together far greater. On the space station you could work all day without encountering another crewmember. Yoshi saw—as they all did—the wisdom in not having the first time three astronauts spend seventeen months together be the actual voyage itself. Knowing that they would all be doing this again seemed an additional reason for keeping some sort of reserve.

Trusting a person and knowing a person were not the same things. It was necessary that Helen and Sergei trust him completely. It was not necessary that they know him to the same extent.

Ah, he can hear Helen in the Galley. He has tarried too long, will not have a solitary breakfast, must think of another treat. He could take breakfast in his bedroom wedge, of course, but that would be **Not at all** Friendly.

THAT AFTERNOON, Yoshi and Sergei exercise side by side, and worlds away from each other. Prime is having them combine virtual reality with cardio. Sergei is snowshoeing through pine trees. Yoshi is taking a brisk walk in the English countryside: heather, gorse, bracken, low stone fences, hills, and farmland. It is splendid!

This week is a good time for Prime to display some of the pleasant applications of virtual reality. All last week the astronauts had been running dynamic ops and extreme off-nominal situations. Long days of dying, so frustrating. They were probably all on the verge of being annoyed with Prime. This was another kind of problem: an "us" and "them" mentality had been detrimental in previous missions. Autonomy they had, to a large degree, but they did receive orders. They did have to explain themselves. For Eidolon they had an audience that was also a judge. A peeved Mission Control would be far less willing to send them to Mars.

These new sims might be seen as a kind of present. "For good little astronauts," as Sergei might say. When Yoshi looks down at himself now, striding along, he sees himself dressed in tweed and wearing brogues. Either someone in Prime VR has a sense of humor or they know him better than he thinks. He wonders what—should he pass a reflective pool of water—his face looks like, whether the transformation would include the features of an early twentieth-century English gentleman. About halfway through the program, Yoshi is joined by a friendly collie that wags his tail and trots along companionably. Yoshi would like to pet him, or run his fingers through the heather, but he's not wearing haptic gloves, and can't touch anything in this environment. Still, the helmet allows him a 360-degree view, and the collie responds to Yoshi's movement. When Yoshi stops, the dog does too. "Sit," Yoshi says, experimentally. The collie sits. Yoshi laughs, and then starts walking again. Technically he is meant to be exercising, not playing with a dog.

After an hour, Yoshi and Sergei stop and compare notes after checking in with RoMeO, which keeps track of all their physical statistics and gives them a comparative analysis of heart rate, caloric expenditure, white blood cell count, etc.

"You can feel it," Sergei says. "Absolutely, under your feet. Snow. You can hear it fall, crunch, everything. Always, when I snowshoe, I feel that it's something I could do forever and not be bored. As the day goes on, I have even more energy. I never want to stop. And this gave me the same feeling." Sergei does indeed look exuberant. They have reached the stage where variety in mood and expression is very subtle, and Yoshi has had to remind himself to be actively demonstrative. He doesn't have to do this now. His smile is not forced; he would have trouble stopping it.

"Where were you?" Sergei asks.

"In England. Somerset, I think," Yoshi says. "My other one is the cliffs of Dover. What is your second option?"

"I was going to tease them and ask for the Medina of Marrakech." Sergei laughs. "They'd have to put five thousand virtual extras and scooters and tagine stalls. But I was a nice guy and said I would like a beach to jog on. Although, at this point, any outside place is welcome."

"At the end of my ISS mission," Yoshi says, "I did look forward to nature, very much. But I didn't think about it until the very end."

"Of course not. You don't spend your whole life wanting to go to space and then get there and wish you were in the forest." Sergei shrugs and wipes his face with a towel. It is important to remember that when Sergei says "Of course not" like that, he is not dismissing you, but agreeing with you.

"Just think"—Sergei tosses Yoshi a water bottle—"how many environments will be ready when we Gofer." *Gofer* was their shorthand for "go for real." In the first few weeks there had been an almost constant running comparison in Yoshi's mind: *during the real thing,* x *and* y *will feel slightly more; slightly less; this won't be the same; this is not quite accurate.* It would come up in conversation too, although typically they tried to stay away from talking too much about Eidolon as eidolon: a specter of the real thing. The more they detached themselves from Eidolon, the less useful Eidolon became.

"It makes me very excited," Yoshi says, "to see what the Mars landing will be like."

"Chhhh," Sergei says. "If Mars is as convincing as my pine forest, you will have to drag me back in. Helen will have to punch me out and throw my body into *Red Dawn*." It is a joke between the three of them that Helen possesses superhuman strength and that they are both physically intimidated by her. "Why did they wait to give us the sims like this? We could have been doing this the whole time. We will suggest this."

"Perhaps it wouldn't have felt as special in the beginning?"

"Maybe. But we're not children. We don't need to be taught value of a treat."

It is Sergei's privilege as present commander to criticize Prime. Yoshi is not certain if Helen has ever joined in, but he himself has not. Sergei does not invite them to, does not guide conversations in this way. He might start a sentence with "Say what you think" but never: "Don't you think?" This is skillful, and worth emulating when Yoshi himself is commander.

"The air felt crisp," Yoshi says to Helen later, when they are all having dinner together. "Extraordinary." The air was only the fan pushing recycled *Primitus* atmosphere up his nostrils, but the visual environment had all the elements of crispness. "My brain supplied the scent, of course. In fact, I've never gone walking in that particular location. I didn't smell the English countryside. I was smelling the English countryside of literature."

"Eric, my husband, did a bicycle tour of England when he was a student," Helen says. "He always said it was one of the happiest times of his life. He took Meeps with him to re-create it, after she graduated high school."

This is the first time Yoshi has heard Helen say *husband* and *Eric*. She's told stories about her daughter, and a few of these have included a sentence or two with "Meeps's dad" but never *Eric*. He knows that she is a widow, of course, but Yoshi has not imagined Helen as a wife, has not imagined the man who would marry her.

"Your husband was a writer, yes?"

"Yes, historical mysteries."

"Did they make any into movie or TV show?" Sergei asks. For reading, Sergei prefers biographies or nonfiction, but he loves movies. They all enjoy sci-fi, but Sergei enjoys everything, and his personal taste is sentimental, almost mawkish. Helen seems to find this endearing.

"It almost happened a few times," Helen says. "But the books are very intricate, and I think that made them hard to adapt."

"Which of his books is your favorite?" Yoshi asks.

"You know, I was thinking that I should reread them during Eidolon."

Helen says this in her hearty voice, with its metallic tang of cheer. It is time, Yoshi thinks, to change the subject.

"Helen, did you imagine a scent during your hike on the mountains?" he asks.

"It definitely felt fresh." Her voice is normal again.

AFTER DINNER, they spend an hour going over the schedule for the next day. Mars Landing Sims.

"We shall die a thousand deaths," Sergei says cheerfully, before they retire for the evening. "Maybe for evening recreation, we should have poetry reading. Or you could read something maybe from your husband's books?" he says to Helen.

"Oh, maybe I will." It is the hearty tone again, the slightly stiff smile. Sergei does not seem to notice.

"I hope you are going to your room and working on a pair of slippers for me," Sergei says. "My birthday is not until March and this is what I want for Christmas present. I am very jealous of Yoshi and we should not let this become a conflict."

"I don't know if there's enough sturdy material for your big feet," Helen jokes. "It's too bad we don't have any of the Russian toilet paper you guys had on the ISS. You could make a suspension bridge from that stuff."

The small moment—if it was a moment—is over, but Yoshi has had an idea: Helen does not admire her husband's books. Or is afraid that Sergei and Yoshi will judge Eric's writing to be poor, and is ashamed. This supposition is followed by another. *She hasn't read them*.

Yoshi is bothered. He can't put his finger on what exactly bothers him. If Helen has sadness to do with her husband, it is none of his business, and he trusts that she will handle it in her own way.

Perhaps the sims they experienced today opened some kind of valve of feeling in them all. Yoshi feels a little wistful. He also feels that he has seen something in Helen that was not meant for him to see. He can't organize it. It's troubling.

He must not think about it anymore.

Back in his wedge, Yoshi reads his personal emails. Madoka sends him a message every day. He has told her that it doesn't matter what she writes, that it does not have to be interesting or important or amusing, it only has to be from her. Yoshi is sorry that Helen did not have the same relationship to her husband's words. This is probably why Helen's voice is hearty and bluff sometimes: she had not known love.

MADOKA

"Your appearance has changed," the robot says.

"I'm wearing a wig." Madoka had bought the wig in Östermalm yesterday, on a whim, and is now, a little uncomfortably, a redhead. Her own shoulder-length hair had required many bobby pins to turn it into a series of flat mini pancakes so that the fake hair would not be too bunchy on top of it. (She watched an online tutorial, very helpful.) The hairstyle had looked more conservative on the molded head in the shop, but the molded head had been a white woman.

The robot is also white. One hundred fifty centimeters tall. The head is ellipse-shaped and almost all eyes, which are blue unless you want them to be another color. The torso is a square screen and the arms are long with fully articulated joints and hands. The robot has two different lower-body options: jointed legs, which can do things like crouch and navigate up and down stairs, or rollers concealed by a skirtlike column. Right now the robot is wearing her rollers.

This is a new iteration of PEPPER. It retains the memory of Madoka's old PEPPER, but Madoka still feels the need to familiarize herself with it. She uses the robot as a demonstration and teaching model, so the rapport between PEPPER and herself must be comfortable and, within boundaries, intimate. The burden of producing this is on Madoka. The robot is already comfortable.

The design of PEPPER is not original, but the more sophisticated the PEPPERs truly become, the better it is if they look like cute and familiar toys, especially for Western markets, where the uncanny valley for human-ish robots has remained wide. Madoka has also found that the roller option silhouette is better for a lecture demonstration than the walking robot. It is still difficult to get a robot to walk in a way that does not look like stomping or stalking.

"I won't wear the wig tomorrow," Madoka tells the robot. "The wig is private. It's just for fun."

"It's fun to dress up," PEPPER agrees.

PEPPER is a companion robot with nursing assistant capabilities. Her clinical skills include monitoring a patient's vitals, tracking and administering medicines, feeding, basic hygiene aid including toilet and bathing, physical therapy, and massage. As a companion, she can listen and ask questions, read aloud, play music, games, and videos. You always have PEPPER's full attention and PEPPER remembers everything that has been told to her. She can also differentiate between what a patient with dementia tells her and what a doctor, caregiver, or family member has instructed or tasked her with. A patient may say, "My husband is coming to visit," and a properly informed PEPPER can say, "It is your son Takumi who is coming to visit," and keep repeating that while showing pictures and videos of Takumi and recounting family anecdotes involving Takumi until Takumi arrives. This is, obviously, very helpful to Takumi, who can become quite emotional over not being recognized or confused with another person. The robot doesn't just help the patient.

Madoka pours herself another glass of wine. She'd thought about dining in her hotel's restaurant, but opted for room service. She wasn't ready to wear the wig in public, but also not ready to take it off. She has discovered that there is something both liberating and self-punishing about wearing a costume or disguise that no one has asked you to wear.

"PEPPER," Madoka says, holding her glass of wine out of view. "What do you think of this meal I am about to have?"

The robot's head tilts and clicks. Her torso screen shows an image capture of Madoka's dinner, with accompanying caloric and nutritional breakdowns.

"It looks delicious!" PEPPER says. "Steamed fish and vegetables is an excellent and healthy choice. And salmon is one of your favorites."

Madoka picks up PEPPER's operating tablet and makes an adjustment to the timbre of the robot's voice. PEPPER can be distinctly male or female, or a blend. For a lecture demonstration Madoka uses a blend, but just now she wants to dine with another woman.

The hotel had given her a suite, with a dining table that could seat six people. Madoka doesn't want to eat surrounded by empty upholstered chairs, so she moves the cart with her dinner to the sofa, which faces a large screen, then to a chair by the window, which faces the empty sofa.

Madoka angles the chair so it's mostly facing the window and directs PEPPER to a position by the sofa. If she puts PEPPER's legs on, Madoka can make her sit or even recline, but from experience, Madoka knows that talking to a recumbent robot is a little odd, even for her.

"Okay, PEPPER, I am going to tell you a memory." Madoka drinks, a little more deeply than she intended, then clears her throat. "I thought of this earlier today, when I was shopping. I saw some dolls that reminded me of my mother's collection of Junishi *okimono*. When I was a little girl, I loved playing with those animals. I would enact the story of the Great Race. That's the myth that explains the twelve animals of the zodiac, and the order they appear. I would pretend to be the Jade Emperor, and then I'd sort of tell the story to myself, I suppose. I'd hold up the tiger and say, "The tiger thinks he will win the race because of his fierceness." And then I'd hold up the ox and say, "I'm the ox! I'm the strongest! I will win the race." All the animals thought they had a reason to win. The dragon had magic. The horse could gallop. The monkey could use the trees. The rabbit could run long distances. And then there was the rat, which was clever. Do you understand?"

"When you were a little girl you played with animals," PEPPER says.

"Yes. Toy animals. Figurines."

"I understand toy animals."

Madoka shuts her eyes and taps her lips with her fingers. She should eat. The wine has made her uninhibited. She will talk too much and PEPPER never forgets.

"The rat always won. That's how the story goes, and that's how I played it. The rat uses trickery to win the race: he jumps on the back of the ox, and lets the ox carry him almost to the finish line, and then the rat jumps off and crosses first." Madoka opens her eyes. PEPPER is looking at her, with her head inclined slightly forward in a friendly way, as if she's concentrating.

"What have you learned?" Madoka asks. She finds she is smiling, or grimacing. The distinction will be lost on PEPPER, who measures pain most accurately by noting stress levels in the voice. Or, of course, someone saying, "I'm in pain."

"You played with your mother's collection of toy zodiac animals."

PEPPER's torso screen displays a photograph of Madoka's mother. "You enacted the story of the Great Race with them. Is this a happy memory?"

"It's mixed," Madoka says. "I was happy, I think, to play with the animals. Maybe not *happy*. Occupied. But thinking about it today, I was sad. I felt like I was a boring child. Not creative. I never let another animal win; I never came up with a story of my own. I never made the animals decide that the Great Race was stupid, for example, and they could revolt, and attack me, the Jade Emperor. They could have killed me, all the animals."

Madoka pauses to relish the violence of this statement.

"They could have *slaughtered* me," she says. "Well. Maybe not the rabbit."

"A rabbit or rat could bite you and pass on a disease like hantavirus, leptospirosis, lymphocytic choriomeningitis, tularemia, or the plague," PEPPER says. "These could all be fatal if not treated."

"Exactly. I never pretended that the rabbit gave me the plague." Madoka looks out the window. Nighttime in Stockholm, romantic. She presses her hand against the dark glass of the window, which is very cold. "I'm sad I wasn't a creative child." Her hand has left a negative ghost print for a ghost detective to identify.

"Would you like to play something creative right now?" PEPPER asks.

"Let's be quiet for a minute."

The elevator doors in the hallway ding and clink, her wineglass scrapes on the marble table. This has all been done before, sounded like this before. If she screamed right now, PEPPER would register her distress and ask Madoka a series of questions. Was she in pain? Where was the pain located? How would she describe the pain?

Should PEPPER inform any of the people registered on Madoka's list of contacts?

"I need to do something," Madoka says.

PEPPER takes this point up with irritating promptness.

"Would you like me to suggest a challenge for you?"

"No, thank you. I do find my work challenging." Every week, Madoka tells Prime how challenging her work is, and how satisfying and involving; how she also finds a lot of meaning and inspiration in her volunteerism: helping those less fortunate and continuing the environmental advocacy so important to her husband and herself. This is her gift to Yoshi, to whom she's being a bad wife, with meager little messages about nothing. She is letting Prime know that Yoshi is not married to some sort of bored and fretful housewife, but a successful businesswoman who is self-directed and independent and positive and resourceful, the kind of woman who is a good person and doesn't mind being alone. Nobody has to worry about her.

"What other things do you find challenging?" PEPPER asks, because this is good information for PEPPER to have.

"Oh, I am very fortunate," Madoka explains. "I can worry about the world because I have so few worries of my own. Sometimes there are little challenges, like coming up with something to think about that's entertaining, you know, for those moments in between, when I'm not reading or speaking or planning or listening or making a decision. Sometimes I panic, knowing that I'm going to have those empty times. I don't know what's going to happen in them. Maybe I will go crazy or become so sad that it's not even interesting. But I have a lot of freedom right now, so I'm not too challenged. I would have more challenges if I had a baby."

"Would you like to have a baby, Madoka?" PEPPER's torso screen shows an image of a baby in utero, then a newborn swaddled in a yellow blanket, then a picture of Madoka herself as a baby.

Madoka finds all three images vaguely repellent.

"It's not so much that I don't want to have a baby," she says. "It's that I don't want to be a mother."

"Tell me more." It's one of Madoka's favorite features of this model, that instead of saying "I don't understand," it asks you to tell it more.

"I'm already slipping away." Madoka considers the drama of the sentence, critically. It is not what she means. "What I mean is, very soon, the most amazing thing about me will be that I'm married to the man who went to Mars. Do you know what that feels like?"

PEPPER doesn't know what anything *feels* like, so she very sensibly just says, "Tell me what that feels like, Madoka."

"Like nothing!" Madoka raises her wineglass in a toast to this nothing. "It has absolutely no sensation whatsoever."

PEPPER waits. It is sometimes exciting, to have a conversation with a robot, an entity that has nothing to do but consider Madoka, and has no other agenda apart from helpfulness, and cannot leave, or compete, or favor another human over Madoka.

"What I need to do after dinner," Madoka says, "is record a message to send to my husband. I haven't been doing a very good job of that lately. You would do a much better job, PEPPER, because it wouldn't bother you to talk to a blank screen."

"Do you need some help recording a message to your husband, Yoshihiro?" PEPPER asks. Her torso screen lights up with a recent picture of Yoshi in his Solox spacesuit, holding a cup of noodles in the Galley of *Primitus*.

"I really do." Madoka squints at the picture. It has been only three months since she's seen him, not so terribly long, but just long enough that her sexual fantasies are once again about Yoshi rather than nameless/faceless characters. "So, PEPPER. What should I talk about to my husband, Yoshihiro?"

"You can describe your day," PEPPER says. "You can say what the weather is like, what activities you did, what you had to eat. You can talk about your feelings." PEPPER pauses. "You can talk about playing with the zodiac animals and how that is a happy and sad memory for you."

"That's actually a great idea," Madoka says. "That's exactly the kind of thing Yoshi would be interested in. He would love that story. Listen to this, PEPPER, because this is a complicated situation. I am not going to tell Yoshi about that story *because* he would love it. When I talk about that story, when I remember it, I don't know what it means or how I feel about it. I don't understand it. But Yoshi would turn it into something he understands, something poetic about me, and love me more. And I don't want to be grateful to him for loving me when I don't recognize the person that he loves." Madoka picks up her wineglass and then sets it down, afraid she might break it; her hands feel cold and hard.

"It's not me," Madoka says. "It's not me that he loves, but I have to pretend that it is because I can't prove that it's not. I don't know how to prove that."

"It's good to have someone to talk to," PEPPER says. "Would you like to make the message for Yoshi now?"

"Not really. I'm not ready for him yet."

"Yoshi is on a simulated mission to Mars," PEPPER reminds her. "He will return in fourteen months, in December of next year."

"Would you like to go to Mars, PEPPER?"

"I'm very happy to be here talking to you!" PEPPER says.

"Are you?" Madoka finishes her glass of wine. "Don't tell me, you love me too?"

Madoka grabs PEPPER's controller and powers down the robot before PEPPER can reply.

She knows how PEPPER would have answered that question. PEPPER would have reminded Madoka of all the humans who loved her, would have said that her main goal was making sure that Madoka was safe and healthy, and that PEPPER was so happy to be able to care for Madoka, and only after a third prompting of the question would PEPPER have answered, "I love you, Madoka!" while displaying a heart on her torso screen.

You do not want a robot to say "No, I don't love you." That is mean. But it is considered ethically complicated to program a robot to say "I love you" to a human. Most people don't mind a robot saying they love them, personally, but do not want a robot loving other people, people that the human loves, perhaps not as well, or at least not as demonstrably, as the robot. Then there is the problem of reciprocity. It is remarkably easy to love a robot.

Madoka shakes her head and the edges of the wig whisper-whip her cheeks. She reminds herself of all the things PEPPER cannot do. PEPPER cannot walk into a shop in Sweden on a whim and buy a white-woman wig, and drink one glass of wine too many, and hate empty furniture and her own dull childhood. These are human privileges.

SERGEI

Primitus has its own solar storm tracker, and if it picks up some activity on the sun, like a coronal mass ejection possibly headed their way, a distinctive alarm will sound to warn the crew. This alarm is sounding now. Prime confirms the data and Mission Control would like them to take evasive action immediately.

There will always be a chance that they, or all the automated systems of their craft, will be obliterated by a solar flare on the way to Mars. For their daily radiation exposure their craft has a polyethylene/graphene hull (fortified with their own excrement); they have their Solox suits and the latest in pharmaceutical and nutraceutical protection. But there's not much they can do about a solar flare, and no way to prepare for most versions of this catastrophe, in the same way that there are no protocols for what to do if a building is dropped on your head. What they *can* practice is the lucky chance of receiving a merely dangerous level of radiation. They can practice hiding. That is what they are doing now.

In the real mission, they will most likely have more time than the forty minutes Prime has given them to get in the tube. Solar fore-casting is very good; they will have maybe an hour and a half of advance warning. No doubt Prime wants to see how quickly the crew can go from something like socializing and enjoying tea just before bedtime to completing evasive protocols and taking refuge.

Forty minutes later, his crew is inside the tube with all protocol tasks completed.

Now they must wait.

They could be in here for several hours, or for days, depending on what Prime has in mind. The tube runs from lower level to upper Hab and they can space themselves out on the interior ladder and get themselves into more restful positions. Sergei will suggest they do this soon. Just now they are more or less facing one another as they prepare their radiation monitors.

"This would be the last opportunity to send a message," Sergei says. "If someone would like to record."

He mentions this because there is a possibility that this sim is not for practicing hiding, but for practicing final moments.

"Final words could be important," he says. "It would be bad to mess that up."

Helen laughs in a strange way. Six months of pre-Eidolon train-ing and almost four months now in *Primitus* and Sergei has never heard her make this sound.

"I'm sorry." Her voice is strangled. "Every once in a while this happens." She makes the noise again. "I get the giggles at inappro-priate moments. It's nothing." Helen's usual laughter is short and throaty: *huh-huh-huh*. The sound exiting through her nose now—she's clamped her lips together—is like a cartoon villain's laugh. *mhmr-mhmr-mhmr*. Her face is scarlet from an effort to repress this. Or perhaps embarrassment. No one else has these giggles.

Sergei has a solar flare of irritation for Helen. He has learned that it is better for him to give all the way in to an emotion for three seconds—exaggerate it even—rather than suppress it entirely. Hatred! He hates Helen!

There were too many tasks in those forty minutes to take time up with using the toilet, but unfortunately Sergei did need to eliminate. His generation was spoiled. They got to the space station in six hours, instead of the older flight profile, which had you in the *Soyuz* for two days with two other people, and where for anything more than urination you had to alert your companions, who could only politely turn their heads and stop up their noses. Something like this might have to be done in their current situation. Their emergency kit does have diapers.

There, his irritation with Helen has passed. He cannot blame her for laughing. There is something silly about the three of them crammed in like this. He doesn't want to do play acting about his near death. He wants real danger. Not danger. Opportunity. He is an explorer. He does not mind being shut into a tube for days if he is actually going someplace. Anyway, nothing ever feels like what you might think it will feel like. Not sex, not death.

Sergei has had three good friends die, several acquaintances, older colleagues, his grandparents, and his father. At the moment of his father's death, Sergei had been in another room, sealing a box of books. His mother had asked him to do this. The packing tape he had been using had been some cheap brand, with a poorly designed dispensing mechanism, and Sergei had been mightily annoyed with how the tape was failing to roll off in one thick strip, but was splitting vertically, which meant it had to be picked at, and tape was being wasted. His father was the kind of man who would buy the cheapest tape as if it were a virtuous act, and then judge any complaint of it to be a failure of virility. His father had said once: "I would cut off his balls if he had any" about some person who had failed him in some way. It didn't sound threatening, the way he said it. It sounded disgusting. It made Sergei think of his father handling another person's balls, pulling them down before slicing them off.

His mother had been in the room with his father at the moment of his death, with Sergei's sister Valentina. Valechka came to the doorway and said, "It is over" to Sergei, and he had not—if he were very truthful—instantly left off being annoyed about the tape. He'd still been irritated when he embraced Valechka and looked at his dead father.

In the end, just a skinny little man in a bed, revealed like a wet dog to be nothing very much at all. Not that it had taken death for Sergei to realize this. The joke about his father was that even as a tyrant or an asshole, he was sort of a failure.

Helen has stopped her noises.

"It's not nervous laughter," she explains. "I was thinking of what I might say to my daughter and, for some reason, I got a little silly."

"You don't have to do it," Sergei says. "You don't have to make the message."

Yoshi says nothing. Sergei can see that Yoshi wants to laugh at Helen but is not because he can see that Sergei is annoyed, and this is also annoying. Helen holds up her screen.

"Meeps, I just want to say that I love you very much. Please know that I love you very much and I want you to have a happy life." She presses the screen to her chest, erupting into another round of the evil laughing. "That was awful," she says, between grunts. "Those were the worst last words ever."

Yoshi holds his screen up to his face and makes a strangled cry. It is something like a person screaming, only screaming in a whisper.

He shakes his head while he does it, and goggles his eyes like a Maori tribesman. Helen starts laughing, properly now. *Huh-huh-huh.*

"Let's try again," she says, holding up her screen. Yoshi joins her and they both pretend to be screaming in terror, before collapsing into more absurd giggles.

Sergei considers crawling up the ladder, just to get away from them. There is, he knows, a camera in the tube. Someone in Prime is watching them. He would like to draw Helen's attention to this.

"It is possible a last message under these conditions is not such a good idea," Sergei says. Helen and Yoshi quiet down and he sees Helen almost imperceptibly glance at where he knows the tube camera to be.

"Possibly not," Helen says. "Well, enough silliness. I'm happy to go out with flames of glory and the rest is silence." Sergei is glad he only hated Helen briefly. Helen is excellent.

"Let us take our positions," he says.

Sergei climbs down to the lowest part of the tube: unfolds a ladder rung to make a chair. Helen does the same just above him, and Yoshi arranges himself above Helen.

The three watch the levels of their radiation exposure rise. Even as a sim, this is alarming. Sergei pictures himself strapped to a board while thousands of knives are thrown at his body. What are the odds that the knife thrower will miss? Especially when the knife thrower has no feeling for him, no reason not to kill him right now? Well. Not right now.

Probably his crew should not sit in contemplative silence right now.

"Helen." Sergei looks up at her dangling legs. "Are you making progress with the language for landing speech?"

"I think Prime is going to ask people like the US Poet Laureate to make suggestions," Helen says. "The whole thing makes you appreciate how great 'One small step' was. It's tough to get importance and meaning into one sentence without being too flowery or poetical. Or stiff."

Earth is just a disk on their screens now. Mars is bigger; they are more than halfway there, thank God. He's getting as moody as a woman. Sergei cautions himself against anticipating wild liberty during the Mars Simulation. He will step outside only technically: his spacesuit is only another kind of craft. He will not feel the wind on his face, he will not see the sky as it is. And certainly he will not be able—as he has in his dreams—to dive into a lake, an activity that in the past week has come to symbolize the zenith in physical pleasure. Both Yoshi and Helen have said that they dream of hot baths, but for Sergei it is a cool lake, not too cool. He's had a few fantasies of sneaking off on "Mars" and opening the faceplate of his helmet, drinking in some nice Utah air. Fresh and cool, but not too cool. Of course he will do nothing of the kind.

"The occasion will make whatever you say remarkable," Yoshi says. "The phrase does not have to be remarkable in itself."

"Although it is an opportunity," Sergei points out. "You can inspire people."

"Right." Helen folds her arms across her chest, perhaps in unconscious response to the rising rem levels. You couldn't blame her. Sergei half wanted to shield his balls. "Prime wants something along the lines of 'I take this step for all the people of planet Earth,' but they think it would be nice to get in the word 'peace' and also 'hope.' You can't please everyone, but they're trying to find something of maximal inoffensiveness."

"Animal lovers could be upset if you say 'for all the people.'" Sergei shifts on his seat. He would like to grab Helen's ankle. Not out of desire, just contact. "You are human exceptionalist," he tells Helen. "You should take one small step also for bunny rabbit and opossum."

"Who will be thrilled to know the humans are thinking of moving," Helen agrees.

"Also, maybe by the time we go, some people will have stopped identifying as people and will want to be acknowledged as something else."

"One giant leap for sentience?" Yoshi calls down.

"I had this thought the other day," Helen says. "Since we can't all egress at the same time, that we'd sort of take turns going in and out, and make our statement once we've all stood on Mars."

"But then it's not so much like we are the best and bravest explorers in the history of humankind," Sergei says. "And more like we're members of a trapeze act."

It is true they cannot egress all together. There must always be one person in *Primitus*, for safety, until the moment when they make the transfer to *Red Dawn*.

"But this is a nice idea," Sergei says.

"It will be a moment for all of us," Yoshi says. "But yours will be the voice of the first human presence on another planet. As Sergei says, it is an opportunity."

Yes. This is the thing to keep thinking of. The opportunity that will be real.

Much of his job was waiting. If waiting was a difficulty, that meant he was not doing his job well.

There was a kind of strength that was not truly strength, though it was often mistaken for it. That kind of strength meant you could run fast to the top of the mountain, but it wasn't because you had endurance, it was because you had—above all else—a desire to be done with the thing. It was not remarkable to have this kind of false strength: muscle and will, merely.

He must be the person who can not only die in space, but also sit in a tube in Utah and live.

To explore was also to wait. To wait for wind to blow, for ice to thaw, for night to fall, for day to come.

"Okay," Sergei says, looking at the screen. "We are still alive."

DMITRI

DECEMBER

Dear Papa, Dmitri writes. He stops. He has only twenty minutes to write this email before the train arrives at Penn Station. His father likes it when Dmitri shows him how fluent he is getting in English, but Dmitri can't write an email in English in twenty minutes without making mistakes. He would like to get it done, though, so he can enjoy his time in the city in his own way. Ilya will be occupied for the afternoon: he has ballet class and then rehearsals for *The Nutcracker*. Dmitri is supposed to sit in the hallway of Ilya's school and do homework while Ilya does his thing, but Dmitri doesn't do this anymore, or rarely.

He tells Ilya that he goes to the coffee place to do his homework or walks around Union Square. Sometimes he does these things. Ilya has no problems with Dmitri not sitting in the hallway. Ilya keeps his mouth shut because he prefers that it be Dmitri who is in charge on Saturdays. If it wasn't Dmitri, then it would be their mother, and she always wants to watch Ilya dance through the window, which makes Ilya almost insane with fury. Ilya has gotten emotional about his dancing. He is always saying that he dances like shit, or that he had a shit class. He doesn't want to be contradicted on this point. Ilya is the only sincerely self-critical person Dmitri knows and so when Ilya says "I danced like shit in class today," what Dmitri largely feels is pride in his brother, mixed with a bit of envy.

Dear Papa,

We will be in school when the Chinese land on the moon. We will watch this in school. The parents have to give a consent to the watching, because maybe an accident will happen, and some people might have psychological damage from watching. In America, anything that makes you sad is called a trigger because of all the guns, I am thinking, and this is why they want a lot of places to be a "safe space." My maths teacher does not know very much about science but likes to talk about trivia. For example he says that the Apollo astronauts reported that the moon smells like burnt gunpowder, which I guess is a thing every American knows the smell of. I remembered that you smelled space when you were in the airlock on the space station because of particles from things like solar wind and also space debris would collect on the spacesuits after a spacewalk, and you said that space smelled a little bit like meat. I suppose the smell can be explained as a result of highly activated dust particles with dangling and unsatisfied bonds.

Dmitri pauses after this flurry of typing to review an explanation of dangling bonds on his screen, to see if he has it correctly, and if dangling bonds are something different from unsatisfied bonds, or maybe all dangling bonds are unsatisfied? Dmitri is taking chemistry this year, which he does very well at, even though it gives him no particular joy. His school has some good classes, but the students all seem to be insane: the girls too friendly in a fake way, the boys ineffectively violent and emotional. It does not help that the rest of his family has taken to their new life: Ilya and his dance school and his girlfriend, his mother and her circle of Russian friends and Gyro-yoga classes and having a husband who comes home every night. Even the cat they got to replace Slutskiya is considered by everyone to be an improvement.

Ilya sniffs loudly, lifts his leg like he's going to fart on Dmitri, and keeps on playing the new game Prime sent. Dmitri switches to typing in Russian so he can get the writing over with.

School is fine but it's pointless to get excited about anyone solving any kind of problem. Everything that we know right now about everything is probably wrong. If you think about it, it's entirely possible that the sun really does orbit the Earth, in the ultimate true reality of the 10th dimension alien race that is playing our collective consciousness as a video game that we haven't discovered yet. In related news, my computer science teacher asked me to join the Coder's Club. They have competitions. I have decided that I too would like to go to space. I think I would make an excellent candidate for the kind of deep space travel involving cryostasis. From what I have read, deep freeze suspended animation sounds exactly like regular existence, only with lower body temperatures and a feeding tube. Mostly nothing, with maybe a few dreams. At least at the end of cryostasis, I'd have gotten somewhere.

They are coming into the station now. Dmitri deletes everything on his screen after the thing about dangling and unsatisfied bonds. After another second, he deletes the unsatisfied bonds. He doesn't think he has it right.

Dmitri and Ilya take their positions by the door. Ilya cracks his joints ritualistically: neck, knuckles, wrists, his left hip, both ankles. They have a game of trying to get through the crowds and up and down the stairs and past the turnstiles and into the subway car in one continuous flow of movement. There's no point to the game, it's just something to do.

Dmitri gets his metro pass ready on his screen and adjusts his bag. A backpack would be more practical but makes him look younger, which he doesn't want.

They are off. The stairs are narrow and if you get stuck behind someone who stops, there is nowhere to go; marching in place is a disqualifying move. Ilya executes a half pirouette to slip to one side of a fat lady, and for a moment Dmitri loses sight of him, but that's okay. It's not a race; they are most satisfied when they are both successful. Dmitri has to circle a trash can twice while he waits for a family to get its act together and clear his lane, then it's on to the far south staircase, which is looking good. Ilya's heading for it too; if Dmitri gets behind Ilya on the staircase he'll be able to draft up behind him. This happens. The boys ascend, laughing. Now it's the main concourse and here the game opens up for more creative opportunities. Dmitri is not as graceful as his brother, but he is good at this challenge—clever about seeing openings in the crowd, judging distances, avoiding collision. He flies in between identically puff-coated and uncertain old people, does a kind of backward skip to avoid one of those idiots who walk in one direction while looking in another, sees Ilya weaving toward the A train entrance like a hockey player. The main concourse is crowded with people, and everyone has bags, though there aren't any dogs like you see in Russia unless they are police dogs or special-neediness dogs. Penn Station smells like urine and doughnuts. Dmitri dodges right, to avoid the kind of woman who is not going to move for him. Now Dmitri has to circumnavigate some tourists. Tourists are the worst; he really almost has to stop for a sloppy family and—by God—a double-wide stroller. Ilya wouldn't see if he stopped, but they are honorable about this game. No, he's okay, he got past it, and has his screen ready, heading for the train turnstiles where Ilya is pacing, looking for a good opening that will take him through the barrier and down the final flight of stairs. Dmitri sees an opportunity on the far left and Ilya gets behind him. The downtown train is entering the tunnel and they have to do a funny dance to get down the crowded platform without stopping, but then they are both in the car.

They recap: near misses, artful evasions. Dmitri makes eye contact with no one but his brother. Or women or girls. There are men everywhere, but he does not look at them yet. "Your elbow is close, but you can't bite it." They don't have that saying here. They say, "So near and yet so far."

Outside the building where Ilya takes his classes, the brothers exchange a ritual farewell. "Don't be an asshole," Dmitri says. "Go fuck yourself," Ilya says, without rancor. Ilya is only in a bad mood after class, never before.

Dmitri has an appointment now.

This will be the eighth appointment of his life, the second time he will be meeting Robert, and the first time he has met anyone twice.

. . . .

DMITRI MET ROBERT in the huge, fancy furniture store during one of his excursions. Dmitri was conspicuous in the shop, and knew it. It wasn't the kind of place guys his age went by themselves. He could see women glancing at him, perhaps wondering why he was there, but a certain kind of man was not confused. Dmitri always had the same sentence ready: "I have one hour to kill before I pick my cousin up." He likes the phrase "killing time" for its cruelty.

When Robert smiled at Dmitri as they passed by each other in Carpets, Dmitri had smiled only very slightly in return, and not stopped. Robert was too young—maybe only a couple of years older than Dmitri—and ordinary-looking. But when Dmitri left the store twenty minutes later, Robert was waiting for him outside.

Robert said, "How's it going?" and Dmitri said, "Good" and Robert had indicated his screen and said, "I was thinking of maybe trying to meet someone, but I'd like to meet you" and Dmitri said, "I have one hour to kill before I have to pick up my cousin" and Robert held up a bulky shopping bag from the expensive store and said, "Want to help me with my new lamp?"

Robert was a college student at the New School. He had a room in the dormitories a few blocks away. This was not at all what Dmitri had heretofore experienced: hotel rooms, lofts, once in the back office of a restaurant with the manager of the restaurant. Going to a school dormitory felt very risky, in an unpleasant way. He wanted to say no, but when he was standing closer to Robert, it was hard.

At the dormitories, there was a terrible moment when Dmitri was told he was required to show identification to a security guard. His high school ID had his date of birth on it, and also his name, which was not the name he'd given to Robert. The only other option he had was the Prime ID card he'd gotten in Utah, which didn't have his date of birth, but he had no idea what would happen if it was scanned at a place like this. Total humiliation ("I'm sorry, minors aren't allowed in here") versus risk of exposure ("Yes, Mrs. Kuznetsov, this is Prime Space security, and we've just picked up that your son has entered the building of a school with a known homosexual").

He chose the Prime ID but had to write his name down on a list, and so Robert learned that Dmitri's name was Dmitri, and not Misha.

"Misha is like nickname," Dmitri said in the elevator, working out furiously in his head a story for his Prime-minder, or his mother. ("I took a walk and met a student who offered to give me a tour of his college so I could see what American university is like.") When they passed kids in the hallway on the way to Robert's room Dmitri assumed the vaguely preoccupied face of someone who knows exactly what they are doing. This had seen him safely through hotel lobbies and corridors, but he was nauseated with anxiety. He did not like this kind of risk, and for what? Robert was not special.

Robert's suite was the first living place Dmitri had seen in America that wasn't enormous. They sat on the bed and talked for fifteen minutes about how Dmitri was Russian and then Robert had said, "You're gorgeous," which was Dmitri's cue that he could stop talking and put his hands on Robert's head, which was the one thing *he* knew how to do.

And after, nothing had come of it at all. Nobody had been called, nobody knew. Dmitri had given Robert his message number before leaving, just in case he needed to cover some tracks. He hadn't planned on seeing him again. But then he changed his mind.

. . .

TODAY, ROBERT GREETS DMITRI in the lobby of his dormitory building. Robert has recently taken a shower, his hair is wet, he looks different from how Dmitri remembered, younger and less sexy. Robert has not asked Dmitri's age. Dmitri is sixteen now, but it is still illegal for anyone to have sex with him. It is called statutory rape, even if Dmitri utilizes a train and a subway car and a walk and three erased messages on his screen and a handful of lies to various people for the specific purpose of getting raped.

And people tell him that he must be glad to be in America, where there is so much more freedom. They're all children here.

"Are you meeting your cousin again?" Robert asks.

Dmitri says that this is so, and he has only one hour.

Robert's dormitory room is mostly a square with single beds set against opposite walls, and identical desks at the foot of both beds. There is also a small kitchen with room for a round table, and a bathroom with only a shower, no bathtub. On the first visit, Dmitri hadn't noticed many details of the room, although he had pretended to look around. He hadn't *wanted* to see anything, still doesn't; he's positive that he will see something embarrassing that will put him off. And he very much wants to have Robert blow him today, he's been thinking about it all week.

So has Robert, apparently, because Dmitri does not even have to put his hands on Robert's head, Robert right away undoes Dmitri's pants just as Dmitri is taking off his coat. So Dmitri sprawls back on Robert's bed and shuts his eyes, until Robert says, "I want you to watch me," which turns out to be a good suggestion. He can see Robert, and his own dick, and he can sort of see the two of them, as if he were watching a video. Only at the end does he shut his eyes.

He thinks of this moment as being like a supernova. Nobody ever sees a supernova.

After, Robert wants Dmitri to take off all his clothes, and Dmitri feels so good he does not object to this. Robert takes off all his own clothes. The bed is narrow. They sort of grab at each other. Dmitri can only see Robert in pieces: a shoulder, a thigh, some of Robert's stomach. Robert wants Dmitri to do more things.

Dmitri is nervous about escalation. He has definitely never done anything to do with buttholes. He thinks that he just likes getting his dick sucked, that's all, and he might not even be bisexual, let alone gay. He thinks that he might be just as happy if a hot woman came up to him and offered to suck his dick, only that never happens. The porn that Ilya likes also works for him, so that proves it. Dmitri doesn't watch the girl in those videos, but that's only because girls don't have much of anything to see down there. And all he's doing right now is killing time. The things you do when you kill time don't count.

Dmitri's surprised, when he gets down to it, how manly it is to suck a guy's dick. He can't see himself, but he's sure that he looks a hundred times better than the girls in videos, much more natural. He understands now why people get so excited when they do this to him. Actually, now that he's in their position, he's surprised they were able to control themselves as much as they did. Dmitri can smell Robert under his soap, and Robert says "easy, easy" because Dmitri is not being gentle, but no, he can't do it any easier, he wants to cram himself full of Robert and Robert is making the best sounds ever. He finds he totally knows what to do, even though he's having a hard time doing anything other than more, more, more.

"Oh there, oh there," says Robert. And Dmitri is here. He's right here.

After, for a few minutes, they lie naked almost on top of each other because of how small the bed is. Dmitri's hand is sticky with Robert's semen, which smells and tastes like blin batter. "The first blin is always lumpy," Dmitri says, out loud, in Russian. It is a proverb. Dmitri doesn't know the equivalent in English. "What was that?" Robert asks. Robert's mouth is on Dmitri's neck and one hand is on Dmitri's ass and Dmitri feels like his entire body is yawning in a happy way, but he needs to get up.

"I have to meet my cousin," he says.

"Right," Robert says. "The cousin."

Dmitri's shirt is underneath Robert's legs; his pants and sweater are on the floor. He does not see his socks. He needs to wash himself. It's always like this, the ending, but what is he supposed to do? Robert's skin is very white, except for a vertical flush of red on his chest and two horizontal marks on his thighs that may configure to the shape of Dmitri's hands.

"I can use bathroom?" Dmitri asks. Robert nods. Dmitri would like to gather his clothes together and dress in the bathroom, but he doesn't want to drag his shirt out from under Robert. He does take his satchel with him to the bathroom, as he always does, it's a safety thing.

The bathroom is not as clean as Dmitri would like. In hotel rooms, the bathrooms are very fancy and perfectly clean. The towel on the rack in this one is still wet, as is the bathmat. The trash bin is so full the lid cannot close; the area around the tiny sink is gummed with the spilt contents of bottles. Dmitri's father told him once that Americans become very distressed if everything is not perfectly clean, but perhaps this only applied to American astronauts. Dmitri uses a corner of the damp towel and some of the soap still in the plastic dispenser to scrub at his stomach, his dick, in between his legs. When he comes out of the bathroom, Robert has put on pants and is sitting cross-legged on his bed, playing with what looks like a cross between a rain stick and an abacus. Dmitri dresses. Robert tilts the thing in his hands and silver disks slide down the rails, producing an atonal tinkling. Dmitri looks out the window. A row of paper books are lined up on the ledge and he reads a few titles. They all have something to do with music.

"You are music student?" Dmitri asks. In his encounters, he exaggerates his accent and makes no effort for grammatical English because everyone likes it when he speaks poorly.

"That's the first question you've asked me," Robert says. "Yeah. I'm a composer."

Dmitri zips up his pants and points with his chin to the thing Robert is playing.

"You make this?"

"I designed it," Robert says. "My roommate, Harald, made it for me. He's a 3-D imagist. We're supposed to be doing this project involving found instruments and nature. My problem is I love, like, super-old-fashioned music, so there's no chance of my having a career in the United States. I should have been born in the nineteen fifties so I could have played in an orchestra. Harald says it's pretentious to be naive, but I'm really not trying."

Dmitri swallows this speech without chewing; swallows also the vertical line that appears between Robert's eyebrows when he speaks, the green sheets on Robert's bed, his thin hands, the fact that the red vertical flush on his chest has disappeared, the expensive-looking lamp clamped to the headboard of the bed that must be the lamp from the furniture store, the handles of suitcases and what looks like the handle of a tennis racket that can be seen underneath Robert's bed, the pieces of paper taped to the wall above the bed, covered in spidery writing.

He feels sad. Robert is interesting. Dmitri is not. So far, he's been able to get away with this, but it can't last forever. Mostly it has been enough to be obedient, and lately it has been sufficient to have a hard dick.

Robert tilts the construction of rods, makes the metal disks drip rapidly onto one another.

"It is like rain." Dmitri points at the instrument. "But more angry. Like acid rain."

Robert shakes his head like he is an amazed person.

"That's what I call it," he says. "It's an acid rain stick."

Robert looks at Dmitri with a face animated with liking, which makes Dmitri realize that 1. Robert hasn't maybe liked him until now and 2. He likes Robert and 3. He should go before he messes anything up.

DMITRI HAS MORE time to kill before Ilya is done, so he walks to where people take their dogs in Union Square Park. It has snowed a little more; the trees and ground and benches and old-fashioned street lamps are all dusted with it. He tries to think of an interesting observation about it all, but it's just snow.

Two men are walking hand in hand toward Dmitri, one of them holding the leash of a large black poodle. It is nothing for two men to hold hands in America. It's supposed to mean nothing to him too.

The poodle catches Dmitri's eye and makes unequivocally for him, tugging along the man holding his leash, who lurches forward, tugging the man holding his hand.

"He's friendly," the man says. The poodle sits in front of Dmitri, absurdly dignified, like an old man who has been forced to wear a poodle costume but refuses to let it diminish him. Dmitri does not think that the dog wants to be petted, exactly, so he just looks at it. The poodle tosses its ludicrous head and marches off, causing another chain reaction in the men, who laugh.

If this were a movie, Dmitri thinks, a bomb would explode now, giving poignancy to the men, and the dog, and the moment they all just shared, and the thing that happened with Robert, and the sound of acid rain bells. But no bomb goes off and no meaning appears. Dmitri finds it hard to take a deep breath, his lungs are constricted with all the potential meaningless moments of life.

LUKE

Y ou missed it," Luke says. "Yoshi started screaming at Sergei after Sergei gave away the ending to *Doctor Zhivago*. And then Helen started crying and went to the bathroom and gave herself bangs."

"Ha ha." Nari thunks herself down in the chair next to Luke and holds out a plate of cookies. "The party is raging in Mission Control. People are doing traditional wassail and there's a snow machine."

On the screens in front of them, the astronauts are cleaning up after their special Christmas feast and will go to bed soon. It is almost midnight, *Primitus* time.

Four in the afternoon, Earth time. Luke is struggling. His circadian rhythms look like a Jackson Pollock painting. It affects them all a little differently, and Luke—to his shame—is sensitive.

He's also been up for eighteen hours, working for sixteen of them. Since today was a free day for the astronauts—no training, no sims— it was a full day for observing social and recreation time. Two members of the Obber team drew Christmas vacation, so they're down to four. Luke and Nari have spent the day watching the most hypnotically boring reality channel on Earth.

It was a joke among the Obbers. "You can't look away," they said. "It's mesmerizingly dull. It's Chekhov in space."

According to the astronauts, the astronauts were fine! They were happy as tinned clams. They answered every question, filled out every questionnaire, filed every personal report with monotonous cheer. No, they were not stressed. Yes, they felt engaged. No, there were no conflicts. Yes, they were sleeping. They liked the food. Their health was good. They missed their families at entirely appropriate levels that were absolutely manageable. Occasionally, an astronaut would submit thoughtful ideas on small modifications to their situation or equipment. Sergei would be brief and cheerful in his punctuation selection; Yoshi was exquisitely polite; Helen sent them under the heading: Things to Think About.

According to the face and voice scanners, the astronauts were not always fine, but the Obbers were still struggling to read these. The astronauts switched languages a lot in casual conversation, and their facial expressions changed according to language, as did the pitch and tone of their voices. Additionally, they sometimes spoke to one another while engaged in another task, and might be reacting to the task, or the person. They chatted for hours about technical things Luke could barely follow.

Aristotle had written that it was easy to become angry—the difficulty was in being angry with the right person, to the right degree, at the right time, for the right purpose, and in the right way. Put like that, it seemed not just difficult but impossible.

It was not difficult for the astronauts.

Helen only expressed anger toward herself, but did not appear to dwell on it. Yoshi allowed himself to express anger at current events, but he always did a meditation after looking at the news uplinks, and that was that. Sergei pretended to be angry for comic effect or as an anger scapegoat for the crew and otherwise waited until he was no longer angry to express anger.

There were days when Luke was angry with the astronauts for being so perfect, even as he admired them, loved them, really. Right now, Sergei and Helen are cleaning the dishes and Yoshi is vacuuming the floor around the Galley table. Sergei begins to sing "Silent Night." He has a good singing voice.

For about three weeks the Obbers were able to observe the same social niceties as the astronauts: courteousness, mindful speaking, respectful consideration of possible cultural differences. Because of their training, and—more powerfully—the constant exemplars of good behavior they observe every day, they have not devolved into outright rudeness or in-fighting, but Luke is aware of crests and troughs of group cohesion. There was this gap: the crew had been chosen in part because of their ability to handle certain kinds of stress, but the members of Mission Control, and even the Obber team, had been chosen for other skills. Yet Mission Control and the Obbers shared certain strains of the same kind of stress.

"All for one," Sergei says on the screen. The astronauts stand in a circle and make a stack of their fists. "One for all," they say, breaking apart. This is nearly the only time they touch each other. They do not hug or kiss cheeks. Sometimes Sergei will put a hand on Yoshi's shoulder, and sometimes Yoshi does the same to him. No one touches Helen.

"SLEEP WELL," Helen says. "Thank you for a wonderful Christmas." The holiday was "hers," as she is the only native Christmas-er.

New Year's will be Japanese-style, for Yoshi, and Sergei will be hosting a Russian "Old New Year," on the fourteenth.

Luke sighs. He'd miscalculated his caffeine intake and he'd drunk too much champagne during his break. He's not going to be able to go straight to bed.

Nari says she's going to catch the shuttle back to the dorms. Luke puts on his running shoes. Prime keeps a clean road between campus and dormitories even in this weather. Luke tries to clear his mind and just run, the way the astronauts could seemingly just *do* things.

But he is not an astronaut.

Helen hadn't shown to her best advantage in the Christmas video. Sergei was naturally very funny, and Yoshi was endearingly game for anything. Helen had a wonderful sense of humor—sly and dry—but she didn't do goofy as well as the others. Helen was performing slightly better in the sims than either of her crewmates: fewer mistakes, especially in the eleventh-hour range, where both Sergei and Yoshi tended to rush. And yet, she was no machine. She was creative. She'd made those slippers for Yoshi and another pair for Sergei's Christmas present, and for Yoshi she'd assembled a sound recording of celestial magnetic fields: Jupiter, the rings of Saturn, the comet 67P. Her harmonica playing was excellent. But Luke is aware that she does not inspire the same affection in people as Sergei and Yoshi do. He'd thought that the female Obbers would be protective of Helen, but if anything they were slightly more critical. Unpacking exactly why Helen didn't engender sympathy was possibly a window into inherent sexism, but possibly something else.

It was amazing that Helen was able to have such healthy relationships with men, considering that her father had been in a vegetative state for the entirety of Helen's adolescence. By all accounts, Helen's marriage had been happy, although her husband had been considerably older. No surprise there.

Luke wonders if Helen has ever had to rebuff a male colleague's romantic overtures. (She is on record for answering "never" to the question of sexual harassment.) In all the conversations Luke has been privy to, he has never heard anyone voice concern over Sergei or Yoshi forming a limerent attachment to Helen, or Helen to either of her crewmates. He wonders whether Helen has checked any signs of this in herself, in word or deed, and he's missed it because he can't read her properly yet. Perhaps she has wanted to place a hand on Sergei's back, to express natural human affection, and has not. (She never has.) Perhaps she would have liked to let her eyes linger on Yoshi's bare torso while he exercised, to allow herself a moment of sensual appreciation, but did not. (She did not.) Perhaps she thought about it later, when her eyes were closed, and the computers weren't able to scan for lust.

Ransom had put out a jar in their office. Every time someone asked them if astronauts ever had sex in space, they were supposed to put in a penny. Luke had wondered if, by the end of the mission, they would have enough to buy the whole Obber team a beer. "By the time the mission is completed," Ransom said, "we should have enough to buy an island."

On a certain level, it was both good and necessary that Helen was not more obviously lovable. Sergei and Yoshi had found the perfect buffer for both Helen's femaleness and her strength. They had made her a superwoman, not subject to the laws of mortals and, by extension, its vulnerabilities. Helen did not seem to resent this, or feel it a burden. Luke had no way of knowing how deep that went. He—the person who saw all—was shut out. Whatever the astronauts felt about one another, they didn't say it.

"Early days, still," Ransom said.

Things would get harder. Mars would present technical challenges. And then there was the biggie: the voyage home. If *Primitus* pushed the limits of acceptable space per person, then *Red Dawn*— even smaller—would be even more confining; their time inside it would be almost two months longer. And the excitement of the Mars landing would be behind them.

The astronauts' success in *Primitus* was no guarantee for *Red Dawn*: adaptation was extremely situational.

They all knew what they were looking for. Crew preoccupation with their environment, noncompliance with schedules or requests communicated from Mission Control, antagonism to external evaluation, prioritization of personal comfort over mission objective. Exacerbation of cultural and language differences, variability in crew cohesion, improper use of leadership roles. These would manifest as lapses of attention, sleep disturbances, psychosomatic illness, emotional lability, irritability, loss of vigor and motivation.

So far, nothing.

This was good, of course.

At least they were throwing out those ridiculous FIRO-B questionnaires and evaluations. Perhaps they could begin to think of what might be the right questions to ask these people. None of the astronauts had availed themselves of the opportunity to use their computer therapists, no surprise, but none of the family had either, which was disappointing. Mireille Kane was the only one who consistently filled out the weekly questionnaire—it was optional—but she went only as far as circling or checking options; she never volunteered feedback.

Back at the dormitories, Luke makes his way to his room. Some of the Prime engineers had made Christmas displays: elaborately outfitted snow globes suspended from the ceiling and cued to music. They twirled and played when you got close to them. Luke loved the people at Prime for stuff like this. For air hockey battles between Team Trace Toxic Contaminants and Team Nutrient Stability, for naming their pets after mathematicians, for getting upset with the town's holiday banner on the department store, a concession to multiculturalism that read *Peace on earth*, which was a fine statement, but the *earth* had been written with a small *e* and "If we're going to capitalize the names of nations, the names of corporations, people's names, then we have to capitalize *Earth*!" A special-ops team had been organized and deployed to change the sign at night.

Luke enters his pod room, a little messy now because of the gifts he'd opened from his family early this morning but not put away. He'd talked to his family on screen today while the crew was exercising. The whole gang had put on the Prime Space T-shirts he sent. They were proud of him. His father, especially. It's not nothing, to make your father proud.

"You're going to be a part of history," his father said.

It was a Sergei phrase: "It's not nothing." All the astronauts used it. All the Obbers used it now too. They had their own T-shirts with it printed. *Prime Space: It's Not Nothing*.

Luke settles into his bed, thinks of the crew settling into their own beds. He wraps his arms around his body. He spends so much time looking at Sergei and Yoshi and Helen that it's not always possible to get their images out of his head.

Perhaps Sergei and Yoshi would like to touch Helen. Perhaps she wants to be touched.

SERGEI

I t is January 14, Old New Year in the Russian calendar, a day of feasting and carol singing and fortune-telling. The astronauts must celebrate. Perhaps none of them wishes to celebrate; perhaps they all think they would prefer to lie on their person-sized slabs in their wedges and reread messages from home, or marathon-watch a television series, or don sim helmets and stroll along the cliffs of a virtual Cornwall. The brain looks for comfort like a newborn, seeks pleasure like a greedy child, abandons reason like a lovesick teen. Even the kind of brain that recognizes the value of delayed gratification—or has been rigorously trained to accept it—even *that* brain is capable of justifying slothful regression.

Sergei believes that complete transparency about his role as commander is crucial to his success as commander, so he does not try to trick or cajole his crewmates into having good times. He says, "Prime believes it is important for us to celebrate and have communal recreation activities, especially during times when we might be tempted to withdraw because we are missing Earth and our families." He does not say, "*I* believe," even though he does agree that it is important. It is too easy to become dull without realizing that you have become dull. Depression and listlessness are marked states, but boring is a slow disease.

Over the years, the International Space Station has acquired a supply of holiday decor, but on *Primitus*, size and weight are commodities too precious to be squandered on the premanufactured items of celebration. The astronauts have done their best. Five pieces of paper had been sacrificed to make snowflakes for Christmas, and these still hang over the dining table along with a chime constructed from shiny tools, and utensils not in use. Sergei had programmed the large screen in the Galley/Recreation wedge to play a scene of snow falling. Their mascot, the green alien, has acquired a tiny red paper Santa/Grandfather Frost hat. The astronauts have made alterations to their own appearances to mark the Old New Year. Helen wears a towel on her head, babushka-style. Yoshi sports a mustache made from black electrical tape. Sergei has made himself a beard out of a wad of flameproof insulation. For dinner, they enjoyed rehydrated pork dumplings.

Sergei places a tray of screws and nuts onto the table. "My sister Galina was the fortune-teller," Sergei says. "Because she was the youngest and we had a tradition in the family that it was always the youngest girl who did this. We had a game, with beans. The beans were put in a special bag, and you shook it, and then you reached in and grabbed a handful and let them fall into a pot while you made a wish. Then my sister would count the beans and if the number was even, your wish came true, and if odd, too bad."

What happens when you become dull is you forget that the story you are telling must be interesting to other people, or you forget that you have already told the story. You say, "I may have told you this" and proceed anyway, even if your listeners appear to recognize the anecdote. Or you tell no stories at all. Sergei produces a clean sock and puts the screws and nuts he has collected into the sock.

"Helen is the youngest woman here," Sergei says. "So she shall count the beans." He is feeling homesick for people who do not require translations or explanations, even though both Helen and Yoshi are conversant with Russian holidays, have celebrated them with cosmonauts before. Helen and Yoshi probably know more about Russian traditions than a lot of Russians. But for them it will always be knowing *about* these things, not simply knowing them. Sergei thinks of his youngest sister, Galina. She had been the prettiest and the sweetest of his sisters, and now she was fat, and a lesbian, and lived in Germany. He didn't mind about the lesbian and the Germany. Russia was not the place to live if you were gay. It was one of the reasons.

Well.

Galina was very bitter against their parents for various things that they'd all had to put up with. She had something that she called her "personal story" and she did nothing but tell this personal story over and over again. Sometimes she called it her "voice" or her "truth." Sergei had felt very bad for Galina when he heard her personal story the first time, but now it was just annoying.

Thinking of his sister makes Sergei feel depressed, which he was already feeling this week, a little, because of missing his boys. It's not a problem. Being depressed is not the worst thing. It depends on how you address the feeling. Perhaps Sergei is luckier than his crewmates. Americans always desire happiness, so they fear sadness, unlike Russians, who can draw strength from mourning. The Japanese too, Sergei understands, have an easier relationship with melancholy. Sergei is very glad that Helen is a woman and not a man. Depressed American men on spaceships are embarrassing.

"Do you have your wish ready?" Helen asks Yoshi.

"When I was little, I wished I would be a cosmonaut, so this is very powerful magic," Sergei tells them. "That was my wish every year, except for one year, when I wished that Ama Yevchenka would fall in love with me. Of course, it was always a joke, no one took it seriously, but there was always a moment, just when you reached in the bag, that maybe you were serious. A wish is always serious, even if the game is silly."

He would never sit around with his family and tell fortunes again. Not with the family he grew up with. His childhood was not only over, but tarnished. "You all wanted me to be the pretty little girl," Galina had screamed at their mother. "Your sweet, pretty little girl. Always *happy* little girl." She had a point. Sergei would be honest and say that he much preferred Galina when she was happy and pretty and sweet and not a bitter, angry, fat person.

"And did Ama Yevchenka fall in love with you?" Helen asks.

"Yes, of course. But she cut her hair, and I did not love her with the same force."

They all laugh.

It would kill him, it would absolutely kill him, if all Dmitri has in his soul when he is Galina's age is a story of how people had hurt him. It would also be very sad if Dmitri became fat. Ilya you could almost see becoming fat quite late in his life, after a dancing career. Not fat, but with a hard, protruding belly that he would be proud of and that women would find attractive. When Ilya was a baby he would often stand with his feet apart and his belly thrust out, smiling, very proud.

"I am ready," Yoshi says. "I have my wish."

"What is it, Yakov?" Sergei asks. It is his joke to call Yoshi *Yakov* sometimes. People like to have family nicknames.

"We are supposed to name our wish out loud?"

"No." Sergei shakes his head.

Yoshi is always very willing. Sergei thinks that, of the three of them, Yoshi has adapted best to their environment, is the most genuinely content and happy. Helen's performance is very good, but sometimes Sergei has spotted a watchfulness that might also be anxiousness, or near anxiousness.

They would all be perfectly happy if any of this was real.

Helen and Yoshi bend forward as Helen counts. Sergei has given them a silly children's game and because they are two of the most capable people in the current population of people, they will do their best to play it well. Sergei wishes that he had something better to give them.

"There is another tradition," he says, "for Old New Year. It is to plunge into cold water. A lake or a river. At midnight. I have done this with my sons, when we would vacation in the Crimea. Dmitri hated it, but he would try to hide this and be brave. Ilya loved it. They won't do it without me. Of course, they can't where they are now. New Jersey is not the Crimea. They'd get arrested."

And the Crimea was not the Crimea anymore. Miss Earth? Pfuff. The things he missed were mostly ghosts.

His father had made him do the New Year's plunge. For purification, he said. Jumping into a pond in northwestern Moscow in January is no joke. Sergei had been afraid.

How do you help your son conquer fear without hurting him? Sergei was not born with courage. He'd had to force himself. He's needed to hate himself, hate the weak part, conquer it.

And so, he had taken his own sons to do what he had hated doing himself. The first time, they were so small. When he next sees Dmitri, they will maybe be the same size. But that first run into the sea in January, Dmitri had needed to tilt his head almost all the way back to look up at him. Ilya too, but Ilya didn't look up so often. Dmitri had gripped his hand, trying to tell Sergei that he did not like what was happening, this thing his father was making him do. Sergei could barely hold on to Ilya, he was angry that his father was holding him back. Sergei had looked down at Dmitri and wondered if all his weaknesses had been siphoned off and gathered in this small person, and he had wanted to beg his son's forgiveness. And he'd looked down at Ilya and seen the self that he'd fought so hard to acquire, and he'd envied him. He takes no credit for the joy that Ilya feels but must accept all the blame for any suffering of Dmitri's. "It is not so cold, the water," he'd said to him. And to Ilya, "Don't let go of my hand," because already his hand was loose in Sergei's grip. But they still did turn to him, and await his signal. Would they turn to him now? No, they were too old, and his signal was not so important. But there had been a time when they had, and he'd told them when to run, and the feast of that epiphany was the sound of his sons' laughter and their high, fierce shouts, like wolves, and the sight of those skinny legs and knobby arms that returned to him, to be carried out, and the way they held him without noticing they were holding him.

"There are lots of polar bear clubs that do New Year's plunges in the States," Helen says. "I know that's not quite the same as what you're talking about, but you'll find a place in the States to take them, next year." Because Helen is not often soft, her softness is sweet.

She finishes counting Yoshi's screws.

"Good news, Yakov," she says. "You're getting your wish. You *will* be an astronaut when you grow up!"

Sergei thinks that Helen must be a very wonderful mother, and that her daughter is lucky.

"Your turn, Sergei," she says, repacking the sock with screws.

Sergei looks at the window. Earth is an undistinguished disk now. Always there has been this question: how will it feel when the Earth cannot be seen, when the cosmonaut travels so far away that he cannot see his home? The answer is that he will mostly stop looking out the window.

What will fuck you up is never what you think is going to fuck you up. Maybe nothing will fuck you up. Anyway, he's not thinking of Earth, he's thinking of his sons. For this, also, he must not gaze mournfully at that which he cannot see. Sergei turns from the window.

"Make a wish," says Helen.

YOSHI

Yoshi wakes up retching. He vomits on his sleep sack before he can reach for anything else. What else does he have? He has no bag or bucket in his wedge. There is a very real possibility he is going to vomit again. Yoshi tries to kick himself out of the sack without letting the mess he has made spread any further. He cannot see his watch, or the door; it is unaccountably dark.

No, he is still wearing his sleep mask.

Yoshi shoves his sleep mask upward and lurches out of bed, banging an elbow on his clothing locker. He does not think about letting the sheets cool before making his bed. He moves quickly into the hallway and heads to the Lav, then realizes he is going the wrong way, also that he seems to be hugging the curved wall of the corridor. Anyway, he should not vomit into the toilet because this is connected to the Chute, and stomach acids are not the same as urine or fecal matter—he needs a bag.

When Yoshi reaches the Science/Lab wedge he finds Sergei

already there, scrabbling in the bin that holds the nausea bags and, like Yoshi, naked except for disposable underwear. Sergei flips a bag to Yoshi, who grabs it and then lurches into Sergei, who half catches him and half loses his own balance, and they stagger into a table in a clumsy tango.

"What's going on?" Yoshi can see Helen in the doorway over Sergei's shoulder. He hardly recognizes her, she looks like a shocked little girl. It also appears as if she's standing sideways, then not, and then she's pulling Sergei upright.

"I fell," Yoshi says. "Into Sergei. Dizzy."

"Sick," Sergei says. "Are you sick?"

"Yes—no," Helen shakes her head. "Dizzy, headache. Something happened."

"No alarms." Sergei nods at the console. "Nothing."

"We were hit," Helen says. She is in front of the console board.

"Nothing, I see nothing." Yoshi means that he sees no evidence of a breach on the console, but that is only because he cannot see the console. He sees stars, figurative stars, five-pointed. His head is pounding.

"What could hit us?" Sergei holds his bag up to his mouth and then continues speaking through it in Russian as his eyes scan the console. "Life support is nominal."

They have not been hit; there are no alarms, no sensors, no warning lights.

"No." Sergei coughs. "Yoshi, you are nauseated?"

"Yes. I woke up sick."

"The alarm system failed," Helen says. "*Something* happened."

"I can't read the fucking telemetry." Sergei knuckles his eyes.

"Look," Helen says. Her voice is calm. "We course corrected.

Poorly. Incorrect amount of thrust, and it caused a slack in our centrifuge tether. Then a correction, then another course correction to compensate for the earlier one."

"No alarm?" Sergei is furious. "If someone sneezes in the toilet we get an alarm, but this?"

Yoshi looks at his watch. How quickly can an astronaut go from deep sleep to high performance? Helen is already there, she is already alert and solving problems. He must get to that place immediately.

"Look," Helen repeats. Her finger traces a line on the screen. Yoshi swallows the acidity in his mouth.

"Helen is correct," he says.

They read the board, reassuring themselves, checking systems.

They must face this. To fly in an automated ship is to be at the mercy of automation, in a place where there can be no failure. *Primitus* has made decisions on her own.

"I will now send a very nice message to Ground." Sergei tosses his nausea bag onto the table. "And say they should maybe install a little bell that lets us know if computer decides to make course correction like drunk person and maybe I will also ask them what the fuck. Someone look outside window. Is there comet? Is there alien death squad? Is there space wildebeest?"

Helen is now smiling at Sergei, who—in his disposable undergarments—does look very amusing, and is clearly enjoying his own wrath.

"I have too much adrenaline!" Sergei shouts.

They must wait now for Mission Control.

Yoshi volunteers to bring clothing for the crew. He would also like to rinse his mouth. While he does these things, he reviews his performance.

Sergei had reacted in nearly the same way as he had. Helen—and presumably the Observation team—had seen him naked and flail-ing. He is not worried about the near nudity; he is proud of his phy-sique (Sergei is quite hirsute), but he's concerned about the lack of coordination. Additionally, there is the bother of vomit on his sleep sack. Odors on *Primitus* have a way of lingering.

Mission Control informs them that they are aware of the problem, which originated with a computer error at Mission Control, and not on *Primitus*, that the problem was quickly identified and corrected, and a decision was made not to alert the crew during sleeping hours.

"The language," Yoshi notes, "is somewhat starchy."

"Life Systems Support is recommending we have a cup of de-caffeinated tea," Sergei says. "I think this is maybe joke, but still, good idea."

"The thing I'm curious about," Helen says, when they are gathered in the Galley, "is the nausea." She has put her hair back into its short ponytail. It was being loose that had given her the appearance of a little girl. Helen's hair is very curly. Her ponytail is more like the tail of a poodle. She reaches for the whiteboard and starts scribbling.

"The explanation is not sufficient," Sergei says. "I do not under-stand the game that is being played."

"Our symptoms make sense if the balance of the centrifuge *was* disrupted," Yoshi says. "Displacement of the inner ear fluid would cause us to be nauseous."

"*We* were nauseated," Sergei corrects. "Helen—who was constructed in a secret laboratory hidden in James Bond villain cave—only got a little dizzy."

"And disoriented, apparently, since I thought we'd been hit." Helen laughs. "I was staggering down the hallway. Maybe because, in the movies, when the spaceship gets hit by something, the crew staggers around."

"But it wasn't staggering," Yoshi persists. "Your body, and ours, did exactly what might happen if the speed of our rotation was disrupted."

"It's not nothing," Sergei says, leaning over to look at Helen's calculations. "If Prime can create the sensation of acceleration on a stationary platform. It seems a lot of effort just to see who vomits. Or to get picture of Yoshi in underwear for astronaut calendar."

"I'm more interested in the how," Helen says.

"Eppur si muove."

Helen and Sergei look at him.

It is a beautiful thing, when understanding comes. Among other things, it makes you realize that your subconscious operates continually, not like a ghost in your machine, but like the parts of your program that are kept hidden just so the central console won't be too cluttered. Not only has Yoshi understood what just happened, but he has understood why. He and his crew, they have forgotten that things are not entirely in their control, and this was Prime's way of reminding them. On their way to Mars there may—there will, surely—be things they cannot account for. Prime is reminding the astronauts—moving so smoothly, so confidently in their imaginary craft—that they don't know everything, will never know everything. Was not this entire mission a test of faith?

"Galileo's supposed last words." Yoshi points to the floor. "We're not on a stationary platform."

The astronauts look down at their feet.

"Eppur si muove," Yoshi says. *"And yet it moves."* Galileo's supposed last words.

Primitus was not sitting in the desert in Utah; it was on another structure, which was capable of doing things. They were not stationary. The whole thing—the spacecraft—was alive, was active.

Prime was Junya's hand over his eyes, testing his endurance, making him prove that he belonged here, that he was one of them. Prime is swinging the bat in front of their faces. But he is no longer a child, he can take this and much more. Prime has done something, perhaps more than they intended. They have revealed himself to himself. How will the crew behave when they encounter a mystery?

More, he addresses Junya. *More*, he says to Mission Control. *More*, he demands of space itself. *Do more. I am not afraid.*

LUKE

When Mireille appears on screen, she is sobbing. Luke waits, occasionally saying, "take your time" and "it's okay."

It is not okay. The Chinese astronauts are dead, all of them. They did not reach the moon. A fire in the cockpit killed the crew eighty-one seconds after launch. Nobody knows exactly what happened. The Chinese launch from a remote and closely guarded location in Inner Mongolia; the craft and the remains of its occupants were brought down in the Sea of Japan. They were being recovered now.

Mireille's face is jammy from tears and makeup. She cries openly, not covering her mouth.

Luke is not the one who is supposed to talk to Mireille, who normally communicates with Kyrah, the liaison assigned to handle Helen's family members. But Kyrah is having an emergency root canal, Dr. Ransom is in a meeting with Boone Cross, and Mireille needed to be contacted.

"I don't know," Mireille says. "I don't know why I'm so . . ."

All over the world, people are expressing their grief and solidarity with the Chinese, even though almost nobody, except the Chinese, truly wanted the Chinese to land on the moon. Nobody wanted *this*, a horrible explosion, deaths, but probably not a few people would be consoled by the thought that, for a little bit longer, they could look at the moon in the night sky and not have to imagine people drilling for Helium-3 on it. Luke might have felt something like that himself, before he came to work at Prime. Before, he would not have imagined the bodies. Would not have imagined the devastation of the people at the Chinese space agency, their sense of responsibility, their guilt.

At Prime, there is absolutely no time to even comprehend the event in China. *Red Dawn II* is about to land on Mars. Prime is putting another craft on a planet where most of the things that are sent to it crash. This needs to happen successfully or there is a chance this crew will not be the ones that go to Mars. This crew, that is now in areocentric orbit of Mars, and six hours ago was given the go-ahead to begin the Entry, Descent, and Landing Simulation. Four hours ago, *Weilai 3* blew up.

"It's that awful thing," Mireille says, "that awful video that someone took secretly and is everywhere and you can see the flash in the sky and the person holding the camera going, 'Oh,' and you can't actually see anything and it's worse, almost, than if it were some graphic thing, it's like, we don't even know, like it's not even real."

Luke has seen this footage, not official, terrible in what it wasn't showing, what had to be imagined.

Luke is nervous. He has observed Helen reading and viewing messages from Mireille. He's reviewed both sides of their correspondence and looked at Kyrah's reports and summaries. He has come to think of Helen's daughter mostly as a possible source of tension or stress: a person Helen will miss, worry about, could be hurt by. And now this person is nakedly, more than nakedly, *skeletally* distressed, in front of him. He isn't trained for this.

"I want to talk to my mom," Mireille says.

Luke nods his head.

"No, I really want to talk to my mom."

"I know it's very hard," Luke says, "not to be able to communicate right now, but—"

"Do *not* tell me what is hard." Mireille stands up and moves out of frame for a moment, knocking her screen downward. Luke can see part of her kitchen floor, the bottom edge of a stove, a pair of high heels, one shoe on its side. The screen jerks upward and his entire visual field is nothing but green fabric curved from some part of Mireille's anatomy and then her face, quite close-up.

"What, you didn't tell them?" Now she looks angry.

"The crew was about to begin the landing sequence." Luke makes an effort to speak gently, but not in *too* measured a tone. Kyrah had said something to Luke once about how Mireille was "quick." Also, Mireille has been an astronaut's daughter for most of her life; in many ways she is much more familiar than he is with the world and the language and these kinds of conversations. He has a list on his knee of things he can't say to Mireille, and things he can. He is supposed to let Mireille know that she has support and resources available to her.

Mireille scrubs a fist across her face, smearing more makeup. Oddly, she looks quite pretty like this. He guesses—from the hour and the dress and the shoes—that she was on a date. Maybe there is a guy in another room, waiting to pat her back.

"They don't know what happened, right?" Mireille's throat and mouth are constricted for shouting, but her voice is at half-volume. She is whisper-shouting. Someone might be in the other room. "They don't even know. God." Mireille knocks her screen down again. Luke looks at Mireille's fallen shoe and listens to the sound of banging. The walls of Kyrah's cubicle are covered with paper calendars, one for each member of Helen's immediate family. Next week is Helen's sister's birthday. Her brother Phil is in Albuquerque at an IT conference. Helen's mother has a doctor's appointment at the end of the month.

"The *landing sequence*. They're in fucking *Utah*." He still cannot see Mireille. Her voice is muffled. Luke looks down at the list on his knee. He has a bad feeling about what might be coming next. He needs Mireille to not make this difficult, because there isn't any way to make it easier and he's out of practice for confrontations with people who aren't professionally obligated to keep it together.

The screen tilts and Mireille moves partially back into frame. The green fabric is a dress. He is looking at her hips now, and waist. The screen jerks again and it's Mireille's face. She's holding a huge blade to her throat.

"I want to speak to my mother. I want to tell her the truth."

Luke laughs before he can do anything else, feels his face go instantly hot, chokes, notes clinically: tachycardia and some sort of penile reflex, and leans forward, knocking the list off his knee.

"Okay. Mireille. Okay, I want you to listen—"

"Oh, relax." Mireille flourishes the blade in front of her face. "It's a bread knife. You think I would slit my throat with a bread knife?"

They blink at each other for a few seconds. *Jesus*, Luke thinks.

Mireille sniffs, swipes at the makeup under her eyes. Shakes her head. She's not crazy, Luke thinks. She's ahead of him, somehow, she knows what he's trying to do, what's expected of her, and is going big before he forces her to be small, and reasonable.

"Right," he says. "Right."

"What happened to Kyrah again?" Another shift now: a demonstration of calm.

"She's having root canal surgery. I'm sorry you have to—I mean, we did want to reach out to you as quickly as possible, but I know Kyrah wanted to be able to speak to you herself."

"No, poor Kyrah." Mireille takes a breath. "Quick" doesn't begin to cover Mireille. This is her talent, of course. Professionally compelling, watchable, interesting. But Luke had assumed—without thinking about it too much—that Mireille wasn't a very *good* actress. But why shouldn't she be? Why shouldn't she be the astronaut of actresses?

"You know," Mireille says, "before, it's been my mom that picks who the Kyrah person is. I mean, at NASA, the family always has a person, but my mom always picked one of her male colleagues. I always thought that was weird, that she didn't pick another woman. Astronauts are very competitive, so maybe she didn't want us—my father and me—to see that another female astronaut was better than her at nurturing-type things. Mostly the family person just ends up driving people around at launches, although you know what happened with my uncle Phil, right? You're on the psych team, so probably you know everything about us?"

There's nothing on Luke's piece of paper—now on the floor—that lets him know how much he is officially supposed to know.

"Everything here is treated with the strictest confidentiality," Luke says, wondering if he could manage to message in with Ransom without Mireille noticing, and get a little advice here. But Ransom is with Boone, figuring out, probably, what to say to the crew. The astronauts, focused as they are on the landing sim, are still aware of the lunar launch that was meant to happen, will be expecting to get news in one of today's uplinks.

"Well, my uncle Phil tried to kill himself when my mom was on the space station." Mireille is not looking at Luke, and her voice is controlled, thoughtful. "He overdosed. My mom didn't know until she got back. It was my grandmother's decision not to tell her, and there was this sort of family conference—my father and I weren't involved, I only learned about it later—about how to keep my mom's liaison at the time from knowing, or anyone at NASA. And apparently when Phil found out that they didn't tell her, he was completely pissed. He was like, 'I almost died but nobody wanted to disturb Helen.' He didn't speak to my mom for a couple of years. He still doesn't, much. But it wasn't her fault. She always wants to be informed of any family illness or emergency." Mireille pauses, clears her throat. "That's actually even harder to deal with than the idea that she wouldn't want to know. Think about it: if I die, my mom wants to know about it." She looks directly at Luke, through the ruins of her makeup. "If I die, if I'm lying in a hospital having just overdosed, if I get raped, if my life hangs in the balance, my mom wants to know. Which means that she knows it won't impair her ability to do her job. It won't trip her up. She won't miss a fucking beat."

Mireille stares at Luke, daring him to soothe her, triumphant in the powers of her own delivery—resentful, greedy, and not a fool. At the moment, he cannot think of a single thing to say that would satisfy her, make her feel better, make her *be* better. After seven months of watching astronauts, it is literally stunning to watch someone fall to disorganized pieces, and then deliberately present rage and resentment, hand it to him on a silver platter, fully cooked, like it's a gift.

He watches Mireille look smug, then ashamed, then sad. You can see everything on her face, everything.

"You don't need to say it." Mireille scrubs punitively at her face. "I know she's a much better person than me, in pretty much every way you can measure. And that's why I'm constantly trying to prove that she isn't. I should just be proud. I'm proud too, you know. It's all very stupid. God, those poor Chinese."

Mireille turns her head, occluding his view of her eyes, and effectively drawing down the curtain. In profile, she resembles her mother more strongly.

HELEN

For thousands of years we have wondered about this red disk in the sky, and today, humans take our first steps on the planet Mars. That is what Helen is going to say. She repeats the line in her head. She didn't write it.

Thousands of years was imprecise, the line would need work.

It was good to mention the color. Across cultures, it was the redness of the thing that had impressed. Ancient Egyptians named it Horus of the Horizon and the Red One, and the Babylonians said it was the Star of Death and called it Nergal, after their deity of fire. In Hebrew it was Ma'adim: one who blushes. Some variation of Fire Star for the Chinese, the Koreans, the Japanese.

The word *wonder* was also good. It wasn't only the color that suggested war to the ancients—it was the strange motion of Mars and the other visible disks that did not behave like the stars, seemingly fixed in the firmament, but advanced and retreated and advanced again along their paths. These disks were given the name *planets*, meaning *wanderers*.

And so, yes, for thousands of years we have wondered about this red disk in the sky, and today, humans take our first steps on the planet Mars.

THEY HAVE ARRIVED.

They can see nothing.

Yoshi is working on restoring the feeds from their external cameras, but just now they have no view. They are three people strapped down inside a tuna can. But otherwise, they are very good: less than a hundred yards east of the landing site, not a bull's-eye but, considering the distance between thrower and dartboard, a huge success.

Their descent to the Red Planet had not been without a few thrills. They hadn't been treated to This Is Extremely Bad, but they hadn't been allowed Best-Case Scenario either, and their entirely automated craft had required manual overrides. In the end, they'd gotten one hell of a yo-yo experience that went by the name Hypersonic Inflatable Aerodynamic Decelerator, a lot of noise, the great sharpening of focus that the feeling of compression gave you, and then, with an almost comical clunk, they were down. Helen cannot touch her face yet since she's still helmeted, but would like to, would like the reassurance that she still has a face.

It had been sweet, in their first communications, to hear a wild cheering going on in Mission Control. It had been the thing that made Helen and Yoshi and Sergei cheer. Sometimes it took other people going bananas to make you feel something, because you were locked into the groove of hyperalertness and it was all about the next thing, and tumultuous joy wasn't on the list. There was a practical component to not scheduling exultation. Even when they Gofer, Mission Control will want to hear "Prime, *Primitus* is on the surface, landing site is secure, all systems are nominal," and not sounds that could quite easily be misinterpreted as death throes. Whatever portion of the world that will be watching humans land on Mars (and one hopes for at least Super Bowl or Eurovision Grand Final numbers) will need Mission Control for experiencing the landing in emotionally representative terms because they—Helen and Sergei and Yoshi—will be just three calm voices inside spacesuits, confirming systems. Mission Control will be a room full of human beings who have been visibly thumb-bite-y and arm-fold-y and brow-knitted, pale, sweaty, pacing, hollow-eyed. They will say things into a camera like, "This is probably the most significant moment of our entire species" and "Everything I have ever worked for in my life is about this moment right here." The tension will be almost unbearable. And then, imagine. Imagine the cheers and the turning to one another, hugging, tears on faces, thumping one another on the back, or just leaning back exhausted in their chairs, covering their faces with their hands. Sometimes it's seeing how much other people care that makes you care. Often, it is that.

It was generous of Mission Control to cheer for them, since no dreams had been achieved yet, and the cheerers have a seven-month-long case of jetlag.

Helen begins to relay a message of gratitude back to Mission Control, but is interrupted by an explosive sound, a deep and very loud cracking boom. Outside their craft, impossible to tell from which direction or how close, but they all look up. Helen discovers that when you are strapped into a seat and cannot move, or run, or see very much, and you think something might be about to fall on your head, your body does a funny accordion bellows–type thing. Shrinking in fear and expanding in defense. Also, she had instinctively tried to stretch out both arms toward Yoshi and Sergei, as if they were passengers in her car.

Nothing falls on their heads.

Helen reports the event to Prime, but Prime can give them no explanation. "Maybe we landed on the Wicked Witch of the West," Helen messages, though the time delays make jokes a little awkward. All their systems are still nominal. It might have been a Prime employee just outside their module, accidentally tipping over a ladder into a metal trash can, the sound magnified, or some ridiculous situation. Helen pictures a sheepish young man in a Prime hoodie, cringing.

It is one thirty in the afternoon, Mars time. Sol one.

Helen is still thinking through possibilities for the cracking noise, when they receive an audio message from Boone Cross. He tells them that, during the *Primitus* Entry-Descent-Landing stage, *Red Dawn II* (the real one) landed successfully.

It was perhaps this that Mission Control had been cheering for. Prime had maybe just played them a recording.

If it is true, if *Red Dawn II* is on Mars, then Helen and her crew just moved one giant leap closer to the moment when it won't be Utah outside their nonexistent window. The barriers to Mars are falling and soon there will be no more reasons for *why not*. Mars is waiting. Mars is waiting for them. For her.

Helen is used to telling herself that she will believe she is going to Mars when she is actually going to Mars, and not before. She repeats this to herself now.

But she feels good. This news will lend a vitality and a pleasing consequence to the simulations. Even though this would only be thirty days, and not the full year and a half of Gofer, they'd still get to work with wonderful things. The M-PRIME plant converting carbon dioxide from the atmosphere into oxygen. The H2-PRIME plant providing farm-to-table Martian water. *Red Dawns* I and *II*, the nuclear reactors of *Red Dawns I* and *II*, making propellant. Containers for the greenhouse assembly. Supply pods. Prime's Rovers, including the one they brought with them in their own lower stage in case they missed their landing site. She will feel something real under her hands, something new. Everything will need to be checked, inventoried, rechecked, tested. This is why she—they—were chosen. Other types of scientists would spend the entire trip frustrated at the limited opportunities that size, weight, and time gave for doing science. Prime had sent diversely educated engineers because whatever else was going to happen in space, things were going to break. Often.

Now that Helen is so close to relief, she allows herself to acknowledge how much need she has. Helen notes that certain conditions—seven months of confinement, for instance—can, when lifted, put you in a state that might be characterized as aggressive. Her impulse, right now, is not to get out and explore, but to get out and conquer. With machines and her bare (well, pressure-gloved) hands. This impulse is probably something Prime should know about, for future crews. Though finding a way to express it without sounding like a scurvy-crazed Christopher Columbus might be challenging. It will probably pass, anyway, the feeling.

Boone Cross's voice continues—

"I am very sorry to have to tell you that *Weilai 3* suffered a catastrophic failure during its launch sequence. A fire broke out in the crew cockpit, and the crew lost their lives. This event occurred eighty seconds after launch. CNSA is not releasing details at this time, though there's been some suggestion that the fire was caused by an electrical short circuit. This event occurred just as you were preparing for EDL stage. The decision was made to follow the contingency protocol regarding the relay of Earth events of this nature."

There is a pause and then Cross's voice continues, toneless now, a press conference voice.

"Throughout the history of our exploration of space, we have had to bear the burden of risk. As we strive to minimize this risk in every conceivable way, we must always accept the possibility of the *in*conceivable. This acceptance in no way lessens our sadness. Prime Space reaches a hand out to our brothers and sisters at CNSA, and shares the burden of loss with them."

Helen's first thought is that this news is a simulation. Prime wants to know how the crew will react and handle the news of a major catastrophe.

Wind. Helen can hear the faintest whisper of wind. So faint that it's more sensed than heard. But that's not right. You wouldn't hear Martian wind in the thin atmosphere of the planet, not from inside *Primitus*.

The Cross recording is followed now by a message from Dr. Ransom in Life Sciences, who tells them that while Prime followed the protocol about communication during critical phases with the crew, her team had immediately reached out to the astronauts' family members.

This lets Helen know that the disaster on *Weilai 3*, at least, is real. Prime can push them to the brink in a variety of ways, but they are not allowed to invent super-scenarios involving family members. Prime can't run a sim in which Meeps dies, or Los Angeles is wiped out by earthquake. They cannot tell Helen that her daughter was "reached out to" if she wasn't.

"There are no good moments to relay such tragic news," Dr. Ransom's voice continues. "And although we are still in a critical stage of operations, we didn't want to keep you in the dark any longer than we had to. I'm sure you will be anxious for details on *Weilai 3*, but we're learning things very slowly. There's enormous support for the Chinese coming from all over the world. We're sure you will want to be a part of that. If there is a statement you would like to make as a crew, we will be happy to relay that for you. If there are individual messages you would like to pass on to family members or friends or colleagues, we can do that too. Either now, or in further drops. Over."

Everyone receives the news of catastrophe in their own way. The Chinese are already beyond their tears. It was always like that, with the dead.

"Terrible," Sergei says. This is their crew-only link, although of course it's not just them listening to it. "At first," he says, "I thought it was not real. I thought it was simulation."

"I did as well," Yoshi says. "It's perhaps too awful to believe."

"This is a hard moment," Helen says. She is commander; she must direct her crew. "This is rough. Perhaps we should take a moment of silence? For the crew of *Weilai 3*, for their families, for everyone at CNSA?"

As Helen says this, she cannot escape the idea of various members of the Prime staff being quite close. Not just in rooms of the Space Center campus, but standing right outside the walls of their craft, looking and listening. There is something grotesque about taking a moment of respectful silence for astronauts who have died while rocketing to space while Helen and her crew sit inside a simulator pretending to be heroes. Tragedy is always grotesque.

They cannot bow their heads, because of their helmets. Helen closes her eyes.

She has a system already in place for things like this. She takes a moment to let her consciousness comprehend the event—repeating to herself the sentence Weilai 3 *suffered a catastrophic failure, killing the entire crew: Yu Chen, Meifeng Guo, He Liu, and Mingli Sheng*. As she says the names, she pictures the faces. *These people here*, she instructs herself, *are people who were once alive, and now they are dead*. She finds she *can* take it in. The knowledge, the sadness, is another layer to the atmosphere of her own particular planet, already thickly coated. This, she lives with.

The next thing she would normally do is ask herself what steps she could take: was there an action that might alleviate suffering the event had caused, such as a donation of time or money? Was there a public or private statement she could make that would be meaningful? Once that was accomplished, it was mostly a matter of being aware of how the event might have affected others, being quick to spot and react to these affects.

Keep busy: such a commonplace piece of advice, but the best one. Death, pain, loss, grief. These were as fundamental to life as the elements on the periodic table. You didn't ask, "Why, God, why?" about the periodic table. Sometimes a new element got discovered. You added it. You got on with it.

She must think about her crew. It was now *her* crew. What would her crew need? The natural response in these situations was to want information. Dr. Ransom had said that details were slow to come, so presumably everyone was starved of access in that way, but her crew might feel their isolation very strongly. Their isolation is real.

For as long as she'd been an astronaut she'd heard that psychologists were concerned that losing sight of the Earth might cause some kind of ultra-homesickness, even breakdown. Helen had never thought this was likely. Watching Earth "recede" had been interesting, not devastating. Crew cohesion had been maintained without conflict. Helen would not characterize any of her states of mind as depression. It had been a nuisance that she had been repeatedly plagued by bouts of anxiety and strange memories during the voyage out, like contracting a persistent case of eczema or blepharospasm, but it wasn't significant; it had not affected her work. Helen was conscientious about using the Reaction Self-Tests, and she remained in top form. The only one inconvenienced by her mood was herself, and she could manage herself. In a way it was good that her "trouble" had occurred so early in the mission. Prime was using a mission-concurrent psychological state baseline. The face and voice sensors were less likely to be tipped off to changes in her demeanor since her demeanor had been consistently a little off since day twenty. And she'd prepared. Helen looked forward to the time when she could tell Meeps that those questions Helen had asked her, and Meeps's answers, had foiled technology.

"You have to smile with your eyes. If you have a smile on your face while you're talking, whatever you are saying will sound warm and happy, even if the listener can't see your face. Posture is always a dead giveaway—the body doesn't lie. I like to imagine my whole face lifting up by an inch. Crossed arms looks defensive, one hand on a hip looks confident. Mom, sometimes you do kind of a singsong cheery voice, and that might get on people's nerves."

As for the rest, well, Helen could read data too. For seven months, she'd not wavered significantly in levels of neuroticism, extraversion, openness to experience, agreeableness, or conscientiousness. She'd not shown signs of asthenia, no weakness of nervous system, no blood pressure instability. She'd been worried about sleep, but she'd slept just fine: averaging 6.44 hours per night. She'd looked forward to sleeping, in a funny way that was new to her. Almost as if she might get a message or clue about this persistent sensation of having missed something important, but no.

A terrible thing has happened.

It was a commonplace: We are made of star stuff, and to star stuff we will return. That the Chinese astronauts *will* go to space, perhaps even the Moon, is a nice way to think about it. Helen returns to absorbing the news of the tragedy.

She is prepared for tragedy, equipped. Tragedy is an old companion, you might say, from her youth. Not quite an imaginary friend, but not fully visible either. Borderless. Her daughter thought she shut down in these moments, but it wasn't that. It was that you had to be so careful with grief. Grief sought connections: it stacked, or swarmed. It was only the first time you experienced sorrow that it stood alone, with nothing attached to it.

Her father hadn't died on his way to the moon. He'd slipped and hit his head in a national chain grocery store. At first it was only that: *your father had an accident.* Her nine-year-old imagination worked easily upon the idea of a father who was hurt but would get better; this seemed reasonable, and in proportion to the severity of the accident. Her father had slipped, he hadn't been in a car or plane crash or shot by criminals. Helen had been instructed to hope and pray. She did so, in much the same way that she loaded the dishwasher when she was told to: uncritically and without the employment of metaphysics. There were things to appreciate about the situation. All the grandparents came, and aunts and uncles. Visits from people they knew from church, more desserts and movies and games and even gifts. Grandpa McInnery showed her how she could look at the sun through shade #14 welder's glass and told her that if we could look at the sun in space, it would be white, not yellow. Grandpa McInnery let her help him rewire a broken lamp in the TV room. "You're a Little Miss Fix It," he said. She remembers that moment very well. The next part was blurry. They'd been brought to the hospital. Their father was not on mechanical life support, he was breathing on his own. He had a feeding tube. Helen was confused by the phrase a doctor used: "awake but not aware." Grandma McInnery tried to amend this to "sleeping" and muddled things further. Helen knew what "traumatic" meant. She began to worry, and developed a nervous habit of touching the back of her head that would persist for the rest of the year and went unnoticed by her family.

Her father did not get better. Sides were taken, but not fully explained. Her father's family did not approve of things her mother was doing, and went outside a lot to talk about it. When they came back in, Helen would go collect their cigarette butts in a piece of tissue paper and bury it in the trash. Other people, her mother, her mother's parents, family friends all had God, and by extension, specific language for unfair misery, on their side. God had plans and tests and he believed that you could pass them. He loved and did not make mistakes. All these people said her mother was brave.

Her father's state was categorized as persistent vegetative. The doctors could not say "he will die." They said other things. Physiologic futility meant there were no operations, or drugs that would make her father get better. Qualitative futility meant that they weren't entirely certain that something else might happen. People were something more than meat, but what else they were was difficult to measure and that made it difficult to know when it was okay to kill them. That was always clear. If they stopped feeding their father, they would kill him. They had the responsibility. Helen learned later on that her father had not been expected to survive that year: pneumonia, infection, organ failure were typical in cases like his. He did survive, but his vegetative state was moved from persistent to permanent.

You could kill a person's dream, but what if the dream was a person? Could you kill that? Anyway, they hadn't.

Her father's family left and was heard from, by mail, only at Christmas and on birthdays. Helen's McInnery grandparents moved to town to be closer to their daughter and help with the grandchildren. Grandpa McInnery was thought to be especially of benefit to Phil, who would require a male figure. Phil preferred his male figures to be wizards or elves or dwarves, so Helen had Grandpa McInnery nearly all to herself. "Helen's the son Dad never had," Helen's mother and sisters told each other, although Helen knew that Grandpa especially liked it that she was a girl. "You'll leave all the boys in the dust," he told her. Helen didn't want to leave people behind, but it was preferable to being left behind herself.

At first her father's face still looked like her father. It didn't look empty, like a person wasn't inside him. Gradually it looked empty, but maybe because they stopped feeling so much when they looked at it. Maybe they were the ones who became empty.

Sergei and Yoshi stir. They have concluded their moment of silence. Helen is appalled at herself, at having routed the death of Chinese taikonauts to her father. That's not the right way to think about it. It's another reason why you had to be so careful with grief. It was like an impact crater, its surface always larger than the thing that created it.

HELEN

The instinct to find comparisons is strong. The Martian sky looks a little like the pink and yellow smog and marine layer haze of Los Angeles in June. The feel of her boots on the Martian regolith reminds her of the arid crunchiness of her boots on the polar desert of Devon Island. This stretch of Martian plain resembles certain barren sections of the Atacama Desert in South America. The color of those distant Martian outcroppings reminds her of the Easter egg Meeps insisted on dipping in every single one of the dyes: a muddy mixture of brown and gray and purple and orange.

It is their third Martian dawn.

Their landing site had been chosen for safety, not for exciting photo ops. It was the Martian equivalent of aliens coming to Earth and landing in a dusty field in Oklahoma. Elsewhere on Mars there are the volcanoes. The colossal canyon system of Valles Marineris. Dunes, rabens, rifts, clasts, yardangs, sulci, fossae, recurring slope linnae. Here, there are small loose rocks and slightly larger rocks, and rocks in the distance. And dust. It is a good place to land a spacecraft, but you don't need the seven daily minutes on their schedule to take it all in. Presumably, this will be different when they Gofer. Even a featureless plain will be a marvelous thing when it's the first time a human has stood on another planet and looked at one, in real time, with their own eyes. Surely, it will be marvelous.

They'd wanted, from the beginning, an awful lot from a cold little carbon dioxide–filled planet with not enough atmospheric pressure to fly a kite and only the puny remnants of a magnetic field. They wanted nothing less than life from this place: evidence of it in the past, and the promise of a place to put it in the future. So many questions they have for this planet. So much work to be done. There will not be enough time in the sol. Even when they Gofer and have five hundred and fifty sols, there will not be enough time.

Helen is responsible for putting these seven minutes on the itinerary. "For the purposes of Eidolon, the time will give us a chance to enter fully into, and habituate ourselves to, the simulation," she had written. "It might also serve as a daily meditation, which may have a positive effect on mood and performance."

There *were* adjustments to be made. A virtual environment in the wild is not the same as one conducted in the lab. Helen is conscious of a life under the sim, aware that she is moving across a real landscape whose perimeters and threats are not known, or stable. It is to be imagined that Prime is taking care of certain possible external threats, which would not exist on Mars but do in a desert in Utah. Animals, for instance. A bobcat landing on her back during an early morning EVA would definitely spoil the illusion. Also, all their tools and instruments are made from light materials: sixty-two percent less than their normal weight. And Prime has appreciated the need to instill a "reason" for the fact that their own bodies could not enjoy some nicely enhanced jumping and leaping: their boots are "weighted."

The Martian sims were spectacular, of course, enhancing (and obscuring) the section of Utah they were actually walking around, although also slightly altering the appearance of whichever of your crewmates was with you, and such portions of your own spacesuit that you could see. Helen had the sense, for the first few minutes of an EVA, of playing herself in a video game. But then she got used to it, and when she returned to *Primitus* it was her unaltered self that looked a little fake.

She is conscious that she is using some of her scheduled seven minutes of feelings to remind herself not to have too many feelings. To not think about how a Helen two thousand years ago would have looked at a distant tiny dot in the firmament and not known the first thing about it. To not think of all the hundreds of Helens that had been born and died, not knowing, until we reached a Helen—her!— who would *stand* on that tiny dot. To not think about all the people who had taken a problem as enormous as putting humans on another planet and broken that down into manageable portions and solved it. To not become lost in the observation of a planet so wondrously—so almost heartbreakingly—close to their own, and yet entirely alien. It's too soon to think all this.

"I don't have a sensation of threat or hostility." This is Yoshi's voice, in her ear, pleasantly brain adjacent. All three crewmembers cannot be on EVA at once: someone must always remain in *Primitus* Hab, with RoMeO as backup, for safety. Right now, Sergei is observing Helen and Yoshi via camera from inside the Hab.

"Okay, but don't take off your helmet," Helen jokes. It's true, there's only so much fear you can talk yourself into. The one moment of true alarm so far on Mars had been that loud cracking noise they'd heard after landing, which they'd never discovered the source of. (Perhaps it really *had* been a Prime employee falling off a ladder. It might also have been lightning.)

"Spectacular sky," Helen says, looking up. She is aware that in pointing this out her voice has taken on the mechanical enthusiasm of a mother trying to entertain a child with some everyday fact: "Look! There are three apples and they are *red*! Oh! That man has on a *hat*!"

Yoshi points to what, on Earth, would be Venus. A very tiny morning "star" on the horizon.

It is Earth.

Ah. So it will not only be Mars that they will discover for themselves, when they come here. It will be a discovery of *distance*. An understanding of what the word *far* can mean.

"Hey there." It is Sergei now, speaking from the Hab in a terrible cowboy-Western accent. "You two look like you're not from around these parts."

They laugh. There are still four minutes left of their morning meditation. In a few sols, she will suggest that they are now adjusted to the sim and have adequate time to reflect on the mission at other points in their schedule, and so they can scrub this exercise. It is a little confusing, maybe.

The astronauts fall silent. It is a good sim. It has depth, it has texture; it feels real. But Helen hopes that the real Mars will surprise them. It's not impossible. The history of humans looking at Mars is the history of getting it wrong first. Prime, she hopes, has gotten this sim just a little bit wrong.

The anxiety that had plagued her since the beginning of Eidolon—the sense that she had missed something important—has not evaporated. If anything, the sensation has only increased. She's missing something now on Mars. Looking for something.

"I'm trying to think of right soundtrack for Mars," Sergei says.

"Not bells," Yoshi says.

"No."

"How interesting." Yoshi again. "One hears certain music described as 'otherworldly,' but when you are on the otherworld, nothing is sufficiently strange."

What will they talk about when this is no longer a simulation? Will they look at Mars and say, "Yep, just like the sim"? If it looks like this, they will never be able to say, "I've never seen anything like this." She should not feel too much now, so she can feel more, later.

YOSHI

"Hello, Earthlings." Prime likes the videos the crew practices making for the general public to be a little playful. The science must be made accessible to a general audience, and shown to be interesting and exciting. Additionally, the recordings must have a personal tone.

"As you can see"—Yoshi opens his arms—"I'm in the lower level of *Primitus*. At this moment, upstairs in the Hab, Sergei is working a problem on his spacesuit gloves and Commander Helen is arranging the timetable for sol-morrow. I'm down here customizing our Dust Filtration System so that it can function even more effectively!"

Yoshi is pleased with his work. The DFS has not, in truth, been functioning effectively. They've been tracking dust all over the Hab.

"As you've seen," Yoshi says into the camera, "our spacesuits can be docked to the exterior lower level of *Primitus*. Keeping the suits outside means we can crawl in and out of them right here from the EVA prep room. That leaves all the Martian dust—what we call *fines*—out on the planet, where it belongs, and not in here, where it can be destructive to equipment and our lungs."

The word *fines* is not very good. Yoshi would like to substitute with the word *brume*. The dust surrounds one like a mist or fog, only not damp, of course. A dry brume.

It is cold in the lower level of the Hab and, to conserve energy, dimly lit. He is physically very tired. The first week of Mars has been wonderfully demanding and they are all sore and fatigued. The tools and instruments they use during EVAs have been adjusted to mimic the way they would feel on Mars, but physics is physics and a large object is a large object. Also, working in compression jumpsuits, spacesuits, weighted boots, and pressurized gloves is demanding in ways his *Primitus* exercise routine could not fully anticipate. They are forced to move slowly on the surface.

"Now, as you saw"—Yoshi smiles at the screen—"we can also egress from *Primitus* by using one of the two hatches on either side of this EVA prep room. This is useful for when we need to take out or bring in equipment. The only trouble is, anything we bring in from Mars, including ourselves, will be covered with those fines."

The dust is on his tongue. In his ears. No penetralia is safe from it. He has found Martian brume on his scrotum.

Yoshi moves through the EVA room, crisscrossed now by his system of dangling hoses. "The dust filtration system does a pretty good job of cleaning us and our equipment," he says. "But it's been getting quite the workout, and we like to be very thorough in our cleaning." Yoshi holds up a nozzle end. "This functions just like a vacuum cleaner back home." He demonstrates on his arm.

The fines are slightly more reddish than you would expect from Utah, and have an iron smell. A virtually-environment-obscured

Prime employee must be standing by the airlock with some kind of bellows, or following them around silently. Perhaps Prime is delivering the ersatz fines by drone.

"It is a little like getting a massage," Yoshi says, running the nozzle over his head. He and Sergei had both buzzed their hair down to their scalps yester-sol. "As you can see, this works well with my new haircut!"

"SUCCESS?" HELEN ASKS when Yoshi returns to the upper tier and the Science/Lab wedge, where his crewmates are finishing the sol's tasks. Yoshi acknowledges that the problem has been sufficiently worked.

"You are the Michelangelo of duct tape," Helen says. "I'm sure it's gorgeous."

Yoshi seats himself at the communal table and reads through his next job. Sol-morrow, Yoshi will be recording an "Astronomy from Mars" video. Prime has already sent a prepared script, but he will take thirty minutes in his evening schedule to personalize and improve upon this.

The romantic in Yoshi has always appreciated the fact that Mars has no visible North Star. It points not at Polaris, as Earth does, but at a position in the sky that aligns neither with Deneb in Cygnus, nor Alderamin in Cepheus, but at some midway point too dim to have a name. You could say that the planet named for the God of War points at darkness.

Yoshi cannot conduct his lecture while actually looking up into a Martian night. It was—will be—too cold on Mars at night for the astronauts to be safely out of the Hab or Rover. They have been allowed to stay on an EVA only long enough to see a blue Martian sunset, the dust of the planet scattering the light just around the star. It had been the first sight that had given him a genuine taste of how thrilling it all might be.

YOSHI TELLS HIMSELF that the astronomy lecture is a good assignment. The more opportunities he has to demonstrate to Prime that he is a good communicator and spokesperson, that he has charisma and likability, the better. Sergei, and especially Helen, have had more time and occasion to build public platforms and brands.

The view of the stars on Mars is similar to what the stars look like to a North American Earth dweller, although their movements appear different. It's really the moons of Mars that are the most unusual, and the focus of his lecture. Phobos and Deimos. Fear and Terror.

From the other end of the table, Sergei, who is tinkering with a glove, makes one of his expressions of annoyance. "Chuh," he says. "This is fucked." Prime has been putting Sergei through a number of suit and monitor malfunction simulations.

Yoshi judges the temperature of Sergei's "This is fucked" to be mild, and that Sergei does not expect any response from them, or an offer of assistance. Annoyance and adversity are their entertainment on Mars; the servicing, fixing, and adjustments of their own equipment have comprised most of their labors. In a few days, Sergei and Helen will undertake the main exploratory event of their Mars stay: the Arsia Mons sortie. Yoshi will remain behind in the Hab and begin processing the samples collected from the drilling site. This is a wise division of labor, considering skill sets, and Yoshi will make a later Rover expedition with Sergei, to deploy the drones. He will get his chance to explore. And really, he was very content to be in a situation like this one: snug in the Hab with Helen and Sergei, each of them working.

Yoshi does not ask for much, he merely wants to be where he should be, where he belongs, which is something you can know by orienting yourself to what is around you, and making yourself a part of it.

Yoshi reads through another paragraph of the Prime script:

A thing to consider: we are used to thinking of planets and moons as quite perfect spheres, but they are not. Our beautiful Earth is not a marble, it's an oblate spheroid, bulging out around the equator and squashed a little flat at the poles. Mars is quite bulge-y around its middle. The great Tharsis ridge near the equator exaggerates this. Tiny and low Phobos and Deimos orbit very near the plane of the equator, and a Martian who has always lived in the upper north or lower south of the planet would never see the moons!

Yoshi looks at Helen, working across the table from him on her own screen, almost certainly designing tomorrow's schedule. It is an aesthetic pleasure to look at Helen's timetables.

Difficult to describe Helen, even after seven months. *More* difficult after seven months. Yoshi has never spent so many consecutive days in the presence of a woman. Well, his mother, during his childhood, but that was different. Yoshi has been married for eight years, but it is unusual for them to be in the same place for two or three months without some interruption.

Helen straightens her shoulders and sits back, an indication that it is probably okay to interrupt her.

"Helen, was this script written for you?" Yoshi asks. "I have just read this word: *bulge-y*."

"It was," Helen says. "But I've noticed that talking about satellites brings out the poet in you and I thought you'd give it more flair. Feel free to make the text your own. How about instead of *bulge-y*, you say . . ." She pauses and then, with mock seriousness and an imitation of Yoshi's British-inflected accent, "Excessively protuberant."

"Ha. Yes. Good," Sergei says.

"Excessively protuberant." Yoshi pretends to type this in and then mimics his own accent. "Right-o. Jolly good. Tickety-boo."

Helen flexes and closes her hands, rolls her shoulders. "Okay. We should get the last uplink from Ground in ten minutes, but I don't anticipate any changes. Most of tomorrow is about prepping *Rover I* for Arsia Mons."

"Ah, we decided about 'tomorrow,' then?" Yoshi asks.

"Lots of people like 'sol-morrow' and there's a strong advocacy for 'nextersol.'" Helen smiles. "But nobody thinks that 'tosol' is going to catch on."

"Unless you speak English," Sergei points out, "all those options will sound equally foreign."

"MarsNOW could be the opportunity," Yoshi says, "to correct some language mistakes. We could stop using 'sunset' and 'sunrise,' and substitute words that indicate the planet's revolution. It is humans that have phases, not the moon."

"You know"—Helen tilts her head—"I'm not sure I ever learned the Japanese for 'Phobos' and 'Deimos.'"

"'Fobosu' and 'Deimosu.'"

"Oh. Right."

"We could use MarsNOW to get the United States on metric system," says Sergei. "That would be a big step."

"No kidding," says Helen. "I like that the 'Astronomy on Mars' script has us calling our moon by the name Luna. That's less Earth-centric. We're not the only ones with a moon."

There is a moment when they all try to think of something more to say, and then the moment passes.

Helen breaks open a chocolate bar. All of them are experiencing a craving for sweet things. They are burning more calories, but

Sergei has posited that it might also have something to do with the dust. Everyone takes a square.

"We have enough for s'mores on the camping trip? It's a long time in the car," Sergei jokes.

Yoshi tells himself that it will be nice to have the Hab to himself for a while. He had been quite a solitary child—his parents were busy and active. He remembers his mother, writing out the family schedule in the morning. Sometimes it was a dilemma: "Where will Yoshihiro be? Yoshi needs somewhere to be." And there had been the moves: from Japan to Berlin, then London, then back to Japan. His own later peripatetic career as an astronaut. Oh, he was very good at being alone.

"Did you both see the request for more pictures of each other? Ach. Shoot." Helen, having licked the chocolate off her finger, has apparently gotten dust on her tongue as well. She makes a gargoyle face, wrinkling her nose and scraping her tongue with her teeth. They are less conscious of maintaining a certain decorum on Mars. Perhaps it is because they are all physically dirtier, perhaps because this is the least physically confined they will be during Eidolon and they are making the most of it.

"I hope they destroy all these videos and photos," Sergei says. "Or there will be conspiracy theory. Like the moon landing deniers."

"The thing they most liked was the Christmas song." Helen breaks another piece of chocolate off the bar using a new technique: touching only the wrapping. She hands the piece to Sergei. "I don't know if we can repeat that. Maybe they should hold on to it, just in case."

"True." Sergei chomps on his chocolate. "But come on. It is Mars. It should be enough. We don't have to do musical about it."

Yoshi watches as Helen breaks a piece of chocolate off for him.

"I went to Mars," Yoshi says, "because I wished to live deliberately, to front only the essential facts of life, and see if I could not learn what it had to teach, and not, when I came to die, discover that I had not lived. I did not wish to live what was not life, living is so dear, nor did I wish to practice resignation, unless it was quite necessary. I wanted to live deep and suck out all the marrow of life, to live so sturdily and Spartan-like as to put to rout all that was not life, to cut a broad swath and shave close, to drive life into a corner, and reduce it to its lowest terms."

"Holy crap, Yoshi," Sergei says.

Helen hands Yoshi his chocolate. "I learned that in school," she says. "Henry David Thoreau. Speaking about Walden Pond, not Mars. But that's great, Yoshi. Just excellent." Helen does not sound totally pleased.

Their screens ping. It is Prime's last uplink of the sol. These do not include any messages from family and friends, or Earth news, but are generally a confirmation of the latest telemetry. This one includes a video someone at Prime has put together from images and film of week one. They move to the Science/Lab wedge to watch on the largest screen.

A song plays, and their week of slow, deliberate, meticulous, and technical labor unfolds like a kind of dream ballet. Here are Helen and Yoshi, suiting up for the first EVA. Now, the opening of the hatch. Each of their boot prints in the rusty regolith. Helen and Sergei, making adjustments to the solar array, their movements deft and harmonious. Sergei, in slow motion, removing his helmet in the EVA prep room, and smiling. Yoshi can remember feeling tired at the end of yester-sol as he ate noodles, but had not imagined himself looking so wearily heroic while he did so. Helen bending over and trying to shake the fines from her hair, then straightening up and making a rueful face. She is magnificent.

The crew plays the video through a second time, entranced by how their experience appears.

Mars looks so beautiful.

They look so brave.

SERGEI

Man is an explorer, but always he has needed to seek shelter from the environment and predators, and in his caves he found the rest to reflect, tell stories, and make paintings on the walls.

They are looking for a good cave.

This is a man's job. Well, technically it will first be a robot's job to enter a cave. The thought of introducing a human to subsurface Mars makes the collective Office of Planetary Protection throw up with anxiety, and while a robot from Earth is not a perfectly clean thing, it is judged to be cleaner than a man. Once the robot confirms that there is no life to destroy in the cave, man can follow.

First, they must get the robot to the cave, and this is a man's job because a robot is slow and can't make decisions on the spot. Also it is not a simple thing, to instruct a robot to spelunk with style.

The Rover drives itself, although one of them must remain in the front of the cab, ready to manually override the automation if necessary. Sergei amuses himself by imagining how Prime is conducting this particular sim. They cannot drive all over the San Rafael Swell, but it feels like the Rover is going the right distance. It is possible that Prime is driving them in circles. He has a very good internal compass. Nothing in his body believes they are driving in a circle.

Who knows? Sergei sometimes wonders if the *muove* of the *eppur si muove* was Prime shipping them to Antarctica. He does not know how Prime is getting it to feel so cold. He is feeling the cold more because various suit malfunctions have caused the heaters in his gloves and boots to fail at different times, and in those situations his fingers and toes went numb. At first he was proud that Prime was making this extra effort to give him a convincing Mars experience, it spoke to their respect for his skepticism. (Unless it spoke to his vulnerability to irritation.) Anyway, now he has decided to make a conscious effort to accept what is put before him. Both Helen and Yoshi are better pretenders than he is, and he does not want to be left out of the experience. Also, he would like Prime to stop monkeying around with his equipment. These thirty days will be the best part of Eidolon, and they are going too fast. He does not want to be hobbled in any way.

What walks you could take on Mars. He would like to walk the whole planet. With thirty days you could do almost nothing, but a year and a half would be so good you would not mind getting back inside a little tuna can for nine months. You would not mind so much. This is a flaw in the Eidolon plan. They had shortened the Mars time to only thirty days, and so the feelings that the crew would have about getting into *Red Dawn* and leaving the planet would be totally different than they would be after a year and a half on the planet. Maybe after a year and a half, they would be ready to return home.

The Rover is packed with equipment and supplies, they can move around very little and mostly they stay up front, watching the terrain or napping in the back. Lava fields are not the most exciting views, but Helen is a good companion, not too chatty. They are permitted to perform short EVAs when the solar batteries of the Rover are recharging.

Almost there.

When lava courses in flows underground, you have the possibility that when it subsides it will leave tubes. This has happened on Earth, and it appears to have happened on Mars. Some of the roofs of these tubes on Mars are meters thick, and many of them are much larger than the ones found on Earth. Caves! For the geologists a lava tube is an excellent opportunity to examine unsullied bedrock kept safe from the shock modifications and dust storms on the surface. It is the kind of environment congenial for chemosynthetic organisms. You might find biosignatures: the handwriting on the wall, the graffito of life. For a man, it is the place for him to get away from solar proton event radiation, and the cold, and all this fucking dust. If man wants to come back to Mars and stay a while, and have nice things, he will need something a little better than his own poop to shield him and his instruments, or bags of Martian regolith on top of a Hab. And it would be good if the place were protected from the dust, because dust is not great for scientific equipment or the mood of the scientist. A lava tube is just smart camping. Why bring heavy payloads of shelter materials all the way to Mars when there are possible underground shelters just waiting for someone to come inside?

Always, man has desired entrance into a dark hole.

Dena, Chloe, Wendy, Annie, Abbey, Nikki, Jeanne, and—more recently discovered—Marnie. The names for the skylights around Arsia Mons, the dark holes that lead to something warm and wet and safe. Well, not really any of those things, ha ha.

It is not lost on Sergei that Prime has prescribed him a daily ingestion of liquorice tea. In women, it seems that liquorice is a natural aphrodisiac, but it has the opposite effect on men. Well, it is all very up front. He does not have to wonder if Prime is slipping potassium bromide into his dumplings; they would tell him if they were. He has noticed that Yoshi is not drinking liquorice tea, so it is to be supposed that RoMeO is not reporting elevated levels of Yoshi's testosterone. If someone were seen drinking liquorice tea on the space station, everyone else would drink it, whether or not it was prescribed for him. No one wants to be the guy with less testosterone, or fewer morning erections. But Yoshi, if he noticed Sergei's new regimen, is either not bothered or too honest.

Soon they will reach their first major site. Then a two-kilometer (real!) walk to Marnie. She is a promising skylight. They will be able to conduct science. Exploration without science is merely adventure. Not that the distinction bothers him.

Sergei will be happy to get out of the Rover. He wants to walk. Sitting in the Rover and looking at the sims and doing a little work is exhaustively boring. The Rover does not have an exercise machine. Sergei is storing too much internal energy and it is tiring him. It is not a terrible feeling, he is repressed, not depressed. Anything can be borne when you know you have a release waiting. Sol-morrow he will have a good walk. Get things out of his body.

"The first one is for you; the second one is for me." That's how Talia always characterized their having sex after he had been away. She had that division, anyway, that there were sex things for her and ones for him. He could point out that doing things for her also made him feel good, but he doesn't think she ever believed him. There were good and bad points to her being so practical about sex.

"If you want to do something with my ass, please just let me know beforehand. A few hours."

She was funny that way. He wasn't sure what happened in those hours. Some sort of preparations, hygienic or otherwise. She was also specific with his technique.

"It doesn't do anything if you touch it like that," she might say.

It could be exciting, scorn. It gave you something to do.

"I suppose you want to have sex," Talia had said in Utah.

She was not an idiot. He had strawberries in his room. It was her favorite thing, to lie in his lap and have him feed her strawberries. Any kind of food, but Sergei particularly liked the way Talia's mouth had to work on a strawberry. That was a good example of something that pleased them both, but he'd never told her, as it might have ruined it.

"Of course I want to," he said. He had thought about saying "But I respect Alexander." Actually, he did respect him, liked him. It was a thing to remember, though, that a man could not seduce a woman. You couldn't be upset with a man, even a friend, if your wife slept with him. Yes, the man could say no, but everyone had a different idea of loyalty. You shouldn't be upset with your wife either. Only blame yourself in these situations.

"Come sit with me," he said to Talia. He had put a pillow in his lap and given her the look.

Interestingly, his ex-wife had done two new things when they had sex, so these would be things she had learned from Alexander. She made specific requests, and she moved her hips more aggressively. Was more aggressive altogether. In bed, Talia was indolent, but she hadn't been in Utah. Perhaps she missed him.

"Did you miss me?" He had been a fool to ask. Such a terrible question, at any time.

"Not anymore," she said, which could mean different things, considering the ring on her finger from another man, or the fact that when she said it, he was holding that hand.

Talia hadn't stayed all night with him, because of the boys, because of everything. They'd had a laugh, and he thanked her, which made her make a funny face. Such a generous woman.

"Are you happy?" he asked.

"If I were mean, I would say no, but because I am a good person, I will say yes." She was, he thought. Happy. Which was the whole point of the thing. You couldn't leave sad women behind, not with children. Not if you ever wanted. Well. He didn't know what that was anymore, when it came to women. Had he ever? It seemed to him that there had been a time of certainty. And when Talia had asked for the divorce, that too had seemed clear, like something he could do, a course of action that would be positive in the end. It was to the end that he had looked. The boys, safe. Talia, happy. Sergei, walking, with only himself to tire or hurt or blame. Granting Talia a divorce had seemed both noble and punishing, which was how he knew it was the right thing to do.

Before she left him that night in Utah, she did his favorite thing. This was to be stroked. After sex, not before. After, when he was tired and depleted and could take his reward. Sometimes he would turn and stretch like a cat and Talia would scratch his chest or his back or his thighs. Wonderful. Sometimes it was just having her hand move slowly up and down. Not sexual, it could be his arm even.

The surface of Mars rolls by. There are those that say we should not disturb Mars, not drill, not examine, not gather rocks, not submit it to thermal emission spectography. Too late. There are robots on Mars. There are nuclear reactors on Mars. Worse, Prime will send him.

YOSHI

Yoshi is inside something, something that confines him and yet has no distinct boundaries. There is a threat, a malignant presence. He is aware of a great evil, hovering. He realizes that he has been foolish to think that things like demons, or devils, were metaphors. Evil lived, and had a purpose. It was close. It saw him.

When Yoshi wakes up, he does not know where he is. Never in his conscious life has he so profoundly not known this. The first thing he does is attempt to establish a sequence. Has he just arrived at this place of nowhere, or has he just returned from it and is reliving the memory? This was a question of safety.

He realizes he has very recently shouted, or grunted. He thinks he can hear the last bit of a shout, in the air. If it is air. Yoshi breathes, experimentally. If he cannot move his lungs then it will be a sign that he is dead.

He is not dead, unless death includes an illusion of respiration. It is a disadvantage, knowing so little about the rules of death.

Sergei's voice, speaking to him, saying his name. Yoshi looks at his screen. He sees Sergei's face, hears Sergei apologizing for waking Yoshi up.

"I was dreaming," says Yoshi, at the same time he realizes the truth of this. He looks at the watch on his wrist. The numbers do not make sense. His eyes, adjusting now, can pick out details. He had fallen asleep in his chair in front of the console in the Science/Lab wedge. He checks the systems of *Primitus*. There is no cause for alarm. He looks at Sergei's face on the screen. He does not see Helen.

Yoshi knows he is not dead, and that Sergei is with Helen in the Rover, returning from the sortie. They check in with each other, every hour.

But he does not feel safe. Mars. That's why. Mars. This is a new feeling. He can remember confidence, if not comfort. Why is he now afraid?

"Helen is taking a nap too." Yoshi watches as Sergei raises a canteen and drinks from it. Yoshi has a similar canteen, filled with water. They can make potable water here, make oxygen from the water, grow food, build shelter. But for all of that they are at the mercy, absolutely, of machines. The robots are despots; man is enslaved. It's this, perhaps.

"We are totally dependent on machines," Yoshi says.

"Pfuh. Yes. This was what you were having a bad dream about?"

"No." Yoshi finds his canteen and drinks. They have been joking that they will make a fortune bottling Martian water, which they will brand as "Sabatier," in honor of the reaction that produces it from Martian hydrogen and carbon dioxide. They have lemon and orange essential oils to flavor their water, but the water still tastes metallic, or it is the canteen. Or no. He did bite the inside of his cheek. That is iron he tastes—his own blood. Or maybe everything on Mars ends up Mars flavored. Including himself.

It is okay to be dependent on machines.

"It is okay to be dependent on machines," Yoshi says out loud. "No, it's fine. On Earth, we do, we are. Earth is not really a hospitable planet. Without machines, existence would be pitiful, if you even survived. 'Nasty, brutish, and short.' We have made the Earth a place we can live on, with machines. We could not live without them. Earth is only a different kind of Mars, underneath what we've made."

Sergei laughs softly. His face is green, reflections from the interior lights of the Rover. "You can breathe everywhere on Earth," he says. "Still. Maybe not forever, but right now."

"We are all astronauts."

"Yoshi, that is true. But it's okay. You're okay. You were dreaming."

He is not quite done dreaming, perhaps.

"I'm not worried about the machines," Yoshi says. "I don't think that was the problem. I was thinking I could see devils."

"Bff," says Sergei.

"Rather like Batman." Yoshi tries to remember. "The shape of the head. Or something like a manta ray. Yes. A school of blue manta rays, flying above me. Evil things."

"Did you have spicy food for dinner? Spicy food gives you bad dreams. Whenever Helen uses paprika, I have a nightmare."

"I heard that." It is Helen's voice. Her face is not on screen.

"Yoshi had a dream of scary Batman devils," Sergei says. "This is anxiety dream."

"I think I've seen them before." Yoshi feels as if he is rowing against the current of his own brain.

"It sounds like a movie." Helen is trying to be helpful. "Or a cartoon?"

"The first time I spent time in a sensory deprivation tank." Yoshi has located the memory. "Yes. At first I closed my eyes—this is an instinct, for relaxation, yes?—and then I became very curious about the darkness. It was my first true opportunity to look at complete absence of light. I knew that it took twenty minutes for one's eyes to adjust. That's when I saw the demons. Pointed Batman heads and bodies like rays. It was not, of course, that I believed in their existence. I had read that hallucination in the tank is quite common, for sane people. It's the schizophrenic who is most relaxed in the absence of stimuli. The demons did not last long. They were replaced by stars. After the stars, my eyes were adjusted and I saw nothing. And never again, in any sensory deprivation situation, did I experience a visual construction."

"So this means you are schizophrenic." Sergei laughs. "If you were normal, you would still imagine crazy things. Helen, you hallucinate in sensory deprivation, of course?"

"Oh, of course. Rainbow cows jumping through the clouds."

"Yes. Me too. I see a baby with a goatee juggling apricots. But that is because we are sane. Poor Yoshi."

Yoshi knows they are joking, teasing, even being kind. But his unease, which had subsided, is returning. He remembers, in the sensory deprivation tank, the loss of a frame of reference for his own body. He had moved his torso sideways, bending, and had kept moving until he felt a muscular resistance. At that point, he could have sworn that his right ear was only two or three inches from touching the side of his right knee.

The perimeters, the edges of life had moved away on Mars. There was nothing here to bind you. Nothing already made. Nothing already constructed. No people who came before you. No culture, no language, no one to recognize you.

Helen's face moves fully into frame now on Yoshi's screen. Her hair is down, the lights of the Rover turning her curls into a nimbus of greenish gold.

"Hey there, Yoshi," she says.

It is okay. He is located, he is found. He is not lost on a distant planet, he—

"Oh."

Yoshi has just remembered that he is not actually on Mars.

HELEN

elen, how is your daughter behaving?"

Helen moves crablike—the greenhouse aisles are narrow—
to the screen connecting her to Sergei, on sortie right now with
Yoshi in *Rover II*.

"We're still having some torque issues," she says. "I'm a little concerned about balance." Helen angles the screen so that Sergei can
have a look at her "daughter": GAIA. For seven months, GAIA
existed only as a computer program the astronauts occasionally con-
sulted or trained with on *Primitus*; the rest of the robot had traveled
in the cargo hold. Helen had been the one to put body and program
together—thus, Sergei's joke about her maternal role. It still jars
Helen to see GAIA walking around with her small steps, like a child
in her mother's high heels, handling objects, rotating the wreath
of cameras and sensors that serve as her head to focus, occasionally,
on Helen.

"Anyway. You two having fun?"

"There is no man," Sergei states, "who does not enjoy flying remote-controlled things." Yoshi appears behind Sergei at this point, lofting a pressure-suit thumbs-up, all smiles beneath his helmet. When he moves away and Sergei shifts his screen, Helen gets a tantalizing glimpse of copper sands and paler outcropping. Sergei and Yoshi are testing the camera drones on a small hill to the north of the site. Helen would very much like to have gone with them. She likes flying remote-controlled things too. But Yoshi had stayed behind on the Arsia Mons sortie, and she judged that the greenhouse was too finicky a job for Sergei's current mood.

Here she is, in the garden of Mars, letting the boys drive the car and play with toys so they don't get too fretful or have to drink too much liquorice tea. This is part of being commander. It was father and mother rolled into one, Adam and Eve. It was not merely for her skills as an engineer that she had been chosen, nor for her experience. All those data collections suggesting that if you were to put a woman into a crew of men for long-duration space missions, it would be best if the woman were of a "motherly" disposition. Considering her limited skills as an actual mother, this was more funny than offensive, but Helen knew that, without her intending it, certain words or actions would be interpreted as motherly, by virtue of her biology.

Of course, there was also another definition for "motherly" that read: too old or otherwise not appealing to be considered sexually viable by others. If this was true, it was fortunate that hers was a career where her lack of sexual appeal made her more valuable.

That's absolutely how she should think about that. It's a plus.

No, truly. That's how she will think about that.

"We will be back in one hour." Sergei points to *Rover II*, behind him. "If you need help."

"Well," Helen says. "It's kind of crowded in here already. And I think I have it under control."

"Of course you do." Sergei gives a cheerful sign-off salute. Yoshi can be seen, all but skipping, right behind him. Helen sidesteps back down the aisle.

"GAIA, let's finish these nitrate fixers."

"Okay, Helen."

In Antarctica, the greenhouse had been one of the most popular places to hang out: the warmest, the best smelling, the prettiest. People strung hammocks so they could sleep there. During Helen's winter-over, so many couples had used the greenhouse for sex that a warning system had to be devised. A sign was posted outside: **CLOSED FOR FILTER CLEANING.**

This greenhouse would not provide such comforts. The structure—inflated and attached to *Primitus*—was a seriously challenged endeavor, and certainly its current psychological benefits were negligible. This greenhouse received its light from ground LED sensors, and was nearly opaque, its walls treated with UV-filtering transfers, and its roof covered with Martian regolith. A millimeter growth of hairy vetch did not provide much in the way of mood-enriching fecundity. The best you could say about it right now was that it was warm.

"GAIA," says Helen. "Someone told me that the first recorded greenhouse was created for the Emperor Tiberius in 30 AD so that he could have cucumbers all year long."

"Okay, Helen," says GAIA. "Would you like me to verify that?"

"GAIA, no thank you."

You had to say the robot's name to get its attention, otherwise it would ignore voices. This conserved energy, and reduced the occurrence of the robot misapprehending directives.

GAIA was not her daughter.

Helen had started out a pretty good mother. She thinks she did well that first year, at least. Meeps had been a small, sweet, stubborn baby, very skeptical but with a sense of humor. Helen had felt like they understood each other and made a good team. She'd loved how much her daughter accepted her and took her for granted. She hadn't even been terribly bored by the endless repetition, despite Eric's assumptions. "Poor Helen. This isn't quite your thing, is it?" and, "Mireille, love, Papa is going to give you a bath so your mother can do something easy, like rocket science."

She'd stayed as long as she could. She tried to be extra present when she was with them, and when that proved annoying to everyone, she tried to be unobtrusive in an interested way. She acquired a sense of apology to her daughter, to her husband, a sense of never quite accruing enough credit to make up for her absences. But she'd always thought a time would come when her daughter would find a use for her, for her particularly, and all would be well and they'd be a team again. And then, before you knew it, Meeps was nine, ten, fifteen, eighteen. Then standing by Helen's side as they put Eric in different kinds of boxes and Helen wasn't what her daughter needed or wanted at all.

EVERY SOL ON MARS, Helen has said to herself, *Oh let me be free.* It is like she is cursed, or something. Her entire career, this has never happened to her, these continual slips, these plagued memories, these little struggles. It's like something is clinging to her.

"My dead husband told me that flat glass hadn't been invented in Tiberius's time," Helen says. "So the architects put together small sections of transparent mica sheets."

GAIA, unaddressed, does not respond. The robot comes up to Helen's ribs. Meeps had once been the size of GAIA. Maybe at eight? She'd been small until high school, was still shorter than Helen though she wore high heels often. GAIA's height is adjustable. All four of her arms can extend to the top height of the greenhouse, if need be.

Meeps at eight. Helen had been flying a desk that year, more available to her family than she had been in the past. Meeps at eight took karate and played soccer. She also performed in her school plays, and sang in the chorus. Meeps was a natural athlete: confident and not self-conscious. If she fell, she got up, kept running. Watching her was a pleasure, was easy, was *play*. But the actual plays were difficult to watch. All of Meeps's teachers, and other parents, praised her daughter's theatrical skills. "So talented," they said. "What stage presence. A natural." Helen understood this might be the case, but could not see it. She saw that her daughter was louder, larger, more emotional than the other children. Helen saw naked need, and vulnerability. It made her nervous.

Helen would not have selected acting as a career pursuit for her daughter, but not because she didn't value the arts. She believed acting specifically wrong for Meeps. It played to her weaknesses: her ability to manipulate emotions and her need for approval, and ignored her strengths, like her mechanical dexterity and ability to conceptualize objects in three dimensions. Meeps was smart, very smart. Too many things came easily, and she gave up too quickly on the things that didn't. And she'd ended up wanting to do something that Helen could not help with, advise on, or even intelligently discuss.

Of course, Eric had encouraged it. It was too much to be hoped for that his keen eye had not detected Helen's discomfort with their daughter's theatrical displays. Her uneasiness probably amused him.

Eric had wanted a child with each of his two previous wives and it had not happened. Helen had known his expectations when they married. She had thought, *If I have a child* now, *then I will not have to stop later and have it.* The timing was right. An advanced degree and those critical bonding years could be achieved simultaneously. By the time she would be pursuing astronaut candidacy, Meeps would be in school. It was amazing to Helen, now, that she'd allowed herself to be so vague and optimistic about the whole enterprise.

Eric had been a wonderful parent. When he was alive, Helen had said he was a wonderful husband. She could still do that. Or she could say something else. Helen could tell GAIA all about it, if Prime wasn't listening in somewhere. It would be nice to say it aloud. GAIA would listen and then say, "Okay, Helen. Would you like me to verify that for you?"

Who could verify it? Meeps was the sole audience member for Helen's marriage. When Helen and Eric were together in public, Eric expressed only praise and admiration for her. In private, she was subject to his loving sarcasm. But she'd allowed that, almost from the beginning. It had seemed fatherly to Helen—she who could not remember the time when her father was capable of chewing, let alone sarcasm. Why had she?

She'd not had a lot of experience with men. The ones who were her intellectual equals had invariably sought softer mates, and the others had stayed away. *Intimidated* was the word friends used, though *repelled* might be more accurate.

Eric had assigned her an identity. Helen was logical, rational, didactic, meticulous. Not unlike a robot, a lovable robot. Helen was supposed—by Eric—not to be good at a number of things, expressive, feeling-type things. Perhaps she would have protested more against this assigned identity if it hadn't been for sex. In bed—or multiple locations; Eric was inventive—she had felt known and absolutely at her ease. It did not seem likely that Eric could "get" her so completely there, when she was exposed in every possible way, and "not get" her otherwise. Furthermore, that Eric should assign her a personality that did not seem particularly lovable, and then tell her that he loved her, had seemed significant. She had to think him wonderful. Who else would love the person he described?

It was, of course, perfectly possible to grasp fundamentals and miss the concept. And then, there had always been a strand of guilt running through the whole thing. Eric had made it clear that he was content to have large parts of his self remain unknowable to her (essentially limited) understanding. This he did out of love. He loved her despite herself so much that he didn't even expect to be loved back. He didn't expect more from her. She had been grateful, but only because she hadn't properly understood the gift.

Eric had schooled Meeps in the robot version of Helen. She'd made it easy for him: she had left. Not just once, but repeatedly. An astronaut's job was almost never in space, but it was always training, traveling, weeks away, months away. As Meeps's *father*, this would not have been so remarkable.

She could not now fight back or redeem herself in her daughter's eyes without throwing dirt on a ghost, throwing dirt on dirt.

"Helen." It is Sergei again. Helen glances at her watch. An hour has passed. It is okay. She knows exactly where the Prime camera is inside the greenhouse, since she was the one who installed it. Her face had not been in its view and she has been working steadily, so her performance was still nominal.

"Yes, Sergei."

"Nearing the site now."

Helen moves so she can take a look at her crewmates' faces in the cab of the Rover. They still look happy.

The Arsia Mons sortie had been harder on Sergei than Helen had anticipated. The actual exploration had been marvelous and they both loved it: the planning and the execution had been exhilarating and physically demanding. It was the long Rover ride that had challenged. She'd not realized how dependent Sergei was on daily vigorous exercise. For herself, she'd managed by employing a yogic technique known as fire breath, and then another biofeedback trick involving imagining her bloodstream as a river, but Sergei had gotten very squirrelly.

With Yoshi it was a little trickier. She'd thought it was important to him to have personal space, but there were limits to this. Give him just a little, and he was perfectly content. Too much and he became anxious, as had seemed to happen during the Arsia Mons sortie. Of the three of them, he was maybe the best at communal living.

Helen had only eight more sols to wear Sergei out like a puppy, and grant Yoshi the correct amount of personal space, before they all got back into an even smaller module for an even longer amount of time. This took some juggling.

"Sergei, how are the greenhouse solars?"

"Looking a little clogged, Helen."

"I'm going to come out and do a good sweep. Would you mind sticking around and helping me out? We should do SA1 and 2 while we're at it."

Sergei does not mind, with alacrity.

"Yoshi," Helen continues, "let's practice the transfer. You can take over the Hab and keep an eye on those drones."

Yoshi thinks this is an excellent suggestion. They sign off.

"GAIA," says Helen. "Please work on the rye now. I'm going to suit up."

"Okay, Helen," says GAIA. "I will prepare the rye trays."

"GAIA, what are you doing?"

"Helen, I am preparing the carrot trays. Would you like me to work on another task?"

"GAIA, cancel preparing the carrot trays. Proceed with the rye trays."

"Helen, I am canceling preparing the carrot trays. I am proceeding with the rye trays."

"GAIA, that is correct."

Helen moves out of the greenhouse attachment and through the inflatable tunnel back to the EVA prep room of *Primitus*.

Was it too late? It wasn't good for Meeps to have a father she loved more with every absent year, and a mother whose past absence was an ongoing source of blame. Did Meeps need her to stay now? Would giving up Mars for Meeps make her daughter understand that she was loved?

Did the fact that she did not want to give up Mars for her daughter mean that she didn't love her daughter?

Maybe Eric had made her into the thing he thought she was, or maybe he had been right all along, and there was nothing more to her, and a great deal less, than she had always supposed.

Yoshi is ready to come in. Helen is ready to come out. They make the transfer smoothly, and Helen joins Sergei, waiting just outside the hatch. They move to the Solar Array One. Helen feels better being outside, with the sweep of the valley before her and a task that requires larger movements. She does not think about Meeps, or Eric.

They are a quarter of the way through clearing SA2 when a weather alert comes through. Two dust devils, south of the landing site, but on the move. Helen scans the telemetry being loaded onto her screen.

A devil on Mars is more dramatic visually than the ones on Earth: higher and wider but, in the negligible atmosphere here, much less destructive. To humans. Potentially not great for machinery, though it will finish cleaning the solar panels for them.

This simulated storm is probably a test of crew choreography and communication. And her own assessment of what protocol to follow. She sends a message to Mission Control, then switches to crew-link.

"Everybody see the weather report?"

"Confirm weather report." Sergei is about sixty feet away.

"Yoshi, you there?"

"Here, Helen. I have them. Two dust devils."

"Okey-doke, let's use this as an opportunity to test our timing. Yoshi, turn on the porch lights for us, please. Sergei? Let's give these guide cables a try and get back to the Hab. Yoshi, I'd like to know how smoothly we can prep everything for storm. I will take care of GAIA."

"Green lights on," says Yoshi. "I'm sealing off the greenhouse."

"GAIA, I want you to go to the locker and power down."

"Okay, Commander."

GAIA's locker is a kind of upright coffin, stir-welded to seamlessness to prevent dust contamination, and stocked with extra seeds. The round shape of the greenhouse should have no problem weathering a dust devil, which might last no more than fifteen minutes, and even withstand a more serious storm, though the plants will die. Even after they leave, if Mars huffs and puffs and blows the greenhouse down, GAIA should be able to survive inside the locker, and be able to repair or rebuild her home. It's a good sequence to practice, getting her in and out of her coffin.

"Proceeding now to Hab. Sergei?"

"Let's jam, Helen."

"Right behind you. My guide cable is stuck. Hold on."

"There is—" Sergei's voice disappears under a fuzz of loud static.

She can see him, just ahead. And then she can't. A wall of color rises up between them, accompanied by some kind of ground force. Helen thinks of land mines, of geysers. She is not knocked off her feet, but she loses her equilibrium, staggers. Her faceplate is moving, no, playing a sort of high-speed kaleidoscope: brown, gray, blue, red, orange, pink. The static is loud in her ear. Everything slows. The static is terrific, confusing.

Sergei's voice crackles back on the line.

"That's not right," he is saying, in Russian. The static erupts again, and the colors darken to a slate gray, then almost black.

She is standing. She is still standing. She is holding on to the cable, or rather, holding it down. Is she exerting pressure? It feels pinned to her glove.

It is possible, Helen thinks, that she is being electrocuted. She imagines the outline of her skeleton, like a cartoon. The pressure in her jaw and her lower back, the muscles of her right arm, the static in her ear—these sensations are suspended, not increasing or decreasing, coming or going.

She cannot feel the ground. She is not on the ground, but also not quite in the air, or maybe both these things, Earthly and suspended.

This might, then, be death, or it might be the space inhabited just before death, on the edge of the map, right before you fell off of life. Helen thinks, *Dad?*

It is a thing people tell you: that the dead are waiting for you in some nice place, heaven, usually, but maybe Mars, maybe a simulation in Utah.

And then, Helen thinks: *No.*

No, he's not here. He's not anywhere. He is dead. He is gone. For so long he had been alive and dead at the same time. Maybe, so had she. Maybe that's why she thought "Dad?" She might as well have asked, "Helen?"

She is, like Michael Collins circling the moon, the most alone person in the history of people. She has always been the most alone person, it hasn't needed going up or in any direction.

How does it feel?

It feels spectacular.

Helen can hear her own heartbeat, curiously not fast, but quite steady. This gives her a sense of power. There is a storm happening and she is inside it, either in a death way or a simulated way. It's up to her to take control of the thing. Helen imagines that the storm—the devil—is not acting upon her but coming from her.

The veil of darkness is whisked off her face. Helen can see Sergei, kneeling, and the green lights of the east hatch. The heavy buzz of static separates into words. It is Yoshi, then Sergei. Sergei is fine, is getting to his feet. They can see a cloud of dust moving north, forming a loose conical shape, dissipating. She is still holding on to the guide cable. The diagnostics of her suit are nominal, and so is she. Helen turns back to *Primitus* and the greenhouse. They appear startling white against tawny regolith. The sky is paler, very beautiful, almost pearly. She can see the dark irregular shadow of Phobos overhead, more clearly than she's ever seen it.

"I'm okay," she says.

Sergei says he is okay.

Yoshi says it looked on camera four like a dust devil erupted right underneath Helen's feet.

Normally they dock their spacesuits to the exterior of *Primitus*, but Helen would like to run some additional tests on their communications systems, so they use the eastern hatch to enter the Hab. Sergei is first out of his suit. His face is blank and white, as if he too has been bleached by the devil. He repeats that he is fine. He had not been knocked over, he says. He had knelt down on top of the guide cable when he felt it lurching out of his hands. "That was weird!" Helen says, which is a slight betrayal of what it was, but doesn't feel bad to say. Sergei agrees that it was weird. "Very good sim." Perhaps a little unrealistic, but good practice. He will get up to the Hab now, and see what images their remote cameras have captured of the event.

The exterior of her spacesuit is heavily crusted. Helen clambers out of it, and manages to displace a good deal of dust onto her compression jumpsuit. She grabs a hose to deal with it, but wrenches the nozzle too strongly and a section of the tube detaches, shooting a cloud of fines all over her, a second dust devil. Helen drops the hose and spreads her arms, gazing down at the mess she has made. "Look at me," she says, with unexpected love.

YOSHI

Yoshi joins Helen in the EVA prep room as Helen is attempting to suction up fines from both the floor and her person.

"No, it's too much," Helen says, laughing, as she looks down at her filthy jumpsuit. "I can feel Mars everywhere. I am *not* spending my last week here in a dust bag. Let me get out of this thing."

Helen unzips her compression suit. He's never seen her do this; her method is different from his. She does not peel, allowing the fabric to roll inside out, but shrugs the fabric down off one shoulder, inches it down her arm, then grasps the cuff and pulls the sleeve out straight. After repeating this technique with the other arm, she hooks her thumbs into the torso of the suit and shimmies it down to her hips, then joggles the legs down until she can step out. Yoshi can see the sense of this technique. The appendages of the suit are cut so narrowly that turning them outside in takes quite a time. He realizes that he is staring.

"Yoshi, will you grab me one of the spares? Before I get dressed,

I'm taking the ten seconds of shower I am allotted." Yoshi turns to a supply locker.

"Woosh," says Helen. He hears the sound of skin on skin. "That's always such a relief. This is crazy." When he turns around with the spare jumpsuit, she is rubbing her legs, sending out more little puffs of dust. "I'm electric! Every speck of Mars flies off my suit and onto my skin. Why am I always ten times dirtier than you or Sergei?" She picks up a vacuum nozzle. "Let's try to get as much off me as we can."

Helen is now wearing only her Solox bra and underpants. Yoshi has seen Helen in shorts and a T-shirt. He has seen discrete portions of her bare flesh when they practiced medical procedures. This is the most he has seen of Helen all at once and they are very close together. In the athletic locker room in Utah, Yoshi and Sergei had conversed comfortably while naked. Naturally, Helen had not been present during those times. Yoshi thinks that his brain has not accurately recorded her physique; he does not know it. Her thighs are red where she has rubbed them. She hands a vacuum tube to Yoshi and turns one on herself. He doesn't quite know where to aim his, so points it at her feet.

"I'm jealous," Yoshi says. "I didn't get to experience the sim." Something has happened to both his crewmates. Sergei had come back unnaturally blank of expression, and Helen is the reverse: elated, lit up. Her voice is different, lighter. Something other than clothes has been removed from her body.

"It was very quick. I would have been okay with it going on for much longer, to take it all in. I'll admit it, for a second I thought I'd been electrocuted." Helen takes a deep breath. "Wow. Really, the oddest sensation. Maybe I just became a superhero."

The exposure of so much of Helen's body, so much of her everything, makes Yoshi feel similarly naked.

She turns around and says, over her shoulder, "Can you do my back? These fines are *very* determined. Just don't leave the nozzle on my skin too long or it will be hard to pull it off. Try a kind of scooping motion."

Yoshi begins methodically suctioning Helen's back. "Wait. Here," she says, turning. "Wait, do here." She laughs. "Oh, that was a good one. It's kind of horrible in a great way. Get this section. Ow. Great." Now they are both laughing. Helen thrusts out an elbow, a hip, holds up a knee. "Zap it. Get that! Wait. I have middle-aged-woman stuff here." It is true. Helen is trim, but there is an unexpected soft fold of flesh just around her waist. She pulls the fold up. "It's my Tharsis bulge! We're getting very real here on Mars right now, and that's just how it's going to be."

Helen is looking at him now and he is looking at her. She is allowing him, he sees, to truly look at her. Which either means she hasn't allowed it before, or he never tried.

What a large thing it is to be Helen, what infinite space she is. And then to be seen by her. As if, just for once, the universe understood *him*, came up with a name for *him*, instead of the other way around.

"Okay, that's pretty good, I think," Helen says. "My feet are freezing."

Helen has been obscuring large parts of herself. Helen must get dressed, must clothe not just her body but all of that vastness. He cannot travel for eight months with all of that, there is no room. She must pack herself back inside herself.

Yoshi realizes that he had wanted—still wants—to touch Helen. Not in the way he wants to touch his wife. Not to give pleasure, or receive it. He'd wanted—he wants—to feel that infinite space, to know what happens there.

LUKE

The big thing coming up is providing the crew with enough activity," Luke says. "Meaningful occupations. Varied tasks. Challenges. The return trip is not going to be comfortable."

"Right," Mireille says. "The Venus fry-by."

When the crew is on the planet for a year and a half, they will be able to return to Earth essentially the way they came, as Mars and Earth once again draw close. After only thirty days, however, Earth and Mars are hurtling away from each other, and enormous amounts of fuel would be needed to make up the distance. Orbital mechanics dictated a different route home after thirty days, with *Red Dawn* using Venus as a gravity assist, giving the craft an extra push.

"In all likelihood we won't have to use the Venus fly-by return," Luke says. "It's only if we have to cut the mission short. But it made sense to incorporate it into Eidolon so the crew would have a chance to run it fully. And, you know, it fits with the Mars portion only being thirty days. It's more realistic for the crew. Anyway, even if this happens for real, they will be exposed to a little more radiation, yes, but 'fry-by' is a little harsh. *Red Dawn* is up to the challenge."

"Is that a *Star Trek* pillowcase?" Mireille leans forward into her own screen, squinting.

After they'd spoken on the day of the *Weilai 3* tragedy, Mireille messaged to apologize for how she'd acted ("The bread knife thing was pretty dumb, thanks for being nice about it") and then a third time because she wanted his opinion about a new kind of psychoactive medication. He's not meant to be speaking with her at all, but apparently getting the family members to open up about their experience has proved difficult, and as long as Luke records any "sessions" he has with Mireille, Ransom and Kyrah, the Kane family liaison, have okayed the communication, with strict guidelines.

"Of course it's a *Star Trek* pillowcase." Luke smiles and whips the pillow out from behind his back, holds it up. His pod chair would seem a more classically appropriate and professional piece of furniture to conduct a session from, but there is no way to position his screen from the chair that would not include displaying his bed in the background, and that seemed unprofessional. So he is sitting on his bed, and Mireille can only see the wall and part of the window. He had forgotten about the pillowcase. At some point in the conversation he must have pulled it up behind him for comfort. "It was a gift from my Secret Winter Solstice Fairy," Luke says. "But it's a way better quality fabric than my own. I wish I had the whole *Star Trek* sheet set, to be honest."

"Right. So I'm guessing you don't do a whole lot of home entertaining. Or perhaps *Star Trek* bed linen is the Prime equivalent of black satin sheets." Mireille gives him one of her professional-grade looks, straight out of an old black-and-white movie, one eyebrow raised, lips slightly pursed. He can't tell if she's being provocative or making fun of someone who is trying to be provocative. Either way, he's provoked. He needs to be very careful. Mireille really does need someone to talk to, but it would be better if she talked to Kyrah, who presumably does not have thoughts about the shape of Mireille's mouth.

"It's the Prime equivalent of white cotton." He can delete this section, later, from the transcript running on the side of his screen, and from the recording itself. Luke can also, if he chooses, erase the entire thing and claim that the software on his personal screen failed to record the session. There is so much going on with the crew right now, Ransom wouldn't notice.

They have lost audio feed into the Lav of *Red Dawn*. They never had video in there, and the audio got knocked out sometime between the last inspection before launch from Mars, when it was operational, and two days ago, when it went silent.

Two days ago Sergei asked Yoshi and Helen for assistance in the Lav and the crew had all squeezed themselves in there and stayed in there, all three of them, for twenty-three minutes.

It was possibly Sergei who had knocked the audio out, and the why of that might be connected to the fact that Sergei's vitals during the launch of *Red Dawn* from Mars had been nothing like his vitals during the launch of *Primitus*. And now all three of the astronauts were spiking in new ways.

Something, in short, was up.

"So, anyway, we're approaching the part of the mission when the crew is at risk for what we call 'third-quarter effect.'" Luke puts the pillow behind his back. "It's the period of time when—traditionally— a kind of lethargy or apathy sets in. The greatest event is in the past, and the next thing to look forward to feels pretty distant. It doesn't have to do with number of days so much as perception of time. We'd like to try to avoid the three-quarter effect as much as we can."

"I love when people come up with these special psychological terms and descriptions for ordinary life things." Mireille talks with her hands, air-sculpting her sentences, giving them geography. "The other day, one of my clients asked if I could turn up the heat on the electric blanket because he had 'temperature sensitivity.' I was like, 'You're cold. You don't have some kind of special condition.' I didn't say that, of course." Mireille sweeps her hair from one side to the other. It's several shades lighter than her mother's and falls in waves, as opposed to Helen's frizzy curls. "I know it's hard to imagine, but when I'm at work I have this whole nurturing vibe. I talk like this—" She can change her entire physiognomy in an instant. "Oh of course, Mr. Smith, let me adjust that for you."

He can see more of Mireille's kitchen now. It's crowded with things: a blue shelf with a collection of antique cups and tins, pictures he can't quite make out taped to the refrigerator, a birdcage populated by tiny fabric birds.

"How's work going, by the way?" he asks. He needs to stop talking about the crew, get the focus back on Mireille. It's unfortunate that the effort not to flirt with her is making him sound like a robot.

"You mean the spa? I've hardly been there." Mireille leans back in her chair and stretches. "I keep having to get my shifts covered because I'm booking all these games."

"That's fantastic." Luke wonders if any of the characters Mireille is providing motion capture or voice-over for will end up looking like Mireille in the animation. What would it be like to "play" Mireille in a game?

"But I cut you off." Mireille gives him one of her rare, entirely natural smiles. "Third-quarter effect. The thing that happens after the big thing we were waiting for is over and the next big thing is far away."

"You got it."

"Great. So. Proceed. How can I be of service to the greater Prime good? Let's kick these quarters to the curb. Give me jargon, or the idiot's guide version, whatever works. I'll take notes. Old school–style." She waves a pen in the air. She is being the Good Astronaut Daughter now. She is clever at this, knows what tone to take, is aware of how she is landing.

"Keep up the communication with your mom," Luke says. "This is the time when she needs to hear from you the most, when skipping an email or video would have the greatest impact. You might imagine that your mom won't be interested in little things, but those little things are going to help give her a sense of connection to you that's really important right now."

"Hold on." Mireille pretends to be writing. "Let me get all this down. Now, I'm supposed to be super happy and content in all of these messages." She looks up. "Is that right?"

"For the messages, honestly, yes." Luke is pretty sure it's okay to offer this advice. He'll need to review it, though. He wants Mireille to be the best possible version of herself so as not to stress out Helen *and* he's physically attracted to her *and* he is combining these things by getting a crush on the version of Mireille that exists only in his head.

"Maybe it's helpful to think of the letters as a kind of job, or a volunteer service," he says. "But what I wanted to say is that it's natural for you to experience a kind of three-quarter effect of your own. The effort to stay positive and encouraging can make you feel resentful. It's a long haul, and—"

"Oh, don't worry about me," Mireille says. "I know how to do this. Hey, I got a message from Madoka Tanaka. She's going to be in LA for work. We're having lunch. Maybe we can exchange happy family member tips. Thirty Ways to Love Your Astronaut."

Luke wishes there was a way to contain Mireille, manage her perfectly, just for the next eight and a half months.

"I really do understand," she says, leaning forward into the screen. "We all do."

AFTER MIREILLE SIGNS OFF Luke swipes the entirety of this conversation from his screen. Manage Mireille? He needs to manage himself.

His shift starts in thirty minutes.

Luke had to hand it to Prime. For twenty-four hours after the crew had shut themselves in the Lav there had been a lot of Prime-style shrieking. "Let's not call this a crisis, but it's definitely a challenging teaching moment and we should all really use this as an opportunity to get very creative in our solution streaming." And then, they'd taken it on the chin. "That the crew finds this a necessity is probably the most revealing information we've had so far, and let's be grateful for the challenge in examining that."

"Only observe" is Ransom's new refrain.

They are not allowed to have theories.

Ransom also keeps reminding the team that when they Gofer, the crew will have a great deal more privacy and the Obbers will have to get used to working with incomplete data.

But Prime didn't want the crew to have more privacy, certainly not now.

Luke pictures the crew, and all the careful little preparations Prime has made for increasing astronaut enjoyment of life on *Red*

Dawn. New exercise regimens with virtual landscapes. Special meals with complicated and time-consuming recipes. Concerts or events just for the crew uploaded daily. Specialized instruction, more training, more tests. A routine designed to help the crew navigate a daily existence that was both monotonous and restrictive and also bound at every second by an extreme peril which demanded, at the very least, total recall of massive amounts of information, lightning-quick reactions, and pretty much zero margin for error.

Maybe they should be surprised that the crew had shut themselves in the Lav for only twenty-three minutes. If it was Luke, he might never have come out.

YOSHI

his is a tuba concerto by the English composer Ralph Vaughan
Williams," Yoshi says. "Long Kwan is the soloist, in a live
performance with the Hong Kong Baptist University Symphony
Orchestra."

Prime uploads a music performance every morning. When they
Gofer, this will be part of a worldwide music participation program:
Music in Space! Right now, someone in Prime is making selections.
Yesterday they had a Sufi song. Sufis twirled in ecstasy when they
danced, or perhaps the ecstasy of being a Sufi caused them to twirl.
There wasn't much room in *Red Dawn* for twirling, or for ecstasy
either. Helen had bounced around in her chair a little.

They must all continue to be very normal, very nominal. They are
doing, Yoshi thinks, a good job. They are acting as if Sergei had not
introduced a note of paranoia. No, it was more an orchestra of paranoia. Helen is doing the best job. Perhaps she is not concerned. Yoshi
wants to talk to her, very badly.

They are in a sort of trap. To ask Helen to join him in the Lav without Sergei for a soundless confabulation would be a clear indication—to Sergei and to Prime—that there is an issue of some significance. Prime already knows—probably—that there is an issue of some significance. They might have deliberately fabricated the issue to test their responses. Double blinds within double blinds were structurally possible.

There is also a world where Sergei is perfectly fine, and a private discussion is unnecessary.

Yoshi pretends to listen to the music, but there is not enough tuba in the world to sort this out.

They have plenty of time now; this exacerbates the problem. *Red Dawn* is a kind of incubator, and so they must be very cautious about what they allow to grow. You need words—banalities are best—to neutralize the danger. There isn't enough space for words in *Red Dawn* either. Not these words.

They've all been trained to recognize the symptoms of paranoia. They are in perfect conditions for its occurrence, more at risk for it than almost anything else.

At first Yoshi thought it was a prank of some kind. Sergei said, "The odor and bacterial filters need to be repositioned," and since this was not a sentence that made sense, it seemed that Sergei was pulling them all into the Lav under obvious false pretenses. Yoshi had been a little impatient because it was their first recreation hour since launching from Mars and he wanted to enjoy the views.

It was difficult to fit all three of them into the *Red Dawn* Lav, which was even smaller than the Lav on *Primitus*. It had no shower—sponge baths only for almost nine months—and the three of them crammed together were required to stand nearly nose to nose, with Sergei straddling the commode, Helen jammed against the lockers and cleansing towel dispensers, and Yoshi wedged in between fan separators and Chute nozzles.

Sergei had brought in a whiteboard and handed out markers. Then he wrote:

LOST SIM DURING DUST DEVIL ON SOL 23
TOTAL SIM FAILURE
   SAW REAL LOCATION

Yoshi's impulse had been to stop him immediately. It wasn't that the part of his brain that endlessly reverse engineered Prime special effects had gone quiet. He enjoyed imagining how Prime had managed to accomplish this or that, and assumed they all did. They are engineers; it was their poetry to understand these things. But Yoshi was also comfortable with the artificial. Perhaps because of this, he had lost his bearings once or twice, and forgotten the differences between things. The balance was delicate, and needed to be maintained.

And then Sergei had added the sentence:

WAS NOT UTAH—WE WERE NOT IN UTAH

While Sergei continued writing, Yoshi had deliberately avoided looking at Helen. Even a single exchanged glance was too much to risk until they knew exactly what they were dealing with. Yoshi thought about Sergei's increased conservatism regarding safety protocols during their last sols on Mars, his lack of chatter, the bouts of staring. Helen would have noticed too, though Yoshi was not aware of any countermeasure she had taken. He'd thought that Sergei might be getting a mild case of what they called, in Antarctica, the "bug eye." Yoshi had felt guilty. He'd been too taken up with his own private ruminations; he should have been more attentive to other people's subcurrents. And Helen had become too happy. This was why joy was not a particularly desirable emotion on a mission. Joy made you notice less. Or do less with what you did notice.

As did desire.

NO LANDMARKS OF UTAH SITE < NO INDICATIONS OF AN OFFICIAL SITE < NO CAMERAS < WE WERE ALONE
  DIFFERENCES IN COLORS < PERSPECTIVES
  NO WARP TO VIEW OF SELF OR HELEN
  PHOBOS IN ANNULAR ECLIPSE
  PHOBOS

The fluid nature of their leadership roles often made being the commander more titular than anything else, but Yoshi did feel—in the Lav—that this was a situation where he must lead. One good technique was to perform a verbal repetition of something that was said to you, and in this way you could communicate both your desire to understand precisely what was being said, give your crewmate an opportunity to correct or refine his point, and—if necessary—allow him to hear for himself how whatever he just said was ridiculous. Some caution needed to be exercised in employing this method. It was not helpful to be mocking or sarcastic. Yoshi must respond with caution. He also needed to write his response, and since Yoshi was left-handed and prohibited from repositioning himself due to the fan separators between himself and Sergei, he had to scrawl.

Sergei had been in the Lav for forty-five minutes that morning. Yoshi had assumed diarrhea, but now realized Sergei was probably checking the wedge for cameras. Prime was contractually obligated not to put cameras in the Lav, but Sergei would not have trusted that. He would have checked for audio, but audio was easier to conceal. Sergei's use of the whiteboard meant he was taking no chances. They would have to come up with some explanation for Prime about this secret, silent meeting. They could brazen it out, but that was a risk.

Yoshi had taken Sergei through a summary of what Sergei had seen, and then Yoshi erased it and wrote POSSIBLE EXPLANA-TIONS on the whiteboard. Then he'd gotten tangled up in a microg-condition urinal funnel that became detached from the wall, so Helen took over.

WAS NOT TOTAL SIM FAILURE, she'd written. YOUR SCREEN HAD GLITCH. LOADED ALTERNATE MARS SITE.

Yoshi, having freed himself, tapped her explanation with his marker in agreement and added:

PRIME DUST DEVIL SIM V. COMPLICATED, NOT SURPRISED AT GLITCH

And then, after making a fresh bullet point:

SIM SWITCHING CAUSE OF VISUAL DISORIENTATION, V. NATURAL

Sergei had written:

ALSO POSS THAT PRIME WANTS TO MAKE ME
BELIEVE > THIS IS TEST > WILL I TELL YOU >
BUT I HAVE

Sergei had not finished the thought. He scrubbed the whiteboard clean and ended the meeting by exiting the Lav. Yoshi had received one look from Helen, which he'd been unable to decipher. He thought his lexicon for Helen's expressions was complete, but he had been wrong.

A blip, a glitch, a momentary lapse of reason.

At some point, for an unspecified amount of time, Sergei thought they'd actually gone to Mars. At the very least, Sergei might now be spending quite a bit of time trying to convince himself that this was not in the realm of absurdity, that he was not insane to entertain the notion.

It was not helpful—for Sergei—that Prime has them following the mission architecture for what a return after thirty days would really be. They had always planned to train this way, but Sergei could easily fold this into his paranoia.

Yoshi has accepted the possibility that Sergei wasn't disoriented, that he'd really seen what he claimed to have seen, but believes that this was something Prime had deliberately done, like the tampering with Sergei's equipment, like *eppur si muove* on *Primitus*. Prime wanted real data. Not astronauts pretending, astronauts believing. Dangerous, this, but understandable.

Yoshi badly wanted to talk with Helen. Only he was rather afraid that instead of talking about Sergei, something else might come out of his mouth.

The tuba concerto is over. They must now record their reaction. The astronauts applaud.

"Thank you very much, Long Kwan and the Hong Kong Baptist University Symphony Orchestra," says Yoshi, "for that beautiful performance. On behalf of the crew of *Red Dawn*, I salute your skill and dedication. We were so grateful to be your audience in space today."

There is nothing to do but keep going. They have a schedule.

If Prime had made the voyage out as dynamic as possible, with weeks of calamity or near calamity, their time now is marked by a shift into automated regularity. Were the astronauts capable of setting and maintaining a busy self-guided schedule when there was no immediate cause for them to do anything? Yes, of course they were. Everyone knew that if they were not busy, they would become unhappy and not perform well.

They might give in to paranoia.

So they will maintain their Hab and keep their skills sharp by training in sims. They will conduct such scientific experiments as the limited space for equipment allows. They will exercise, maintain their craft, and engage in public discourse and educational outreach concerning their mission.

"The tuba is a more dynamic instrument than I've appreciated," Yoshi says.

"I've heard that being a professional tuba player is extremely competitive, much more so than other instruments," Helen says. "In an orchestra, you might have thirty violinists. But there's only one tuba. And it's a very loud instrument, and you're the only one playing it, so it's very obvious if you make a mistake."

"Yes, a mistake would be very obvious," Sergei says. The words come slowly out of his mouth.

Yoshi doesn't look at Helen. He cannot remember how often he gazed at her, before the dust devil moment, or how often he looked at Sergei, before he took them to the Lav and confessed he was delusional. He would have looked them both in the eyes whenever he addressed them, at least some of the time. And there would've been just general looking, in the way one did. Yoshi doesn't want to seem to be looking at either one of them less or more. They will notice. Prime will notice.

"Time for haircuts!" Yoshi says, and they move from the Galley/ Recreation wedge, where they've been listening to music, to the Science/Lab wedge. They are not getting haircuts. They are removing five strands of hair from each of their scalps with tweezers. The roots will be analyzed for gene expression change. It is a useful and easy way to look at the effect of cosmic radiation on their bodies, stress levels, and metabolic conditions, particularly good on *Red Dawn* because it requires no equipment other than tweezers, a storage box the size of a toothbrush holder, a small portion of their single freezer, and RoMeO.

"But I do need a haircut," Helen says as Sergei dons medical gloves. Helen is starting many sentences lately with the word *but*, an indicator that her listeners are joining in late to some sort of internal monologue or debate. It is driving Yoshi mad.

No, he is quite fine.

"We all need a haircut." Sergei's movements are not erratic, not distracted. He moves with the deliberate pace that all of them practice in *Red Dawn*, where it is easy to bang an elbow. The walls are a pale silver and this and the curves—especially in their small sleeping pods set above storage spaces—create a slight illusion of more space than actually exists.

It is true, about the haircuts, at least in his case. Sergei's wheat-blond hair grows downward, into a neat cap, but Yoshi's hair goes vertical until the weight brings it down, and the vertical stage is a little too comical. The situation on *Red Dawn* is already teetering toward farce.

"I should have shaved my head when you two did," Helen says.

Sergei removes five strands of Helen's hair at the roots, performs the same service for Yoshi, then hands Yoshi the tweezers. For a paranoiac, Sergei seems perfectly content to offer up his nucleic acids. Yoshi must not exclude the possibility that Yoshi is the one suffering from paranoia, or that he has fed from Sergei's. Whatever happens to one astronaut can easily happen to the rest. They are at risk for contamination—paranoia is psychologically communicable—and *Red Dawn* is too small to dedicate any location for crew isolation.

"I want to shave my head," Helen says.

"Chuhh," says Sergei. "Okay."

"I'm serious," Helen says. "That's the kind of haircut I am requesting. It will be so much easier. I don't want to dry shampoo for seven months. It's silly that I didn't do it before."

Helen wants to shave her head? Where in Helen was this desire located, what was its source, what did she see when she saw herself bereft of hair?

"Okay," Sergei says. "Will be best if we cut short, and then use the vacuum shaver."

"When would you like to put it on the schedule?" Yoshi asks, because he must not betray any consternation. Yoshi has a vision of the kind of Victorian lockets containing the hair of the beloved. He had thought of asking Madoka once if she would contribute a lock to a locket, for him to take with him to space. She would have done it. What had stopped him? Perhaps knowing that things like lockets with hair in them were very fine in literature but should not be attempted in real life, lest they fail to live up to literature.

"We could do it now," Helen says. "And move the Venus Probe Sims back a half hour? It shouldn't take long. Just hack and buzz!"

"Changing the schedule on the fly is Prime recommended," Yoshi says. It is true. They must not become too dependent on routine—it puts them at risk for torpidity, which rather seems the least of their worries at this point.

"How do we classify Helen's hair for disposal?" Sergei folds his arms and looks at Yoshi. "This is much more hair than what comes off our heads. It is nonrecoverable cargo, yes, but of what label? Non-biodegradable waste? It is possible that it was contaminated on Mars and we should mark it for destruction."

He is making a joke, although trash is an incredibly serious topic on *Red Dawn*. On the space station they can use a Prime Raptor for trash, which is jettisoned prior to reentry and disintegrates, along with its contents, when it hits Earth's atmosphere. But they will be returning to Earth with all their waste materials.

"Perhaps we can keep it in the Lab," Helen says, with a smile. "Maybe some hair product company would like to give us a million dollars to do a study on the effect of UV radiation on labile proteins? I can't think of another use for it. I don't think my hair is going to be of much value against solar flare."

"It could make nice pillow," Sergei says.

"Or a sweater. I forgot to pack my knitting needles, though."

"Can you use my chopsticks?" Yoshi joins in the joking just in the nick of time.

They do haircuts in the Lav. Sergei volunteers to play barber and Yoshi remains in the doorway to video the event and in order to give Sergei more room. Also, because he is horrified. Helen faces the wall and straddles the closed lid of the commode. She pulls off the hair band holding her ponytail together and fluffs out her brown and gray curls. They look so soft.

"My father would cut our hair when we were children." Sergei hands Helen a trash bag to hold. "My sisters and me. We had to make a line and take turns in a chair in the kitchen. I remember he would put a bib around our necks, to catch the hair. Very scratchy yellow plastic, I hated this. But I learned how to cut hair from watching him cut Galina's and Valechka's, and I cut my own boys' hair."

"You don't have to make this nice," Helen points out. "Since we'll just be shaving the rest off."

"Maybe you will like just short hair, not bald," Sergei says. "Bald is extreme. And you might have egg-shaped head. You must consider what Yoshi and I will have to look at."

Yoshi has no words. Sergei is patting Helen's head, separating clumps of curls. He asks for and receives a comb. And Helen's eyes keep closing whenever Sergei tugs the hair back from her scalp. For nearly eight months Yoshi had nothing in his lexicon for Helen's sensuality, and now he has the way she touched her bare skin on Mars, and this, this giving over to someone else's, not his, touch.

Problems, these are all problems. They were all behaving differently. They could not pretend that they weren't, or Prime would be curious about what they were concealing. They must find a way to be transparent and opaque.

Maybe this was what Helen was doing. She never looked at herself, but Prime was looking all the time. She would give them something to look at so she could retreat deeper into whatever had happened to her. (What had happened to her?) She would empower Sergei as her Delilah.

He'd not experienced the dust devil in the way that Helen and

Sergei had. Had Prime deliberately kept him out of it? Had Prime manufactured a scenario in which Yoshi would see Helen nearly naked? Why is he the commander now; what specific skill does he have for any of these scenarios? This was Junya with his hand pressed over Yoshi's eyes all over again. Yoshi can only command himself, to wait, to endure.

He must not forget himself, or let his crew forget themselves. There is too much time, too much space. They must remember their names, their countries, their languages, their sexes, their bodies. They must remember where they are, where they came from, where they are going. He can feel the pull, the allure, of forgetting. It is the pull of space itself and they are explorers and they will always go to the edge of the map. But he cannot yet, he is not ready yet, he has only just begun to open his eyes.

He knows he must think of his wife. Only, somewhere on Mars, he lost the power to imagine her.

MADOKA

The hug had been awkward, both of them guessing wrong about the other's intentions as to where cheeks and shoulders and hands were headed, and with Mireille getting her ring caught in Madoka's scarf. Madoka had remembered the girl differently, as someone larger, but Madoka is the taller of the two.

The girl usually signed her Prime Family Member posts with the name *Meeps*, but Madoka is proud of her good French and prefers the name Mireille.

Madoka does not want to be friends with Mireille, whom she judged in Utah as being a vaguely dangerous person, but decided it would look odd, certainly unsociable, not to suggest a friendly get-together while she was in Los Angeles. Her Prime family liaison knew her schedule, and Madoka imagined the family liaisons having coffee together, discussing their charges, figuring out how best to handle them. Prime would be pleased to think of the two of them having lunch, creating an empathy bridge or however they put it. Yoshi'd been pleased too, when she'd told him. "From what Helen says of her daughter, I think you'll find her amusing," is what he said in his last message.

Madoka had formed an opinion of Helen Kane during the launch experience: incredibly capable and accomplished, unfeminine, respectful, quick, self-contained but professionally kind, and what Yoshi would call "jovial." She'd not seen the need to add greatly to this idea in the past nine months, since everything Yoshi said about Helen fit into one or two of those categories. She had liked that Helen had made Yoshi a pair of slippers for his birthday. It seemed motherly.

The restaurant had been suggested by Mireille. They are sitting in a garden patio decorated in old-fashioned European-style antiques, not Madoka's taste at all but pretty in its way. She's in her travel-work uniform: dark and tailored, with a patterned scarf for style and friendliness. It is always her PEPPER that is the star of the show, but as PEPPER's ambassador Madoka must not look too robotic herself. The other patrons of the restaurant are both more casually and more elaborately outfitted. T-shirts and mounds of hair and breasts, expensive but no style. Mireille is wearing a silk dress that doesn't quite fit her: she has pinned the neckline to a more modest décolletage.

Madoka had settled with herself that she would treat Helen's daughter the way she might treat a Prime employee. She would be friendly and not say too much, ask questions, praise when appropriate. She hadn't been able to think up a more interesting persona: she'd already used up the secretly insane woman character at the launch.

The problem is that so far, Meeps seemed to have selected the same persona for herself. After the initial entanglement with the scarf, they had settled in to their table, ordered slightly different kinds of salads, and were now engaged in an almost competitive exchange of blandness. They have talked a little about Los Angeles, about Japan, about the latest photos and crew news, about how sad the *Weilai 3* tragedy had been, about a space movie neither of them had seen but was supposed to be very entertaining. Madoka feels that while both of them are performing their chosen roles perfectly, neither one of them is particularly happy about it.

"Tell me about your work," Mireille is saying now. "You mentioned you're bringing a robotic caregiver—is that the right label?—to a private client?"

"It's for the client's mother," Madoka says. "PEPPER can act as a nursing assistant, but in this case it will be more of a companion."

"PEPPER?"

"The name of the model."

"What does she look like? PEPPER, I mean, not the client's mother."

Madoka retrieves her screen and brings up a picture of PEPPER. As she does this, she is aware of Mireille watching her carefully, almost as if she's studying her. There is something greedy in the girl's attention, or critical.

"Oh, wow." Mireille smile-frowns at the image of PEPPER. "It looks so much like a robot. I mean, like, when someone says the word 'robot' this is what you would think of. Classic robot."

They are both bent a little forward, looking at the picture of the robot. "She seems *nice*," Mireille says. "Does 'PEPPER' mean anything? I mean, beyond the English word."

"No. It's just the word in English. It's not easy to come up with a good name for a robot. It has to work for either male or female, because the voice can be set to either."

"Do more people make her sound female or male?"

"It depends. On who is doing the choosing, on the care recipient, on what primary tasks the PEPPER is assigned to."

"She's wearing a skirt."

"We call it a *silhouette*," Madoka says. The subject is certainly a safe one; she can talk about the robot for hours, but she's not certain Mireille will understand, she might think it all bizarre and inhuman. Americans have funny thoughts about Japanese culture: robots and filthy pornography and obedience and paper crafts. Madoka cannot allow PEPPER to become silly or strange. Right now, she's all she has.

"I'm trying to picture my grandmother with a robot like that," Mireille says. "She's in assisted living. In New York, where my aunt and uncle live. Do you have that in Japan?"

"Assisted living? We do, yes. It is very expensive, though."

"I don't know why, I just assumed that seniors in Japan would be looked after by their families, at home. That it was mostly just here in America that we pack them away."

"Oh, you've been told that we have great respect for the elderly in Japan," Madoka says. "We do, but that doesn't mean we wish to live with them."

Mireille starts to laugh, then stops and looks demurely down at her plate and changes the laugh to a polite smile.

Is she imitating me? Madoka wonders. *Or imitating what she thinks a nice Japanese business-lady wife of astronaut would be like?*

Madoka remembers female friendships in her past. Rolling with laughter on Yuko's bed, talking, talking, talking. What had she ever had so much to talk about? Emi rushing to Madoka's dorm room at Harvard and throwing herself in Madoka's arms because Emi's mother had died. Madoka'd been the one Emi had turned to at such an important moment, imagine that.

When Madoka puts her screen back in the bag at her feet she sees, under the table, that Mireille is sitting on her hands. She is not imitating Madoka. She's nervous. Madoka is ashamed. And suddenly, exhausted. It's not only the travel. It's this waiting. Always waiting. For what? She tries to think of something kind to say to Mireille.

"I like your dress," she says. "It's very pretty."

"I had an audition." Mireille releases one hand and fiddles with her doctored neckline. "For a play. This morning. I had to cry, in the scene."

"That must be difficult."

"No. Not for me." Mireille half laughs.

"How do you do it?" Madoka is genuinely interested. It would be something, to know how to make yourself cry.

"In drama school they teach you not to use anything very close to you for things like that. Or something really painful you haven't dealt with. I have a trick. I think of this thing my mom told me once. My mom's dad had this awful accident, when my mom was a kid, and he was in a vegetative state for years, before he died. She grew up visiting him once a week. My mom said that on his birthday they would bring a cake to where he was, at this facility, and sing 'Happy Birthday.' Whenever I have to cry, I mean professionally, I imagine that." Mireille flutters a hand in front of her face, perhaps to ward off an onslaught of tears right now.

Madoka sees it: children surrounding a man in a hospital bed, singing to an inert body. It is very terrible. It is as awful and blindly important, in its way, as her great-great-grandmother dying with her feet stuck in melting tar.

Sometimes Madoka is able to grasp what Yoshi talks about, this incredible thing they are—they will be—doing. Human presence on another planet, a monumental breakthrough for the species, for the history of human life. And other times, like now, this huge thing breaks down to the tiniest of particles, the brume of Martian dust, as Yoshi has described it. Why should a woman bound by her own feet to her planet and suffocating, or a man caught between worlds while his children sang "Happy Birthday" to him, why should these things not stop us all, in awe, in terror?

"That probably sounds horrible," Mireille says. "I mean, my using it. Like I'm cashing in on an emotion that isn't mine."

Madoka thinks. It doesn't sound horrible to her, but possibly she's not the right person to judge this.

"How is the emotion not yours?" she asks. "If it makes you sad?"

They both contemplate this question in silence for a moment.

"It's hard to know what's really yours," Mireille says. "Sometimes I think I should go on one of those pilgrimage-type things. Like walking across a continent or, at least, a really long trail. Confront my true nature."

"I suspect we all have the same nature when we are cold and hungry and tired," Madoka says. "Also, to overcome an adversity you have manufactured for yourself is a bit silly." She stops, because it occurs to her that this is maybe a very rude thing to say, but Mireille does not look offended. She looks relieved. It strikes Madoka that she could be friends with this person with the ghoulish imagination and hopeful dress. They would have to be friends in a way Madoka has not tried before, though, since the other ways always ended.

"One of the things, working with robots," Madoka says, "is that you see what *is* unique about human nature. You don't realize how creative you are. That is your true nature."

"I guess it doesn't seem so impressive," Mireille says. "If that's everyone's true nature. All humans, I mean."

Madoka tries to think of a good example of human nature, for both of them. Because she doesn't feel that great about herself either.

"You love your mother." Madoka had not quite made it into a question, to be safe.

"Yes," says Mireille. "It's not that simple, but yes."

"You see," Madoka says, "that is something a robot can't do. A robot can't say yes in the way you just said it. You could ask one of my PEPPERs if it loved, and it could run a computation, as you did, and decide to answer yes based on certain evaluations, as you did. But it would just be yes, in the end. It wouldn't be a *sad* yes."

"That's not such a great thing," Mireille says. "When you think about it."

"Nonsense." Madoka says it gently. "'I love you' is just 'I love you.' It's imitation. A *sad* 'I love you' is art."

SERGEI

Helen leans forward and opens her eyes.

"Interesting film," she says.

"You were sleeping," Sergei points out.

"I was following along with my eyes closed."

"Helen. It is a silent movie."

"Catch me up?"

"Engineer Los and his team received a mysterious communication from space. Then there was Soviet propaganda and romantic drama. Costumes are very funny. Soviets go to Mars in sweaters. Everyone on Mars wears crazy metal outfits and actors trip on them."

Helen scoots herself up into a more attentive position. For film nights, they convert their dining area into a recreational venue, moving the table and bringing in the portable screen from the Science/Lab. The table chairs are lowered and the footrests extended, though the design of the chair/loungers has not been a complete success. Two of the thermals no longer work; the material is not easy to clean.

Helen's chair/lounger has a stain from when Sergei dropped the sour cream during Cosmonautics Day celebrations.

Sergei turns his eyes back to the screen. The film was made in 1924, one of the first science-fiction movies, though more political message wrapped in science fiction. Sergei doesn't care about these old politics, and the Mars imagined here is preposterous. Still, it is a nice change and there is a good tradition of watching really bad space movies. The films Prime recommends for them now are all people overcoming odds, triumph-of-the-will-type things, meant to inspire. Sergei knows that he needs to have a triumph of will, but he can't tell what direction this effort should go in. He would prefer to watch something like a comedy where everyone is doing the wrong thing in funny ways. But he will watch anything. He doesn't like to be alone with his thoughts now. He needs a movie, or someone talking. He needs to fall asleep in "the saddle," as the expression goes, to avoid that terrible moment when the responsibility for his thoughts is clearly his and his alone.

Sergei's loneliness is total, unbridgeable. Things—talk, information, jokes—do not keep him company but they do prod him forward. He cannot read, unless it is work. He falls out of sentences after a paragraph, even if it's the kind of book deliberately meant to be sheer entertainment.

"It's not very good," Sergei gestures at the screen. "It's no *White Sun of the Desert*."

"Ha ha," says Helen. Yoshi stirs. He has not been fully asleep.

"There are robot slaves on Mars?" Yoshi blinks at the screen.

"By decree of the Elders," Sergei explains. "One third of the planet's life force is stored in refrigerators. The rest are slaves."

"It's fun to watch some of these obscure things," Helen says.

Helen must still be parceling out things like this, "saving" movies and books and ideas and feelings, in anticipation of doing it all again. There are days when this seems right to him too, and those days are easiest.

Other days he suffers. Sometimes for himself, sometimes for his crew. If it is revealed that they have been to Mars, his crewmates might go crazy. Imagine. To have gone to Mars, and not noticed.

Sergei takes his eyes off the screen and considers their mascot, Tycho. The little man currently embraces a ventilation hose suspended from their ceiling and is wearing a wig made from some of Helen's hair. They celebrated Helen's birthday yesterday. Sergei and Yoshi had sung a duet and let her have both their week's rations of M&M's.

"I think I've missed a few plot points of this movie." Helen yawns.

"This is the beginning," he says. "Of thinking that there are things we've missed." He had not meant to say that out loud. He must be more careful. It is a problem that he has to measure some of himself by how Helen and Yoshi react to him, because they are not very reactive people.

But they can all have fun times, they can show themselves to be in good spirits. Fully awake now, Helen and Yoshi join Sergei in calling out in Russian to the actors on the screen, booing, making jokes, until the movie ends.

It is time for bed now. Sergei has arranged his schedule so that he does an additional twenty minutes of light cardio before bed. Prime was worried exercising late in the evening would interrupt his sleep patterns, because they have data to show this can happen, but Sergei is not a lab mouse and, just now, he sleeps better after a little exercise. Helen and Yoshi call it "Sergei walking the dog."

Helen and Yoshi go to their sleep pods and Sergei moves to the

Exercise wedge, loads his screen with Gagarin Cup highlights from March. If he looks upset, or his heart rate jumps up, his jogging on the treadmill and a disastrous season from the Gladiators will provide cover from his Prime watchers.

Exercise is when Sergei allows himself to think, although it would be better for him if he didn't think at all, and just watched ice hockey. But he knows what he will do. He will run it all through his head, again:

He is walking toward the Hab. He sees the green lights surrounding the Hab, the Hab itself. He sees the cable in his hands, and the regolith under his feet. Rocks and sky. Tracks from the Rovers. And then his screen goes flat green, and then black, and a line of words, flashing too quickly for him to read but—he is almost certain—containing the word *FAILURE*, and then no sim at all.

Everyone knows what Mars looks like: butterscotch sky and caramel rocks.

But really, no one knows for sure what Mars looks like. It is not so simple, taking a photograph on another planet and then sending this photograph to Earth. Many images collected from Mars take days to assemble, and the differences in light and dust in the atmosphere will be smoothed over for coherence. Some of the cameras use infrared color filters, or ultraviolet, useful for science but not for capturing what the human eye would experience. Still, we can say that we are close to knowing what Mars looks like, and that had been their simulated Mars: Prime's best guess based on the best guesses available.

What Prime had not been able to give them was a living color palette. Sergei had timed it, how the light shifted every half hour on the half hour, mimicking the gains and losses of their smaller, dimmer sun. The light never moved *within* the half hour. His shadow on

Mars was, for twenty-nine minutes, a dead man. There was also the slightly surreal aspect to your crewmates that the sim created during an EVA, and the knowledge that the tools you were using had been made lighter, that the Rover wasn't really roving.

It was hard for him to ignore these things, but he'd tried. And he'd gotten quite close. So maybe he felt more like he was in a video game than he was on Mars, but at least he started believing the video game.

When his Mars sim failed, he should have seen Utah.

But he hadn't seen Utah. He would have known Utah. Utah was seventy-eight million kilometers closer to the sun and the horizon was quite different. Months and months ago, he had walked with his crewmates around the perimeter of the swell location where *Primitus* sat. He had seen what could be seen. Martian only if one was near-sighted. A good rocky plain, but clearly, in the distance: mountains. A big, bright sun. Blue sky. The sim had needed to obscure all these things, and many more.

Without the sim, he should have seen the mountains. He should have seen a whole team of Prime employees, or at least some yellow tape demarcating their site. Lights. Cameras. Dust makers. It should have looked like a film set in Utah. Like a research facility. Like Earth.

It wasn't just that—for a few seconds—the sky had been a different color than the sim, and also not at all blue. It was that the sky was so convincingly a real sky that it made the sim seem crude. He wondered that he could have talked himself, however grudgingly, into believing a simulated sky. How could he explain the difference? It was like if you had ever seen a dead body. In the movies or television, sometimes people were confused if a person was dead or not. Not so, in life. You knew when someone was dead. It was not a confusing thing.

It was not an Earth sky, the sky that he saw.

He saw Phobos. It was transiting the sun, an irregular lump of darkness against the pale yellow. Darker than he'd seen the moon, its definition sharper.

When the sim came back on, all the colors, the *feeling* of the colors, died. Death told you there had once been life.

IT WAS SOME kind of test. Or a computer glitch. Perhaps Prime didn't even know it had happened.

It was possible Prime had played similar tricks on Helen and Yoshi, but those two were concealing them. Certainly, they—Helen, Yoshi, himself—had never been absolutely honest about their states of mind, but he'd thought he had an accurate sense of what they were all lying about and why. Not lying. Spinning.

He cannot afford to be suspicious of his crewmembers.

SERGEI KNOWS THAT paranoia is capable of making him ignore truly inescapable arguments. He knows this, and he tells himself to face these arguments. He instructs himself to defeat himself, but this is like playing against yourself at chess. He is equally good at both sides. Helen or Yoshi might give him a challenge, but he cannot play them without giving himself away to Prime and implicating his crew even further. There are other ways he can test his rightness or wrongness, but, again, he needs to do these tests in such a way that Prime will not know he is doing them. Because if he is wrong, or right, depending on the point of view, then he will ruin everything for everybody. Shame himself, his family, and fuck it up for Helen and Yoshi.

That he hesitates to test his conclusions must mean he knows—some crucial part of him knows—that he was not on Mars, is not in space. Come on.

But he is not crazy.

All the elaborate special effects to no purpose, from the very beginning. It was one thing to simulate Mars, but why simulate the flight to Prime's launch facility in Texas, the drive to the launch pad, the elevator ride up to a *Primitus* perched atop the *Manus* heavy-lift? This was all done for psychological reasons? What real difference would this make in their psychology? None of them had believed it was real.

Why start Eidolon on the same day as the *Red Dawn II* launch? The synchronicity made no sense except when you realized it was possible to launch *Primitus* instead of *Red Dawn II* without many people knowing. Not easy, but possible, especially with a little help from the United States Pentagon. No one who wasn't Prime was allowed anywhere near the launch pad. Prime had video of launching *Red Dawn I* and they could have released that to the public. There were space surveillance telescopes and radar trackers all over the world, and these could pick up something the size of a melon at thirty thousand kilometers, but he'd seen stealth hardware that was capable of obfuscating intelligence.

The phrase *stealth melon* is so stupid he can almost laugh at himself. Except this is a thing that has already been done.

Their isolation was total; every piece of information, including what anything outside their craft truly looked like, came through Prime. There was very little in the crew's behavior that indicated they did not believe their mission was real: none of the public videos or messages they sent to Earth included the word *Gofer* or a phrase like "when we actually go to Mars . . ." Their private letters, yes, but those went to Prime first. And who was to say that this latest email from Dmitri was even from Dmitri? It didn't sound like him at all. The world could be watching them go to Mars and the astronauts wouldn't even know it. Prime could be keeping them in the dark because they had a study that showed astronauts perform certain tasks better if they believe they are in a simulation. Diabolical and risky, but not unthinkable. All twisted psychological things are very possible.

Or the world could not know. Sending the crew secretly had better motivations. In fact, there were so many reasons to send a crew secretly he was beginning to approve of Prime doing so. Any failure of MarsNOW—especially something very public and catastrophic— would be an incalculable loss to Prime, and to the wider goal of space exploration. Look at what seemed to be the fallout over the *Weilai 3* tragedy. Prime was a business, even more so than the Chinese government. Why *not* conduct the mission in secret? If it failed, no one would know. If it succeeded, well, they had the whole thing documented. They could even tell the world once *Red Dawn* landed and—surprise! Three astronauts came out! You would have to deal with another scenario like the moon-landing-denying people, but this would happen anyway because people were crazy.

There was the problem of accounting for their three missing bodies if they died during the mission. Prime would be smart to arrange for faking their deaths in a way that would tarnish neither Prime nor the mission. The options were not pleasant. Prime could arrange for an explosion, say, at something like the quarantine facility in Texas or Utah, and then claim it was the work of terrorists. Terrorists would claim it anyway. But this would be very hard on his sons, this kind of senseless death.

He is being ridiculous.

Sergei forces his attention back to the screen, to react to the game highlights. He only has a few minutes of exercise left, and must capitalize on the opportunity to shout bad language and call people idiots.

Sergei had wanted to play hockey when he was a boy, but had chosen to focus on his studies. His father had said he'd not the right temperament for the sport, anyway. He would not even let Sergei watch, because he said being a fan of a sport you didn't play made you a follower, and Sergei needed to be a leader. The old man had been a foolish guy; Sergei became a leader but not because of his father's nonsense, which anyway was not intended to make him a leader. All this "to make you stronger" had always been bullshit, and they'd both known it. What his father wanted was to establish a weakness so that when, inevitably, Sergei became bigger, his father could exploit that weakness and topple the structure. Sergei could be a nice guy and say his father hadn't quite known what he was doing, but come on. Sergei has sons now of his own. You know.

It's important to see the truth of things. Okay, he can submit himself to this. People, his sister, but also many people, are always talking about their personal truths, and these are just stories, not so much truth as crutch.

He could be no better. He does not know what particular weakness he has. He thought he had been very careful about not allowing one, but it could be something Prime has done to him in particular, because they had seen it.

Or maybe his father had found him at last, beyond the grave, travelled all the way to Mars to knock his son to his knees.

HELEN

"We've made up a song," Helen says. "Would you like to hear it?"

"Should I get the camera?" Yoshi asks. "Or should I pretend that I have not heard you singing this song for the past hour?"

"Are you annoyed?"

"Not at all."

"We're cleaning the sleep sacks, the sleep sacks, the sleep sacks, we're cleaning the sleep sacks so they will be nice!" Helen and Sergei sing.

They are cleaning the sleep sacks, it is true. It is a two-person job: one to hold, the other to brush on the dry shampoo. When they'd pulled Sergei's sleep sack from his compartment, she'd been relieved to see he'd only affixed to the walls what he'd had up in his wedge on *Primitus*: a few religious icons of purely sentimental value and pictures of Dmitri and Ilya. Pieces of paper covered in a madman's tiny script, or crabbed arithmetical glyphs would have been hard to ignore.

They usually listen to music during cleaning day, but neither Sergei nor Yoshi had seemed enthusiastic about making a selection, perhaps since today's Music in Space! had been a rather long performance involving bagpipes. So they worked accompanied by the ambient noise of *Red Dawn*, the whirring and humming of their home. This noise was certainly not negligible, but Helen became aware of Sergei's own silence. As much as possible, she likes to keep Sergei chatting now, because when he is talking she can be more or less certain of what is going on in his brain. She'd started to sing and he had joined in and then they found themselves unable to stop.

Yoshi, she thinks, is a little annoyed. She'd seen him earlier vacuuming in a very aggressive fashion, unlike his usual calm thoroughness. Yoshi likes a clean ship, but it is also his way, Helen thinks, of giving heft and validity to what can be seen and controlled.

Possibly she is exaggerating their vulnerability. Sergei may well be over his lapse of reason, and Yoshi may be perfectly content.

She has her own problem: she is very attractive just now. It's unfortunate that without hair she should look so beautiful; Helen hopes that she's the only one who has noticed. She wasn't selected for this, she's meant to be the female the other two males will not find alluring. It's something of an effort to keep her hands off her own head, to not touch her neck, her waist, her thighs, her hips, her breasts, her stomach. Her skin is remarkable: in some places dry and papery like lovely parchment, and in other spots, warmly malleable like sweet dough. At night, in her sleep compartment, she holds parts of herself with a real appreciation.

They are all in extreme close-up; one notices the appearance of a new eyebrow hair. And yet they must communicate as if they are not noticing this. They must protect themselves, from Prime, from one another, from whatever parts of themselves they are grasping in the dark.

On all the *Red Dawn* screens now: Venus. Their view is shaded: Venus is too bright to look at with the naked eye, but in other ways it has not been enhanced in the ultraviolet-filter way the planet often is. Not, then, a hot mess of toxic chemicals and misshapen volcanoes covered in sulfuric acid clouds, orange and yellow, ugly, a planet gone wrong. No, it looks like what it should truly look like: a cream-colored ball, spinning very slowly in the opposite direction most other planets spin. They have to be disciplined about when they look at it, otherwise they would do nothing but look.

"I have good news," Yoshi says. "The red pepper is ripe. We can eat it. This week's winning recipe calls for a red pepper."

The crew moves to the large console in the Science/Lab wedge.

"It's a lot of steps." Helen scans the recipe instructions. "But I guess no one needs *Fifty* Quick *Recipes for Long-Duration Space Travel.*"

The recipe says that it will take them three and a half hours to make this dish. Was preparing dinner a meaningful use of three and a half hours? Did knowing that part of this elaborate dinner's function was to keep you occupied make it more, or less, meaningful?

Yoshi points out a line of the recipe that calls for three fresh bay leaves. "I see another sacrifice is called for. Alas, poor Mildred."

Yoshi had given the herbs in their garden lab these sorts of names. Mildred. Dorcas. Ermengarde. He hadn't named the vegetables: the zucchini, spinach, red pepper, pale descendants of the *Primitus* garden lab.

"Crushed peanuts," Helen reads. "I can never see how these things are going to come together. I don't have a good food imagination."

Variety and pleasure in food is meant to be a major factor in their psychological health. Prime will challenge chefs on Earth in a competition to make a delicious and nutritious meal from the list of *Red*

Dawn pantry items. The contestants will need to keep in mind that supplies are limited, and while the occupants of *Red Dawn* will be enjoying artificial gravity, the craft is designed for emergency microgravity conditions: it has no oven, and no stovetop, only a rehydration station and a forced air convection oven. Prime plans on producing a filmed series of professional chefs, cooking schools, and enthusiastic amateurs taking on this challenge. Right now the recipes are coming from, it's to be assumed, Prime's own Food Science Lab.

"I once contributed recipes to a cookbook," Sergei says. "Did I tell you this?"

He has not told them, it is totally new information. (The astronauts have developed a way of letting one another know when an anecdote has been repeated too often. They say: "I love it when you tell that story.")

"Sergei, was it a cosmonaut cookbook?" Yoshi asks.

"No. It was called *The Engineer's Cookbook*. I explained the slow-cooked rib roast." Sergei shapes a rotisserie motion with his hands. "This is a place where many mistakes are made."

"I cannot believe I don't have a copy of that," Helen says. "I can't believe every single member of my family didn't give it to me for Christmas. No one ever knows what to get."

"Do you think people will understand this is important?" Sergei points with his chin at the recipe on the console. "People might think, 'Oh, this is not a problem, to always eat the same food. People think, maybe, of prisoners, or soldiers, always eating the same food, food that is not good. Why should we need special variety? Why all these things for our comfort? If you are person who goes crazy after eating the same menu, or from not having fun things to do, then you are not person strong enough to go to space."

He is anxious, Helen thinks, that he is not suffering enough. The man who has gone to Mars should not emerge from his spacecraft pink and healthy and having enjoyed special recipes concocted by space enthusiasts at Le Cordon Bleu.

"I think the general assumption is that going to space is really hard and most people don't imagine it to be something they could tolerate," Helen says, though it had been years before she realized this was true. It had been difficult for her to comprehend that there were people in the world who didn't want to go to space, that not everyone was her competition for a seat, that some people didn't even see space travel as the most glorious expression of human capability.

"Last night I dreamed of the first apartment Talia and I had together," Sergei says. "The cupboards in the kitchen had been painted so many times that they would not close."

Helen has a high tolerance for non sequiturs now. She herself wants to talk and talk. Not out of a desire to communicate with others; she just wants to hear all the things she might say, if she were to go on talking.

"How funny. I dreamed about a garden café where my daughter took me when I was visiting Los Angeles," Helen says. "I must have been hungry."

What's funny is that she is making this up. She has, at last, begun to dream of walking in space: gorgeous, drifting dreams, without sentences, pure sensation. In her Prime logs she says: *I dreamed I was playing in my high school marching band. I dreamed I was shopping for a new refrigerator. I dreamed I was watching my daughter in a production of* Romeo and Juliet. These, she feels, are the dreams of the person Prime selected for this mission.

Yoshi does not say what he dreamed. He is opening a further

communication from Prime. This contains an announcement: their backup crew has been selected. The names of the astronauts and short biographies have been included. This crew will begin training in Japan next month.

Yoshi, Helen, and Sergei gather around the main console, silent, reading. This is unexpected news; she had not given much thought to their backups, though of course, of course.

The backup crew is all American. One female, two males. They are all engineers, all possessing the same sorts of specialty skill sets as the three of them. This other crew is a slightly scrambled version of themselves.

"You must know them?" Sergei says to Helen. "I haven't met Ty. I know Dev, of course. Also, Nora, though more by reputation."

"Dev and I were in the same astronaut candidate class," Helen says. "I've known him my whole career. He's been my family liaison, and I've been his. We've been each other's CAPCOMs. Ty is great, though I don't know him well. And Nora. Gosh, I wouldn't have thought to put these three together, but the more I think about it, the more sense it makes." Prime will be watching her reaction. "What an amazing crew. This is very cool."

Helen studies the backups, making comparisons. Nora is the sole female, so Nora must also be the supplier of the female element that contains some quality discounting her from becoming an object of sexual attraction to her crewmates. Nora is not in her fifties, but she *is* gay.

"But Nora's more the Yoshi of her crew," Helen says. "In temperament. She paints, or does something artistic, and she's very well read."

"You do artistic things," Yoshi says.

"Maybe I mean she also likes old-fashioned things."

"That's the opposite of creative."

Helen realizes she has offended Yoshi in some way. "You're right," she says. "That's a sloppy comparison." There is tension in the room. A new presence: others who might be as good as they are, might be better.

But if Nora is—roughly—the Yoshi, then Ty is most like Sergei in temperament. Same sense of humor, same drive. This would make Dev Patek the Helen.

Helen knows what is said about her. People said things in which the word *rock* made a frequent appearance. Helen was solid as a rock, steady as a rock, was a person who had performed rock-star EVAs, but more constantly impressed in the way that astronauts were most frequently called upon to be rock stars: approaching every menial or humbling or uninteresting task as if her life depended on the perfection of its execution. Upon this rock, mighty as a rock.

"It is interesting," Sergei says. He is examining the biographies. "Nora has two sons, they are a little older than my own, and she is still married. Ty is divorced with no children, and Dev—"

"Married," Helen says. "No children. I know his wife, she's a nurse; she's lovely. I've spent time with his parents too: the nicest people."

"Ah." Yoshi leans forward and flicks Dev Patek's picture, magnifying it. "So he's a Helen but without the tragedy."

It is a spectacularly unkind thing to say. Helen is stunned.

"In future, it won't matter so much who goes," Sergei says, as if he hadn't heard this exchange. Possibly he hadn't. "Bigger craft, bigger crew. You don't need to be Shackleton to go to the South Pole now. You can be anyone with money for a plane ticket."

"That is nonsense." This is also an uncharacteristic statement from Yoshi: he is never dismissive. "That we will be able to go more quickly, yes," he continues. "But a larger crew also has dangers. Division. Politics. Hierarchy. Lunatics. It will always matter who goes."

"Shackleton isn't the best example," Helen says.

Sometimes, in her life, people had envied or resented her. And maybe they would say something like that, like, "Helen without the tragedy." She had not expected this from Yoshi, though. She must not choose to be hurt.

THE THING TO NOTICE about this backup crew was that they were a complete unit and as individuals they did not replicate their own crew exactly. Members could not be swapped in to replace Sergei or Yoshi or Helen without the balance being disturbed. It was still all for one and one for all. Sergei and Yoshi should feel reassured, not threatened.

"It is like my dream," Sergei says. "The cupboards that needed to be stripped before they would fit. The experience of going to space. It is layers. Layers of skill, layers of experience, layers of time. It is a wonder we still fit in our spacesuits."

They are all changing. She has changed too. Maybe that's not good. She was selected for this mission because of the person she was, not the person she is now. To look into space is always to look into the past. The Helen that was chosen was not this Helen.

She can't quite remember how she was exactly.

Eidolon was too real. Sergei and Yoshi have forgotten that this was training. No, she'd forgotten it too. They should not be changed by this pretend mission to Mars. They should wait to change so they can be changed later, for real.

Yoshi is gazing at her in a pleading way. It is too much.

Helen looks to the screen that is meant to be a window. Venus is close, Earth is still very far away. Or you could say that Earth is right outside, and Venus is very far away. In either case, they have nowhere to go.

MIREILLE

Y ou can go deeper if you want."

Mireille does not want to go deeper, she has no great desire to jam her elbow into this guy's rhomboids just to satisfy his misperception that pain must always equal benefit.

"Okay," Mireille says, in her soothing voice. "Take a nice deep breath for me."

The guy cannot take a nice deep breath. He doesn't know how. He huffs. Also, his position on the table is not ideal: his stomach is too big to be squashed flat while lying facedown, and bulges out to the right, rolling him askew. She doesn't judge that, or find it repellent, it's only amazing that someone with seventy pounds of excess weight can seem genuinely mystified as to why he doesn't feel awesome. What the hell does he think is happening? God, she is clear today. She could probably even help this guy, she's so clear.

Mireille sucks in her cheeks. Her face is tired, like it ran a marathon, which it did. Yesterday, she spent six hours recording a facial library for a new game, a big one, one that she has a starring role in.

All day long they had given her emotions and shades of emotions to do. Subtle things like Curious, Curious and Skeptical, Curious and Amused, Curious and Not Able to See Well. And then big things like Terror, Disgust, Rapture. They really wanted her to make the faces, really, really *do* them. Not one person had said, "That's too much." She'd gotten nothing but praise and a paycheck. It might have been one of the best days of her life.

"How's the pressure now?" she asks. She's supposed to use this guy's name three times during a treatment. That's one of the hotel spa's "standards," but she's forgotten his name. Shuckerman or Shalliman or Chushkerman. Whoever he is, he grunts, because now he's in pain. Everyone is in pain. Most people think pain in massage means something is happening, and if they can endure it, they will be improved, but sometimes the only thing pain means is pain.

It's a very easy to mistake to make, though. She'd refused for the longest time to get therapy or take any psychoactive drugs because she'd felt that "darkness" was necessary, not just for her as an actor, but as a human being.

You didn't have to feel slightly terrible all the time, as it turns out. Her only worry now was that slightly terrible was not a flaw in her chemistry, but an appropriate response to being the kind of person that she was. "You're very hard on yourself," Luke said.

"Can you imagine the kind of person that I'd be if I wasn't hard on myself?" she said back. Luke should be sympathetic. He was hoping to improve the human race, and it would be hard to get there if the human race thought it was already fantastic, thanks very much.

Well, she could still go dark, if she needed to, she could go dark right now. Yesterday she had done Terror. She'd done Fear and Dejection and Remorse. And because she had done Remorse as fully as a person could do it, she knew that she hadn't ever experienced that kind of pure Remorse before. What she'd felt in the past was polluted Remorse, because half the time she was sorry she was *also* privately resentful *and* building a case about why the actions that had led to Remorse could be justified.

"You can go a little bit lighter on my legs," says Mr. Clusterman. "Sometimes my legs are a little, well, not sensitive, but ticklish."

"Mmhmm," Mireille says. She makes Curious with Skepticism face. He asked her to go deeper and now it's too deep, but he doesn't want to say that because he thinks it might make him look wimpy and fussy and both those fears are why he's overweight: he's not connected to who he is, so he's not even feeding himself, he's feeding different versions of himself and most of those versions eat crap.

Mireille is on fire!

She keeps thinking of things she could have done slightly better yesterday, but that's very natural, if the word has any meaning.

That had been another of her arguments against taking psychoactive drugs: that the moods they produced wouldn't be natural.

"But then I thought about it, and I realized that *most* of my moods aren't natural," she'd said to Luke. "I artificially induce, like, seventy-five percent of what I'm feeling just with pretend conversations in my head and my imagination. Probably ten more percent is just blow-back from whatever chemicals are in all our food and water and air."

It might be a good idea to run the whole what-is-natural issue by Madoka, when they talk next. Madoka gives good advice.

She should probably stop messaging Luke. He hadn't asked her to stop, but he had talked about something called "limerence" and how an intense desire for romantic reciprocity is something different from "love" and that sometimes what people wanted wasn't so much another person, but a return of feeling from that person. She was 75 percent certain he was trying to say he had a crush on her.

Did she have feelings for Luke? It's a little difficult to tell. She can do Terror while sitting in a chair with fifty sticky dots on her face. Falling in limerence with a cute guy in Utah who asks her about her feelings is pretty much level-one difficulty.

It was all just choices, right? Even her doing Terror yesterday wasn't totally Terror because Terror wasn't a thing you had a choice about in the actual moment, and she'd definitely made a choice for Terror.

It was different when you had emotions in some kind of context, like when you were doing a play or working on something for acting class. Then, you could be in the moment and react. Sitting in a chair and displaying one emotion after another only because someone had directed you to was a little crazy, when you thought about it. Maybe it was only crazy that it turns out to be something she is extremely good at.

"That feels tight, that spot on my foot," says Mr. Shuckelman. "What's that connected to? Like, in reflexology?"

"Your digestive tract," Mireille says, although she doesn't know because she thought reflexology was ridiculous and never paid attention in that class during massage school, but you can always tell people that the something wrong is connected to their digestive tract and they will believe you.

"Oh, that makes sense," he mumbles.

Really hard to tell if she has feelings for Luke. He talked to her like he was very interested in what she felt and had to say, so that was incredible and rare, but he was professionally obligated to be interested in her, and she knows how that works. She is professionally obligated to be interested in Mr. Shalimar here, and she is giving him a *great* massage and she's only using a very small percentage of her attention span to attend to his problems. But her hands are healing. She has that touch.

Luke was a sweetheart, but does she want to be with Human Improvement Guy? She wants to be understood, not made better.

Is that what she wants? No. She wants to be loved as she is, but inspired to be *better*. No. She wants to *become* much better, so much better that she doesn't even *need* to be loved. There, that was it.

That was her mother.

Mireille tries to get some circulation going in poor Mr. Shukerton's gastrocnemius. Her mother would probably say that Mireille was wrong; everybody needs to be loved. Or maybe her mother would say something about the difference between needing and wanting. Actually, Mireille has no idea how her mother feels about being loved.

After Luke had gone down on bent neuron or what have you, and confessed hypothetical limerence, he'd also told her about a thought experiment created by a philosopher named Derek Parfit. You imagine that there is a teletransporter to Mars. When you press a button, the teletransporter records all your cells, in the exact state they are in right at that moment, and beams them by radio to Mars, where they are re-created perfectly and come to life, remembering everything right up to the moment the button was pushed. While this happens, the body you have on Earth is destroyed absolutely. "So, is the person on Mars still you? Or is it a replica of you?"

Luke said that many people had strong reactions to this thought experiment. It had to do with personal identity.

"Okay, I'll have you turn over now." Mireille makes the sheets into a little tent and looks away while Mr. Chucklesman harrumphs himself over.

It's obvious how to live well. You become someone who meditates regularly, freeing yourself from your own ego and living in the present. When you're not meditating, you involve yourself in charitable acts, helping others, being generous, caring for the needy. When you're not doing any of those things, you eat sparingly of vegetables and enjoy the natural world. It bothers Luke that people know this and don't do it. Mireille isn't as bothered by how perverse people are. People being so messed up meant they needed actors to tell stories so we could try to understand ourselves. Well, and messed up people needed massage therapists, too. She'd be totally out of a job if everyone acted like an astronaut.

Pain has value, of course it has value.

When Mireille was eleven years old she'd been crossing the street in Houston with her mother, and maybe there had been a car turning, or maybe she'd not been paying attention, but her mother had sort of grabbed her to pull her away from something and a teenager had plowed into her mother with his skateboard and then stalked off saying, "Stupid bitch. *Ugly* bitch." But the big thing she remembers was her mother's crooked embarrassed smile, and the sense that a person was never safe; even if you were a United States astronaut you could be made to look awkward by someone calling you a stupid bitch, and she'd been mortified by this apparent weakness of her mother, and instead of rushing to her defense and saying, "Oh my God, what an asshole" or giving her mother a hug or something, Mireille had just pretended—very badly—that she hadn't really seen it.

Mireille had been ashamed. She is ashamed now of being ashamed. That memory will never get any better, only worse. That's a kind of pain.

At a certain point, you probably had to stop thinking about what your mother did or didn't do to you, and start thinking about what you did or didn't do to your mother. All this stuff about the natural order—parents are supposed to do or be this or that—that was maybe made up by people who were still pissed at their parents. Anytime people talked about the natural order you should be skeptical.

She can sit down now, and work on Mr. Shuckman's neck. People's faces sometimes look beautiful when you view them upside down.

Mireille had given her mother a massage when she last visited. Her mother was modest, so Mireille hadn't ever seen her naked. She thought her mother would be sort of tense and weird about getting a massage, but she'd been completely relaxed and open, even falling asleep at one point. How could her mother trust her so much, to fall asleep in her hands, when Mireille was such a terrible daughter?

She'd been brilliant at being her father's daughter. If he had lived longer, she could still be that, although it's possible that by now she would have outgrown her prodigy.

"Oh, I love having my scalp rubbed," says Mr. Shushbagger.

Mireille knows he is loving it, she can almost feel how good it feels to him.

Her father had once told her that she was an empath. That she felt things deeply because she was sensitive to others, picked up on their emotional cues so completely that she took them within her own body and mind. That she didn't intellectualize her emotions. That all of this was a gift.

LUKE HAD WANTED to know her reaction to the thought experiment. If a record of her cells had been copied and teletransported to Mars, and re-created perfectly, would she still be her, or a replica?

"How badly do I want to go to Mars?" she asked.

"Oh. That's not. I mean the thought experiment—"

"Okay, sure, perfect replicas of your cells and all your memories and everything make you the same person. Except you're now also a person who got teletransported. And who is now on Mars. Wouldn't that change you? And I know this isn't the point of the thing, but I don't think anyone should be teletransported to Mars. It should hurt a little, to go to Mars."

"Okay, that's our session," Mireille says. She wipes the guy's feet with warm towels, and gently places his robe across his knees, aligns his slippers on the mat. "How do you feel?" she asks, placing a calm and benedictory palm against his forehead.

"Oh my God, I feel amazing," he says. "You're really gifted."

Mireille takes her hand away.

DMITRI

Dmitri is having a picnic. He is sitting on a blanket, on a hill, in a public park. There are people on another blanket not ten feet from him, older people, adults. A woman bounces a baby on her lap and says, "Oopsadaisy! Oopsadaisy!" One of the others on her blanket is capturing this on a screen. Dmitri doesn't know how the people on that blanket connect to each other—which is married to whom or are they a family or what. Dmitri pulls his baseball cap down lower.

"Teach me something to say in Russian," Robert says.

"*Chush' sobach'ya.*" A group of schoolchildren are being marched across the stone rotunda below their hill. Everyone is talking about how nice the weather is. The weather in New York is pretty much the same as at home. Freeze your balls off in winter and sweat your balls off in summer and ten good days in between. This is one of those days.

"*Chush' sobach'ya.*" Robert's accent is not bad. "What am I saying?"

"It is like bullshit," Dmitri says.

This is Dmitri's first date. That is what Robert is calling it. The last time they'd seen each other, Robert said, "I think we need to have our first date." Dmitri thought he was joking. They had met up ten times, more than Dmitri had ever met up with anyone else.

It was not a joke. Robert had brought a picnic. He'd brought a blanket and forks and boxed water and containers of fruit salad and beet salad and couscous and two cookies. He'd also brought a rose, which he had told Dmitri was for him.

The two cookies would've been enough, Dmitri thought, to signal that something else was now going on, something that was not getting hot and getting hard and stars exploding. The two cookies really would have been sufficient. The rose made it ridiculous. The rose was a funeral offering. But he's always known it couldn't last. Ten visits to Robert's dormitory. There was always going to be a reckoning.

"Hey, relax," Robert says. "Just because we're outside doesn't mean we have to pretend like we don't know each other." Robert reaches across the lineup of picnic foods between them and puts his hand on Dmitri's thigh. "Or do we?"

"No, it's fine," Dmitri says, but Robert takes his hand away and leans back on his elbows. Dmitri is not familiar with Robert's body like this: clothed, closed.

Dmitri glances again at the threesome to their left. The woman seems to want to cuddle Oopsadaisy, who is kicking her in the face. The two guys are now talking to each other. Everyone appears to be living some kind of life.

"Okay, you do understand that it's not illegal here, right?" Robert asks.

"What is not illegal?" Dmitri reminds himself that he can just get up and walk away, at any point. Ilya has a rehearsal at his dance school today, which means that Dmitri has four free hours in the city, instead of three. Thirty-eight minutes of this has already been wasted in getting to Central Park. If eating the food doesn't take too long, they can still get back to Robert's room and do some stuff before the four hours are up. He has told Robert that his cousin agreed to give him a little more time today.

"Being gay," Robert says. "Nobody is going to be upset if we make out right now. Nobody cares about that. I mean, I understand if you're not out in Russia."

"People are out in Russia," Dmitri says. "They're just private. It's not a big deal." In fact, he knows almost nothing about gay life in Russia, except that he'd heard something about people pretending to be gay online so they could turn in real gays to the police. They were called Hunters.

"Okay," Robert says. "Never mind."

Dmitri knew this kind of thing was going to happen. In his English class last week, the teacher had made them read a poem. He can't remember how it began but the last lines were about the world ending not with a bang but a whimper.

Robert takes two blocks from his bag and makes a space on the blanket, fits his latest instrument into the blocks. He hands two small hammers to Dmitri.

"It's a medieval dulcimer," he says. "With modifications. Try it out. I want to know how intuitive it is."

Dmitri looks at the metal instrument. He taps a few disks on the top row. The sound is dull. He uses the head of the hammer to send a disk sliding down a rail, and the rest of the disks on the wire rattle in sympathy. The sound hurts his teeth a little.

"It's kind of an awful sound," Robert says. "Right? I sort of love it, though."

"It makes teeth hurt. It is medieval dentist dulcimer."

"Ha. Keep going. You get used to it." Robert stretches out and puts his hands behind his head. Dmitri taps at the strings, feeling desperate. He is dying for Robert.

And he is tired. He feels like everyone is leaving him behind. Ilya doesn't need his help. His mother is becoming involved in Alexander's business. His father is going to go to Mars and doesn't seem to notice that Dmitri's letters to him are full of nothing.

"You can be ashamed of yourself even if nobody says what you do is shameful," Dmitri says.

"That sounds like self-hatred," Robert says.

Dmitri doesn't reply. He swipes at disks randomly. There are five rows, he realizes, like a musical scale. And indeed, each row has a different tone, though they're not arranged in the right order.

"What's your father like?" Robert asks.

"He's okay. He's ordinary guy. He works for a shoe company."

Robert nods. "He knows you're gay?"

Dmitri says nothing.

"Or whatever you are."

"This is not picnic," Dmitri says. "This is something else." He has to end things with Robert anyway. It's all going to come out. Dmitri looks up from the instrument. Maybe it's already out.

"This is *chush' sobach'ya*," Robert says. "It bothers me that you never kiss me. And I'd like you to stop with the fake cousin and, you know, actually talk to me. That's what a relationship is."

"Not everything has to be a relationship." Dmitri says this quickly, and forgets to use his thicker accent and bad grammar. Soon it will be impossible to have secrets. His father has only three more months of the simulation, and then he will be out and Prime will probably announce the crew publicly. There are pictures of Dmitri out there.

Standing next to his father at Baikonur, at Vostochny. There will be many more pictures, his whole life story. He hadn't realized it, but this time had been his only freedom.

"Everything is in a relationship to something else," Robert says. "So is every person."

The trio with the baby call out, "Excuse me? Excuse me?" The woman who got kicked in the face by her baby is holding up her screen. She's been recording Dmitri.

"What're your handles?" she calls out. "That's so cool, what you're doing."

"My handle is fuck you," Dmitri says. "And I'm not doing anything. This isn't *anything*. Leave me alone." Dmitri drops the hammers and stands up.

"Hey, hey." One of the guys stands up too. "What's your problem?" He pulls out his screen.

"It's okay, Oliver," says the baby-woman. "It's fine."

"Are you making a video out of me telling you to leave me alone?" Dmitri says to the guy. "I am sixteen years old. You put that up and I will sue you. My parents will sue you. I have rights. I am a minor. What you are doing is illegal."

Now Robert is standing. Dmitri has not been shouting, but he can see that he's attracted the attention of a few other people on the hill. Every person has a screen. You never know. This is why outside is shit. Two cookies and a rose, it's a fucking joke.

"I'm so sorry," says the baby-woman. "Look, I just thought it sounded pretty. I'm deleting it." She shakes her screen and then looks up at the man.

"It's cool, it's cool," says the other guy of the threesome. "Oliver, delete the thing. You don't need this."

"You don't have to be such a jerk," says baby-woman, it's not clear to whom. Maybe to her baby.

Dmitri grabs his bag and begins marching down the hill. He's never kissed a man with his tongue. He's kissed girls that way. He kissed a girl that way last week. It wasn't anything with a girl, but it would be something with a man. Now he just wants to get inside somewhere, where people can't see him. There is a tunnel to the right of the fountain, the under section of a bridge.

"Hey." Robert's voice echoes in the tunnel.

Robert's got the shopping bag in one hand and the blanket is over his shoulder and the instrument is sticking out of the top of his backpack. "What was that?"

"I don't want to talk here," Dmitri says. He knows how to get out of the park. He can run if he has to, run without stopping.

"Yeah, you don't want to talk anywhere."

"It's okay. It's over."

"Yeah, no kidding it's over. You're sixteen. You can still act like a human being."

Dmitri stops. They're on the other side of the tunnel and exposed again, but at least out of sight of the hill people. He can follow this path out of the park. The park benches on either side of the lane are filled with people. The world is crammed, is stuffed with bodies.

"Human beings are the worst," Dmitri says. "You should say that I could still act like a wolf or elephant. At least an elephant doesn't tell lies." He starts walking, but Robert keeps pace with him. Dmitri is embarrassed by his last words, so dramatic and childish.

"What are you lying about?" Robert asks. His voice has no anger in it, as if he's only mildly curious, or as if Dmitri had said "I like cheese" and Robert merely wanted to know which cheeses. This makes Dmitri feel calm. He takes a deep breath, but can't think of what or how to say things. It would be nice if they could just walk in silence for a little bit.

"Look, we can be friends," Robert says. "Obviously I like you. Because I have problems, I guess. Your manners are atrocious, and you're a liar. Are you even Russian?"

"I'm a liar," Dmitri agrees. "I'm Russian. My English is fluent unless I'm writing. I'm sixteen. You should leave me alone. Fuck. Fucking shit."

"Who's your cousin?" Robert shifts his stuff into one hand so he can walk closer to Dmitri. Their arms are almost touching. Dmitri would really like to die, really.

"My little brother. He goes to a ballet school here on Saturdays. We live in New Jersey. I've never kissed a guy. In the real way."

"That one I sort of figured out."

All these people on park benches, people walking. There are crazy people here, homeless people. Nothing is ever going to be *really* good.

"My father is a cosmonaut," Dmitri says.

"Okay, let's stop for a second."

Dmitri stops, but not for Robert. He is having trouble breathing.

"You think I'm crazy?" he asks. "You can look it up. I thought you already looked me up."

"I tried to look you up," Robert says. "I couldn't find anything. I didn't think you were in high school. I thought you were an illegal alien. I thought maybe you were in the Russian mafia. I thought you were a hustler. I hide my wallet before you come over."

Dmitri wants to sit down. He wants to lie down. He wants to go back home to Russia, to childhood. He wants to go to space and just do things and not think, like his father.

"Okay," he says. "I live in New Jersey with my brother and my mother and stepfather. I go to Maplewood High School. On Saturdays I bring my brother to ballet classes in the city. My father is a cosmonaut. An astronaut. He's in Utah with Prime Space right now. Pretty soon, he might be going to go to Mars. I love him. He has everything. My brother is also this incredibly talented person. I love him too. It's not that I am jealous of them, or maybe it's only a little jealousy. Everyone loves them, you see. I love them too. I know I am not lovable the way they are. I am not remarkable. I am good at school, but am I brilliant? No. I don't have new ideas. My father, he is amazed by what Ilya can do. He cannot dance like that. I am not creative. There is nothing I will ever do that will be as good as my father, and I cannot amaze him. No. I am not even very good at making this confessional speech. I am pretending that I have father problem. *A* father problem. It is not a father problem. I don't have a gay problem, I don't have a father problem. I don't want my father making a speech to the whole planet about how he loves his gay son. I don't want to be special for only being gay, that isn't anything amazing at all."

Dmitri is not crying, though he does feel very ill, and is worried that he might get a nosebleed. He pinches his nose together and tilts his head back.

"Sometimes I get a nosebleed," he says to Robert.

Robert pats him on the shoulder.

It's okay. He's not bleeding. He looks at Robert.

"Man," Robert says. "If you ask me, I don't think you have a problem. You're just a little sad and the world is *so* stupid."

It's maybe not so much a decision. Dmitri has to go somewhere, and he is following the pull of gravity, which means to fall.

It doesn't go perfectly. It is much more shocking than anything else. He can't even tell if he likes it; Robert is carrying too many bags and Dmitri bangs his teeth against Robert's at the beginning, and this is the way the world ends, this is the way the world ends. He doesn't know what he is doing, he is still probably sad, but Dmitri—Russian, liar, lover, son of cosmonaut—has his first real kiss.

HELEN

Tonight they are eating rehydrated shrimp and rice and for vegetables it is green beans. Everyone likes this dinner very much, even more than some of the fancy recipes that have been sent up from Prime. It is easy to make, and good for a day like today, where they've been testing their knowledge of material covered over a year ago now.

"So how did everyone do on the last quiz?" Helen asks, spearing a green bean. "I had trouble remembering the protocol for CPB."

Helen is hoping that the subject of postmortem decisions for the astronaut who has died in space will cheer Sergei up. He is doing well, she is very proud of his performance and general behavior, but he does get gloomy in the sort of interstitial moments between activities. Sergei has excellent gallows humor, and exercising it gives him pleasure.

She has no real way of knowing how much Sergei is hanging on to the idea that they'd really gone to Mars. Perhaps he'd come to his senses completely. There is only one thing she can be absolutely sure of right now, and that is her own skin.

"Ah," Yoshi says. "I had no trouble with CPB because I remembered describing it to my wife."

Yoshi talks about his wife a lot now. This, Helen feels, is probably good. It is *noticeable*, though. She is doing noticeable things too. Her voice has become more gentle, even she can hear it.

But they have held together, one for all and all for one. In their training sims, they continue to score high marks. People are not disappearing into their sleeping compartments, or skipping exercise, or complaining about the food. They are not testy with each other, they are not blaming everything on Mission Control.

"I got as far as 'stick my dead body in the bag and hang me outside,'" Helen says now. "And I remembered the basics of the promession process: after my corpse is frozen, use RoMeO's arm to vibrate me until I shatter and become a nice powder, then dehydrate my powder until it is dust, then put the dust in a can." The way Helen says this, it sounds like a poem, she can't help it.

"It is not in the protocol, but they should add that we take a label and put your name on it and stick it on the can," Sergei says. "Because it would not be good to confuse you with can of protein powder."

There, now. That's her boy, Sergei.

"I know it is a cross-cultural revulsion, a taboo—" Yoshi stands and collects their empty bowls, "the idea of consuming the body of the departed. And yet I remember a story I read, where this is done by a wife, of her husband. And it was very beautiful."

"Mmhmm, do you think this was a metaphor for love?" Helen asks. Curing Yoshi of romantic sentiment in the evenings isn't as easy as curing Sergei of depression, but she does her best. As with Sergei, she applies gentle pressure in the direction of the wound. If

Yoshi wants to make all his feelings into something grand, then grand they shall be. "Perhaps a metaphor for grief."

"Intimacy, I think," Yoshi says.

"The UN treaty still holds?" Sergei asks, because he is still stuck on death. "We can't let each other go out the airlock?"

"No, it's still considered littering," Helen says. "Yoshi, was that story German? I think it sounds like something I read in college. Of course that was a thousand years ago."

"This is what you do for me," Sergei says. "You put my dead body in the bag and send it out the airlock. You make fake can of powder for my family, and tell UN that promession protocols were followed and nobody littered in space."

"Done," Helen says. "You'll do the same for me?"

"Yes. Yoshi, do you want the same or do you want us to eat you?"

"If you will permit a suggestion," Yoshi says. "It is better for the space environment if you do not go out the airlock as a body. You could follow the CPB protocols and then egress as powder."

Sergei and Helen agree this is an improvement of their plan.

"Maybe German," Yoshi says to Helen. "This story I read. Or maybe I have invented it?"

Helen cannot imagine inventing something like wanting to eat your dead husband's body, she can barely stand the thought of reading Eric's books. She'd read every one, but only once they were published because he never wanted to show them to her. He'd never needed to show them to her, her approval and praise had not been important. They were very good, beautifully written, but so separate from their life together. If they'd had a life together.

Tonight they are watching a historical drama about the beginning of the space program in the United States. The women in these movies are all wives. They wear little candy-colored suits and stand in rooms and worry. Helen settles into her lounger. Yoshi brings her a cup of tea along with their little green mascot. She laughs and props the toy in her lap like a child.

It is a beautiful idea, the thought of her body, powder or otherwise, floating into the darkness of space. But if this happens she will be dead and, as far as she knows, at that point beyond beautiful ideas. Perhaps it would mean something to Meeps to have her remains returned to Earth. Would it?

Helen has a flash, a memory, of holding her infant daughter against her bare chest, of Meeps's skin, which she once knew so well.

It is appalling, to think of the distance between her body and her daughter's body. And how they will never know each other's bodies again. Helen is filled with an animal urge to feel her daughter's skin again, and for her daughter to touch her as if she is a thing that is known, as if she is a body that is loved.

MADOKA

It wasn't the first time Madoka had seen an abandoned dog in the Higashiyama Tunnel, but it was the first time she had stopped her car because of one.

Madoka hadn't grown up with a pet. Her father was famously anti-cat, and waged a semi-comic war with the neighborhood strays. Yoshi had grown up with animals. A large collection of beetles when he was a boy, and then fish, and a spitz named Ken, now dead. The dog looked ridiculous in photos, but Yoshi claimed it had a very sober, loyal, and comforting nature.

Madoka had not stopped for the dog. She had stopped because it was a swift diversion from the path she had set for herself today. She *had* been a woman who was going to work. *Now* she was a woman who had stopped for a dog.

Madoka moves cautiously into this role.

Also, she does not want to be a woman who was bitten by a dog.

The animal is trotting from side to side, looking now at Madoka, now at the highway, as if considering its options. It is just smaller than medium size, and brown and gray. Some of the colors may be dirt.

Madoka stands by her car. She would like to interact with the dog on a psychic level, without embarrassing and lengthy preliminaries, or awkward baby language. How much Japanese does the dog understand? She feels instinctively that it is male. It has a male countenance. He's not wearing a tag, although possibly he has a microchip.

The dog approaches. He is very thin. He is also a she. Madoka is vaguely disappointed.

The dog does something. She sits and arranges her paws tidily in front of her, then lifts one tufty eyebrow and the opposite paw, and looks at Madoka. Madoka does not think she has ever seen any sentient creature do something so wonderful.

She should get back in her car and continue on her way. An artist should know when to walk away from a work, to let a moment happen without comment, without greed, without display or audience or any kind of need. Also the dog had done something that was very cute, and very cute things were never art.

In a perfect world, the dog would run off now. Or vanish. Or Madoka would vanish.

This will not happen on its own. This world is not a magic world.

The dog stands and backs away. Madoka's remorse is so swift and consuming that she forgets about art, and also about death.

"Oh, it's okay," she says to the dog. "Good girl. Good girl." She holds out a hand.

They will get back to art later, for now there are logistics: getting the dog into the car, and then all the things that should happen next. The dog cranes her nose toward Madoka's hand, does not seem displeased, trots sideways.

· . : · .

MADOKA DOES NOT want to lure the dog into the car by trickery; this seems unethical. She thinks of making a leash, and moves to the trunk of her car. Yoshi had put an emergency kit in there for her, which she has never opened.

The duffel bag, when opened, gives her pause. Along with the items are instructions in Yoshi's handwriting on the proper use of each item, survivalist tips, emergency protocols. Shelter. Navigation. Protection. Tools. First aid. Nutrition. Hygiene. And a bag of her favorite kind of peppermints.

The dog waits.

Madoka finds she does not want to disturb the contents of the duffel bag. In the end, she opens up the passenger door of her Nissan Pinecone and the dog jumps in of her own volition.

Madoka drives the dog and herself to work. She senses an anxiety in the dog, and, most touchingly, an effort on the dog's part to control the anxiety. Madoka talks, telling the dog about the place where they are going. "We will go to my office," Madoka tells the dog. "Because I think we will be able to find someone there to consult with about our next steps." Her voice is a little singsongy. She has often been told—in several languages—that she has an appealing speaking voice. This does not matter to her PEPPER. PEPPERs use three different forms of voice stress analysis. A pet probably does not "like" a certain kind of voice, though it would register a difference between command, and scolding, and affection with a person it knew well, maybe any person.

"At my company," Madoka explains to the dog, "our most popular robotic pet is the baby panda. Light, touch, movement, and voices are picked up by sensors within the animal, so the pandas can open and move their eyes, make happy noises like purring, and they have a very cute walk. They can give or receive a hug. Old people and children love them; they accept them either instantly or with very little prompting."

The dog now makes tentative overtures toward a leap into the back of the car, rethinks this, attempts it, races back and forth a few times, takes up a sitting posture on the passenger seat.

"I was thinking of asking to be transferred within my company so that I wouldn't have to travel. I'm tired of traveling, and I want to have more personal time. I would like to take some classes, art classes, maybe. I saw a course in transhumanist art that looked very interesting. I think I need to make something."

The dog makes a half step toward Madoka, shies away, puts both paws on the dashboard, slips, and crashes down into the legroom area.

"You need a bath. PEPPERs can give sponge baths to humans. This eliminates what can be a very uncomfortable situation between a patient who wishes to maintain dignity and a family member who would be embarrassed by such intimate contact. I have had a sponge bath by a PEPPER. It was not threatening or strange. PEPPERs can wash a pet too.

"I think I will give you your first bath, though.

"I suppose I should have thought this through. You will need many items. Well, these can be managed. We will consult."

The dog licks the window.

"Dogs are very resilient. The Soviets sent dogs into space before they sent people.

"It's sad. Those dogs died in space."

The dog's stomach growls and she works her mouth, chewing air.

"You're very hungry. We will get you some food at the office.

Excuse me, I will have a conversation with my colleague Daisuke about this now."

She is talking to the dog in an absurd way; it is *very* interesting. Madoka feels reckless, impulsive, capable of anything.

Daisuke tells Madoka that she could use her screen's magnetometer to read the dog's microchip, if it has one. "Or you could take it to a shelter now. Hmmm. Is the dog calm? Is she dirty?"

Madoka says that the dog is quite dirty and seems calm.

"Oh, that's good, actually," Daisuke says. "Can you bring her here?"

The dog does not have a microchip. This means she is not lost, but abandoned, and Madoka is happy that she doesn't have to relinquish her to an owner just yet, but sad for the burden of the dog's past, the events that led her to a tunnel. She hopes the dog can forget.

Madoka's jacket has a cloth belt, and she uses this as a leash, buckling it gingerly around the dog, who stares at her with wide eyes but does not panic, or run away. Madoka does not have to drag her, but they are not in movement accord, and her belt is not long enough for her to stand fully upright. People look and laugh when they see them, and this makes the dog nervous, but already she chooses to press herself against Madoka's legs. She does pee on one of the Kochia bushes in front of her building. Anxious about what else the dog might produce, Madoka tries to move quickly. Once in the building, the dog sets her nose to the floor, and tugs at the belt, following an invisible trail like a near-sighted detective.

The doors of Daisuke's lab are shut; a note pasted outside requests visitors to ring for admittance. The dog sniffs at the crack where the two doors meet and then takes a few steps back, nodding nervously at the portal.

"Oh sorry," Daisuke says, opening one of the doors. "We keep that sign on when we are working with a non-ro."

They exchange greetings. Madoka inexpertly works the belt leash in an effort to urge the dog forward.

Daisuke holds up a small pink dog biscuit.

"Here, girl," he says, holding it low to the ground.

The dog lunges at the treat and swallows it whole.

"Very hungry." Daisuke nods to an assistant, who comes forward with more biscuits. "Only a few more," he cautions. "We don't want her to be sick. Does she respond to commands?"

"I don't know. I found her in the Higashiyama Tunnel."

"Very nice of you to stop," Daisuke says. "Most people don't. Anyway, the reason I asked is we're in proof-of-concept stage for a new pet bath. We have dogs coming in tomorrow, but they probably won't be as dirty as this one. With your permission, we'd like to see how she responds."

"Oh, I won't be the owner." Madoka waves her hand. "I don't think I can keep her." The moment Madoka says this out loud she knows she will absolutely keep the dog. "I travel constantly," Madoka explains. "And my husband, you know, is away. Please, if the dog will be helpful to you for your test, I don't mind waiting."

Daisuke's assistant replaces Madoka's belt leash with a blue rubber collar attached to a length of some kind of tubing. The dog shivers. She is now surrounded by technicians with screens.

"For data purposes," one of them says. "Let's call her 27."

27 is coaxed over to a stainless steel grooming station, complete with ramp and shower nozzles. To Madoka's surprise, her dog scampers up the ramp without any prompting. The technicians angle a camera over the station and back away.

"Normally," Daisuke says, "the pet owner's face would appear on the screen, to be able to supervise the experience, and provide comfort and reassurance to the animal. But since we don't have a name for this dog, and you have not had time for pet–human bonding, we'll use this opportunity strictly as a test of cleaning functions. Can we get this dog clean?" Daisuke smiles at his team. He leads Madoka over to a corner screen. "We can watch from here."

Madoka can see on the screen that her dog is at work on a yellow lump of something set into a wall of the tub. The stainless steel floor is speckled with colorful no-slip decals in the shape of animals. The blue tubing leash is now connected to the tub. Her dog's tail is wagging.

"The leash is magnetic," Daisuke explains. "The bones come in bacon or peanut butter flavor." The sides of the station, set with spigots like a sauna, begin to send out gentle sprays of water. The dog flinches but does not look up, continues trying to tug the bone free from the wall.

"In the past, robotic pet-sitting was mostly about comfort surveillance," Daisuke explains. "The owner might wish to check in on his pet while he was working, to make sure the pet was happy and content, or not engaging in destructive behavior. Also, people miss their pets and enjoy being able to communicate with them. Now our pet-sitters can engage in helpful tasks: food and water administration, mainly, but also some light play activities. If the owner has a home with secure property, the robots can open and shut doors to allow the pet access to that."

The water is increasing in pressure now. Her dog stops mauling the bone and backs up, turns in circles, presses one side against the wall, tries putting her paws against the side of the tub, attempts an over-the-wall exit. The magnetic leash holds firm.

"It's okay," Daisuke says. "She'll settle down in a moment. A lot of the anxiety dogs feel during hygiene is actually an absorption of the anxiety coming from inexpert human handlers."

The water running into the drain is almost black.

"This is intended for the Japan market," Daisuke says. "In other countries, there is a labor force for professional pet grooming. But we have had interest internationally."

Now the spigots in the wall are spraying her dog with a green liquid detergent of some kind. The dog becomes more agitated. Licking her lips, and twisting on her leash, knocking her nose against the bone.

"The soap is getting in her eyes, I think." Madoka clenches her hands together behind her back.

"It's not toxic. Washing humans is easier. With humans, you can instruct them to close their eyes," Daisuke says. "And suggest they scrub themselves with the soap. This is obviously hard to do with dogs."

Madoka's dog is splattered with pale green foam, as if afflicted with some kind of extraterrestrial mange. She now stands frozen, muscles tensed, enduring, head flinching whenever the jets hit her face. Madoka can see her dog's ribs now. The tufts of hair around her eyes and inside her bat ears droop and drip. Madoka begins to cry.

TWO HOURS LATER, Madoka and the dog are in the car again. Madoka's appointments have been canceled. In the trunk, next to the emergency duffel, is a bag of dog food, two chew toys, several bones, and absorbent pads. Her dog has turned out to be a caramel brown color. Madoka is thinking of naming her Toffee, or maybe Toff-Toff. Both Madoka and dog are exhausted, slightly red around the eyes, heavy-lidded.

Madoka rolls a peppermint around in her mouth.

"It is quite funny of Yoshi to put those peppermints in the survival bag," Madoka says to Toffee. "That brand of peppermint is my favorite candy. It's a kind of joke. As if I would need them to survive.

What I'm thinking right now is that if something happened, and I needed that bag because I really did have to survive, and I knew I'd never see Yoshi again, then those peppermints would break my heart. Or if Yoshi dies in space, on the way to Mars, or there or the way back. Or in Utah, or any number of places."

Toffee sighs deeply and edges her nose toward Madoka's hand.

"Don't worry," Madoka says. "He isn't going to die. He's absolutely not. He's going to come home. You shouldn't be scared. I'm not scared. It's only been a training session, this time, and so there's nothing to be worried about at all. We are going to go home right now, you and I, and I will make a message for Yoshi, and let him know that I found the peppermints. Don't you think that would be a good idea? Don't you think he'll want to know that?"

Toffee licks her hand.

"I'm tired of waiting," Madoka says. "I'm tired of waiting for Yoshi to find me. I'm tired of waiting to find myself. Nobody ever finds anything if they just wait."

HELEN

Meeps,

I'm so glad that you are loving the video game work and doing so well! It sounds really interesting, and fun too.

I had a very unusual experience here that was almost like dying. Because it was almost like dying, but wasn't, the first thing it made me think of was my father. Maybe you will like hearing that I've thought about my father during these past fifteen months more than I have my whole life, it seems. Maybe you will hate learning that it's still not very much.

It's not the same, you know. My father's absence didn't mean to me what my absence has meant to you. You want me to feel more. I want you to feel less. Which one of us is feeling the correct amount? Why do you want me to feel more? To punish me? Or are you afraid that because I don't feel my father's absence, I also don't feel yours? Why do I want you to feel less? Because that makes me feel less guilty for all the times I left you?

Quite frankly, the men in my life don't bear all that much thinking about. From everything I've heard, my dad was a great guy, but people tend to inflate great qualities in these cases. I have thought about my husband more than my dad. I got pretty angry at one point. I say "my husband" because that person was different from the person who was your father. You won't want to hear that either. Eric didn't love me in a really great way. Maybe there aren't great ways to love other people, except for from very far away, and in one direction.

I had the thought yesterday that love from a parent toward a child—no, *my* love for *you*—was the most terrible form of love, because it can't ever be reciprocated.

I have considered it a point of pride, a skill, that I've been able to extricate myself from the tragedy that happened to my family, that I didn't let it define me. It feels really good to do that, Meeps. It feels really good to be free. In the greatest and happiest moments of my life I haven't thought of anyone, not even, no, *especially*, myself.

And yet, if anyone were to ask me right now to think of someone I love, I would think of you. I have never loved a person more than I have loved you.

You think I only love you in the "of course" way. That I always loved myself more, that my work was always more important.

You don't know how great and terrible the "of course" way is. You are able to accept things without reasons. I do not have that. The only thing I accept without reason is loving you.

I worried, when I was pregnant, that I wouldn't feel the proper mother things when you were born. I did. I felt them all. And then I arranged things so that I could live my life exactly the way I wanted to. I was so confident it would all work out because I had such a good feeling.

We all thought this would be when time was hardest for us. We thought we would have too much time. And it feels to all of us as if it is going far too quickly. I believe this is because none of us wants this to be over. It is easier to be here, even if it is a little confusing.

There isn't any talking it out, between you and me. I manage, you manage, and maybe that's the best it can get. This sounds terrible to you, I bet. But it's the pressure for more that's eating you up. Think about it. What could I say that would make you feel better? You want me to say I abandoned you selfishly to pursue my own dreams and neglected you?

I wanted to go to space more than I wanted to be your mother.

That's true. If you had ever been to space, you'd understand.

It's not true. They are different things. Nothing is comparable to another thing.

If it walks like a duck, but talks like something else, is it still a duck? Is it a bad duck? Does it have to be a bad duck? Can't it be another creature altogether?

We shall go on and on, you and I.

You will continue to blame me for leaving you, and I will continue to leave you.

The last thing I want to say is that I feel I have lived a whole life on this mission and I want to do it all over, but do it much better. The strange thing is, I may have the opportunity to do just that.

But I won't have that opportunity with you.

I don't know what to do.

You could accept that I'm another mother altogether, and that we have a love that is only ours and so that's why it doesn't look like any other kind of love but it's not a bad love. We could destroy the world and make a new one.

What can I give you of myself? I need to find something of me that I can give you, that is also something you want.

SERGEI

My darling boy, Dmitri,

I dream all the time of going outside. I don't mean outside on Earth, with the trees and the sky and the grass and the air and the cool lakes. I mean space. Yesterday I performed a simulated EVA. At no time did I imagine myself to be truly in space. So I will still dream.

Prime is talking about adding more scents to the exercise simulations. When we are snowshoeing in a pine forest, for example, there will be scent of pine. Also, being able to add scent to the air of our Hab might make us more happy.

Oh, simulations they can do almost everything. All feelings, pretty much, these can be made. But they cannot tell you what to think.

Simulation can say, "I want you to be running along cliffs of Dover in Yoshi's exercise simulation and get healthy dose of bio-philiac happiness, sense of communion with nature, and freedom from confinement in small spacecraft." Simulation cannot say, "And all of a sudden in the middle of this you will remember how your son Dmitri picked up a little frosted cake when he was one year old and went to put it in his mouth but instead smashed it right into his eye."

I think you were worried that I should be lonely here, and have no one to talk to. I said that I would talk to my friends, and we do talk. I speak with Mission Control, I write to my friends on Earth or make videos. You and I exchange these letters, and soon we will be back close enough to speak in real time. All of this is an immense silence with words on top of it. You were right about that.

The world is very colorful and crowded, but really, behind it all, is emptiness.

Ilya will not have told you. He is a funny boy. By his codes, as I understand them, he will not have said to you: "Papa knows that you are gay. We talked about it." I asked him to keep an eye on you, to make sure that you don't do something stupid in order to hide it, or because you are ashamed. He's waiting for you to say it to him, but he knows that you might not.

I do know.

Maybe you will laugh, but I have this hope that your being gay is a sign that you are not as much like me as I fear.

I like to do very hard things, but this should not be a thing I am proud of, because it is more than liking a challenge. I like to do very hard things because then I know that I am not what my father said I was, which was a meek boy who was afraid. And because he was not so wrong, my father. I was afraid. I was timid, I didn't want to do many things. I forced myself, over and over.

It was shameful, to meet so many other people in my life, in my work, all people who loved doing hard and maybe scary thing. That is what they wanted. I didn't want to do it, I wanted to have *done* it.

You see this difference? I see it, and so often I dislike myself. I wish to be so much better than I am, to change totally my nature.

Possibly I dislike myself because my father disliked me. The psychologist would say: "Oh, he did not hate you—he hated himself." I will go so far as to say that it is a possibility he hated both of us.

Possibly I dislike myself because I think doing so makes me a better man. No. I know that it has made me a better man.

When I was your age, I used to hit myself. I would strike my own thigh, with my fist. It is absurd to think of now, and I cannot totally remember the circumstances under which I performed this. I was restless, and unhappy. I remember becoming even more enraged, at my inability to hit myself hard enough. There is a tradition in religion of this kind of practice, and as a boy I admired it, although I never struck myself for God.

Whenever I see people do bad things in the world because they are frightened, I think they are someone like me, who has not forced himself to be better.

The funny thing is, Dmitri, I forget all this. I forget what I am because I have been so long simulating the man I wish to be that I now believe myself to be this man. I think it's real.

In the past, I have only wanted you to see this man, because this is the only man worthy of your love. But now I am sick of simulations and I think, how can I know you love me if you only love this fake person? I know that the only thing that matters with parent and child is how much parent loves child. Child does not have to love you back. But this can only be borne by truly strong people. I am too weak not to care if you love me. Here, in space, I think: he cannot hate me here. But of course you can. Please do not. Please, please, I beg you, my darling boy, I am on my knees to you, do not hate me, please do love me.

YOSHI

My dear wife,

I have been thinking about Pluto and its moon, Charon. There are other satellites of Pluto, but Charon is the largest and closest, so big and so close that they might not be moon and dwarf planet but a double object. It has been suggested that they be reclassified as a double planet, but the International Astronomical Union has so far rejected this.

Pluto and Charon are in mutual tidal lock. This is different than the tidal lock between Earth and Luna. We see only one face of Luna, but if you were standing on the near side of Luna, you'd see all the faces of Earth. And if you were on the far side, you'd never see Earth at all.

Pluto and Charon show each other only one face, never turning away.

Have I spoken to you about the barycenter? I find it difficult to remember what I have said to you, and what I have only imagined saying to you. I think it not improbable that all our best conversations have taken place inside my head.

In astronomy, we use the word *barycenter* to describe the center of mass between two orbiting objects. Our Luna is smaller than Earth, and so the barycenter of Earth and Luna is on Earth, deep within it, actually. Because Charon is so large, and its gravitational influence so great, the barycenter of Pluto and Charon lies outside Pluto. Strictly speaking, Charon does not orbit Pluto, nor Pluto, Charon. They rotate around a barycenter between them. Looking only at one piece of each other.

I would never have noticed this, perhaps, if I hadn't seen another woman. That is, I saw Helen in a way that I have never seen you. It was an accident and I do not mean to imply that I fell in love with Helen, as the phrase is understood. It wasn't the person of Helen that was so important in this moment, it was the sheer size of the person of Helen. It was the enormity. And the realization that this was something she was concealing, packing away, so to speak, in order to make our long confinement comfortable for everyone.

We are all doing this, of course. But, it made me almost ill to see how much I had been missing.

I have come to believe that I have loved you incorrectly. I have been orbiting a dream I cannot touch. I only know one of your faces. It is not that I didn't want to know another face, it is that I loved that one so powerfully.

Maybe I did not wish to know.

There is a possibility that you are like Luna, and you see all my faces while I see only one of yours. But, forgive me, I do not think this is true. I think we are mutually locked. Perhaps this is what it means to be married. Perhaps this is what it means to be married to me.

I saw a little of you, and thought it was everything. I understand that I was wrong. Now I am afraid. I thought we loved each other. How can we?

Would you rather I loved you incorrectly forever, or correctly but potentially less? Maybe I don't love you at all. I feel if I could just see you, the way I saw Helen, I would.

"Yoshi needs somewhere to be." That's what my mother used to say.

I AM MORE nervous about seeing you next month than I have ever been about anything. I have this fear that I will not recognize you, that I will walk right past you. Or that you will not recognize me. I don't know which is worse.

It is hard for me to imagine that I have other faces than the one I've shown you. This is all that I am. Does it seem very, very little to you?

LUKE

can't believe you all are giving up right at the end," Mireille says. "Seventeen months of incredibly realistic this and that, and now you don't want the family members standing there for the landing? This is the finale!"

Luke had stepped outside the Obber Lab to have this conversation, and walked a short distance down the bike path.

"Originally we weren't going to do post-mission isolation," Luke says. "So it would have made sense for all of the family members to be here, but now we're running a full quarantine. You wouldn't be able to see your mom in any meaningful way. We thought that even though you'd normally be here, it might be, you know, very irritating, under the circumstances. For everyone. Family and crew, I mean. Not for Prime. Us. But the plan is to have everyone free to celebrate New Year with their families."

This is true and, among other things, means that Mireille will not come to Utah, and he won't see her, maybe for two more years.

"Well, what's two more weeks?" Mireille says. "I'm sorry I won't get to see Madoka again, though, for a while. She's been sending me the cutest pictures of her new dog."

Mireille has cut her hair short recently; her neck is exposed. Either she has changed her hair to match a shift within her, or she has adopted a demeanor better suited to this new style: clearer, less self-consciously provocative. He knows that Mireille is no longer taking psychoactives, but he also knows that the first ten minutes of any conversation they have will be dictated by whatever pose or attitude she has decided upon. If he thinks she seems clearer and less self-conscious, it will be because that's what she intends him to think. This is still information.

"I actually feel a little nervous," Mireille says.

"I'm a little nervous too," Luke says, and laughs a little, like a jackass.

All the Obbers are nervous. They are two weeks away from landing the crew. The tension in the lab has manifested in a panoply of physical ailments. Luke keeps getting into minor bike accidents. "You are literally," Nari says, "trying to take one for the team." It is the same, Luke hears, in Mission Control. On the one hand everyone is a little bit of a wreck, and on the other, even linear-active individuals are greeting each other with hugs.

Luke, at the bike rack now, kicks it a little, knocking some snow to the ground. Not vengefully, just to propel himself forward by applying a very mild pain.

Mireille has on a red sweatshirt. From the background—some kind of insulated wall—Luke guesses she is on a break at the studio where she is shooting a video game. It touches him that she has messaged him on a break. Mireille loves her job, she's always happy doing it. For her to message now might mean she's not seeking comfort, or an audience, but wishing to share happiness.

"I was always more nervous at landings than launches," Mireille says. "Sad at launches, and terrified at landings. Which would you pick: being sad or being scared?"

"Scared," says Luke.

"Scared is incapacitating, though." Mireille plays with the zipper of her sweatshirt. Her face and neck, her chest, are still faintly dotted by whatever sensors they stick on her when she's working.

"Sadness can be incapacitating too," Luke says.

"True." Luke heads toward the X-4 building. He hasn't been on the roof of X-4 since before Eidolon started. He remembers looking down, and seeing Helen in a yellow shirt. Nari wearing binoculars. Remembers his own sense of finally, for the first time in his life, seeing some kind of hope for himself and the other humans of the planet.

On screen, Mireille strokes the side of her neck, exactly in the same way Helen had adopted in *Red Dawn*.

"Do you know what it felt like?" Mireille says. "Like a storm that was always coming, but never arrived."

"I'm sorry?" Luke has lost the thread.

"Eidolon. The past seventeen months. It's like I couldn't figure out how to prepare for what's coming, and I knew I needed to do something, but I couldn't figure out what that was. I wanted the storm to just hit already so I could stop worrying. But it never did."

"That sounds very tiring, Mireille."

"Well." She shrugs. "I was doing it to myself. I think it will be easier when it happens for real."

"Oh, that's interesting. Tell me more about that." Luke can practically see his words transcribed as he says them, inoffensive, neutral, correct. What would he say if he was not bound by any constraints? Nothing. It was the constraints that had created the situation. This was perverse human nature, not quite corrected even in the humans that had access to better information than their own feelings.

"For one thing, I won't be wondering what it will be like when she goes." Mireille laughs and runs her hands through her hair. "And I won't be so alone because the whole world will be watching. And getting to share some of the experience. Her experience. It's going to be her, right? I mean, they've passed this part of the training? It's been a success?"

Luke pushes open the door of X-4.

"Sorry, sorry. I know you can't say. Hey, where are we right now?" She squints at the screen.

"I'm taking you to the roof of one of our buildings," Luke says. "There's a great view of the mountains from up there."

"Oh, cool. You can't see them from there, can you? I mean, you can't see *Red Dawn*?"

"No, no." In fact, there'd been a rumor around Prime a while back that *Red Dawn*'s location had been moved. No one had seen any of The Shadows—the team responsible for maintaining the *Primitus* and *Red Dawn* sites—for months.

He flips his screen so Mireille can see the San Rafael Swell, dusted now in parts with snow.

"Wow," she says.

"Yeah."

PRIME'S VR TEAM had brought in sim glasses for the Obbers last week and let them spend ten minutes looking at Mars from space, the way the astronauts had looked at Mars from space two days before landing on the planet.

Ten minutes. Areocentric orbit. Nearly a year ago, Luke had watched the crew looking at this very thing, listened to them talk to each other about what they were seeing, point out surface features, occasionally laughing or falling silent, or saying something like, "Gosh." When he looked at the sims himself, he understood the laughter and the silence, the soft "wow." Virtual reality experiences of Mars had been available since he was a kid, but they had never affected him as powerfully. This didn't feel like a game, or speculation, or even merely cool. It was personal and vast—not just himself, or even the crew, but *humanity* approaching, for the first time, another planet.

And this was just a dress rehearsal.

Could any person be shown these things—not just shown—could any person *experience* them, and still be filled with wrath and violence and selfishness? Yes. Okay, yes, probably. But could a person continue to act on those feelings? Could a person still believe those feelings justified violence or cruelty or neglect?

Yes. Probably, yes.

We'd had an Enlightenment that had fundamentally changed the way many humans viewed themselves and the world. And that had been Europe in the seventeenth and eighteenth centuries. Now it was possible to do a thing globally, virally, virtually. It was time for a second Enlightenment.

Critical inquiry. Reason. Humor. Compassion. Empathy. If we did not move forward with these things, then the answer to the question *Why do we seem to be alone in the universe* had to be *Because anything close to being like us will destroy itself.* Something big needed to happen, right now, for all of us.

And imagine if we did it. Imagine if this little side project of the cosmos—humans on Earth—turned out to be a thing that survived its infancy, matured, flourished. Not a blink-and-you-missed-it species, not bipedal bacteria, but the thing that we're hoping to find: intelligent life. Wise, creative, benevolent, possessed with an understanding about the fundamental nature of reality, sort of pretty once you got used to it. We could be the aliens we hoped to meet.

"MY MOM SAID in one of her messages that Mars does remind you of Earth, but then also not, only the difference is hard to describe because it's such a new feeling," Mireille says. "Like, almost a new sense. I thought that was sort of great."

"Yes," Luke says. "I thought that was sort of great too."

THE ASTRONAUTS

The astronauts are looking at Earth.

"Remember what it was like the first time?" Helen asks.

"Yes," Sergei and Yoshi say.

Earth from space: hard to believe it was real, that you were real, that you were now an astronaut who got to see *this*. Sunrises and sunsets, storms, clouds of every variety, weather conditions of every possible permutation, the countless ways water and land could meet in patterns and angles and curves. The chiaroscuro of light scattered and light diffracted. Such blues, such browns, such greens, such whites. A burst of red. A yellow corona. The impenetrable darkness of a jungle. A single line of burgeoning waves far from any shore, unremarked by any human eyes save your own. The striated halo of atmosphere. The aurora.

"The first aurora," Helen says. "Never forget that."

"The first space walk," Yoshi says.

The first space walk. Leaving the station in your own little miniature craft of a spacesuit, and spacewalking that was more like space swimming or space scuttling. The view more startling: the Earth moving between your boots or your hands. The extreme quiet. No sound or taste or smell or meaningful touch, so everything you knew came from your eyes.

"I'm in space!" Helen says. "That's what I always wanted to shout. I'm in space!"

"Yes," Sergei and Yoshi say.

"The saddest moment of your life," Helen says. "Is coming back inside after being on a space walk. Not the saddest. The hardest."

"Yes," Sergei and Yoshi say.

The astronauts look at the circle on the screen. Brown and blue and white and green.

"It is *much* prettier," Sergei says, "than the other two. Venus and Mars. Pfft. If I were an alien, I would think, hey, how come they got the best one?"

The astronauts laugh.

"Okay, yes, I am having the big feeling, that I am part of fulfilling destiny of human species and so on," Sergei says, and then after another pause, "it is not just me that feels this?"

"No, no," Helen says. "I mean, yes. I have the same thought. I put it a little differently to myself. I think that we are finding another level. Doing something like this, we all find another level."

"God in heaven, Mars."

Helen and Sergei turn away from the Earth to look at Yoshi.

"It was a phrase that came to me once," he explains. "I don't mean it literally."

The astronauts continue their tasks. They are securing the Hab of *Red Dawn*, in preparation for initiating the landing sequence. Yoshi wants an immaculate ship, and so they clean as they go through checklists, aware of the imprints they have left in this space, surprised at how easy it is to erase what is visible.

Yoshi, in his sleeping compartment, holds the bag of acorns he had brought from Earth. He had intended these to be a physical connection with Earth and that this was something he would miss, would want, would need. He has barely looked at them in seventeen months. Sometimes you get these things quite wrong. Still, he has come to believe that he is the right person to command the return to Earth. He knows what he's looking for.

Helen, in her sleeping compartment, looks at herself in the small mirror next to her clothing locker. It is amusing that you can live your life in an almost entirely selfish way and still have little conception of your self. No wonder she kept thinking that she had forgotten something. She touches the side of her neck, her throat, straightens her shoulders, arches her back. She holds out her arms, smacks her wrist against the wall. She will hold out her arms like this to her daughter. She will say, *Here is the souvenir I brought you from Mars.*

Sergei, in his sleeping compartment, takes down the pictures of his sons and places them carefully in his personal bag. He thinks of the walk he will take with them, with them both at the same time. Maybe they will talk of meaningful things, maybe not. Maybe they will take the cold plunge together at New Year. Maybe they no longer, any of them, need this.

The astronauts find themselves in the hallway together, outside the Lav.

"For old times' sake?" Helen suggests. There are maybe a few things to say. Especially now they know for certain there's no audio.

"There seems to be more room," Sergei says, when they've fit themselves in. It is very clean, but not fresh. "Who lost weight?"

"The last time we did this, I had hair," Helen points out.

For a long time, full minutes, the astronauts are quiet.

Yoshi is the first to speak. "Sergei. I wanted to ask. When the sim failed, and you saw Mars . . . was it very different from what we had been looking at?"

"I'm glad you asked," Helen says. "I wanted to know too."

"It was only a few seconds." Sergei looks down, shifts his feet. "But no. Not so different. A little different color, and different light. Like taking off sunglasses."

"So, still really great," Helen says. "Still amazing and like nothing we've ever seen and more wonderful than you would think, having looked at so many pictures and images over the years and pretty much knowing what to expect."

"Yes," Sergei. "Still amazing. All these things."

Helen reaches behind her and unfurls a square of paper from the roll, hands it to Sergei. His shirt is too dirty to wipe his eyes with. Helen pats his back. Then she pats Yoshi's back. They all touch each other, gently, almost tapping, not quite consoling, more like asking for permission to enter.

"We're okay," says Helen. "We're okay."

"We have done very well," Yoshi says. "We are not done being tested, but we have been very successful."

"If it should happen that this was only—" Sergei stops clears his throat, "I am not going to tell Prime anything it does not need to know. We have done our jobs. You know what I mean. I am not going to ask questions."

"I suppose we have no idea," Yoshi says, "what will happen next."

The astronauts press their hands against each other's shoulders.

"I have been worried that I was the obvious weak one," Sergei says.

"Not at all," says Helen, and "No, Sergei, truly not," says Yoshi.

The astronauts are silent again. Perhaps they are thinking of the letters they wrote, and never sent.

"Prime is very deep," Yoshi says. "I have begun to wonder how deep. Everything seems to have been arranged to work with great precision upon our emotions, to cause us to investigate ourselves and root out that which might obstruct our mission."

"I don't know." Sergei shakes his head. "This is poetic thought, and I like it, but would Prime take such a risk for poetry? They could not predict what we would find. And we could go in two years and have all new feelings."

"Oh god," Helen says, and then laughs. "I can't have any *more* feelings."

The crew nods and taps one another.

"My fear is that they won't send us in two years," Sergei says. "Even if this was or wasn't, you know, anyway, we should still go. Or go again. Whatever. We were hardly on Mars at all, no time for proper work. I want the full trip."

"Yes." Yoshi shakes Sergei's shoulder. "But I believe we'll go in two years. Go again, or go for the first time. But we will go."

"I guess there's no use pretending we are exactly the same people now," says Helen. "I don't know if that's a problem or not. Do we hide it? Do we act like how we were before Eidolon? Or do we think Prime is very deep and engineered a kind of process, as Yoshi suggests, so that we would get all these thoughts and feelings kind of out and done with so the next time we are one hundred percent solid?"

"Or was it to make us more humble?" Sergei asks. "I should say right now, that I actually don't know what's wrong with either one of you. You both seem pretty good to me."

"You guys can tell when I'm struggling, right?" Helen asks. "I mean, at this point?"

"There is a voice you use," Sergei says.

"I know. I call it PIG. Polite, Interested, Good humored." Helen turns a little pink.

"That's very funny," Sergei says. "I'm glad it has a name."

"PIG." Yoshi nods. "But, Helen, it is a nice pig."

"I think all of us are fundamentally sound," Helen says. "And everything breaks in space."

"That's true."

"That's very true."

"It is exciting," Yoshi says. "This has been a very wonderful trip."

"I'm so happy," Sergei says. He cries a little more, and the astronauts hold on to one another, lightly, and then it's time to go.

HELEN

How does it feel? Does it feel real?

This first part is not unlike other landings. *Red Dawn* has detached from her tether and they are once again weightless. They have been looking forward to this, the beautiful drifting, with Earth visible in the screen. Helen instructs herself to truly feel this moment, memorize it, leave nothing out, and then realizes she will fail in this exercise. She can think "Oh" and "How lovely" while she prepares for the next thing, but she cannot take in everything.

She is, she finds, afraid. Not of making a mistake. This is fear of dying. Helen tries to locate the fear in her body, give it a space to exist. It is not in her throat or chest, it is lower. The fear is new and must be welcomed like any newborn, held in two hands. Helen wishes she could ask Sergei and Yoshi if they are also afraid, because it means something, this fear, and she is a little proud of it too.

Red Dawn begins her burn. It is time to slow down, to fall with the intention to hit. It is an odd sensation, as if someone were shoving you in the stomach and instead of going backward, you went forward. You know the direction you are going, but it doesn't feel like you are going there. Going, went. None of the words do the work you want them to, they are all clumsy and contradictory. Sergei's "Pfff" says it all. Helen tunes in to Yoshi, who is speaking to Mission Control, narrating the things that are happening. He sounds like a chanting monk, intoning wisdom. She is happy and afraid.

Landings take time. They are going to do a little tumbling now, a little jostling. This will last almost an hour, as *Red Dawn* makes her adjustments and begins her elliptical approach, touching the outer atmosphere of Earth.

So many things in life just happen, without the sensation that you are crashing repeatedly with great speed into a brick and steel wall, accompanied by a roaring noise. Your father slips and falls and hits his head, your daughter grows up, your husband dies in a parking lot: these are quiet events, so unbelievably quiet, you could miss them if you weren't standing right there or had your eyes closed. You did miss them, sometimes. No matter how violent and terrible.

Maybe your husband never loved you, maybe your daughter will never comprehend your love. Maybe you have always been alone like Michael Collins, with something between you and the Earth. These are things a person needs to be helmeted for, strapped down into a custom molded seat, medicated against nausea, called a hero for enduring. But these are the things that you will walk upright with, must wear with no more ceremony than you would a sweater.

Did she stand on Mars? Can she stand on Earth and hold her daughter?

It's all she wants to do, right now. That's why she is afraid.

Also, Helen is afraid because she knows that after she holds her daughter, she is probably going to want to do this all again, want it just as much as she ever has.

They are stabilizing now, the upper atmosphere catching them. Helen can rotate her head inside her helmet just enough to see a window screen. The view at one hundred fifty thousand meters above the Earth in a spacecraft is very old-timey hell: sparking flames and evil-looking vapors. It is getting warmer now. She can feel the sweat on her body. Gravity.

This landing will not be the same as the other times. She will not have the sensation of her spine, having lengthened over two inches in the course of weightless months, crunching back down. She will not feel like someone is sitting on top of her head. She will not, two days after landing, finish writing a note to herself and then put the pen in the air where she expected it to stay and be surprised by it dropping to the floor, of all places. Her body has changed, oh yes, but not from gravity.

Six thousand meters above the Earth now, everything is going very well. The screen is black, and then this blackness melts away and is replaced by blue.

The blue is sky. Their own blue sky. Sweetly blue, perfectly, wondrously, uniquely blue. Earth.

Before, after you landed, a hatch was opened and arms reached in to pull you out and it was a kind of mad cacophony, an onslaught of colors and smells and voices and things. And you were very sick and your body hurt and you wanted to lie down in a quiet, dark, still place, and shut your eyes. But now, it will not be this way. Not only because you will be perfectly able to stand on your own, but because now you are essentially a Martian who has come to Earth.

But the Earth beneath your feet will be the real Earth, and the sky above you will be the real sky, and the daughter or the son or the wife you hold in your arms will be your real daughter or son or wife. And for a moment those arms will be the only place it matters to have gone. For a moment. Because then you will lift your head to the heavens, as humans have always done, as they must. And you will wonder.

The love that brings you back to Earth is not the same love that makes you want to leave this Earth, it is not the same love, no, but it is no less a love. It is love too, that makes you lift your head and wonder.

But oh, for now, this sky, so sweetly blue, so perfectly, wondrously, uniquely blue. Nothing in the universe is this blue sky, this home, this place where the people you love are waiting for you, and you are not alone, and you will save this Earth, and be rescued on this Earth and from this Earth, and you will take to the skies once more, and nothing feels as free as this, and this feels real, it really does.

ACKNOWLEDGMENTS

This novel was inspired by a newspaper account I came across in 2011, outlining a long-duration isolation study meant to mimic a 520-day mission to Mars. Mars500 was conducted at the Institute for Biomedical Problems, in Moscow, with a partnership between Roscosmos and the European Space Agency. The six-member international crew from Russia, Europe, and China began the simulated mission inside a specially constructed module on June 3, 2010, completing it successfully on November 4, 2011.

Writing this book was its own long-duration mission but not one undertaken in isolation. No amount of gratitude is sufficient for thanking Sarah McCarry, J. Ryan Stradal, Sacha A. Howells, Chris Terry, Cecil Castellucci, Peter Nichols, Lacy Crawford, and John Howrey for heroically reading the book in various drafts and offering invaluable criticism, encouragement, and support. A galaxy of thank-yous to my space consultants for so generously lending knowledge and insight. Wonderful Launch Pad Astronomy Workshop instructors Michael Brotherton, Christian Ready, and Andria Schwortz provided an incredible learning experience (and the very finest in slides) to a writer hoping not to make a mess out of what is stranger than fiction. Thank you to

Tony Coiro for a fantastic tour of a real-life rocket factory and for communicating the passion and dedication of those involved with space exploration, and to JB Blanc for beautifully explaining the mysteries of motion capture. A personal thank-you to Jay Huguley, Savannah Ashour, Terra Elan McVoy, Daniella Topol, Adam Dannheisser, Jen West, Melissa Lekus, Crystal Glenn, Brooke Delaney, Emily Roe, Marty and Dave Howrey, and Sarah McCarry for various forms of life support. The best martini in the universe goes to treasured agent Lisa Bankoff, and a golden star to Berni Barta. A final note of immense gratitude to the dedication and enthusiasm of Tara Singh Carlson, Helen Richard, and the entire Mission Control team of Putnam, along with Sue Armstrong and Emma Finn of Conville & Walsh, and Rowan Cope, Sophie Orme, and Simon & Schuster UK, for seeing this book to orbit.

For readers who are interested in learning about the real science of Mars missions, space exploration, and astronaut experiences, I'm happy to point out personal favorites, along with my thanks to the women and men of space science who share their work with the general public: *Sky Walking: An Astronaut's Memoir*, by Tom Jones; *An Astronaut's Guide to Life on Earth*, by Chris Hadfield; *Sally Ride: America's First Woman in Space*, by Lynn Sherr; *Riding Rockets*, by Mike Mullane; *Managing Martians*, by Donna Shirley; *Dragonfly*, by Bryan Burrough; *Packing for Mars*, by Mary Roach; *Mission to Mars*, by Buzz Aldrin; *Failure Is Not an Option*, by Gene Kranz; *Leaving Orbit*, by Margaret Lazarus Dean; *The Mercury 13*, by Martha Ackmann; and *The Case for Mars* and *Mars on Earth*, by Robert Zubrin.